SF Bo

LOST STARSHIP SERIES:
The Lost Starship
The Lost Command
The Lost Destroyer
The Lost Colony
The Lost Patrol
The Lost Planet
The Lost Earth
The Lost Artifact

DOOM STAR SERIES:
Star Soldier
Bio Weapon
Battle Pod
Cyborg Assault
Planet Wrecker
Star Fortress
Task Force 7 (Novella)

EXTINCTION WARS SERIES:
Assault Troopers
Planet Strike
Star Viking
Fortress Earth

Visit VaughnHeppner.com for more information

The Lost Artifact

(Lost Starship Series 8)

By Vaughn Heppner

ISBN-13: 978-1985736450
ISBN-10: 1985736454
BISAC: Fiction / Science Fiction / Military

-PROLOGUE-

-1-

Yen Cho—the oldest of the Yen Cho Series Androids and likely the oldest android, period, in Human Space—hunted an assassin in one of the most secure buildings in London in the England Sector of Earth.

It was the Queen's Tower, a gleaming skyscraper soaring over the rest of the city. The android was on the 101st floor, moving through a carpeted corridor. He wore a Star Watch Intelligence uniform but possessed a questionable pass.

If that wasn't bad enough, two Queen's Tower security agents guarded the door he needed to get through at the end of the corridor.

Yen Cho wore a disguise, a Captain Maddox faceplate with elongated legs, for this mission. He attempted to mimic the captain's customary swagger and impatient stride. If the agents questioned him, though...

Yen Cho ran through his parameters as he neared the two agents. One watched him closely. That agent used his left elbow to nudge his partner. The other looked up, seemed perplexed and grabbed a hand monitor hanging from his belt.

Yen Cho did not like that.

His logic processors churned at incredible speed and precision. One hundred and sixty-seven years ago, Yen Cho had gained Builder-grade upgrades, making him unique and possibly the most lethal of the androids.

1

He increased his pace, as he was seven doors away from the guards.

The second agent—a man with heavy sideburns—must have seen something he didn't like on the hand monitor. He let the monitor drop, reached for his holstered sidearm and spoke rapidly to his partner.

Yen Cho broke into a sprint. He could have drawn his own weapon. But it was a dart gun with special tranks and only contained a few shots. He could not afford to waste the darts on these two.

The first agent froze, if only for a moment. All hominids had that tendency, which Yen Cho had hoped to engage. That gave him his chance, except for one unforeseen problem.

The second agent must have been a speed-draw artist. He cleared a Churchill automatic from its holster, flicked off the safety with his thumb and pulled the trigger before Yen Cho could reach the man.

Then, one of those quirks of fate gave Yen Cho a hand. The automatic must have jammed. It took a moment for the agent to realize that nothing had happened. Using two hands, he began to clear the misaligned bullet—

That was all the margin Yen Cho needed. He reached them and punched the gun-wielding agent in the throat, crushing the human's windpipe and bones with an exoskeleton-enhanced feature of his metallic frame.

Yen Cho had a pseudo-skin covering, and thus appeared human to anyone without a scanner. But that made no difference to his incredible strength.

As the second agent crumpled to the floor, the first agent finally came out of his funk. He swung at Yen Cho. That was a mistake. The android absorbed the strike against his face. It did not hurt. He only feared that it might damage the pseudo-skin, marring it and thus wrecking his disguise.

Before the agent could recover from his mistake, Yen Cho grabbed the man's head and twisted so the neck bones snapped. The man joined his compatriot in a heap on the floor.

The android did not need to check a watch to see how much time he had left. His internal chronometer told him that he had less than seven minutes left—if his calculations were correct. And Yen Cho was quite certain they were.

He used a key, unlocked the door and dragged the two corpses into a hallway. He stepped back outside, staring at the blood on the rug. There was nothing he could do now about the mess left there from the ruptured throat.

"I say," a woman called from deeper in the apartment. "Is everything all right? I was told no one would enter without my permission."

Yen Cho knew he was out of time. He shut the door, locked it and hurried down the corridor. Something warned him then. It wasn't intuition, as androids did not possess such an ethereal function. It must have been the upgrades running through various scenarios.

He knew that the woman was a highly skilled credit-thief. It seemed unlikely she would have called out as she did in an innocent manner. She must have done that to lull whoever had come in.

Yen Cho threw himself onto the floor as he turned the corner. His assessment had been correct. The credit-thief hid behind a sofa with a spring-driven needler in her hand.

She'd fired as soon as she had seen him, and several steel needles pin-cushioned the wall behind Yen Cho.

"You're fast," the thief said. She had short red hair and what humans considered a pretty face.

Yen Cho hadn't expected her to keep her cool so well. As he scrambled up, a half-dozen steel needles pin-cushioned the pseudo-skin of his face.

The android was aware of the strikes, of course, but he did not feel pain like a man would have. He moved fast, and the thief blanched as he charged her.

She shot him again, in the torso this time, tearing his Star Watch Intelligence uniform.

By that time, Yen Cho had gone over the sofa, grabbed the credit-thief and pinned her shoulders against the wall so her feet dangled above the floor.

"You're hurting me," she said.

Yen Cho regarded her with the steel needles embedded in his face.

3

"Obviously, you're an android," she said.

"Where is he?" Yen Cho asked in an imitation of Captain Maddox's voice.

She stared at him without replying.

"You will talk to me," he said.

"Listen," she said, not frightened yet, but seemingly considering if she should be.

"I am out of time," Yen Cho said. He threw her onto the floor, turned her over and put a knee on the small of her back.

"Upstairs," she gasped. "He's upstairs."

"I know that. What floor and room?"

"Does it matter?"

"Yes. He plans to assassinate the Lord High Admiral of Star Watch."

"You're lying," she said. "Everyone knows Admiral Cook saved humanity. He saved us all from the Swarm. Why would anyone want to kill him?"

Yen Cho did not have time to debate. He had withdrawn a hypo from his kit. He pressed the end against the woman's neck and with a hiss of injected air, gave her a full dosage. Afterward, he removed his knee from her back and stood up.

She turned around groggily, blinking at him.

"I know," Yen Cho said. "It hurts. The pain will not go away until you are dead. If it is any comfort, you are going to die soon."

Terror widened her eyes. The fear should help the drug loosen her tongue, which was why he'd told her.

"Who...are...?" she whispered.

"I am Captain Maddox."

"No. Disguise... You're...android."

He pulled out an energizer and pressed it against her neck. It caused her body to heave upward with a massive jolt of electricity.

She began talking, babbling as fast as she could concerning what she knew about the assassin.

Yen Cho listened, his cybertronic brain recording everything.

In 56 seconds, it was over. The credit-thief drummed her heels on the carpet as her seizure worsened. Half a minute later, air wheezed from the corpse as all the muscles relaxed.

Yen Cho was already in the bathroom, using the mirror to pluck the steel needles from his face. He removed the ones from his torso as well. Could he reach the assassin in time?

He ran through possibilities and saw that he had one chance. It was a risk, a big one considering the man's location and the event that was taking place near Big Ben. Soon, the Lord High Admiral would give his speech.

Yen Cho whirled around, moved back into the living room, passed the dead woman and came to a large window overlooking London. It was a long drop to the ground 101 floors below.

Yen Cho smashed one side of the glass. He then yanked the windowpane inside. Some shards would have rained down. He hoped no one noticed. Without hesitation, the android climbed up to the window frame at the right side.

He manipulated his hand. Spikes appeared at each fingertip and each toe. He had already kicked off his boots. Like a human fly, Yen Cho drove the finger and toe spikes into the outer wall of the gleaming Queen's Tower. He scaled the outer wall as the wind whipped at his garments. This was seriously compromising his human disguise. He would have to discard the pseudo-skin soon and replace it with a new covering.

The android's right foot slipped and he almost lost his grip.

"Concentrate," he told himself.

He did, and he climbed to the second highest floor. While clinging to the wall, he used his left foot and hammered the glass of another window. It was a tricky maneuver, but he made it into the room.

It was empty. Good. He had less than thirty seconds left. Admiral Cook would soon come up on the podium. Given the assassin's motives, he would want to kill the Lord High Admiral at the psychologically worst moment.

The android ran through an empty corridor and slowed down as he neared the fated door. A hiccup in his logic processors came to Yen Cho as a moment of doubt. He shoved that aside. If he was correct, this could lead him to the greatest

5

discovery of his long life. That was why he did this. He did not care about the Lord High Admiral or the unity of the Commonwealth of Planets.

The Swarm Imperium was going to conquer Human Space. It was just a matter of when. The Imperium had sent one invasion fleet. Eventually, they would send a second, third and fourth, however many were needed.

No. This was for a possibly greater prize, one that Yen Cho had secretly yearned to achieve almost since he had gained self-awareness.

The android opened the door and slipped within. He moved soundlessly, and in seconds, he saw the assassin.

He was a wizened old man hunched over a long-range beam rifle. A force screen shimmered in place of the window someone had taken out. The man's ability to reach this location at this time was unbelievable considering the security that had gone into locking-down the city of London and the Queen's Tower in particular.

How did the assassin think he could get away with this? Surely, he wanted to live afterward.

The android advanced upon the assassin. The other adjusted his big beam rifle. It was on a stand while a targeting computer made minute adjustments.

Something must have alerted the assassin. He whirled around, and his eyes widened in astonishment.

"Captain Maddox...how?"

The android smiled. "Strand," he said. "Fancy meeting you here."

The old man, who looked exactly like the Methuselah Man Strand, licked his lips. He seemed to be calculating madly.

The android drew and fired the dart gun, putting three tranks into the man's chest.

The Strand lookalike blinked at the darts, looked up at the android, and faded into the influence of the tranks, wilting onto the hard floor.

Yen Cho moved up and looked through the beam-rifle's scope. He saw the podium down there. He saw the Iron Lady, the Lord High Admiral and Captain Maddox, all sitting in the front row of a vast crowd. If he wanted, Yen Cho could assassinate them all.

Would that be what humans called ironic?

The android's internal chronometer told him he lacked the time for such thoughts and pauses. Taking out a hypo, he revived the man who looked like Strand.

Yen Cho knew the real Methuselah Man was locked on the Throne World, a prisoner of the New Men. Who was this man and why was he here?

As the Strand lookalike woke up, Yen Cho bent down and put a device on the man's forehead. He then sat on the floor cross-legged beside the man. The interrogation would take fifteen minutes, and it would cause the lookalike much pain. But Yen Cho wanted data. If he was right about the reason for this Strand-looking assassin, this little talk could be the most important one of his exceedingly long life.

What was funny about it, in a way, was that he—Yen Cho—had just done the Commonwealth a great service. They might or might not learn about the greater danger to the Commonwealth that this lookalike and his assassination plot represented.

That, though, wasn't the android's concern.

"Ready?" Yen Cho asked the man.

"Please, don't hurt me."

Yen Cho chuckled. Then, he began the intense process of extracting the assassin's data.

-2-

In Galactic terms, Human Space was a tiny region several hundred light-years in circumference. Within the Patrol-charted area were several multi-star-system political bodies. The Commonwealth of Planets was the largest, containing hundreds of Earth-colonized worlds. Before the Swarm Invasion Fleet a year ago, the Commonwealth had been busy integrating planets from the Windsor League, the shattered Wahhabi Caliphate, the Chin Confederation and the Social Syndicate Worlds, among others.

Since the alien invasion, since the billions of slain people lost in the Tau Ceti, Alpha Centauri and other star systems, since the hundreds of destroyed Star Watch and New Men warships and hundreds of thousands of dead service men and women, several severe political quakes had shaken the Commonwealth of Planets to its core.

People were tired. People were scared, and people were hiding their money because the taxes to pay for such powerful space defenses had started to become too burdensome.

Despite all this, there was a greater, hidden problem. While many of the quakes—the revolutions, the nationalist rebellions and the quantum leaps in incidences of piracy—seemed understandable, there were *other* problems with a different source, a calculated and possibly evilly premeditated source.

Brigadier Mary O'Hara of Star Watch Intelligence had sensed this hidden hand. She'd pored over charts, graphs and secret reports indicating this veiled malignance, and she had lost far too many of her best agents in the oddest places.

She finally asked the Lord High Admiral for the services of Starship *Victory* and for her favorite Intelligence officer to return to her stable of operatives. That officer, of course, was Captain Maddox.

Brigadier O'Hara, aka, the Iron Lady of Star Watch Intelligence, summoned Maddox to her office in Geneva, Switzerland, Earth. She briefed him, listened to his thoughts, and then sent him on a secret mission to a No-Man's-Space between the Chin Confederation and the former Social Syndicate Worlds.

After Maddox left, O'Hara studied a different report, a troubling one that she hadn't considered yet. That report led her to request the use of a special Builder communication device.

Three days later, the Lord High Admiral granted her permission.

Two and a half hours later, O'Hara spoke to the tall, urbane and golden-skinned Emperor of the New Men.

The Emperor lived on the Throne World many hundreds of light-years away from Earth. Star Watch did not know the precise location of the planet. However, Star Watch did know that it was in the region of space commonly known as the Beyond.

Quite simply, the Beyond meant *beyond* Human Space. More than one hundred and fifty years ago, the last two Methuselah Men—Strand and Professor Ludendorff—had started a colony world of genetically superior people, hoping to create a defender race of supermen for the rest of humanity.

Things hadn't quite worked out that way. The New Men were faster, smarter and stronger than the old, so that part was a success. Unfortunately for the rest of humanity, the New Men had understood their superiority over *Homo sapiens* humans. Seeing themselves as the rightful rulers due to genetic brilliance, the New Men had decided to subjugate those they considered as sub-men. Those sub-men had proven more stubborn than the New Men had expected, and the initial New

9

Man invasion had been beaten back by ferocious and desperate fighting.

Due to a number of strategic factors, the New Men had come in their star cruisers to help against the Swarm Invasion Fleet. With the climactic victory over the aliens, the star cruisers had departed Human Space and returned to their place in the Beyond. However fragilely, the uneasy peace between Star Watch and the New Men still held.

One of the reasons that the Emperor of the New Men had agreed to help Star Watch was that Captain Maddox had given them a special captive, their genetic creator, as it were, the Methuselah Man Strand.

Strand was also the reason for O'Hara's special long-distance call. She had achieved the call through a unique Builder communication device, its duplicate on the Throne World.

After O'Hara completed the pleasantries, she came to the point of the call.

"I cannot pinpoint the exact reason, your Majesty," O'Hara told the Emperor. "But I have a feeling that a Methuselah Man works against the Commonwealth."

The Emperor nodded. They spoke via screens. He seemed to nod, however, only out of a sense of common courtesy. In truth, the golden-skinned superman seemed bored with O'Hara.

"Do you suspect Professor Ludendorff?" the Emperor asked, most likely out of a sense of obligation and not because he cared what happened to the sub-men.

"I do not suspect him," O'Hara said. "You may not know, but Ludendorff has left our service. I believe the professor is recouping from injuries gained during the Swarm Invasion. What I'm saying is that he did not seem to be in a belligerent frame of mind the last time I saw him."

"I see," the Emperor said. He straightened the slightest bit. "Obviously, then, you suspect Strand. That is why you have called me."

O'Hara nodded.

"I assume you realize that Strand is still in our custody," the Emperor said.

"I do, Sire."

"You must also realize that he has had no outside contact with anyone but me."

O'Hara became cautious. Those the New Men considered inferior easily offended them. "I am in no way suggesting that someone can trick you, Sire. I was merely wondering if it is possible that some of your people could be secretly helping Strand."

The New Man smiled indulgently. "Brigadier, my people hate Strand. Most would like to strangle him with their bare hands. Those who think otherwise would like to torture him to death for all the indignities he has heaped upon us. There are none among us who would help Strand."

O'Hara wondered how to bring up the next question. She finally blurted out, "May I ask, Sire, why you don't kill him, then? Strand is dangerous. He may be the most dangerous human alive."

The Emperor's dark eyes swirled with passion. It's possible he considered himself to be the most dangerous human alive.

"If I have overstepped myself…" O'Hara said quickly.

"You have," the Emperor said. "Yet…you are a substandard model of—"

O'Hara understood that the Emperor had just cut himself off out of what he must think of as politeness. New Men were insufferably arrogant. They couldn't help it.

"I realize that fear motivates your rudeness," the Emperor said, taking a new tack. "Know, Lady, that I study Strand as I talk to him. He is full of unusual insights. He is restless, though. He hates captivity. Rest assured that prolonged confinement is better revenge than killing him. Strand seethes inside. He desires to be out creating mischief. He also fears what I will eventually do to him. There is another point to consider, one I believe you are intelligent enough to perceive."

"You are gracious," O'Hara managed to say.

The Emperor showed off his white teeth in a feral grin. Clearly, he understood how she really felt about New Men.

"I believe there may come a day that we desire Strand's insights," the Emperor said. "That is the key reason I permit him to live."

O'Hara nodded. She didn't like hearing that.

"But I shall watch him even more closely," the Emperor said in a condescending tone. "If I learn anything that shows he is actively plotting against the Commonwealth, I shall inform you at once, Brigadier. You have my word on this."

O'Hara nodded. She couldn't ask for more than that. "Thank you, Sire. You are most gracious."

He smiled indulgently, clearly waiting for the interview to end.

"I wish you well, Sire," O'Hara said.

"Yes, yes," he said with a wave of his long-fingered hand and no pretense of returning the sentiment. "If that is it then…?"

"It is, Sire. Thank you once again.

The Emperor nodded a last time and cut the connection.

O'Hara sat back as the screen went blank. She believed that the Emperor had told her the truth. So…if Ludendorff wasn't plotting against the Commonwealth, if Strand could not because he was a prisoner of the New Men, was there a third Methuselah Man out there working against humanity? How could another one have been hidden this long, from her agents and from the other two Methuselah Men?

O'Hara did not know. She hoped Maddox found a clue at Smade's Asteroid. Star Watch needed to find this hidden foe if they were going to keep the Commonwealth intact. Humanity needed the Commonwealth because mankind needed Star Watch. For one thing, the terrible Swarm Imperium was still out there.

We defeated one small Swarm Invasion Fleet, O'Hara thought to herself. *And it took everything we had. What if the Imperium sends another fleet through the hyper-spatial tube? What if the Imperium sends two or three fleets, each of them three times the size of the first fleet?*

O'Hara took a deep breath. Star Watch had a lot of work to do before humanity could sleep safely. A lot of hard and ceaseless work if they were going to keep the human race alive in this part of the galaxy.

PART I
SMADE'S ASTEROID

Ninety-seven days later

-1-

Captain Maddox abruptly returned to consciousness and tasted blood in his mouth. He didn't know where he was. He didn't know what had happened to him. He did, however, have a sense of danger.

Was *he* in danger? Was someone close to him in danger, or was it broader than that?

He tried to assess his surroundings, but that proved difficult, as he was groggy and disoriented. He lay on something cold and hard. The coppery-tasting blood came from a cut in his mouth.

A cut in his mouth…? Yes! He'd been in a fight. He recalled…three blows. The first had smashed his inner cheek against his teeth, cutting skin. The second had badly staggered him and the third had presumably knocked him out.

Maddox tried to bring his right arm around in order to touch his jaw. A jolt of pain caused him to open his eyes.

It was dark. He couldn't tell if it was night or if he was in a building. He was breathing hard from the pain in his right arm.

He lay on his face on metal. Slowly, carefully, he shifted onto his left side. Then he tried to move his right arm again. That sent pain shooting up and down the limb. Was it broken?

He didn't know but was beginning to suspect so.

Maddox concentrated on moving his right arm; he clenched his teeth so he wouldn't groan. He refused to, for a number of reasons. The first was a matter of safety lest he give himself away. The second was a matter of pride. He did not like to give in to pain.

Soon, his right hand touched his face. With his left hand, he tested the right arm. He did not find any ripped cloth or jagged bone ends. The muscles were tender, though, as if someone had repeatedly wrenched the arm back and forth.

He was wearing boots, pants, a shirt and a jacket. He suddenly remembered why he *wasn't* wearing his Star Watch uniform. He did not want anyone to know that he belonged to Star Watch.

Star Watch—

Abruptly, Maddox groaned as he remembered the Battle of Alpha Centauri. Star Watch had fought the Imperial Swarm and an ancient spirit-entity Ska. The good guys had been on the verge of defeat. Maddox had saved the day by engineering the explosion of the star Alpha Centauri A. It was a tri star system. The exploding star had annihilated most of the enemy fleet and the Ska. Unfortunately, it had also killed every human inhabitant of the Alpha Centauri System.

The guilt of slaughtering hundreds of millions of humans—

As he lay alone in the dark on the cold metal floor, Maddox ground his teeth together.

He could logically process the idea that he'd saved the greater Commonwealth. He had also rid the universe of the wicked Ska. He had not yet found a way to process, to personally accept, murdering hundreds of millions of people to achieve those ends.

None of that mattered to him here…wherever here was. It was time to figure that out.

Making as little noise as possible, Maddox worked up onto his knees. He cradled his right arm. The injury couldn't have occurred too long ago. Like New Men, contributed by the New Man who'd impregnated his mother, he healed faster than a regular human. He had a slightly higher metabolism and definitely had quicker reflexes than a normal person.

He stared into the darkness but saw nothing. He craned his neck. There were no stars or sky or visible cloud cover. No breeze stirred against his face. Given the taint in his nostrils, the silence and the darkness, he could be in a basement or an underground garage.

It has a metal floor.

That could indicate a spaceship or satellite. He did not sense any vibration that would have revealed an engine. Could he be drifting in a dead spaceship?

With a surge of determination, Maddox climbed to his feet, swaying for several seconds. The last blow, the one that must have knocked him out, must also have scrambled his brains more than a little. He waited, and the feeling of disorientation passed.

He searched through his clothes. He did not have a gun or a link to Galyan in Starship *Victory*. No gun, no brass knuckles, he had nothing to defend himself, not even his monofilament knife. The empty scabbard was hidden under his jacket. He must have lost the knife somewhere.

He listened but there was still nothing to hear.

Maddox picked a direction and began to slide his feet. He did not step in case he might trip on something. His slid his feet—and bumped up against something.

Crouching, Maddox felt a prone body. He searched for a pulse, but found none. He leaned near the mouth, but could not hear any breathing nor feel air move against his cheek. The skin was cold and clammy. He discovered the handle of a knife with the pommel pressed against the chest. Right. The blade was in the torso, possibly in the heart.

Ah. Maddox recognized the handle of the knife; his monofilament blade, a weapon so sharp it could cut almost anything.

Maddox must have stabbed this man for striking him.

With a tug, Maddox removed the knife and, working carefully in the dark, wiped the blade against the man's garments. Afterward, he slid the ultra-sharp blade into the scabbard inside his jacket.

Turning around, he slide-walked back the way he had come until he reached a wall. His right arm didn't hurt quite so badly now, although he had no intention of trying to use it yet. He felt left-handedly along the wall until he reached a hatch.

Hatch?

This wasn't a door. It was a hatch. What did that indicate? A spaceship? A satellite? A submarine?

Maddox bent his head but no memory came. Wait! He did remember something. He—

With a sick feeling, Maddox felt his scalp. Someone had shaved him bald. They had done so in the past few hours, as he did not even feel bristles of hair.

He felt along his scalp until he stopped at the back of his head. He felt stitches.

For a second, rage surged through him.

He fingered the stitches. He was going to yank them out and tear out whatever had been implanted in his head. Before he could, the hatch slid up and a blinding flashlight shined in his eyes.

-2-

"Don't move," a mountain of a man growled. "Don't even twitch a muscle."

Maddox squinted as the harsh light blinded him. He raised his left hand to shield his eyes and backed away from the bigger man.

There was a popping noise. A tangle capsule struck Maddox's chest and flung sticky strands around him, webbing his arms to his torso. Another popping sound occurred. A second capsule struck his legs, tangling them. Then a third sound, a sharper one, heralded a solid rubber bullet striking his chest. It knocked the air out of his lungs, and it caused him to attempt to stagger to keep his balance. He couldn't because his legs were webbed together. He toppled backward and hit the deck.

"You don't listen too good," the man told him in a gloating voice.

The bright light moved into the chamber. A second light appeared. The two beams centered on Maddox.

A third man cursed. His light shined on the corpse in the chamber.

"He killed Yunnan," a higher-voiced and weaker-sounding man said.

Despite his tangled position, Maddox turned his head. Through the beams shining in his eyes, he saw a massive corpse.

17

The dead man looked like a pro wrestler from a 2-G planet. That would explain the power of the blows. The corpse had close-cropped hair, a mashed Asian face and wore an unfamiliar black uniform. Blood had welled from the chest like an old-fashioned oil gusher.

"I'll be damned," one of the men said.

Something clicked and light flooded the chamber.

Maddox squinted in the glare and looked around a bare room. He didn't remember it, and he didn't understand why he wouldn't remember. But he wasn't going to worry about that now.

He focused on his adversaries. Two of them looked like Yunnan clones. They were massive, wore black uniforms and had mashed Asian faces and ugly dispositions. One cradled a tangler, a shotgun-looking weapon, while the other had a pistol slugthrower. Each had a flashlight, which they now snapped off.

The third member wore a white lab coat. He was much shorter and thinner, and had copper-colored hair that he wore like a bowl.

"Why did you kill Yunnan?" the tangler-armed mountain man demanded.

Maddox had a vague recollection of the fight. It seemed like a dream; he had trouble remembering.

"Look," said the scientist, the thin man in the white lab coat. "Yunnan hit him. There's a welt on Maddox's face."

The armed men looked closely.

"Yunnan broke the rule," the scientist declared. "Maddox is in a delicate condition—" The scientist stopped talking, possibly because he noticed the captain watching him intently.

"Did you operate on me?" Maddox asked.

The tangler-armed mountain man laughed, but choked off the jeering sound at a frowning glance from the scientist.

"What is this place?" Maddox asked.

"You're going to be all right," the scientist said in a soothing voice.

"Did I escape?" Maddox asked.

"Now, now," the scientist said. "You're upsetting yourself with these questions. That's not going to help you recover. You've been injured and we're helping you."

"He killed Yunnan!" the pistol-armed Asian shouted, his features having turned red. "He killed him!"

The massive Asian rushed Maddox. With a steel-toed boot, he kicked the Star Watch officer in the stomach.

Maddox twisted in pain, tightening the sticky strands webbing him and making it harder to breathe.

"Stop that!" the scientist shouted.

The huge pistol-armed Asian cursed bitterly, kicking Maddox a second time.

"No," the scientist said, reaching into a lab-coat pocket.

"Please, Doctor Lee," the tangler-armed mountain man pleaded.

The huge Asian went for a third kick, drawing back a tree-truck-like leg. Then, he stiffened as his eyes bulged outward. He turned stiffly toward the scientist, Doctor Lee presumably.

Doctor Lee held a small device, pressing a switch with his thumb.

The huge Asian raised his pistol at Lee.

Lee frantically pressed the device a second time.

A hiss sounded from the massive Asian's skull. Smoke trickled upward as his eyes rolled up into his head. A second later, as the stench of burnt flesh filled the room, the huge man collapsed bonelessly onto the metal deck.

The tangler-armed man's head whipped around as he stared at Doctor Lee. "You killed my friend," he accused.

"He was going to shoot me," Lee said.

"You panicked. That's not an ordinary gun, but a slugthrower firing rubber bullets."

Doctor Lee shook his head.

"You bastard, you panicked and killed my friend."

"Don't swear at me," Lee snarled, stung, it seemed.

"I—"

"Don't *ever* swear at me," Lee shouted, raising the device as his thumb hovered over a switch.

The massive Asian with the tangler turned away from the scientist. His shoulders hunched.

Maddox glimpsed the mountain man's face. He was furious, but Doctor Lee had cowed him.

"I have a question," Maddox said.

The tangler-armed man focused on Maddox. Hatred burned in his black eyes, but he kept his back to the scientist.

"Yes?" Doctor Lee asked.

"Who are you?" Maddox asked.

Lee seemed shocked by the question. Then a sly smile stole onto his face. "Interesting," he said.

Maddox did not find it interesting. He found Lee's smugness annoying. It was time to begin playing his adversaries.

"I'm finding it hard to breathe," the captain said. "Could you loosen these strands a little?"

Lee eyed him. Finally, he focused on the armed man. "Guard him, Jand. On no account will you touch him. If you harm Maddox in any way..." Lee glanced suggestively at the newly dead 2-G corpse

The tangler man, Jand, nodded without looking up, although he had turned to face Lee.

"I'll be back with the stretcher team," Lee said.

This time, Jand did nothing.

Lee seemed as if he was going to add something. Finally, he pocketed the device, headed for the hatch and stopped.

"Oh," Lee said. "Don't talk to him, either. His memory loss...that is quite interesting. The Master will want to test this, I'm sure."

Lee moved through the hatch and continued walking, the sound of his footsteps soon dwindling.

Maddox had a premonition. This was it. If he was going to do something to get out of this, now was likely his sole opportunity.

-3-

"Where is this place?" Maddox asked.

The huge tangler-armed man, Jand, looked at him. Then, the heavy—a term for a 2-G person—sneered and turned his back on the captain.

"The little guy always tell you what to do?" Maddox asked.

There was nothing, no response.

"Seems like Doctor Lee is a little prick with a big weapon," Maddox said.

Jand glanced at him, shrugged.

"Lee also murdered your friend with his little device," Maddox said.

There was nothing again, but Maddox had the sense his words bothered Jand.

"Just pointed the device, pressed his thumb, dead," Maddox said. "That was a Hell of a way to go. It wasn't even a fight. Your friend was angry I'd killed his friend Yunnan. I can't blame him. If someone slew Sergeant Riker, I'd kill him, or her, if that were the case. But no. That little prick Lee took out his control unit and fried your friend's brain with it. I can still smell it. Can you smell it?"

"Shut up," Jand said. "Just shut your yap and wait for it. You're not going to be talking soon."

"I get that," Maddox said. "I just don't understand your place in this. I mean, two of you are already dead. I killed one. The little Doctor Lee burned your friend's brains, not that he

21

had much of a brain to start with. But if I had a burn unit in my head—"

"You do, you idiot," Jand said savagely. "It will do more than just *burn* you, though."

Maddox was silent a moment as if pondering that.

"That shut you up," Jand said with a sneer.

"That doesn't make sense," Maddox said. "Why use the tangle gun on me, then? Just press a button to stop me. I don't know why you're lying about that, but you obviously are."

"You think so?" Jand asked, staring at Maddox with hot beady eyes.

"I know it," Maddox said.

"You have stitches in the back of your head, you fool. Why do you think they're there?"

Maddox raised his eyebrows as if surprised.

"That's right. They put a control chip in your head. A better one's going to go in deep later. Right now…"

Jand suddenly seemed worried that maybe he'd said too much.

This was the moment. Maddox could sense it. He also felt that he'd gotten a handle on Jand's personality. It was time to twist the metaphorical knife.

Maddox chuckled.

Jand's face soured. "What's so funny, huh?"

"You and me," Maddox said. "What do you think I'm going to tell the little guy about you?"

"If you're smart, not a damn thing."

"Wrong," Maddox said. "I'm going to tell him how you told me about the deep implant. That's good, because it gives me information. You're screwed, Jand. I'm going to watch Doctor Lee burn you. I'm going laugh while he does it, too."

"You're a bastard."

"I'm Captain Maddox."

"Yeah…" Jand said. "I know about how you think you're tough because you're half New Man. You ain't crap, though. I could twist you like you're a child."

"I doubt it. I killed your friend easily enough. Now, I'm going to watch you die. I'm going to—"

"Shut up!" Jand shouted, stepping close, looking as if he was going to kick Maddox in the face.

Maddox looked up into Jand's eyes. The heavies were obviously powerful, but they were not bright. They were also far too emotional, which seemed strange given their background.

He wondered if they were from the planet Shanghai. He'd read a report once about the lush Earthlike planet with two crushing gravities at the surface. Hadn't there been Chinese colonists? He seemed to recall experimental drugs that had promoted massive muscle growth along with tougher tendons. Most of the second generation had died on Shanghai. The few that had survived were incredibly strong compared to regular 1-G raised humans. Could Yunnan and Jand be from Shanghai? Doctor Lee had also looked Asian, but he clearly wasn't from a 2-G world.

Jand crouched in front of Maddox. The gunman held the tangler under his right armpit as he flexed his huge fingers in front of Maddox's face.

"I know what you're doing," Jand whispered with his bad breath. "It ain't going to work, though. I'm going to watch them shove an implant deep into your brain. I'm the one who's going to laugh, not you."

"You're not going to laugh after I talk to Doctor Lee," Maddox said.

Rage boiled in Jand's black eyes. He stood, deliberately turned his massive back on Maddox and stepped to the hatch. He leaned against the frame as if indifferent to everything.

"And another thing," Maddox said.

Jand began whistling as if to show Maddox that he wasn't going to listen to any more provocation.

That was fine, as that was what Maddox had been trying to achieve. He didn't think he'd have long, though, and he had no doubt Jand had hair-trigger senses. Low-IQ gunmen often had the best hearing.

"You can whistle all you want," Maddox half shouted.

That only made Jand whistle louder.

As Maddox continued to goad the big man, he strained his left arm. Tangle strands were capture tools. They weren't meant for long-term confinement, though. The sticky web still held him, but not quite with the same ferocity as earlier. The trick with tangle strands was to relax. The harder one fought them, the more they tightened.

Maddox had relaxed and fraction by fraction he'd been repositioning his left arm. Now, he strained. Now, he had run out of time. He strained until his head pounded. He strained so his right arm throbbed with renewed agony. By a monumental effort, he forced his left hand under his jacket. He'd stopped talking. If he tried to speak while he did this, his voice would sound too strained. Jand would surely turn to investigate then.

In truth, Maddox needed some luck. Jand could turn around at any moment. The man could also realize that Maddox no longer spoke. The loud whistling helped a little. That might be the margin that allowed him to—

Maddox's left hand clutched the handle of the monofilament knife. He jerked back. The sticky strands fought him. He jerked back again, and he grunted.

The whistling stopped.

Maddox took a slow deep breath, tried to slow his jackhammering heart, and said in a rush, "I knew that Lee was going to fry your friend's brain. I have to say that I really enjoyed—"

Jand hunched his monstrous neck and began whistling again.

Gritting his teeth, Maddox heaved, yanking his left arm back enough to free the monofilament blade from its sheath. He had to be careful or he'd hack himself.

He brought out the blade and sliced several sticky strands. He ended up shaving some of the uniform, but he didn't slice into his flesh. He cut more strands, giving him a little more control of the left arm.

He worked frantically, slicing, freeing more of himself.

The whistling stopped again. "What are you doing?" Jand asked as he turned around.

Despite the agony, Maddox rolled, using his right hand to push against the floor. That hurt like blazes, but it worked. He heaved up as Jand stared at him in surprise.

24

Then the mountain man brought up the tangle gun. Maddox lunged. Jand pulled the trigger even as the captain clapped his right hand over the barrel mouth. The capsule struck his hand with terrible force.

Maddox growled at the pain. He stabbed left-handed, the blade entering Jand's flesh. The blade cut effortlessly through Jand's clothes and flesh, bones and blood vessels. It was a sickening weapon if one had time to think about it.

Jand screamed, flinging himself backward in order to get away. Remorselessly, Maddox followed, killing the enormous man by slicing off the top of his skull.

As the captain did so, he found himself looking out of the hatch and down a long corridor. It was lit now, and it seemed like a ship's corridor with metal bulkheads. The corridor went for a ways. At the far end appeared two more heavies. They carried a stretcher between them. Bringing up the rear was the thin Doctor Lee.

Maddox did not hesitate. He knelt, felt around Jand's bloody jacket and grabbed a magazine of tangle capsules. Then, he was up with the tangler, moving into the chamber where he'd first woken up.

"Stop!" Lee shouted in the distance. "I'll shock you if you don't stop."

Maddox did not stop but charged through the chamber, heading for the hatch on the other side. Lee might or might not shock him. Probably the scientist would, but while he was free, Maddox was going to try to escape.

-4-

As Maddox passed through the hatch and entered a different corridor, a buzzing sensation caused the back of his head to tingle.

Maddox hesitated. Would he drop, convulse or simply go unconscious? None of those things happened. Abruptly, the tingling stopped.

Maddox began to run.

The first mountain man must have hit him too hard when they'd fought. The heavy must have jarred something loose in Maddox's control chip. Instead of smiling at his luck, a fierce resolve built in Maddox. Someone had shaved his scalp and operated on him. According to Jand, Doctor Lee or his team planned to put a deep implant into his brain.

The brain surgery sounded like Methuselah Man Strand. Maddox knew that Strand was a prisoner of the New Men, of the Emperor on the Throne World. Maddox knew because he'd captured Strand on the Junkyard Planet Sind II and given him to the New Men as a gift.

Maddox turned a corner. He still felt strong.

Could Strand have escaped from the New Men?

Maddox seriously doubted that. Could the Spacers be behind this? They surely hated him enough.

The captain glanced back but couldn't see any pursuers. If this was a spaceship, there should be monitors everywhere. He did not see any security cameras. He still did not feel any vibration on the deckplates.

Maddox reached another hatch. He panted. For all his vaunted self-control, he had been running too hard. The control unit in his head might have something to do with that. The remembrance of Strand's horrible practice of having a controlled crew of New Men added a touch of horror to Maddox's predicament.

He let himself pant as he put away the monofilament blade and loaded the tangler. He had three shots. He had to use them wisely.

Maddox cocked his head, listening. He heard footfalls in the distance. The two stretcher-bearers and the scientist were coming after him.

An alarm began pulsating. The sound came from the other side of the hatch before him.

The hatch slid open, and Maddox saw two new Chinese heavies in black uniforms. They were too close for a good tangle shot. Maddox automatically reversed the direction of the shotgun-like tangler and used the stock, smashing it against the nearest face. There was crunching, and the big man staggered backward as blood gushed from his broken nose.

The second heavy's eyes widened with surprise. Maddox drew back the tangler and tried the same stock-smashing tactic. The man was fast despite his size. That confirmed Maddox's suspicion that the heavies came from Shanghai, from a 2-G planet, like his wife Meta had.

The heavy yanked the tangler out of Maddox's grasp. Maddox moved in aggressively and brought up his left knee in a vicious groin shot. He didn't have time for anything more elegant. At least the heavy had unprotected and normal balls. The man's eyes bulged outward as his mouth opened and he made gobbling noises.

Maddox shoved the man. The Shanghai bruiser toppled backward and curled into a fetal ball, clutching his groin as he did so.

In those seconds, Maddox examined the chamber. It seemed like a guard station. There were video screens, coffee cups, rice snacks—

On one screen, Maddox saw the two stretcher-bearers racing down the corridor. He presumed they were running after him. Doctor Lee huffed and puffed, falling farther behind despite his labored running.

On another screen, Maddox saw what seemed to be a bazaar with stalls, sellers and milling crowds. What was interesting about the bazaar was the ceiling. It arched high, but it seemed artificial, as in a satellite or possibly an interior asteroid.

Maddox had normal weight, which meant normal gravity. A satellite or a rich enough asteroid base would have gravity control.

None of that jogged his memory, but he wasn't going to worry about that now. The point was if he went through the next hatch, he could possibly mingle with the bazaar crowd, losing himself among them.

The captain did not like to kill needlessly. He did not consider himself a murderer, except for the hundreds of millions who had died due to his actions in the Alpha Centauri System a year ago. In personal situations, he did not casually murder the helpless.

But this seemed different. He was lost. He did not have all his memories, and a nefarious group was trying to control him with brain implants. Since he didn't know what this was about, he would assume the worst. He had to believe this was an attempt to infiltrate Star Watch, maybe help overthrow the government of Earth.

Maddox drew the monofilament blade and swiftly slew each guard. He did not think he had much time left. He could not afford any mistakes.

He took both men's IDs from their wallets. Then he buckled on one gun belt—fortunately adjustable for a thinner man—with its blaster and secreted the other gun on his person.

Afterward, he moved to the hatch and automatically touched his shaved scalp. Would that make him conspicuous out there? It was possible.

He made a last glance around, saw a felt hat on a console, grabbed it and slung it onto his smooth head. Then—

He picked up the tangler and used the stock to smash each screen. The others wouldn't be able to use the guard station to track him. Finally, Maddox went to the hatch and opened it, heading down a short corridor, which he hoped led to the outer bazaar.

-5-

One of the first people to notice Maddox was a young woman with long dark hair and a veil that only revealed her brown eyes. She wore an ankle-length dress and was flanked by two gunmen wearing slick jackets. The gunmen weren't like the Shanghai heavies. They weren't even Asian, but they looked stocky and competent enough.

The woman's eyes registered surprise at the tangler in Maddox's hands. She stared at him as if he was a man of low morals. She backed away until she bumped up against a stall. One of her gunmen noticed, turned and spied Maddox. The gunman had a dusky complexion and hard eyes. He squinted at Maddox as his gun-hand dropped to the butt of his holstered weapon.

Maddox turned away, putting his back to them. He'd just slipped out of a hatch from a building beside the bazaar. He could feel the man's gaze against his back. He tucked the tangler horizontally inside his jacket, hiding it from view. He had no idea why the woman or her guard should look upon the tangler with suspicion.

The bazaar had countless stalls packed in an open area under a high arched ceiling. There must have been more than three hundred people milling around and in the stalls. It was crowded, busy and much quieter than he would have expected. Everyone seemed…careful and watchful of his neighbor. Otherwise, the people seemed ordinary enough. The men primarily wore pants, jackets and boots and were all armed in some fashion. The women wore long dresses and all were uniformly veiled. None of them were Asian that he could tell.

Maddox stepped behind a stall and was momentarily out of sight of everyone. He set the tangler against the stall and moved away. He went deeper into the crowd and watched the hatch.

Thirty seconds later, two Shanghai heavies burst out. They each gripped a gun. The two looked around, searching, angry and maybe even a little desperate.

Maddox eyed the crowd near the two men. Several people noticed the two heavies and hurriedly looked away. That indicated they knew who the heavies were and were frightened of them.

Several more heavies rushed out of the hatch. They conferred together in low whispers as they eyed the large crowd.

Maddox had seen enough. He faded back. He had no doubt the heavies or their employer would soon offer a reward for his recapture. That told Maddox something important.

This was not a spaceship.

If this had been a spaceship, there would have been a captain. A captain could easily order the passengers to help the crew track down a dangerous fugitive. The arched ceiling, the intense crowding; Maddox was now certain this was an asteroid port of some kind.

Maddox tugged the felt cap lower over his eyes. A memory struggled for his attention. He couldn't quite grasp it, but it told him that he was correct about this being an asteroid base. He was also quite sure this place was not in the Solar System.

As he processed that thought, another certainty surfaced. He had come to this star system for a precise reason. He had first spoken to the Iron Lady. Yes. Maddox had come to this star system at the Brigadier's request.

Did that mean Starship *Victory* was in the star system?

A nondescript little man moved away from a stall while holding a sizzling shish kabob. He was an older man with thinning white hair, a gun at one hip and gripping a beer in his other hand. He gnawed a piece of meat, obviously enjoying it.

Maddox moved near the man, looming to the side.

The older man looked up at him.

"Where is this?" Maddox asked quietly.

"Get away from me," the man growled.

Maddox grabbed an upper arm, applying pressure. The older man winced and tried to twist free.

"No," Maddox said in a low, dangerous voice. "Don't make a scene. Tell me what I want to know."

The man eyed Maddox, and there was cunning in the gaze.

Maddox increased his grip.

"Smade's Asteroid," the older man hissed. "Now, let go of me."

"What star system?"

"What kind of question is—" The older man cried out, dropping his shish kabob because of Maddox's cruel grip.

"The Tristano System," the older man whimpered.

Maddox's forebrain began to throb. He let go of the man to rub his forehead.

The man picked up his shish kabob and hurried away, blending into the crowd.

This is a pirate base, Maddox realized.

More memories surfaced. The Tristano System was outside of the Commonwealth of Planets. It was a no-man's space between the Chin Confederation and the Social Syndicate Worlds. The planet Shanghai was in the Chin Confederation. The Social Syndicate…they used to bother Doctor Dana Rich's home planet, Brahma.

According to recent reports, the pirates here preyed on both the Social Syndicate Worlds and the Chin Confederation. The people of this place would likely regard a Star Watch officer as a weasel, an officer of the law in a lawless land.

For the first time, Maddox took stock of his garments. He wore a mercenary pilot's leather jacket and ordinary shirt and pants. His boots looked worn but they were still serviceable enough. This was anything but his Star Watch uniform. Maddox was taller than most of the people around him. He looked over heads—and saw a Shanghai gunman barreling through the crowd toward him. The heavy effortlessly shoved people out of his way. Their eyes met. The heavy spoke into one of his cuffs. He was obviously communicating with someone about having spotted the prisoner.

Maddox drew a blaster, raised it—

Two men by his side moved in. One yanked the arm down. The other tore the gun out of Maddox's grasp.

Maddox tried to resist. Pain stroked his side, half paralyzing him. The two men spun Maddox around, forcing him to walk away from the Shanghai bruiser, propelling him through the crowd.

Maddox drew a breath to shout for help. Another stroke of pain rendered him speechless. At that point, the two men shoved him into a stall, following him through, closing a door behind him.

The door almost immediately opened. A veiled woman stepped in. Her brown eyes seemed familiar. She was the woman who had stared at his tangler earlier.

"Send him down the tube," she said with authority. "No one must ever know that Captain Maddox was here."

-6-

Maddox struggled. The woman shocked him with a riot baton. The two men lifted and shoved him feet-first into the mouth of a tube. He dropped, sliding down metal, picking up speed in the darkness.

They had manhandled him much too easily. Were they slavers? Had they noticed the Shanghai ruffians hunting for him? He should have been paying more attention to his surroundings. His lack of awareness—

He slammed against a mattress, bouncing off it and tumbling onto a deck. It took him a second to get his bearings.

He was in a small metal room. He spied a portal and tried to force it, but it wouldn't budge.

Because he had light down here, he went to the mattress, listening carefully at the tube exit lest someone or something else—

Maddox jerked back, as he heard someone coming down. If it was his captors, maybe he could disarm them.

The woman dropped out of the tube, striking the mattress and bouncing onto her feet.

Maddox snatched the pain wand from her belt. It was a riot control weapon and what she'd been using to shock him.

She no longer wore the ankle-length dress, but pants, shirt and jacket like the men, who had not come down yet.

"I had to use it," she told him, referring to the baton. "We'd run out of time and you were resisting. You almost made a scene."

34

Maddox ingested the words. She seemed to think that he should know her.

"Do you want to get off the asteroid or not?" she asked, searching his eyes.

He nodded. Of course, he did.

"Then get out of my way," she said, pushing past him.

Keeping the pain wand, he stepped aside and watched her. She moved decisively, touching the portal's handle.

Maddox heard a click. It must be thumbprint activated.

She opened the portal, looked back at him with her eyebrows raised, and he followed her into a larger chamber. It had sleeping cots, lockers and an assortment of carbines in a rack.

"Just a minute," Maddox said, grabbing one of her arms.

She spun around fast and raised her other hand. It held a needle with a glistening green drop of poison on the tip.

Maddox let go of her. The pin-jabber brought back a memory…but not about this woman or this place. Maddox recalled that his mother had once used a weapon like that to protect him as a baby. He'd seen the memory while—

"Who are you?" Maddox asked.

"Where did you go just now?" she asked, seeming interested. "Your eyes went blank and then suddenly you were back. You seemed so sad—"

"Enough!" he said. "Answer my question."

She searched his face. She was tall for a woman, although shorter than he was. She was slender and pretty in a hard fashion, with calculating brown eyes. He wondered what had happened to her veil.

He did not think Meta would like her, not because the woman wasn't a decent person. Meta would not like the woman because she had a way about her, a way that Maddox liked.

"I warned you not to come here, remember?" the woman said.

"Yes," he said, not knowing if that was true or not. His instincts told him she was telling the truth. He was usually a good judge of character and good at telling when others lied.

"You don't remember me, do you?" she asked.

35

He shrugged.

"They did a number on you, didn't they?" Her eyes widened. "Did they tag you?"

Maddox almost said no. In the midst of a mission, lying came second nature to him. But in this case...

"Yes," he said. "They tagged me."

The woman swore, seemed about to run—

Maddox grabbed an arm again. She brought up the pin-jabber—Maddox knocked it out of her hand. The needle-weapon shattered against a locker.

"Who are you?" he said. "Give me the truth."

"Finlay Bow," she said in a deadened voice.

"What are you?"

She hesitated before saying, "I'm a merc, a pilot."

The way she said that, it probably meant smuggler.

"You have a ship?" Maddox asked.

"Great," she said. "That's just great. They mind scrubbed you, too. They're probably moving in on us even now. Look," she said in earnest. "Your name is Captain Maddox. You didn't tell me that, but I found out just the same. I lifted this—"

She tried to reach back with her free hand and then winced as Maddox squeezed her arm with considerable force.

"Do it slowly," he warned.

She nodded, slowly reached back and produced a small leather wallet.

Maddox released her, opened the wallet and saw his ID.

"You lifted this from my pocket?" he asked in disbelief.

"No. On the way in, you stashed a small bag in my ship. I saw it, even though you tried to hide it without me seeing. I opened the seal."

"Give it," he said.

"If you mean the rest of your stuff, it's on my ship."

Maddox studied her. If Finlay was correct, he'd hired her to bring him onto the asteroid. That meant she could likely take him off it.

"How much did I pay you?" he asked.

"A hundred thousand credits," she said, "with a bonus if I brought you out."

She'd probably inflated the price in order to try to get more credits from him later, but that was fine.

"What is this place?" he asked.

"Look," she pleaded. "You said they tagged you. That means they can follow you with a locator."

"Maybe," he said. "The tag shorted earlier."

She stared at him.

Maddox took a risk, half turned and pointed at the back of his head.

Finlay swore again, with greater force. "We're screwed," she added. "You're a freak, one of Chang's zombies. What are you supposed to do, infiltrate—"

Maddox shook her so her teeth rattled. "It only tingles when he presses the pain button."

She blinked at him several times.

"If it tracks me…" Maddox paused. Could that be true? Was the Master—was Chang the Master?—tracking him even now.

"You're a mercenary pilot," he said. "We have to leave."

Finlay shook her head. "I want to leave, but there's no freighter scheduled for another three days. If we leave now, as you say, Chang will send out his scouts. The scouts will blast us so our remains will float in space for the next million years."

"No. I have…people out there."

"I don't believe you."

"If…Chang is tracking us—"

"Chang won't care," she said, interrupting. "His bouncers will, though."

"Bouncers?"

"Don't you remember anything?"

"Just a little," he said.

Finlay appraised him again. "You're a slick one, all right. It looks like you escaped after they caught you. All right. If you're tagged, I'm already screwed. But we won't go down without a fight, right?"

"Right," he said.

"Then let's make a run for the hangar bay. If Chang's bouncers are there, maybe you can kill them and we can grab my ship, get clearance and go."

37

"What about your gunmen?"

She sneered. "They're not mine. They're local protection. I thought you said you remembered at least a little."

"I did. So it's just you and me, then?" Maddox asked.

"You're finally getting it, aren't you? We're totally screwed. I never should have listened to you."

"Don't worry," Maddox said. "We're going to make it."

"Why do you think that?" she asked.

It was a reasonable question. Instead of answering, Maddox spun Finlay around and pushed her toward the hatch. In situations like this, speed often counted for everything. And he didn't know why he thought that.

7

Finlay received a lesson in Captain Maddox efficiency. He used the pain wand and a sap like an artist, leaving cracked heads and unconscious questioners everywhere. If Chang's men were hunting for them, they should be easy to find by following the trail of snoring bodies.

"The trick is speed," Maddox told her.

Finlay shook her head, bewildered by his performance.

"It's time to really run," he said.

Finlay was already running down a corridor with Maddox beside her. She ran as fast as she could, her feet pounding against the floor. The corridor led toward the asteroid's main hangar bay. Maddox had stolen tech IDs, a beam carbine and a headset. The captain wore the headset, but Finlay heard hangar personnel alerting the tower for two fugitives worth half a million credits each from Chang.

Half a million credits? Who was this guy? Why would Chang pay that much, and why for her, too?

Finlay's feet tangled and she would have gone down, slamming her nose against the floor, but Maddox grabbed an arm, keeping her upright. Once she got her feet back under her again, he sprinted even faster while keeping hold of her. The air burned into her lungs as sweat dripped from her face.

What had she gotten herself into?

***

As the two ran, Maddox cocked his head. According to his headset, the guards ahead said they were ready. Maddox had debated with himself to ditch Finlay. He could do this without her, but he owed the woman. She could have faded into the woodwork. Instead, she'd nabbed him as he'd no doubt instructed her to do before Chang's people had captured him. Her action had his signature style and had likely saved his life. He wouldn't ditch her. He paid his debts, good or bad.

"No matter what happens," he shouted, "keep following me."

Finlay glanced at him with glazed eyes.

After releasing her, Maddox began to truly run, sprinting faster than any Olympic athlete. In seconds, he raced around a corner, spying two guards outside a security hatch. Despite what they'd said on the comm earlier, they must not have expected him like this or so soon. Instead of kneeling, aiming their weapons, each guard watched the corner but kept his weapon down by his thigh.

Now, the guards tried to bring up their carbines.

Maddox fired from the hip. A beam drilled the first guard in the face. The captain hadn't aimed for the chest because the guard might have been wearing armor. The second man went down almost as fast as the first, his face burned off.

It was brutal but effective and took pinpoint accuracy.

In moments, Maddox dragged the smoldering corpses to the side and opened the security hatch with one of their recognition codes.

Finlay finally staggered around the corner looking sweaty and beat. As a pilot and asteroid dweller, she'd probably never run this fast or far before. That couldn't be helped.

As she lurched near, Maddox once more grabbed one of her arms and half lifted her as they ran through the open hatch, down a short corridor and entered what had to be the asteroid's main hangar bay. They slowed to a walk then. This was a back way in, which was why they'd needed the tech IDs earlier.

The cavernous hangar bay was full of docked shuttles and ships. Crews dragged fuel hoses to some. Deck workers repaired others.

Finlay groaned as she stared into the distance.

Maddox followed her gaze to an obvious smuggler's craft.

40

"Are those Chang's men?" he asked, indicating a group of black-clad heavies beside the ship.

"Yes," Finlay panted.

Maddox looked around. He saw a coaster to his left that could work. It was a two-man craft, a little bigger than the flitters he sometimes used for landings on alien planets.

"We'll use that," he said, pointing with his chin.

Finlay shook her head. "You're crazy. We'll last a day out there, tops, in that. Then what do we do? There's nowhere else to land in the system. Now if there was a freighter coming—"

"We're gambling that there is," Maddox said.

Finlay gave him a horrified look and must have seen the determination in his eyes.

"Listen to me," she pleaded. "I'll take the beating. Maybe Chang will have me tagged. At this point, I don't care. I'd rather be alive than not."

"You're going to live, and live untagged, but only if you stick with me."

"I don't think so. You're crazy, and believe me, it shows."

"You're rated a comp tech, right?"

"So…?" Finlay asked nervously.

"Don't look over there—"

"Hey!" a Shanghai heavy shouted. "That's Maddox. Let's get him, boys."

Seven Shanghai gunmen standing guard around Finlay's smuggler craft turned toward him. Each was massive, but broke into a faster run than any normal could do, proving their 2-G heritage.

Maddox didn't hesitate. He knelt on one knee, powered up the battle carbine, sighted and burned down the last man in the group. He did not target the first man, as the others would see the person drop. That might make the others more cautious. He did not want them cautious. He wanted them racing like charging bulls so he could cut them down.

The second-to-last gunman flopped onto the deck So did the third. That was when the first runner looked back, shouted in dismay, and watched the fourth member of the team smash onto the deck with a smoldering burn hole in his face.

"I'm going to be sick," Finlay said.

A hangar siren began to blare.

Finlay moaned in dread.

The remaining gunmen fired back, sending a fusillade of bullets. Finlay hit the deck as slugs whined and ricocheted everywhere. One of them tore Maddox's jacket at the shoulder of the previously injured arm, sending up a spray of blood. The captain kept beaming. He seemed impervious to pain.

Then it was over, the Shanghai heavies dead on the main hangar deck. Everyone else had disappeared, having ducked out of sight.

Maddox stood and waved the end of the carbine back and forth as if cooling the tip. He hadn't checked his shoulder yet. He turned and regarded Finlay with eyes that seemed to be made of steel.

"Who are you really?" she asked, awed but still in panic mode.

"We'll talk about that later," he said.

"You still don't get it," she said, beginning to sound hysterical even to her own ears. "Sure, we can steal the coaster and fly into space. But now, Chang will order all his strikers after us. We won't stand a chance against them. Our only chance was slipping away quietly."

Maddox did not seem to listen as he peered into the distance.

"What now?" she asked in growing dismay.

He looked at her. "I was going to suggest we grab the rest of my equipment from your ship. We can't now. More of them are coming."

"What?" she said, whipping her head around to look where he had been staring.

More of Chang's black-clad heavies burst into the hangar bay. They looked around, shouted and pointed at Maddox.

Maddox grabbed Finlay, slinging her much too easily over his bloody shoulder, and sprinted for their chosen craft. Well, his chosen craft.

8

Maddox shoved Finlay at the coaster's main hatch.

She tried the outer combination, but the hatch wouldn't open. "No…" she moaned. "It's over. We're dead. We're—"

Maddox spun her around and slapped her across the face. She blinked at him in shock as pain jolted her mind. Outrage flared next.

He put his face an inch from hers. "Get. It. Open. Get the thing running. Now."

A light snapped on in Finlay's eyes, indicating the terror had taken a back seat.

"Right," she said.

Maddox faced the charging bulls, once more took a knee and fired the battle carbine.

The new Shanghai heavies scattered, jumping behind ships or dropping and sliding on their torsos as they tore out their guns. A few fired back, but they were too far away for effective pistol shots. Maddox drilled one guy in the face, killing him. The rest of those who'd dropped to the floor scrambled for cover.

Behind him, Finlay laughed with glee.

Maddox glanced back as the hatch opened. Finlay darted into the coaster. Maddox followed as he fired the battle carbine.

"Hurry!" Finlay cried.

Maddox came through. She slapped a control and the hatch snapped shut.

This wasn't like a shuttle. It was much smaller. The woman squeezed into the pilot's chair and began pressing panel switches.

"We got a break," Finlay said. "These are easy to warm up."

Maddox stowed the carbine as he squeezed into the other seat. He began activating a weapon's board.

"I don't know what you think you're going to do," Finlay said, as she continued to manipulate the controls. "We don't have clearance. Tell me again; why is the tower going to just open the outer bay door for us?"

"Just get us airborne," Maddox said. "I'll do the rest."

The engine whined as the coaster began to vibrate.

"We have plenty of fuel," Finlay said.

"But we're not airborne yet," Maddox said.

She shot him an accusatory glance, tapped the controls and the flitter began sliding along the hangar bay deck.

"That make you happy?" Finlay asked. "I tried to lift us too soon."

"Don't give me excuses," Maddox said coldly. "Just do your job."

Her jaw muscles bulged as she ground her teeth together. Her fingers seemed stiffer as she punched controls. The small coaster lifted off the deck.

"Turn us," Maddox said. "Aim us at the gunmen."

Finlay licked her lips and did as the captain ordered.

Maddox's fingers blurred across the controls. From the underbelly of the coaster, a cannon chugged 20-mm shells at the Shanghai gunmen.

"What are you doing?" Finlay cried. "You'll damage some of those ships. That's going to get a lot of people seriously pissed off at me."

Maddox ignored her as he continued to rain heavy shells at the hidden locations. Some of the gunmen broke, racing for the exit. Maddox targeted them—

The coaster swung about as it headed for the main closed hangar bay door.

"Don't do that again," Maddox said. "I was killing them."

"I'm the pilot."

Maddox stared at her.

Finlay hunched her head. "Okay, okay," she said. "Don't be a grouch about everything. Now, how do we get that hangar bay door open again? It's shut. In case you forgot."

Maddox flipped a switch, turning on the comm. He tapped the selector for long-range communication. "Bring in the space marines," he said. "If the bay doors remain closed, blow them open. I repeat, blow the main bay doors open unless the authorities cooperate."

"Who are you talking to?" Finlay shouted.

Maddox did not answer. He was too busy staring at the hangar bay door.

"Why are we racing for the door like this if space marines are ready to storm Smade's Asteroid?" Finlay asked.

Someone else must have thought the same thing. The comm crackled as the screen blinked.

Maddox pressed a switch. The screen activated. A bearded man with gray eyes regarded him. The man wore a tower uniform.

"Who are you?" the operator asked.

"Open the outer bay door," Maddox said. "If you don't, I'm not responsible for the people on Smade's Asteroid."

The operator seemed queasy but stubborn. "I heard your message. I think I was supposed to hear it. Our scanners don't pick up anything out there. You know what I'm saying? There are no space marines waiting to enter."

"Suit yourself," Maddox said, seemingly indifferent to the situation. He turned to Finlay. "Start blowing up spaceships. I have orders not to let anyone escape."

"That doesn't make any sense," the bearded operator said from the screen. "If you don't want anyone to escape, I should keep the hangar bay door shut."

"Get off this frequency," Maddox told the operator. "I'm expecting a call any second."

"Come on, get real," the operator said, looking more worried. "My scanners would have shown stealth ships by now if they were out there."

Maddox scowled as he gave his full attention to the tower operator. "I know what you're thinking, that this is a Star Watch operation. But you're wrong. I'm with the Dominants."

"What?" the man said, obviously perplexed.

"The Dominants, the New Men," Maddox said dryly.

The operator stared at Maddox, and the man's eyes widened with horror. Maybe he noticed that Maddox looked like a New Man.

"W-W-Why are the New Men here?" the operator stammered.

"Can't you guess?" Maddox asked in a sneering manner.

The operator glanced elsewhere, stared as if listening to someone and finally regarded Maddox again. "I don't see anything out there," he whispered.

"I know," Maddox said with a smirk. "You're not supposed to."

The operator wiped a sleeve across his sweaty brow. "You'll put in a good word for me?" the operator whispered.

"I have already memorized your face and speech patterns," Maddox said.

The operator whispered something under his breath and began to tap controls.

"The hangar bay door is opening," Finlay shouted.

Maddox had immediately clicked off the comm at her first syllable lest she give away his scam.

"Go," Maddox told her. "Keep accelerating once you exit the hangar bay."

"What direction should we head?" Finlay asked.

"In-system," he said.

"What about the waiting space marines?" she asked.

"Don't worry about them. Just do what I tell you."

Finlay stared at Maddox a moment longer. "There are no space marines waiting out there, are there?" she whispered. "You make everything up as you go along."

Maddox nodded. She had that right.

"Oh, crap," Finlay said, turning pale as the little space-coaster shot out of the hangar bay opening.

-9-

On Smade's Asteroid, several minutes after the operator had opened the outer hangar bay door, his tower hatch opened and three massive black-clad Shanghai heavies entered. These three were subtly different from the other heavies, seeming smarter somehow, like big male lions instead of snorting bulls.

"You're not supposed to be in—" the operator said, abruptly silenced as one of the bruisers grabbed him by the throat, lifted him out of the seat and crushed his windpipe.

The huge Shanghai heavy twisted the operator's head for good measure, snapping the neck bones and tossing the puny man aside to expire on the floor.

Only then did Strand the Clone enter the control chamber, looking like a stunted dwarf compared to the threesome. The clone's eyes burned with passion as he studied the main screen. The stolen coaster zoomed away at what must have been full speed for the craft.

Strand had followed Maddox's performance throughout his time on Smade's Asteroid. According to his calculation, the hybrid had had decreased in efficiency since the original Strand's capture in the Sind System.

That decrease was interesting and heartening.

The clone pulled out a small tablet-type unit, punching highly advanced symbols into the logic processor. The unit was connected to a larger computing system on Strand's ship.

"Ah," Strand said, as he observed the results. The tiny screen showed strange symbols that almost seemed like

Egyptian hieroglyphics. Strand knew what the symbols meant, but no one else would have.

"Give me that," Strand said.

The biggest of the three Shanghai bruisers held a control unit close to his massive chest. The man had a bullet-shaped head and hot beady eyes. He was Chang, a different kind of pirate lord with the deadliest crew on Smade's Asteroid. Even so, like a second-rate cowed punk, Chang handed the unit to the wizened Strand.

Strand inspected the device. Chang had been using units like this for two years already. The original Strand had taught Chang a few interesting tricks as well as modifying the space pirate to near-perfect obedience. The pirate lord did not realize that he now dealt with a different Strand, and that didn't matter in the slightest.

The clone flipped open the unit's shield and pressed a red button. Nothing happened that anyone could see. He dropped the shield back into place and handed the unit back to Chang. After that, Strand turned and headed for the hatch.

"Just a minute," Chang managed to say.

Strand raised an eyebrow that no one else saw. This was unexpected. How had Chang managed to resist his programming? Strand stopped, turning to study the huge man.

Chang tried to match the burning gaze but failed. "That's it?" the pirate lord asked. "That's all you wanted?"

Strand assessed Chang's inner struggle. It surprised him to realize that the pirate felt demeaned. If pushed too hard…Chang might conceivably test his powers. Strand wasn't ready for that just yet.

"What did you expect to happen?" the clone asked.

"When you pressed that," Chang said, "I thought the coaster would blow up."

Strand almost sighed at the stupidity of the thought. He had believed Chang was intelligent in a positive sense. But such inferior thinking as this…no. Why would he, Strand, have gone to all this trouble just to blow up Maddox's ship? It made no sense. Besides, it didn't follow Chang's usual method of putting controlled officers back aboard a targeted starship.

Instead of berating the pirate, Strand shook his head and started for the hatch again.

"Wait," Chang said.

Strand paused. This time, he did not sense any challenge. Chang sounded confused.

"Should I send strikers after Maddox?" the pirate asked.

Strand became impatient, scowling at the bigger man. "Would you normally send strikers?"

"Of course," Chang said.

"Then do so now."

"But…why did you let Maddox escape, then?"

"The primate is curious about my motives, is he?"

Chang flushed crimson, finally saying, "No one talks to me like that, not even you…sir."

This was amazing. The mouse roared at him. But Strand didn't have time for such antics. The crew of *Victory* was a deadly enemy. He had to leave this place *now* while he could.

"Don't worry about your prestige among your men," Strand said. "It is quite intact. And don't worry about Star Watch, either. Everything will work out perfectly for you."

"What if my strikers reach the coaster?" Chang asked.

"Believe me, they won't."

The confusion showed again. "Should I *try* to intercept the coaster?" Chang asked.

"Yes, yes, try. Try your best," Strand said peevishly. "It won't matter, though, as you won't capture or destroy the coaster."

Chang studied the tracking screen. "I can destroy the coaster easily enough. I could probably order the Syndicate head to launch missiles right now."

"Then do so," Strand said.

Chang raised his eyebrows. "And if I destroy the coaster?"

Strand massaged his forehead. He had fed the various possibilities into the advanced computer, and it had spit out the answer. He knew what would happen, to a ninety-nine percent probability. Chang was never going to destroy the coaster. If he did…Strand would have to reassess his entire strategy. Still, it was an interesting test. Therefore, he decided to goad Chang by shaking his head and leaving the tower control room.

Chang watched him go, unaware of Strand's control over him via inner compulsions. He did not like Strand. He did like the credits Strand paid him, though, and he had salivated at the advanced sensing gear that Strand had offered him as part of the latest deal.

The space pirate chewed his lower lip. Why did Strand think destroying the coaster would prove so difficult?

Chang shrugged. He wasn't going to worry about that. He wasn't going to call up the Syndicate head, either. He was going out there himself in a striker to collect Captain Maddox. If the Star Watch officer was worth so much to Strand, how much more would the fleet captain be worth to Chang's hidden New Man contact?

"Let's go," Chang told his guards. "We have work to do."

-10-

Maddox sat in the passenger seat of the two-man coaster, pressed back because of the high-Gs of Finlay's acceleration.

She struggled because of the high Gs, fighting to remain conscious. The coaster lacked any gravity dampeners to make the acceleration easier to withstand.

Because Maddox was part New Man, he could stand many more Gs than she could. He thus studied his monitor in relative comfort.

Smade's Asteroid dwindled on his private screen. So far, nothing had left the asteroid after him. Maddox had half-expected missiles to launch or maybe a beam weapon to fire. Two larger spaceships were in orbit around the asteroid. They had done nothing either.

The star system seemed nondescript. It had a G-class star, three terrestrial planets in the inner system, an asteroid belt and four gas giants beyond. According to his monitor, there were four useable Laumer Points in the system.

No new vessels appeared on his screen. He hadn't expected any. Where was Starship *Victory*? He would guess behind one of the larger moons of the nearest gas giant. If the Star Watch vessel was out there, it hadn't left any signature.

Maddox turned toward Finlay. As he opened his mouth, a signal reached him. The signal had originated from the control device Strand had taken from Chang. The button Strand had pressed activated something in the chip implanted in the back of Maddox's skull.

The embedded chip buzzed—and Maddox slumped unconscious against the safety straps holding him in his seat.

***

Maddox's consciousness faded, burrowing deep into his unconscious mind. The captain dreamed strangely.

It felt as if he zoomed down an incredibly long corridor. This might not have happened in the past. The process had something to do with his war against the Ska in the Alpha Centauri System a year ago.

The Ska had been an ancient spirit-entity trapped on one of the Destroyers of the Nameless Ones. Those Destroyers had been in a null zone that had been separate from regular time and space. The Nameless Ones had been through this part of the Orion Arm many thousands of years ago. Maddox had freed several Destroyers from the null zone for use against the Swarm Fleet. He'd also inadvertently released the seemingly un-killable Ska.

Later, he'd faced that Ska in the Alpha Centauri System. The fight against it had altered something in his mind. At this point, no one was aware of that, not even the captain.

Maddox felt as if he raced through the corridor going faster and faster. The ride was enjoyable, as Maddox liked speed— the faster the better. Then, it seemed—in his dream state—as if he frowned. There was a noise outside the corridor. It was a harsh sound, a commanding one growing more insistent by the moment.

"Hello?" Maddox asked in his dream.

The rush down the vast corridor continued, but so did the harsh commands hammering against his mind.

Maddox scowled. He did not like the words. He did not like the manner in which they were spoken. Who did this person think he was, trying to give him orders?

"If you have something to say," Maddox shouted, "say it to my face."

For a second, the harsh commands stopped. In their place, a superior sort of chuckling began.

That infuriated Maddox, but it would not have shown on his features. It would have made him seem a little sterner, perhaps, his eyes a little more squinted, but that would have been it.

In his dream state, Maddox concentrated. He realized that this was a memory. The commands had a hypnotic quality. They sought to...

"Control me," Maddox told himself.

As the captain sped through his dream corridor—unconscious in the coaster—he realized that someone had strapped him down in a chair earlier. Doctors had rotated the chair. A saw buzzed, cutting his skin. There had been pressure as a doctor had implanted the device in the back of his head. It had not gone deep into his skull. The doctor sewed the cut.

The chair had rotated again, and a small wheel in front of Maddox's eyes had moved in a bewildering way. The pattern sought to numb his mind while a person spoke beside him.

In his dream state, as Maddox still seemed to zoom down the endless corridor, he concentrated on the voice. He'd heard this person before. He knew the voice. It was the sound of—

"Strand," Maddox said.

In the coaster, Finlay finally noticed that Maddox was unconscious when he mumbled in his sleep.

The dream state altered. Maddox no longer sensed anything. He heard no words. He saw no corridor. Instead, his consciousness departed his unconscious mind, and he went to sleep, no longer even dreaming.

-11-

Maddox had been correct about something. Starship *Victory* was behind the third moon of the most inward-system gas giant, a pink-colored Saturn-sized planet.

The double oval-shaped warship had been behind the moon in relation to Smade's Asteroid for a week. The crew had one more twenty-four hour period to go before they went in after the captain.

Lieutenant Valerie Noonan sat in the captain's chair on the bridge. During Maddox's absence, she was the acting commander.

Valerie had let her hair grow longer since last year. Unfortunately, she'd also let her waist get a tad bigger due to comfort eating during the terrible battle against the Imperial Swarm Invasion Fleet. The battle was over, but the comfort eating had continued.

Keith had been glancing at her stomach more often lately. He hadn't said anything, but she'd felt the pressure of his eyes hinting at his displeasure.

Valerie sat in the command chair, staring at the main screen while thinking about chocolate cake. She hadn't eaten any chocolate cake for a long time. She hadn't eaten anything this morning, as she was in the midst of a new diet attempt.

It wasn't only Keith's glances that had been bothering her. Valerie did not like the way her clothes fit too snuggly. Maybe it was more than that. She was starting to feel older. When studying her face before a mirror, she'd noticed the tiniest of wrinkles on her brow. That horrified her. She tried not to frown anymore, and not to smile too much, either. She worked at keeping her features even-keeled so no lines would develop.

"Do you notice that coaster, Valerie?"

The lieutenant looked up. The holoimage of Adok Galyan had addressed her. The holoimage had ropy arms and an alien face with many crisscrossing lines. Galyan didn't have to worry about getting fat because holoimages didn't eat.

Valerie glanced at the main screen.

While *Victory* was behind the moon, a sensor drone orbited the stellar body on the other side. The drone was linked to the starship by several other drones at different locations.

"What about the coaster?" Valerie asked.

"It accelerated out of the asteroid at a considerable rate," Galyan said. "It has acted like a vessel on the run."

"Okay…"

"Now, several strikers seem to be in pursuit," Galyan said.

"You think Captain Maddox is in the coaster?" Valerie asked.

"The captain has not contacted us for some time, Valerie. Maybe he is in trouble."

"He would let us know if that was him," she said.

"Not necessarily," Galyan said.

Valerie rubbed her chin. "That isn't Finlay Bow's smuggler ship."

"The asteroid authorities might have discovered that Finlay is in the captain's pay," Galyan said.

Valerie made a face. The "authorities" that Galyan referred to were the Social Syndicate overlords of the asteroid. She hated space pirates with a particular loathing. Actually, because of letters of marque from the Social Syndicate, the base personnel called themselves privateers. But that was just a fancy term for pirates.

To Valerie, privateers or pirates were exactly like the gang members of Greater Detroit, scavengers that preyed on the weak and helpless. She'd grown up dealing with gangbangers and had learned to hate their ganging-up tactics. To her, they were like hyenas. Space pirates were just like that, too. In fact, she didn't have any use for smugglers like Finlay Bow either. But that was another matter.

Valerie had seen gang members beat up on each other. That was probably what this was. She didn't think Maddox would get himself in such a pickle as to have to run in a tiny coaster pursued by larger strikers. Maddox would know better than to try that.

Galyan could be such a worrywart at times. The holoimage was at his worst when it came to the captain's safety.

"What if it isn't the captain?" Valerie asked Galyan. "What if, instead, the captain is in danger inside the asteroid, and us appearing out here to help the coaster makes everyone inside the asteroid go crazy against Maddox? They hate Star Watch over there, remember?"

"I am familiar with the mission parameters," Galyan said. "Look, Valerie, the strikers are gaining on the coaster. I have detected radar lock-on. They appear ready to fire on the vessel."

Valerie stared at the situation on the screen. Maybe if she ate a ham sandwich, her mind would clear up. How was anyone supposed to think clearly, if she were hungry all the time?

"We're too far away to make any difference," she pointed out.

"Keith is not too far," Galyan said.

"He's waiting where he is for emergency action only," Valerie said. "No. You have to give me evidence that the captain is in the coaster. Otherwise, I'm possibly harming him by showing our hand too soon."

"Hail the vessel," Galyan suggested.

Valerie considered that, and shook her head. "Hailing them will give us away just the same as if we showed them *Victory*."

"May I make a suggestion?" Galyan asked.

"Save it for later," Valerie said, irritated. Yet, despite her hunger and despite her certainty that the coaster held scummy pirates instead of Maddox, Valerie bent forward in the command chair to watch the ongoing events.

-12-

The Clone Strand also watched the action. He did so from his secret ghost-ship. It was a unique vessel, hardly bigger than a Star Watch shuttle. It was, however, of Builder design with many revolutionary systems.

The clone sat in the command chair, using gravity waves to build up speed. He observed the fleeing coaster and the three following strikers. Slender craft, the strikers were mostly fuel and engine with forward compartments for the two-man crews. Each striker had twin cannons capable of firing 30-mm shells. Sometimes, a striker carried a few missiles. These three did not.

They were the perfect pirate ships, small, maneuverable and easy to hide behind stellar debris. Like ancient pirates, the asteroid looters did not use large spaceships. The strikers were more like canoes on ancient Earth during the time of sailing vessels. In those days, pirates had often used a mass of low canoes to sneak up on an unsuspecting anchored merchantman until the canoes bumped up against the wooden hull, and then the pirates swarmed aboard.

The strikers had much greater acceleration than the coaster. They would be in firing range in less than two minutes.

As Strand watched the situation, he made a face. He did not see why his advanced computer had said Maddox would get safely away ninety-nine times out of one hundred. Chang seemed to hold all the advantages out there.

Could the computer be that off? If so...he might have to alter his plans.

Strand knew very well, of course, that Starship *Victory* was behind the largest moon of the nearest gas giant. Had the original Strand been wrong to trust the advanced computer? After all, the original had failed in the Sind System. Captain Maddox had captured him there.

Was there something...different about Maddox that upset the incredible Builder software?

Strand's ghost-ship continued to drift in-system through the asteroid belt. So far, everything had proceeded smoothly enough. Strand had followed the computer's suggestions and by them, lured Starship *Victory* out here between the Chin Confederation and the Social Syndicate Worlds.

Strand the clone had woken up in a distant star system during the grim Swarm invasion of Human Space. He had learned that the original Strand was a captive of the New Men on the Throne World. His activation was the key to a revenge plan on the original's part. Strand the clone had reached the Solar System twenty-six days after Star Watch's last battle with the Swarm. Strand had begun his secret work shortly after that.

The clone had labored hard, only using a few secret assets left on Earth and Mars. He had been one man working across many months to achieve his careful purpose. Professor Ludendorff's sullen anger had greatly aided him. The professor had left the Solar System in a huff, taking Doctor Dana Rich with him.

Strand smirked as he remembered. Ludendorff might have understood certain signs. The old fool was cunning. Now, though, no one on the other side truly understood his genius. The New Men no longer had spies on Earth. The Spacers had departed...

Strand cracked his knuckles. His only worry was the advanced computer's reliability. If Chang caught or destroyed Maddox...

The wizened clone stabbed a switch on his console. When nothing happened, he pressed it again.

A moment later, a hatch slid up. A hovering Builder robot moved through the hatch. It looked like a large upright artillery shell.

Strand the original had found the robot and the advanced computer long ago. The original had left both in storage, fearing to use Builder tech. Now, with no other tools available and due to the parameters of the Samson Option, the clone had decided to activate the complex machinery.

"Maddox is in danger," Strand told the robot.

The robot neither said nor did anything.

"The computer said Maddox would survive his mission to the asteroid," Strand told the robot.

"Your statement is incorrect," the robot said in a stilted voice. "The captain will escape ninety-nine times out of one hundred."

"You're telling me we're watching the one time the computer is wrong?"

"The computer is correct," the robot said.

"Chang is easily going to destroy Maddox."

"No."

"No?" Strand asked.

"The computer has rendered its verdict. Maddox will escape."

Strand looked up at the screen. The strikers were closing in fast. What was he missing? What did the Builder computer know that he did not?

A queasy feeling of doubt touched Strand. Had it been a mistake to activate the Builder robot and computer? He would never have done so, but under the Samson Option, he could use such tools. What did it matter if the tools became uncontrollable? The Samson Option meant that he was supposed to destroy everything he could.

"Chang's strikers have achieved radar lock-on," Strand said.

"Wait," the robot said. "It is not yet over."

Strand scowled, nodding, hating the churn in his guts. He'd staked far too much on the computer's computations. If Chang captured Maddox or even killed him, the privateer would

59

become unbearably smug, to say nothing about Strand's future success with his greater goals.

A second later, Strand shrugged. Well, if Chang did become too smug, at least it wouldn't be for very long.

-13-

Maddox's head swayed back and forth as Finlay tried one jink after another. His eyelids fluttered as his neck muscles finally stiffened, keeping his head from flopping all over the place.

The captain smacked his lips as consciousness slowly returned to his brain. He sat up and noticed Finlay giving him a quick glance.

"Glad to have you back," she said. "You're just in time to watch them kill us."

Instead of responding, Maddox reached up behind his head and felt the stitches. He should have ripped them out some time ago. Could he shove his fingers into the wound and yank out the device?

Maddox frowned. There was something else, something he wasn't remembering…

The comm beeped.

Finlay glanced at him again. Terror filled her eyes. "Chang is going to demand our surrender," she said.

Maddox wiped his lips with the back of a hand, squeezed his eyelids closed and then opened them. He clicked the comm switch.

On the screen, the bullet-shaped head of Chang appeared. The man seemed inordinately pleased with himself.

"We have radar lock-on, Captain Maddox," Chang said.

Maddox said nothing, although he nodded in agreement.

The massive privateer showed off his index finger. "All I have to do is press the firing switch and you're dead."

"Do you mind if I verify the validity of your statement?" Maddox asked.

It took a half-second. Chang smiled grimly. "No, no, please, be my guest."

Maddox tapped his controls. On his screen, he saw the three tube-shaped strikers closing in on the coaster. There was an asteroid fifty thousand kilometers away. The asteroid was nine kilometers in diameter, a pygmy compared to Smade's Asteroid.

Maddox noted the radar lock and the 30-mm cannons on each striker. The privateer was right. Chang had them dead to rights.

The comm beeped again. Maddox tapped his console. Chang's gloating face reappeared.

"Well, Captain, what's it to be?"

"I want to live," Maddox said in a plaintive voice.

"That's not an answer."

Maddox seemed to hesitate. As he did, his manner changed. He became quite meek. "*Please*, let me live."

Chang laughed heartily. "I wish Strand could see us now."

"Strand?" asked Maddox.

"That's right, Captain, Strand, Star Watch's terrible nemesis."

"That's impossible."

"Is it? Shall I put you to sleep again by pressing this?" Chang showed off the control device.

Maddox's mouth dropped open in shock as he reached back and touched the stitches.

Chang leaned nearer to his screen, and his manner became intense. "Jettison your cannon, Captain. Turn your ship and began deceleration. If you don't immediately comply, I will obliterate your vessel."

"We are complying," Maddox said.

"No," Finlay said beside him.

Maddox reached across his console into her space, and slapped a switch. The coaster shuddered. Outside the viewing bay, the vessel's cannon tumbled end over end.

"Very good, Captain," Chang said. "You're being wise."

"I want to survive," Maddox explained. "And I want to add that I'm worth quite a ransom."

"Is that so?" Chang asked in a smug manner.

Maddox nodded.

"It will cost Star Watch plenty to get you back," Chang said. "...if I ransom you to them, that is."

"Why wouldn't you?" Maddox asked. "They're the only ones who would want me."

"Do you think so?"

Maddox's eyes widened. "No," he said, sounding terrified. "You wouldn't ransom me to the..." He let the last hang because he didn't know who Chang referred to.

"The New Men," Chang said.

"B-But, the New Men are our allies," Maddox said.

Chang laughed again while rubbing his hands in glee.

"Should I rotate the coaster?" Finlay asked him quietly.

Maddox turned to her, scowling thunderously. Couldn't the little smuggler keep her mouth shut?

On the screen, Chang stopped laughing.

Maddox faced the privateer, his features nearly unrecognizable as he began to beg, "Please, don't ransom me to the New Men. Star Watch will pay you a bonus for me."

"What do I care about that?" Chang asked.

"Sir," Maddox said.

From her pilot's seat, Finlay was staring at Maddox in shock.

"Rotate your vessel," Chang said. "You must begin decelerating at once."

Outside the coaster, one of the strikers pulled up less than five hundred meters from them. The striker had rotated and decelerated with hot exhaust so it wouldn't overshoot the slower-moving coaster.

"Do you have any idea when the ransom talks would begin?" Maddox asked.

"No more stalling," Chang said. "Rotate your vessel."

"Yes, at once," Maddox said. He faced Finlay. "Rotate us," he said, while giving her a minute headshake.

"What's that supposed to mean?" Finlay asked.

63

Maddox closed his eyes almost as if in pain. "Rotate the ship," he shouted, opening his eyes and leaning toward her. That leaning took him slightly out of sight of the comm screen.

"Don't do anything," Maddox whispered to her.

Finlay stared at him as if the captain was going crazy. Her hands hovered over the controls.

"Why isn't your pilot rotating the coaster?" Chang demanded.

"I'm going to throttle her," Maddox said. "Give me a second."

"You'd better hurry, Captain," Chang said. "My patience is limited."

Maddox unbuckled his restraining straps. Then he stood in the tight confines of the cabin and loomed over Finlay. By doing so, Maddox put his back to the screen.

"What's wrong with you?" she whispered.

"I'm buying us time," he whispered back. Then he shouted, "I don't care what you think. Chang gave us his word. He said that he'll ransom us. You will not self-destruct this ship. That's an order."

"Rotate your ship," Chang said from the screen.

"I'm trying, sir," Maddox shouted.

"I think he's trying to trick us," someone said from Chang's screen.

"Maddox, do you hear me, Maddox?" Chang shouted.

Maddox slid back into his seat. "We're rotating now, sir. We're doing it now."

Several seconds ticked by. As they did, Maddox buckled his straps back into place.

"You're not rotating," Chang shouted. "Rotate now or I'm firing. Do you hear me?"

"I do, sir. I don't know what's the matter." Maddox twisted in his seat to stare at Finlay. "Turn hard right and keep doing it. Go down and right and don't stop. It's our only hope."

"What?" Finlay said.

"Now," Maddox said insistently. "Do it this instant or we're dead."

-14-

Lieutenant Keith Maker had been watching the four vessels. He was behind the nine-kilometer-diameter asteroid, "behind" in relation to Smade's Asteroid and to the fast approaching spaceships. Just like Starship *Victory* behind its moon, Keith used an independent sensor in front of the asteroid to watch the ongoing situation.

The lieutenant was a small, sandy-haired Scotsman noted for his daredevil flying skills and a penchant for whiskey, buried out of loyalty to Maddox. He had a thing for Valerie Noonan, despite her pent-up personality. She was a babe, and there was something anchoring about her personality that appealed to Keith. She was the opposite of him, and he liked that. He felt he could trust her.

Keith nodded to himself even as he powered up his experimental fold-fighter. He had monitored the communications over there. Captain Maddox was in the fleeing coaster. The wily captain had been using one of his trademark methods to get out of danger. It was a good thing he—Keith—was here. The captain must realize that only Lieutenant Maker could save his life.

That was why it was so galling that the fold-fighter was failing to fire up its jump capacity.

The fold-fighter was a modified heavy strikefighter common to Star Watch. The strikefighters were like old-fashioned jets, but they flew in space and attacked like a swarm of angry hornets.

Modified was the key word here, as the fold-fighter lacked the regular strikefighter's racy lines. This baby was a tin can—almost literally—a tube of metal with hundreds of sprouting antennae, cannons and laser emitters. In the past, a tin can like this would have had a matter/antimatter missile. Keith did not have one of those today. The bulk of Star Watch's antimatter missiles had been burned up during the Swarm Invasion.

Not that Keith would have used an antimatter missile in this case.

"Blast your balls!" Keith shouted at the machine, banging a fist against the console.

That didn't help a thing except it made Keith feel a tad better.

He shook his head, telling himself to think this through. He was the best strikefighter pilot in Star Watch. That was a fact. That didn't mean he was a good mechanic, but he knew how these things operated.

He'd been behind the asteroid for several days already. He slept in a separate attachment pod, ate, played endless video games and waited for the captain to show up.

Keith had been in the pod when the four spaceships had spit out of Smade's Asteroid. On the possibility that Maddox was in the coaster, Keith had immediately transferred to the tin can.

The thing had been powering up ever since. Now, with the open transmission between Chang and Maddox—

Keith floated to another panel, his fingers blurring over a console. He ran a diagnostic—

A red light blinked on his board.

Keith gave it three seconds' thought, pushed himself away and floated to a different board. He sat there, hesitating. Abruptly, he overrode the safety feature that was blocking the jump. It could kill them all. It could cause the jump mechanism to malfunction and throw them who knew where.

"Them are the risks," Keith muttered.

He landed at his piloting seat, strapped in and began running through the fold sequence. The countdown began.

"Right," Keith said. "Now, you're going to see."

Lieutenant Maker kicked in the thrusters. The ungainly-looking tin can began to move, picking up velocity as the thrusters roared hotter.

The tin can aimed at the asteroid. Keith turned so he curved around the asteroid's edge, building up speed and calculating his attack plan. This was going to be sweet. He hoped Maddox got out of his way, because if the captain didn't…

"Balls to the wall," Keith said, activating the fold.

For two seconds, nothing happened. Then the tin can disappeared as it folded through space, making a short hop in the proverbial blink of an eye.

During that time, Finlay banked the coaster hard right and down. It zoomed out of the direct path of the three strikers.

On the coaster's screen, Chang shouted in outrage. "Don't think that's going to help you, Maddox. We're—"

Chang stopped talking because a spaceship literally appeared out of nowhere before the three strikers, barreling directly at the tri-formation.

It was Keith's fold-fighter.

The lieutenant had passed out due to Jump Lag. He'd taken his drugs, of course. With a shudder of air, Keith lifted his head. He felt a little groggy, but his mind started functioning almost right away.

The coaster was still pulling hard Gs. It was possible the pilot had blanked out with such a violent maneuver. If she had, maybe Maddox could reach over and bring them out of it.

Keith cackled in a sleepy manner.

The strikers headed straight at him. One slowed down, shedding its velocity. The other two took aim at him.

A light blinked on Keith's board. One of the strikers had radar lock-on. Its cannons fired 30-mm shells that headed straight at Keith's vessel.

The fold-fighter had heavier armor than the coaster. It could probably take a few of those shells.

Keith's cackle rose in pitch. He slapped a button. Anti-personnel guns tracked the approaching shells, beginning to chug solid shots. Ah-ha! An enemy shell exploded prematurely. So did another.

By that time, the fold-fighter was almost upon the two nearest strikers. Keith had yet to target anything. His mind was sharp enough, so that wasn't the problem.

"Three...two...one..." he said. Keith slapped a switch.

As the tin can accelerated, reaching the two nearest strikers, a new pulsar weapon radiated a pulse. The pulse traveled outward from the tin can like a rough-edged smoke-ring. The edge of the pulse struck the two strikers, and bulkheads crumpled.

One of the strikers began to tumble end over end.

Keith studied his screen. "It worked!" he whooped. "The son of a gun really worked."

The fold-fighter began to shiver.

Rage entered Keith's eyes. The last striker fired at his precious vessel. The Scotsman activated his cannons, targeted—and a laser sliced through the striker's skin, reached a fuel pod—a fiery explosion told the end of the story.

The fold-fighter absorbed various particles as it passed the former striker's location.

"Chalk up another victory to the ace," Keith said.

At that point, he began braking and turning. He had to make sure the other two strikers were out for good. Maybe one of them had a kamikaze switch and would try to take out Maddox with them.

-15-

Strand sat back in wonder as his ghost-ship continued to accelerate from Smade's Asteroid. Maddox had evaded capture and destruction. A fold-fighter had literally appeared out of nowhere and saved the day for the captain.

"You miscalculated," Strand told the robot.

"Maddox survived," the large artillery-shell-shaped robot replied.

"Yes, but not of his own doing."

"Is that positively reasoned?" the robot asked.

Strand stared at the Builder construct. "Are you going to tell me that Maddox foresaw such events and planned in advance?"

"I am not suggesting that."

"What then?"

"Captain Maddox preplans, he acts promptly in emergencies—these factors are all weighted and applied to the greater calculation. In this instance, given all the possibilities and probabilities, Captain Maddox would survive. Thus the computer reasoned and thus occurred."

"In other words," Strand said, "he got lucky."

"Luck is a fairy-tale concept for weak minds," the robot said.

Strand leaned forward in his chair as he studied a screen.

Starship *Victory* had left its hidden location by the third moon. The huge warship accelerated for Smade's Asteroid.

Now, Star Watch would want to rip apart the entire asteroid in order to find evidence. Luckily, he had foreseen the move.

The clone turned to the robot. "There is no such thing as luck?" he asked.

"The computer does not factor for luck, which is not real. It factors evidence, giving everything a number."

"Random events—"

"Are not luck," the robot said, interrupting.

"A random event can help or hurt an individual."

"That is not luck."

"Maybe your software is lacking in subtlety," Strand said.

"The computer's software is the greatest in the galaxy."

"I retreat from your flawless logic," Strand sarcastically told the robot.

"The computer knew you would," the robot said.

Strand stiffened, although only for a moment. Was the Builder computer analyzing *him*? He did not like that, and he wondered if the robot had made a slip.

There was a worse possibility. The robot had not slipped but had deliberately told him that in order to goad him toward some future action that the computer already desired.

How could Strand ensure that he remained in control of the Builder robot and computer and not vice versa?

While scratching his right cheek, Strand wondered if he should turn off the robot. He finally rejected the idea. He needed the robot for a little while longer. Until then, he would have to act cautiously around it.

***

The robot had been watching Strand as the human contemplated possibilities. The robot was a master at body-language reading, at the science of *kinesics*. Satisfied with the human's condition, it now turned around and floated through the hatch.

Strand was acting within the normative parameters set by the computer. Thus, the robot did not yet have to eliminate the amazingly gifted human. The computer needed the fantastic human mind for a little while longer...

-16-

From the hard-banking coaster, Maddox witnessed the ace's brilliance as Keith defeated the strikers. The captain knew the ace could do it.

Finlay saw the victory, too. She straightened their small spacecraft so the excessive Gs from hard banking bled away.

Maddox touched the back of his head, fiddling with the stitches. The good feeling from seeing Keith win faded some but did not altogether evaporate.

Was Strand behind the implant operation? The Shanghai heavy, Jand, had said as much. Yet that should be impossible. Strand should be in captivity on the Throne World. There were three possibilities concerning that. One, Strand had escaped from the New Men. Well, the Methuselah Man could have struck a deal with them, but that seemed unlikely. Two, the Methuselah Man Jand had spoken about was a clone of the original. Strand had used clones of himself before. Thus, a clone Strand was well within the realm of the possible. The third possibility was that Jand had been incorrect about Strand being the Master.

Maddox tended toward the second possibility. It made the most sense given Strand's—and Ludendorff's—past actions, and the New Men's hatred toward Strand. The New Men were the least likely people to make a mistake regarding Strand.

"Look!" Finlay shouted.

Maddox looked up. She pointed at the screen. One of the drifting strikers exploded. Several seconds later, the last intact striker also detonated.

Finlay turned to him in accusation. "Why did your man do that?"

"Keith?" Maddox asked. "He didn't."

"You saw those strikers."

"I did."

"They blew up!" Finlay shouted.

"I'm right here," Maddox said softly. "I can hear you just fine."

She glared at him.

Maddox was perplexed. "I just said that I saw the strikers. Why would you assume that Lieutenant Maker fired at them while they were helpless?" Maddox finally recognized the cause of her bewilderment. "I see. It doesn't occur to you that they might have self-detonated."

"That's crazy," Finlay said, sounding more agitated than ever. "Why would they do that?"

"Yes. That's an excellent question. One I don't intend to leave unanswered."

Finlay stared at him until she noticed her sensor panel. She bent forward as her fingers tapped against the console. "Do you see that?" she asked.

She obviously referred to Starship *Victory*, which accelerated from behind the third moon of the pink-colored gas giant.

Finlay glanced at him with understanding. "Do you belong to them?"

"No," Maddox said. "They belong to me."

"What? You're telling me that you're the starship's captain?"

Maddox said nothing.

"No. That's not reasonable. Starship captains don't go alone onto enemy asteroid bases, certainly not a pirate asteroid base."

"Privateer," Maddox said.

"Whatever. It's the same difference."

"Wrong," Maddox said. "From all indications, the Social Syndicate is behind the base. That's quite a bit different from an independent actor. Of course, that might also be a front." Maddox nodded to himself. "Yes, the Social Syndicate angle is most probably a front."

Once more, he touched the stitches at the back of his head.

Finlay noticed. "You said Chang tagged you. Now, Chang is dead. What's next on the agenda?"

Maddox pointed out the small port window. "We're going to board the fold-fighter. It will take us to *Victory*."

"And then?" she asked.

"Then you get paid your bonus."

Finlay blinked several times until finally a smile broke out. "I like the sound of that," she said.

Maddox had thought she would.

***

Keith contacted the coaster, instructing the merc pilot on docking procedures with the tin can.

The self-destruction of the pulsar-wrecked strikers seemed odd. According to his sensors, nothing had been seriously out-of-whack with the strikers. They shouldn't have blown up like that due to a malfunction. That left the grisly option of the pilots killing themselves.

That didn't make much sense for pirates or privateers. Keith shrugged. It wasn't his problem. He was the gifted pilot doing what no one else could do in the pinch. That was why Star Watch paid him.

He noticed that Finlay was okay at docking, but he had to compensate for her…twice.

In a bit, a hatch slid up and Captain Maddox floated through.

"Welcome aboard, sir," Keith said. "What's with the goofy hat?"

Maddox gave him his trademark stare. Sometimes, the captain didn't like people asking him questions.

"They shaved him bald," the merc said as she floated in after Maddox. "That's what's with the hat."

73

Keith couldn't help it. He turned sharply to stare at Maddox. He was smart enough to keep any remarks to himself, though.

"Get us home," Maddox said, stiffly.

"Aye, aye, sir."

"That was some terrific flying earlier," Finlay told him.

Keith grinned. "It was a piece of cake, but I'm glad you liked it. I could have taken out twenty of them with the new pulsar wave—"

"Lieutenant," Maddox said, interrupting.

Keith looked at the captain expectantly. The captain said no more. Finally, Keith got it. The pulsar weapon-system was new, experimental. Finlay was a merc. A Star Watch lieutenant wasn't supposed to give away fleet secrets to a mercenary.

"You can sit there," Keith told the merc. "And you'd better take an injection."

"What for?" Finlay asked.

"We're going to jump."

"In this thing?" she asked.

Keith glanced at Maddox. The captain was studying something on a screen.

"This is a fold-fighter," the ace said.

Finlay shook her head.

"Take the injection," Keith said. "You'll find out soon enough, and be glad you took it."

"Yes, do hurry," Maddox said. He shut off his screen. "I want to get onto *Victory* as soon as possible."

-17-

The holoimage Galyan studied the asteroid base.

He was an ancient AI program run from the engrams of the last Adok starship captain. This had been his command—his starship, once, over six thousand years ago against the Swarm. The insect-like creatures had annihilated his world, detonating it into many floating rock chunks. The Swarm had committed racial genocide against the Adoks. It had left Galyan with a bitter taste, so to speak, against anyone committing genocide against any other race.

The Adok AI program had many Builder functions within it. Six thousand years ago, the Builders had intervened against the Swarm, although it hadn't been enough to save Galyan's race.

Galyan loved the crew of Starship *Victory*. Captain Maddox and his wife Meta, Lieutenant Valerie Noonan, Lieutenant Keith Maker, Sergeant Treggason Riker and Doctor Dana Rich were all his best friends. Galyan did not quite feel that way about Professor Ludendorff.

The Methuselah Man was gone, though, having taken his lover, Doctor Rich, with him.

Galyan would have liked to know how Dana was doing. The holoimage was quite sure a peeved Ludendorff could take care of himself.

Galyan stood at a bay window as he peered into space. He used the starship's sensors to study the Tristano System.

He had watched Keith perform another fold-fighter miracle. It was the ace's characteristic move. The tin can was making another fold, bringing Captain Maddox and his mercenary pilot to the vessel.

There was a lot of comm traffic at the asteroid base. A few ships accelerated away, the most notable being the two bigger spacecraft that had been parked outside.

Galyan cocked his head. This was interesting. There was a new stream of data flowing from the base. It seemed that some of Chang's people had just died en masse from exploding heads.

Obviously, that meant brain implants, since they had all exploded at once…

Galyan ran an analysis. Methuselah Man Strand had been notorious for using brain implants on his top people. Strand was presently in custody on the Throne World. But that didn't mean agents in Strand's former employ couldn't have used his old methods.

Galyan ran further computations. Strand had another noteworthy habit. He liked moving about in a cloaked vessel.

The small holoimage nodded, recalibrating a few ship sensors. He began the time-intensive process of searching the system for cloaked vessels. There was a vast emptiness of space to check. He began the sensor sweep by concentrating on the asteroid base and working outward in a growing circumference.

***

Maddox's wife Meta was a strong woman from a 2-G planet. But she was also shapely, blonde and a trained assassin. Like Galyan, she stood at a viewing port on *Victory*. She concentrated on the approaching fold-fighter. Her husband was coming home after a dangerous infiltration mission on Smade's Asteroid. Meta had been against the mission from the beginning.

"Why is the captain of a starship going undercover?" she'd asked Maddox a little over a week ago in their quarters aboard ship.

"Because I'm the best Intelligence field agent here," Maddox had told her.

"That doesn't matter. You're too important to risk on something like this."

"No," he'd said. "The situation is too critical to let anyone but our best Intelligence operative go undercover."

"I don't like it."

Maddox had not said anything to that.

They had had a furious bout of lovemaking afterward. She'd held him so tightly. He meant everything to her. He was a maddening husband, imperialistic, demanding, far too full of himself and brilliant and strong, with a hidden sensitivity that few ever saw. He loved her. Absolutely, unequivocally. That was the important thing. He would risk anything for her. But he would not let anything stand in the way of his duty. He had a...terrible need to win at whatever he did. He seemed to square off against the universe. His unique nature had marked him, often in an unkindly fashion.

For one thing, Maddox wanted to kill his father for what the man had done to Maddox's mother. That didn't help the captain in the least.

Meta smiled in relief as she saw the fold-fighter braking as it neared the main hangar bay entrance. Maddox had survived his undercover mission. She wondered what he'd discovered this time.

She sighed. He'd almost died out there in space. He had—

Galyan materialized before her. It made Meta jump back while her right hand snaked to the hidden gun on her person.

"How many times have I told you not to do that?" she demanded.

Galyan's eyelids fluttered. "One hundred and thirty-two times in total," the holoimage answered.

"Then why did you still pop up like that?"

"You must hurry to medical," Galyan said. "Valerie sent me. I urge you to hurry."

"Why?" Meta asked, worried now.

Galyan hesitated.

"Tell me," she shouted, moving closer, trying to grab him. Her hands went through the holoimage. She backed up,

77

shaking her hands, finding the experience troubling, highly unsettling.

"Is it Maddox?" she demanded.

"Yes," Galyan said. "During the fold…"

"Yes, yes, what? Spit it out, Galyan."

"The captain went into a seizure. They are rushing him to medical."

"Is he going to be all right?"

"I do not know, Meta. That is why I think you should hurry."

Meta stared at the holoimage a second longer. Then she whirled around and began to sprint.

-18-

Captain Maddox felt weak.

He didn't know how much time had passed. But for some time, it had felt as if he was falling down into an endless abyss.

Fortunately, the sensation had ceased. He lay on something soft as people murmured around him. He tried to dredge up the strength to open his eyes. He did not understand this weakness. He hated it. He was Captain Maddox. Nothing was beyond him. He needed to concentrate, to force his will…

By slow degrees, Maddox forced his eyelids to flutter open.

"Look," a woman said. "He's coming out of it."

Someone rushed near. Warm hands grasped his right arm. "Darling!"

Maddox looked up into Meta's sweet face. She was beautiful, and she seemed concerned.

Maddox moistened his mouth. "What…?" he whispered.

Meta looked back at someone else.

"Tell…" Maddox said weakly.

"Please, allow me," a woman said from behind Meta.

Reluctantly, Meta released his arm and stepped to the side. Maddox had difficulty tracking her.

"Captain," a woman said.

Maddox's gaze slid away from Meta, making him feel sad. It took time for him to refocus on a thin-faced woman with a beak of a nose and a high forehead. He felt he should know her.

"I'm Doctor Lister," the woman said. "I'm *Victory's* chief medical officer."

Maddox continued to stare at her.

"You had a seizure," Lister said.

Maddox moistened his mouth again. "When did...it...hap...?" he whispered ever so slowly.

"We believe the fold caused it," Lister said.

Maddox let that sink in, and he finally noticed the worry in the doctor's eyes.

"Implant..." he said, too tired to finish his thought.

"We know about that," Lister said. "We believe the implant had something to do with the seizure. In fact..."

Maddox started to fade away, which made him stubborn. He refused to pass out. Fear nibbled at him, but he was going to face down the fear.

By slow degrees, Doctor Lister's narrow face reappeared.

"He's coherent again," Meta said from somewhere.

Doctor Lister regarded Maddox. "Can you understand me?"

"Implant trigger...?" Maddox whispered.

Lister glanced at Meta before focusing on Maddox. "Yes. We've tested the linkage. This implant is subtle. It is...booby-trapped I believe is the correct word. I have to tell you, sir, I don't think I can take it out."

Maddox understood what she was saying, and the implications. A grim smile tugged at his lips.

"I'm quite serious," Lister told him.

"He knows that," Meta said.

Maddox managed the slightest of nods. "Listen... Operate. Take...out..."

"I'm not sure you understand the risks of my doing that just now," Lister said.

"Don't...care," Maddox said. "Take...out...now."

The worry in Doctor Lister's eyes turned into fear. "I'm not sure I'm skilled enough to do that."

"Do...it...anyway," Maddox whispered.

"Sir—"

"Just a minute," Meta told the doctor. "Let me talk to him."

Lister seemed relieved. She backed away from Maddox.

Meta took the doctor's place. She put her warm hands on his right arm again. She leaned near as she stared into his eyes.

Maddox smiled. He loved Meta, and he knew she would force the doctor to operate.

"The operation could kill you," Meta said.

He already knew that.

"It could cause permanent brain damage," she added.

That gave him pause. The idea that he would be less than he used to be was galling indeed. But in the end, that didn't matter. He wasn't going to have a Strand control unit in his head. He would rather die than allow such a thing to stay.

"I understand," Meta said quietly, as she searched his eyes. "And I'll honor your wish, my husband. But if you die on me…" Her grip tightened on his flesh.

"Must…fight," Maddox whispered.

Meta nodded, and tears welled in her eyes. The tears began to drip onto his shirt. "Say it," she whispered.

"Love…" he said.

"Yes," Meta said, letting the tears continue to drip. "I love you, too."

Maddox smiled once more. Then, he faded away. Meta had understood his desire. He no longer had to fight to remain conscious. They did what he wanted.

***

"You don't understand," Doctor Lister said. "I—"

"Listen to me," Meta said, interrupting the doctor. "Captain Maddox wants you to take the risk. He trusts your skills."

The high forehead of Doctor Lister wrinkled in concern. "What if I fail?"

"Then you fail," Meta said grimly. "He cannot stand the idea of anyone or anything controlling him."

"I can appreciate that," Lister said. "But let's wait until we reach a better facility. This is too important for any of us to take such an unneeded risk."

Meta shook her head. "That's not how Maddox thinks. He has a task to perform. He—"

"He's sick," Lister said, interrupting. "He's in no condition to make such a demand. I'm the chief medical officer. I'm the one who decides these things. He's going to have to wait."

"Maddox doesn't wait for anything if there's a faster way to do it," Meta said. "You have your orders. Now, perform them, Doctor."

Lister became stubborn. "Not from the captain, I don't have any orders. I have your interpretation of what you *think* he wants."

Meta's face screwed up with outrage. "Are you saying I don't know what my husband was trying to communicate to us?"

Lister looked down. "No…I suppose not. It's just—"

"Listen to me," Meta said earnestly. "You signed up for Starship *Victory*. Here, Captain Maddox expects everyone to do their assigned duty. You're the surgeon. That means this task falls to you. You cannot escape the risk because you think…you *fear*…you might fail."

"Do you understand what you're asking me to do?"

Meta snorted. "Doctor, Star Watch has had its back to the wall with the Swarm Invasion. The present bug assault might be over, but there might be more Swarm fleets readying to invade the Commonwealth. We've all had to do things that frighten us. You signed up as a doctor. Now, you have your back to the wall with this operation. You'd better do this surgery to perfection. Because if you don't—"

"Just a minute," Lister said, interrupting. "Are you threatening to kill me if I fail to perform the surgery correctly?"

Meta's face took on a cold, hard cast. "Yes, Doctor, that's exactly what I'm saying."

"Are you insane?"

"No," Galyan said. The holoimage had popped into existence. "Meta is a former assassin. Killing those who disappoint her is Meta's way. Meta loves the captain. If you fail to save the captain, Meta will follow her emotions and kill you."

Lister stared in disbelief from Meta to Galyan. "You're all crazy."

"Meta is correct in saying this is a trying time," Galyan said. "I suggest you listen to her and do the best you can. I will attempt to assist you to the best of my ability."

"How can a holoimage help me perform a surgery?" Doctor Lister demanded.

"I have been tracing the implant's connectives," Galyan said. "I believe I can be of great service to you in mapping out his brain."

Lister took a deep, perhaps calming, breath. "All right, I'll operate." She looked as if she wanted to say more but seemingly decided against it.

"You're going to have to leave, though," Lister told Meta. "I can't do this if I feel as if you're standing behind me with a knife in your hands, waiting to plunge it in my back."

It took Meta three seconds. She nodded. She also determined that she was going to find the person who had ordered the implant put in Maddox's skull. Once she found the person, she was going to kill him or her in a yearlong process filled with intense agony.

-19-

After the injections prepping him for the operation, Maddox traveled much closer to death than the doctors had anticipated. This happened because of the soul-energizing weapon he'd used a year ago against the Ska in the Alpha Centauri System.

The ancient Builders had dreaded the day a Ska would roam freely among the weaker races. They had put a deep memory in Professor Ludendorff. The Methuselah Man had constructed a weapon to slay the Ska. Maddox had used the weapon, burning up much of his personal soul energy to power the weapon. The Ska and he had been in close contact during the fight. That contact had changed something inside Maddox's soul.

Maddox hadn't perceived the change, however. No one had. It had been at a deep and fundamental level. After the soul-draining battle, the captain had struggled to *want* to remain alive. In the midst of that anguish, a wall in his subconscious had come down for a while, exposing his earliest memories as a baby. For the first time in his adult life, Captain Maddox had remembered his mother.

As the captain once more plummeted toward death, as the doctors operated on his brain, trying to sever the implant from every invaded nerve fiber in his mind, something strange happened to Maddox.

He remembered some of what had occurred to him less than a week ago in the operating theater inside the asteroid base.

Medical personnel had inserted an implant into the back of his brain. Afterward, he had been placed in a chair with his head strapped into place. A colored wheel had spun around and around before his eyes, playing tricks with his mind. Someone unseen had injected drugs into his system.

The wheel turned. The drugs battered his mental defenses. The implant was a distraction. It was not the true danger. Strand spoke to him. Maddox recognized the smarmy voice all too well. He recognized that the Methuselah Man attempt to bend his will through a form of alien hypnosis.

This is what had caused the growling noises earlier in his dream state. He had been trying to remember what had happened.

"Strand," Maddox said in his near-death dream-state remembrance of what had happened inside the asteroid base.

"Captain Maddox," Strand said, "I congratulate you, sir, as you have an uncommonly stubborn will."

While his head had been strapped into place, Maddox had managed to shift his gaze from the spinning wheel. With a grunting effort, he'd shifted his strapped-down head enough to see the wizened bastard standing nearby.

"That is quite amazing, my dear hybrid," Strand said.

"How did you escape from the Throne World?" Maddox asked.

"I'd worry about you, hybrid, not me. You're the one in mortal peril."

"No," Maddox said. "There's something different about you. Your skin is too smooth. Why is it so smooth, Methuselah Man?"

"You will not goad me, Maddox, not when I know how to adjust your personality so perfectly. You are going to do something quite amazing for me. I need you to break into a place on Earth forbidden to me."

"I get it," Maddox said. "You're not the real Strand. You're a clone of him."

The wizened features scowled. "I am Strand."

"You're a clone of Strand."

"Clone or not, it makes no difference."

"It makes all the difference. I will defeat you, Clone, just as I defeated the original."

Strand grinned evilly. "I doubt that, hybrid. You're my tool. You made a mistake coming here alone. The computer knew you would."

"What computer?"

"It's a Builder device," Strand boasted. "With it, I have been predicting your every action. You're an open book to me now, Maddox. Isn't that funny?"

"You're a fool if you think you can use a thing like that—"

"Enough," Strand said, interrupting. "We will proceed to the next lesson. Listen closely, hybrid. You are going to have to remember a great deal. Are you ready?"

Maddox had tried to resist. The drugs the doctors had injected had proven too strong, the wheel too intoxicating and Strand's hypnotic abilities bordering on the miraculous.

As the captain floated in the death-dream state, he pondered the clone's instructions. He saw the cleverness of the plan, and he began to deduce the clone's real objective. Before Maddox could pinpoint it perfectly, though, his consciousness began to shoot upward out of the realm of death.

The conflict with the Ska a year ago had changed things in Maddox. It had opened inner doors, making it seem as if Maddox possessed an inner eye. That gave him insights he never would have had otherwise. The only problem was that he had to sink near death to see with this inner eye.

At that point, Maddox began to convulse on the operating table.

-20-

Galyan assisted in the operation as best he could. That was mainly in the opening procedures, giving Doctor Lister information about super-thin nerve-threads leading away from the control chip into the captain's brain.

Once Lister was underway with the actual operation, Galyan departed the theater. It was unexplainable, but the holoimage could not watch, finding it too distressing. He did not like seeing Maddox in such a vulnerable state, especially since the captain might very well die.

What happened to one's soul after death? Galyan had often pondered the idea. Had his Adok soul passed on to a different place? His engrams had given the AI program life. Yet, was he truly alive like those with souls? It was a terrible dilemma. Everyone had their own opinion on the matter. No one he knew had come back to report. How did one find out the unequivocal truth?

It was a thorny problem, to say the least.

To take his mind off the operation, Galyan continued to scan the Tristano System. He'd widened the search in a growing circle. The continuously widening scan had already departed the Asteroid Belt. It had also headed out-system and in-system at the same time. The growing circular scan went above and below the star-system ecliptic, the path that the majority of the planets followed as they orbited the Tristano star.

Time passed as Galyan searched for a cloaked spaceship. As he scanned for such a vessel, he continued to monitor the situation aboard Smade's Asteroid.

It was quickly devolving into chaos over there. *Victory* could have used its star-drive jump to get to the asteroid quicker, but such a jump or fold might worsen the captain's condition. Valerie was not willing to risk that.

It appeared that Chang's elaborate setup had gone to pieces on Smade's. Too many of his key personnel were dead. According to the comm messages Galyan was picking up, some of Chang's employees were looting his former premises. Other asteroid personnel—other space pirates—had also smashed into those premises and looted the riches as well. That had started gun battles that became hotter the longer they progressed.

That likely meant that much useful data had already been destroyed over there. Maddox's original plan—once he returned from Smade's—had been to use *Victory's* space marines to take over the asteroid base. Before that could happen, the starship had to get in range to launch the regular shuttles to ferry over the space marines.

There were several fold-fighters in *Victory's* hangar bay. Valerie could send elite marine teams onto the asteroid. She was not yet ready to order such a maneuver. Galyan was certain that under similar conditions Captain Maddox would have led the away teams over there himself.

"Humans are quite different from each other," Galyan said aloud.

At that point, one of the sensors pinged. It indicated unusual gravity-wave readings. Such readings could indicate—

"A cloaked vessel," Galyan said.

***

Lieutenant Noonan stared at Galyan as the holoimage gave his report.

Valerie abruptly turned in the captain's chair, giving orders to various bridge personnel. In thirty seconds, the Kai-Kaus Chief Technician, Andros Crank, confirmed Galyan's find.

Andros Crank was a stout, short, older man with thick fingers and unusually long gray hair. Maddox had saved Andros and ten thousand other Kai-Kaus from a Builder Dyson Sphere a thousand light-years from Earth.

"The concentration of gravity waves indicates a cloaked vessel," Andros declared.

"Do you have the ship's precise location?" Valerie asked.

"It is at this location," Galyan said.

On the main screen, a tiny green circle appeared. No doubt, Galyan meant to encompass the so-called cloaked vessel.

"Yes," Andros said. "I detect a heavy concentration of metals at that location. It's a spaceship all right, a cloaked one."

Valerie nodded slowly. The location was several million kilometers from the system's nearest Laumer Point. That made it quite a ways from *Victory*, over three billion kilometers.

"What is the ship's heading?" Valerie asked.

Galyan indicated the heading with an arrow on the main screen. It showed that the cloaked vessel headed directly for the Laumer Point near the third terrestrial planet.

"Any idea who's inside it?" Valerie asked Galyan.

"Yes."

Valerie waited a second before saying, "Well. Who?"

"The probability is that it's an old confederate of the Methuselah Man Strand," Galyan said.

Valerie blinked with surprise, and her gut clenched. Methuselah Men and their confederates were notoriously difficult to deal with.

"You think that because it's a cloaked vessel?" she asked.

"And because Captain Maddox had a Strand-like implant in his brain," Galyan said.

Valerie slapped an armrest. "Of course. I should have seen that. Good work, Galyan."

The little holoimage stood a little straighter. "Thank you, Valerie. It is kind of you to say so."

"Open channels with the vessel," she told Andros.

Crank hesitated.

"Is anything the matter?" Valerie asked him.

"We know he's there," Andros said. "He doesn't know we know he's there. Why not send a fold-fighter or two near his position before we let him know we know?"

Valerie's gut clenched again. She didn't like the idea of sending Keith anywhere near a Methuselah Man's confederates. She remembered Ludendorff's slarn hunter all too well. Keith was a terrific pilot, the best, but this was a cloaked vessel with hidden properties. She was sure of that. She could actually feel that part of it.

A hunch, Valerie realized. *I'm having a hunch.*

Normally, she was a by-the-numbers officer. She wasn't the kind to have hunches. Now she did. Now, she had to figure out how to play her hunch.

"Do you still want me to open channels with the cloaked ship?" Andros asked.

"Give me a second to think about it," Valerie said.

Even as she said that, she knew she was being too wishy-washy. A confident starship captain made snap decisions. The others expected that from her.

Remember, she told herself. *Do things your way. You're not Captain Maddox. So don't try to be Captain Maddox. Be Lieutenant Noonan.*

What was the right thing to do?

Valerie knew it as soon as she asked herself. She should use the star drive and jump beside the cloaked vessel. Then, she should use a tractor beam and pull the hidden ship into the hangar bay. The space marines could take the Methuselah Man's confederates captive. She would put them in the brig for Intelligence people to interrogate later.

But she couldn't use the star drive right now. Maddox had gone into a seizure during a fold. He had come out of surgery. She had to give his body time to heal before the starship attempted a jump.

She frowned. Was that right, though? Wasn't her first duty to Star Watch and the protection of the people of the Commonwealth?

Andros cleared his throat.

Valerie scowled. Why did the Chief Technician think he knew how to do everything? He wasn't the one having to make the decisions.

I'm responsible. It's why I'm a command officer. I have to make the hard choices.

"We're going to capture that ship," she said.

"You're going to use the star drive?" Andros asked, sounding surprised.

"I have to," she said. "We must capture whoever's aboard the cloaked vessel. It's why we came way out here in the first place."

"The captain—" Andros said.

"Would expect me to use the star drive," Valerie said, interrupting.

"You cannot do that, Valerie," Galyan said. "The captain is in critical condition. If you use the star drive—"

"I already know what will happen," Valerie snapped. A second later, she said, "I'm sorry, Galyan. We're all worried about the captain. But we have a duty to perform."

Galyan did not look convinced. "I am much older than you, Valerie. It is a terrible thing to give a command that results in the death of those you love. If I were you, I would wait to see what happens."

"If I wait, we might lose the cloaked vessel."

"It is not presently accelerating," Galyan said. "We have many hours before it will begin decelerating to enter the Laumer Point."

"It might not decelerate to enter it," Valerie said. "The vessel might zoom in."

"That is true," Galyan admitted.

Valerie took a deep breath. She should order them to jump to the cloaked vessel. If she first called to see how Maddox was doing—

The main hatch slid open.

"Captain on the bridge," a marine said loudly.

Valerie swiveled in her chair. A chalk-white Maddox supported by Meta slowly stepped onto the bridge. The captain had one arm draped over Meta's shoulders. One of her strong arms was clasped around his waist. He looked exhausted, his eyes staring and faraway-seeming. Sweat stained his face.

"Sir," Valerie said. "You should be in sickbay recovering."

Maddox did not give the slightest impression he'd heard her. By slow degrees, Meta maneuvered the captain toward the command chair.

Valerie's stomach seethed. She couldn't give command back to the captain while he was in such a weakened condition. Regulations clearly stated that the captain had to be in sound medical health to resume command. She didn't want to do it, but Valerie was going to have to send him to sickbay whether he liked that or not. Afterward, she would have to order Victory to jump to the cloaked vessel. But if she did that, with the captain in his present condition, Maddox might well die.

Valerie didn't know what to do.

-21-

Maddox felt horrible, had felt horrible ever since he'd woken up from surgery. He was weak, disoriented and ready to dry heave whatever was in his stomach onto the deck.

The implant was gone. Doctor Lister said a nerve fiber or two, or two hundred for all she knew, were still embedded in his gray matter. They might or might not cause him trouble. The implant had powered the fibers. Now, the implant was gone so, theoretically, it couldn't power those nerve fibers anymore.

The medical team had fused his skull bone back into place, but according to Lister, a hundred things could go wrong. He should sleep for three or more days, at least, before he considered returning to active duty.

Now, Maddox slowly worked his way across the bridge. He did not like this look. He clung to Meta, but it was her strength that kept him upright. If she lost hold of him, his arm would slide off her shoulder and he would crash onto the deck.

He hated being this weak, but there was nothing he could do about it at the moment.

"Sir," Valerie said, her features pinched with distaste.

Maddox knew his lieutenant. He knew what she was going to tell him.

"Did you...?" he panted.

"Sir?" Valerie asked.

"Did you...find the cloaked vessel?" Maddox asked.

The bridge personnel had been watching his slow and agonizing journey across the deck. Some had been looking away. Now, all of them concentrated on him with amazement.

"Did Galyan talk to you?" Valerie asked.

"About the cloaked vessel?" Maddox asked.

"Yes, sir."

"Ah. That means you found it. Good. What is its location?"

Valerie's mouth had opened with surprise. She closed it and shook her head. "I don't understand, sir. If Galyan didn't tell you about the cloaked vessel, how could you know about it?"

"Through deduction," Maddox said. He'd meant to say it in a quick two words. Instead, it had come out slowly, syllable by syllable.

"Sir?" Valerie asked.

Maddox tore his gaze from her and painstakingly looked up at the main screen. He saw the green circle around nothing. That green circle slowly moved toward the nearest Laumer Point.

"Have you contacted the ship yet?" Maddox asked.

"No, sir," Andros said from his place.

"You'll have to move out of my chair," Maddox told Valerie.

Her pinched look tightened. "I'm afraid I can't do that, sir," Valerie said. "You're in no condition to resume command yet. You should be in sickbay."

Meta's grip tightened around his waist. Maddox wanted to stand under his own power, sweep over to Valerie and yank her out of his chair. Her not instantly moving out of the command chair was intolerable.

"Where's Riker?" Maddox asked.

No one answered him.

That told Maddox all he needed to know. The others agreed with Valerie. He must look terrible indeed.

"Let go of me," he whispered to Meta.

Meta looked up at him. He could see the concern in her eyes. He could also see that she wasn't going to let go of him. He could see that no one would back him up.

94

For a moment, Maddox breathed through his nostrils, thinking.

"I suggest you report to sickbay at once, sir," Valerie said.

Maddox gave a dry whispery laugh. "You have no idea what's really going on," he said in a thin voice. "You think...I don't know what you think. Strand is in that cloaked ship."

Valerie stared at him in astonishment.

"That or his clone," Maddox said. "Most likely it's his clone."

"How can you possibly—?" Valerie cleared her throat. "Can I ask how you know that, sir?"

"I remember from Smade's Asteroid," Maddox said. "Strand spoke to me while I was there."

"Why didn't you say anything about this earlier, sir?" Valerie asked.

Maddox disliked anyone under his command questioning him like this. But he had to convince the others that only he really knew what was going on.

"Because I only remembered seeing Strand once I went under for the operation," he said.

"Ah...say what?" Valerie asked.

Maddox was getting frustrated, but he couldn't afford that. He was too weak as it was. If he let frustration sap any more of his limited strength, he'd pass out.

"How did Captain Maddox know about the cloaked vessel?" Galyan asked Valerie.

"Say...that's right," Andros said. "How did you know, sir?"

"Because I spoke to Strand while on the asteroid base," Maddox said. "I know his ways. He uses cloaked vessels—" The captain suddenly stopped talking.

"What else?" Valerie asked. "You were going to add something else."

"The brain implant was only part of Strand's plan," Maddox said. "The key was first getting me to go undercover to the asteroid on an Intelligence mission."

"I don't understand," Valerie said

95

"I don't know all the parameters," Maddox said. "But this clone of Strand's has a piece of Builder equipment. It allows him to predict people's actions."

"Go on," Valerie said.

That peeved Maddox, but he swept that aside. He had to concentrate on the task.

"Strand's clone set up the conditions so *Victory* would come to the Tristano System," the captain said. "Strand was able to do that because his Builder computer has a remarkable ability to correctly predicate many things. One of those was that I would go in undercover to first investigate the happenings on Smade's Asteroid. Strand wanted me there—"

"I get all that," Valerie said, maybe frustrated by his slow speech. "Strand's clone wanted you there so he could put an implant in your brain just like he did to his former New Men crew."

"Wrong," Maddox said.

"But you just said—"

"Valerie," Maddox said, and he almost swayed out of Meta's grasp as his knees badly sagged just then.

"Move aside," Meta said, surging toward the captain's chair, dragging Maddox with her.

Valerie darted out of the chair because she could tell Meta was going to throw her out and because Maddox really needed to sit somewhere before he collapsed.

Meta gently deposited the captain onto the command chair. He slumped back, gasping, turning whiter than ever.

Valerie chewed her lower lip. She'd never seen Maddox like this, and it upset her.

"Hang on," Maddox mumbled. He'd meant to say it under his breath to himself, but he could see that Valerie, Meta and maybe even Galyan had overheard that.

"Listen," Maddox said. He pulled himself upright, took several steadying breaths and almost puked. He felt worse, not better. He wasn't sure how much longer he could hold onto consciousness.

"Strand's used advanced hypnosis on me," Maddox said slowly. "That was the point. I'm…I'm supposed to do something for him back on Earth."

"What's that?" Valerie asked.

"I can't quite remember," Maddox said. "The clone is destabilizing the Commonwealth. That's his mission. I don't know why that's what he wants, but I know I'm right."

"Sir, in your condition—"

"Listen," Maddox said, and his voice broke at the strain.

"I'm listening," Valerie whispered, feeling terrible for Maddox.

"We can't let the clone escape," Maddox whispered.

"I agree with you, sir. I'm afraid I'm going to have to order a star-drive jump—"

"No," Maddox whispered. "That's a bad idea."

"I'm going to have you board a shuttle first—"

"Strand is counting on that," Maddox said, interrupting.

"What do you mean?"

"He's predicated all this. Don't you see?"

Valerie shook her head. "That's impossible."

With an effort, Maddox raised a hand and swept it side to side. Then he focused on the bridge crew.

"Weapons," Maddox said.

"Sir," the man said.

"Launch two antimatter missiles at the present cloaked ship coordinates," the captain said.

"Sir," Valerie said. "I'm still the acting captain. I have not yet—"

"Sergeant of marines," Maddox said in a whispery voice.

A bulky space marine sergeant hurried up. The tough-looking marine gave his total attention to Maddox.

"Escort the lieutenant to her quarters," Maddox whispered.

"You can't do that," Valerie protested. "By regulations, that would be mutiny. I'm the acting authority on the starship."

The space marine looked indecisive.

"Carry out your orders," Maddox told the marine. Then, the captain deliberately turned his chair so he no longer looked at the sergeant.

"Please, captain," Valerie said. "I hate to—"

Maddox raised a hand and slowly snapped his fingers.

Taking a deep breath, the space marine approached Valerie. "If you'll come with me, Lieutenant."

Valerie debated physically punching the marine, realized the futility of that and—her shoulders slumped. Maybe she should have given command back to Maddox. In the end, he always got his way. This was against the book, though. She was right in doing what she had. And yet, she had lost to Maddox once again.

Valerie wanted to tell Maddox that he was in deep trouble, but she couldn't get the words out. She'd never seen him like this. Couldn't the others tell that he wasn't fit right now to command a starship?

Feeling keenly slighted and extremely embarrassed, Lieutenant Noonan left the bridge under armed escort.

-22-

Maddox might have felt bad for what he'd just done, but he was too tired to focus on more than one thing at a time. He did not have the energy to keep arguing with the lieutenant. He also knew she would never willingly go. He had to do this right. He had to break the Builder computer's ability to predict his actions.

"Weapons," Maddox whispered. "Are those missiles underway?"

"Ah...not yet, sir," the weapons officer said.

Maddox could feel the chills hitting him now. He was even sicker than he realized.

"Sir," Galyan said. "Might I offer a suggestion?"

It took Maddox time to notice the holoimage. "Yes?" Maddox asked.

"Would it be better to load a fold-fighter with the missiles, have the fighter jump near the cloaked vessel, launch the missiles and—?"

"Yes," Maddox said. "That is better. Weapons—I mean Communications, get me the deck officer presently in charge of the hangar bay."

It took ten seconds. In that time, Maddox dozed off. Meta jostled his arm. He raised his head, looked at her in surprise and needed time to figure out where he was.

"Sir," Galyan said. "You really do not seem well. You have just been in a difficult surgery—"

"Galyan," Maddox whispered. "Do you know what I'm doing?"

"I do not understand the question, Captain."

"I know what's going on, what's *really* going on. I know how dangerous the clone is, how deadly his cloaked vessel and computer is. Valerie is a good officer. But…"

Maddox felt Meta shake his elbow. It took longer this time, but he looked up at her. What was going on? Why was he nodding off each time?

Maddox cleared his throat. He didn't know how much longer he could do this. They were listening to him because everyone was used to obeying his commands. But if he dozed off again, Valerie would soon be back in the chair. He had to make sure Strand died. The clone was more deadly than anyone realized.

With anyone else in command, the clone might be able to talk his way out of death. Maddox wasn't going to let that be a possibility.

"Launch two fold-fighters," Maddox whispered. "Each should have an antimatter missile. We must stop the clone now."

The comm officer looked up. "The fighters will launch in fifteen minutes, sir."

Maddox acknowledged the words, wondering why it would take so long. Then, he realized that wasn't long at all. Since they were not in a state of war, the antimatter missiles were in a special set of lockers. The warhead would have to be fitted to the missile, and after that—well, the process took time.

He didn't think the clone knew what was going on yet. Just how clever was the Builder computer?

Maddox had a feeling it was much more clever than anyone realized, maybe even the clone.

The captain sat back. He refused to shiver. Why was it so cold in here? He forced his eyes open and waited. He could do this. For the sake of the Commonwealth, he'd better.

***

Lieutenant Maker found himself heading back in the tin can. That surprised him. Of course, he was the best. But he'd just come in from a mission. He'd folded. A person needed time to let his body adjust to all the skipping around through space.

Star Watch had refined the drugs that let people fold and jump without the old Jump Lag. But still, extended folding in a short amount of time took its toll.

Soon enough, Keith was in the tin can. They'd loaded up an antimatter missile this time.

"Incoming message from the captain," the flight officer said on the comm screen

"Roger that," Keith said.

Maddox appeared on the screen. What the heck? The captain looked terrible. Maddox should let Valerie do this.

Keith hadn't yet learned that Valerie had been confined to quarters.

"This is it, gentlemen," Maddox whispered, addressing both fold-fighter pilots. "I have reason to believe that you're going up against the clone of the Methuselah Man Strand," the captain whispered. "He has a unique vessel, along with...Builder equipment."

Keith nodding with understanding, realizing now why they'd wanted him in on this one.

"Your mission is critical," Maddox said.

Keith already knew that. Why was the captain stating the obvious?

"No matter what happens," Maddox whispered, "you must destroy his vessel."

Keith cocked his head. It seemed they ought to try to capture a ship with Builder equipment. But his wasn't to reason why. His was to do or die, with the emphasis on do.

Maddox continued the briefing. The captain looked as if he was going to pass out at any second.

"Any questions?" Maddox finally asked.

Keith licked his lips, almost asking why they weren't going to capture the clone and his ship, but he decided the captain didn't look healthy enough to answer.

"Get him, gentlemen," Maddox finished. "I'm counting on you."

"Aye-aye, sir," Keith said. "Consider the clone as good as dead, sir. You can take that the bank."

-23-

Strand's clone slept in his quarters aboard his ghost-ship. He was catching a few winks before the Laumer-Point jump. An alarm rang. The clone opened his eyes, sat up, stretched—

The hatch to his quarters slid up. The big artillery-shell-shaped Builder robot floated in. That worried the clone more than the red-alert klaxon. He'd given precise orders some time ago. The robot was *not* allowed to come in here.

"You must hurry to the bridge," the robot said.

Strand's hand slipped under his pillow. He gripped a powerful blaster hidden there. He didn't know if the Builder robot had a good defense against the blaster or not. But he felt that he was about to find out.

"Why are you in my quarters?" Strand demanded.

"Because this is an emergency that overrides your former commands," the robot said blandly.

"I gave you unequivocal orders."

"If you do not reach the bridge soon, your probability of surviving the danger will dip below sixty percent."

"What are you talking about? What's gone wrong?"

"*Victory* has launched two fold-fighters. The craft have folded and are less than three hundred thousand kilometers from us."

"Are they headed for the Laumer Point?"

"Their trajectory is toward us. Captain Maddox is likely aware of our ghost-ship."

"That's impossible. Maddox is in no condition to know that. Besides, he has powerful post-hypnotic commands. He cannot lift a hand against me."

"You must reevaluate your belief, as two fold-fighters are racing toward us. Each of them carries an antimatter missile."

Strand's mouth went dry.

"If you do not reach the bridge soon…"

Strand sensed a threat from the robot. His fingers tightened around the blaster. What if the robot had a force field that was proof against the blaster's heavy beam? Surely, at that point, the robot would retaliate. Should he risk everything by destroying the robot? He would lose his link to the incredible Builder computer, then. Without the computer, how would he achieve his master goal?

"Why are you hesitating?" the robot asked.

"Don't you know why?" Strand mocked.

"In truth, yes," the robot said. "You are deciding if you can destroy me with your hidden blaster. You cannot, but if you need to make the attempt…"

Strand went cold inside. "And if I fail to destroy you?" he asked.

"Then you will die."

The fear wriggled in Strand's gut. He couldn't believe this. Had the robot and the computer been using him all this time?

He released the blaster and removed his hand from under the pillow. He couldn't worry about the robot now. He would later, but not now.

"Maddox knows we're here?" Strand asked.

"I give that a seventy-eight percent probability," the robot said.

"That means Maddox broke my hypnotic conditioning?"

"Most likely true," the robot said.

"How did he do it?"

"I do not know. It is an interesting mystery, one I intend to solve."

"Well, that's something. You don't know everything"

"I never claimed I did."

Strand shook his head. The robot was giving him a migraine. He couldn't believe this. Maddox was on to him. How had the blasted captain managed it this time?

Strand stood up, leaving the blaster under the pillow, for now, at least.

"Can we beat the missiles?" the clone asked.

"If you act with haste," the robot answered.

That was all Strand needed to hear. He hurried to the hatch. How had Maddox broken the hypnotic conditioning? The hybrid had more tricks up his sleeve than seemed reasonable.

"Not this time!" Strand shouted, and he began to run to the ghost-ship's small bridge.

-24

Keith came out of the fold feeling groggy and disoriented. He threw up on the floor of the tin can.

The tin can kept on its original flight pattern as programmed before the fold. That was away from what was supposed to be a new heading. His flight screen blinked on and off, trying to alert him. Finally, a klaxon began to blare for his attention.

With a sleeve, Keith wiped the vomit from his lips. His head pounded. He knew he'd overdone it. He'd been right. He should have skipped this fold, this mission.

"Get a grip, now," he whispered.

"Lieutenant Maker," his comm squawked.

Keith slapped a switch.

Second Lieutenant Roderigo Hernandez stared at him from the screen. The man had a V-shaped buzz cut and the narrowest, most intense face among the strikefighter pilots aboard *Victory*. "What's wrong with you?" Roderigo asked.

"Not a damn thing," Keith said.

"Your voice sounds hoarse."

"What has your panties in a bunch?" Keith asked.

The man's intensity dialed up. "You're off course. *Victory* has fed us new coordinates. The cloaked vessel has changed heading. It's not heading for the Laumer Point anymore, but trying to slip away from us."

Keith scowled. Something seemed off about that. They had just made a fold. That meant they had crossed through or jumped from one part of space to another. *Victory* was three billion kilometers behind them…

Light traveled 300,000 kilometers per second. That meant in ten seconds, light traveled three million kilometers. Ten ten-seconds was one hundred seconds or one minute and forty seconds. In that time, light traveled thirty million kilometers. Ten times that was 300 million kilometers. Ten times one minute and forty seconds was something over sixteen minutes. Ten times sixteen minutes—to reach three billion kilometers away—was something over two and half hours.

All of that meant *Victory* could not have possibly sent them new data about the cloaked ship's new heading. The math was all wrong for a signal to have reached them this soon.

"Is something wrong, Lieutenant?" Roderigo asked.

Keith wiped his eyes, blinked several times and studied Roderigo Hernandez. He tried to remember exactly what the man looked like. Right, Roderigo had a mole over his left eye. It was no longer there.

"Damn it," Keith hissed. He slapped another switch, activating a powerful comm pulse. It was meant to burn through enemy jamming.

The image on his screen dissolved. A second later, Second Lieutenant Roderigo Hernandez stared at him. This one had a mole over his left eye.

"Back already?" Roderigo asked.

"What's that mean?" Keith asked warily.

"You just said—"

"No! That wasn't me," Keith shouted. "You must have received false communications just like I did a second ago. Remain on the original target and launch your missile. Do it now, man."

"What are you talking about?"

At that point, heavier enemy jamming blanketed the comm signal. Roderigo's image became a blizzard of screen snow.

"Strand is messing with us," Keith said.

He made a fast course correction. As he did, he primed the antimatter missile. He typed in commands. Once launched, the missile would shut down its comm link. It would only follow its prearranged flight path, nothing else. Strand would not be able to feed the missile or the warhead false data. Well, if this was really a Methuselah Man, he shouldn't be able to mess with the missile. With these super-geniuses, one never knew.

The tin can shuddered as Keith launched the missile. Then he began to bank hard, activating the gravity dampeners. He had to get out of here as fast as he could, but he dared not use the fold again. He was already messed up enough as it was.

-25-

Strand sat back, frustrated with the fold-fighter pilot, the one named Lieutenant Keith Maker. The ace had been with Maddox for a long time, the captain's wiliness rubbing off on him in a bad way.

"The second pilot is too wary for your tricks," the robot said.

Strand glanced back at the pesky construct.

"You're in this with me," the clone said. "If I die, you die."

The robot did not reply to that.

"So if you can't come up with a plan, don't mock the one who has one."

The robot still said nothing.

With a soft grunt, Strand resumed scanning. The first pilot was on course with the new heading, going the wrong way. The pilot's antimatter missile was still onboard the first fold-fighter. It was the second missile barreling on a beeline course for the ghost-ship that frightened the clone.

"It has an antimatter warhead," Strand said. "It doesn't have to hit us, just get close when it ignites."

"I am familiar with the parameters of a Star Watch antimatter missile," the robot said.

"You're a fussy little robot, aren't you?"

"Your mannerisms indicate that you are worried. Do you fear extinction?"

"Yes!" Strand shouted. "You should fear it, too. Or are you too stupid to realize how precious your life is? This is the only one we get, you know."

"Do you truly believe this?" the robot asked. "Do you not believe in an afterlife for sentient beings such as yourself?"

"No!" Strand shouted.

"Your voice patterns are off. Why are you lying? Do you fear that your unbelief does not make it fact?"

Strand turned fully around, giving the robot a scathing glance. Then he faced his board and pressed a switch. That activated an outer relay, which sent a powerful and precise pulse toward the two varying missiles—the one heading for the ghost-ship and the one going away with the duped fold-fighter pilot Roderigo Hernandez at its helm.

***

Strand's signal to the antimatter warheads had taken a long time for the Builder computer to create. That signal now sped at the speed of light to the warheads.

The special signal momentarily showed the ghost-ship's exact position to anyone with the proper sensors. Giving away their position was a risk, but it likely wouldn't matter in the larger scheme of things. The coming antimatter blasts would act as two perfect jamming devices. The blasts would whiten the area, in sensor terms.

The special signal reached the first fold-fighter and its antimatter missile in the launch tube. The signal activated the warhead's firing sequence. Three seconds later, the antimatter warhead detonated. Antimatter mixed with matter, creating a vast explosion. The detonation annihilated the fold-fighter and Roderigo Hernandez, and everything else in the immediate vicinity.

The antimatter blast billowed outward, sending heat, gamma, x-ray and other radiation.

Keith saw the blast, cursed and initiated the fold-mechanism. He didn't have to look at the numbers. In that split-second, he knew that Strand had screwed them, somehow fooling the warhead. He had no doubt that, despite his precautions, his warhead would detonate as well.

The fold-fighter banked and turned, almost completing the maneuver so it would head back to the starship. That was three billion kilometers away, so it would take time to reach *Victory*.

Keith knew he couldn't outrace the antimatter detonation. He wasn't far enough away from his missile yet. He tensed up as he readied to hit the fold switch.

The warhead on the missile he'd launched ignited.

Keith cursed once more, pressed the fold switch, and nothing happened.

"No!" Keith shouted. "What's Valerie going to do without me?"

At that moment, the sluggish system activated. At the same moment, the first gamma and x-rays from the terrible antimatter blast reached his tin can.

Destruction occurred while Keith's fold-fighter began to fold, heading back in the blink of an eye toward the ancient Adok starship.

-26-

While *Victory* had searched for the clone of Strand and then sent out its fold-fighters, conditions inside Smade's Asteroid had worsened with growing intensity. First, the heads of key Chang personnel had literally exploded, raining skull fragments and brain tissue everywhere, which included onto nearby confederates. That had created instant panic inside the large Chang facility. The panic had loosened authority until certain opportunists had begun to loot, favoring high-tech equipment and military grade weaponry, and stealing billions in credit transfers and valuable items such as platinum, gold, gems and various jewels. The panic and the sense of grab-what-you-can-while-you-can had jumped to the regular space pirates outside the Chang compound. Many of them had broken into the fabled stronghold. Gunfights between looters quickly turned savage, and many people were murdered.

The chaos worsened as key asteroid life-support computer systems activated a strange protocol. The asteroid's main stations cycled to hidden canisters of XT Chlorine, a highly toxic gas. The life-support systems began injecting the mutated chlorine into the main halls and corridors. Shortly thereafter, people had begun to drop like proverbial flies. Many vomited first. The survivors soon realized that the interior asteroid air had been poisoned.

That intensified the gunfights as the survivors who'd managed to find gasmasks clawed and struggled for the few remaining spacecraft. Smade's Asteroid was turning into a charnel house. The survivors wanted off as quickly as possible, and they were willing to murder anyone who got in their way.

Deep inside Chang's highest security area—with private cyclers pumping fresh air into the chambers—was a roomful of frightened scientists, medical techs and surgeons. They were primarily of Asian descent and predominantly men. Among them was the scientist with the bowl-cut copper-colored hair, Doctor Lee, who had ordered Jand to watch Maddox and had later chased the captain into the main bazaar.

Only one humanoid in the large room did not tremble with fear. He was a dark-haired individual, slightly taller but much heavier than average. The greater weight did not come from his stature or from bulky muscles. He looked ordinary enough. He simply seemed slightly heavier than average. The greater weight and density was due to his construction. He was an android made to resemble a placid Asian man with unremarkable features. The placid features were a good touch, since the android did not emote feelings the same way flesh and blood humans did.

He happened to be one of the oldest and possibly *the* oldest android who commonly resided in Human Space. His name was Yen Cho, and he'd been on Starship *Victory* several voyages ago when he had taken a "data gulp" for Maddox and the crew, and later bargained to give up the data for a head start against Star Watch Intelligence operatives.

This Yen Cho android had his own agenda, which did not always coincide with the "Rull" of the Android Nation as discovered on Sind II by Professor Ludendorff.

In any case, the most-premier Yen Cho-model android sat at a console. He wore camouflage military gear and seemed to be in his mid-thirties, in human terms. He studied the image on his screen, watching the approaching double-oval starship, *Victory*. His acuity sharpened as a badly damaged fold-fighter abruptly appeared in space near the starship.

With swift taps, he adjusted the controls, zoomed in on the fighter and attempted to break into its communication. All he got was a standard mayday signal.

Despite his obvious interest, Yen Cho's black eyes seemed unusually deep and unusually calm. He was processing all the data he'd gathered so far together with the sight of the combat-damaged fold-fighter.

It had been quite some time since Yen Cho had interacted with Captain Maddox and his people. He had learned several interesting pieces of data during Maddox's internment on Smade's Asteroid. For instance, cunning Professor Ludendorff and his lover Doctor Dana Rich were not aboard the starship. That was important.

Indeed. As Yen Cho sat at the console, he nodded decisively.

He had taken considerable risks by coming to Smade's Asteroid. Officially, he was part of Chang's carefully collected science team. The greatest risk had been discovery by the clone Strand. As far as Yen Cho had been able to discern, the dangerous clone hadn't sniffed him out. There was no possibility that Chang would have. Now, the Shanghai heavy leader was dead.

Decision made as what to do next, Yen Cho stood, and he whirled around as someone hammered insistently outside the armored hatch.

The noise badly affected the scientists and medical personnel crammed in the room. Almost to a person, they jerked in fear. A few pulled out small handguns, aiming the weapons at the armored hatch.

"Put those away," Yen Cho said. He did not want a bloodbath in here, one that might incapacitate him. He didn't fear their small caliber weapons, but what the hammering marine might do in response to enemy gunfire.

Unfortunately, no one paid his order any heed; he was not highly ranked on the former Chang pay scale.

The hammering changed, becoming a heavy clanging that produced dents in the armored hatch. It must have become obvious then to the others what Yen Cho had already divined.

"The knocker is wearing combat armor," the android shouted.

A few of the scientists and medical personnel turned to stare at him.

114

"If you shoot at a combat suit," Yen Cho said with remorseless logic, "the suited heavy will surely kill you out of hand in automatic response."

The people in this room were an unsavory lot, having committed horrid deeds on other humans in order to receive high pay. The Shanghai heavies were equally immoral. They were also brutal and savage when given their choice. If the suited heavies indulged their whims, they would use suit-contained cannon-fire to massacre everyone in here, including Yen Cho. The android hoped to forestall that.

The hammering intensified once more, creating deeper dents in the hatch.

"What should we do?" asked Doctor Lee.

"What can you do?" Yen Cho asked. "Surrender is the wisest option. Perhaps these heavies want your technical expertise for something. That is our greatest hope."

Doctor Lee blinked several times as his gun hand and weapon shook. With an effort of will, Lee slid the small caliber pistol back into a hidden holster.

The others began to do likewise.

At that point, metallic fingers eased between the battered hatch and the doorjamb. With a whine of servos, a heavy combat suit tore the hatch from its moorings.

The scientists and medical personnel cried out in fear. The fear had two sources, the heavies and possible poisoned gas. They cringed against the farthest wall. Yen Cho stood at the very back, although he did not cringe like the rest. He kept studying and analyzing.

Three exoskeleton combat suits clanked into the chamber. Two of them aimed heavy 30-mm autocannons at the mass of scientists and medical personnel. The other combat suit's faceplate whined as it descended. A Shanghai heavy peered out of the armored helmet. He was a cruel-faced soldier with a deep scar over his left eyebrow.

"Which of you is Doctor Lee?" the heavy asked.

Several of the cowering people turned to the copper-haired scientist.

"You," the heavy said. "Step forward."

Doctor Lee pushed past the others. Just like the time he'd chased Maddox, Lee wore a white lab coat. He did not cower, although he seemed tense. He also seemed calculating.

"You are Doctor Lee?" the combat-suited heavy asked.

The scientist nodded.

The cruel-faced soldier did not smile, but became even more intense, more concentrated.

"There is madness in the asteroid," the heavy said. "The air is poisoned. Worse, a Star Watch battleship approaches the asteroid."

Lee said nothing.

"We wish to escape," the heavy said.

Lee nodded.

The heavy abruptly clanked forward until the combat suit loomed over the scientist.

"You will take us to the hidden spaceship," the heavy shouted. "If you do not take us there this instant—"

"I will take you," Lee said.

The heavy quit shouting, and seemed to lose much of his hostility.

"How many…soldiers are with you?" Doctor Lee asked.

"Eleven, including me," the heavy said.

Lee turned around, studying the anxious scientists and medical personnel. He seemed to be counting their numbers. Maybe he was counting in order to see how many would get to leave the asteroid and start anew somewhere else with him.

Yen Cho pushed through their number. "I am an engine tech," he told the doctor.

Lee squinted, and he shook his copper-haired head. "I do not know you."

Yen Cho understood. The doctor would not take him along. That was unfortunate. He had assumed one of the scientists knew the whereabouts of a special escape ship. Yen Cho's problem was that he hadn't known which one. Now, he did.

Yen Cho had gained several interesting upgrades throughout the millennia. He did not have the same goal as many of the other Yen Cho-series androids. He was, in most cases, far less bloodthirsty than others of his kind. This, however, was an emergency. That changed his protocols.

116

Yen Cho moved closer to Lee. As the android did so, he slumped his shoulders in a cringing manner while his features took on a pleading cast.

"Please," Yen Cho whispered. "I am a space tech."

"Go away," Lee told him.

Although Yen Cho dipped his head in submission, he knew his precise location in the room compared to the heavies in their combat suits. Yen Cho fell to his knees, as might a frightened human who had lost all hope. His shoulders shook as if he was weeping in abject fear. What he was really doing was hotshotting his special laser pistol. The heavy-duty pistol could now fire three intensely hot rays. That would burn out the pistol's laser circuits and might possibly cause a deadly explosion afterward.

"We must go," the combat-suited heavy told Lee. "We are running out of time."

"Yes," Doctor Lee said. "I understand. I am choosing the ship's crew. You said there are eleven of you. That means eight of our group can fit into the escape ship. Now—"

At that point, Yen Cho looked up and fired from his kneeling, hunched-over position. An intensely hot laser-beam burned against the armored faceplate of the most faraway-standing exoskeleton-powered armored suit.

The hotshotting had worked. Because of the short range, the super-heated laser-beam penetrated the faceplate, spearing into the face of the heavy inside.

Yen Cho shifted targets and fired his second beam. It, too, burned through the enemy faceplate. As the weapon did that, the first combat-suit clanged against the floor as the slain heavy inside fell down.

The scientists and medical personnel, still crammed against the back wall, began to shout and scream in terror. Many pressed farther back as though they could get away from the conflict. A few braver souls began drawing their small hand-weapons.

The combat-reflex from the last heavy was almost instantaneous. The two-ton suit opened fire with its arm-integral 30-mm. The autocannon chugged shells, mowing down the cringing crowd.

At the same time, Yen Cho could no longer use his laser pistol, however. The hotshotting had only lasted for two shots, as the inner circuits had burned out.

From his kneeling position, Yen Cho straightened, drew back his right arm and threw the overheating pistol. As the pistol flew through the air, smoke began chugging from it, the plastic melting into a blob of uselessness. That blob flew through the opened faceplate and struck the firing heavy in the face.

The heavy howled in agony. He must have instinctively activated the faceplate. It now snapped shut, keeping the melted superhot pistol pressed against his face.

The exoskeleton-powered suit began to dance in a macabre fashion. Yen Cho darted aside from its path, and he grabbed the back of Doctor Lee's lab coat, barely yanking the man aside in time so the two-ton combat suit didn't crush him.

A second later, the combat suit banged against a wall, fell onto the floor and began to writhe back and forth. It was horrible and obscene as pitiful cries echoed inside the helmet.

The doctor turned in Yen Cho's grasp. He looked at the android's right hand. Yen Cho grabbed the lab coat with the left. Some of the pseudo-skin on the right-hand palm had burned away, revealing gleaming metal underneath.

"What are you?" Lee whispered in horror.

"You can obviously see what I am," Yen Cho replied.

"An android?" the doctor asked.

While keeping hold of the doctor's lab coat, Yen Cho examined the weeping scientists and medical personnel who had survived the autocannon onslaught. Less than a third lived, and many of those were badly wounded.

"A moment," Yen Cho said.

The android released the doctor, hurried to the dead and hurting, and searched two of them. He came away with two handguns. One of those he shoved into Lee's hands.

The doctor stared at him, the question obvious in his eyes.

"We're going to your escape ship," Yen Cho said. "We want to leave the dying asteroid before the starship arrives."

"Just the two of us?" Lee asked.

"No."

Lee waited a moment longer, maybe waiting for Yen Cho to add something. Finally, Lee said, "I don't understand."

"For now, you do not need to. You can trust in the knowledge that I am Grade 'A' strategist and tactician. You can also trust me to get you to your ship and to get us away from here undetected."

The doctor scanned the dead heavies, took stock of the dead and wounded scientists and medical personnel and, finally, regarded Yen Cho again.

"There are other heavies in our path," Lee said.

"Good. We need some of them."

"I do not understand why we would need them."

"Come," Yen Cho said. He grabbed one of the doctor's sleeves. He was going to have to do this the hard way, as it was taking too long doing it through coaxing and explaining.

At that point, Doctor Lee began to train his gun on Yen Cho. The android had been expecting that. He slapped the gun out of the doctor's grasp. Then he picked up the struggling human and darted out of the hatch.

He'd lied to the man. Yen Cho had no intention of escaping from the approaching starship. Quite the contrary, in fact.

-27-

There was gun- and autocannon fire in the halls and corridors. Lights flickered in places. In others, a red emergency glow gave the corridor an eerie feel.

"Put me down," Doctor Lee shouted. "You'll get us killed with your carelessness."

Yen Cho did not respond. He had a plan. He had a mission. He needed the doctor's knowledge. He did not have time to torture it out of Lee, either.

Throughout the centuries, the androids had moved undercover through the human populations. Sometimes they did it to protect humanity from its stupidest impulses. Sometimes they did it to help the underground community of Builder-made androids. This was one of those times where both reasons motivated Yen Cho.

Strand had set up a horrible situation. He had gone much too far this time. If Yen Cho and his brothers were right about Strand's ultimate desire...

Yen Cho skidded to a halt before his quarters in Chang's underground dormitory. The fingers of his metallic-looking hand blurred over a control pad. The hatch slid open.

Setting Doctor Lee onto his feet, Yen Cho unceremoniously pushed him within. Lee crashed against a chair, sprawling onto the floor. The doctor yelped in pain. He'd caught himself, so his face hadn't smashed into the floor, but at least one bone in his left wrist had snapped from the force of his descent.

Yen Cho ignored the mewling doctor for the moment. He rummaged in his locker, pulled out a pair of gloves and shoved his hands into them. Then he withdrew a medical kit. It seemed innocent enough, but it was not.

He went to Doctor Lee, who lay on the floor, cradling his broken wrist. The man had turned white from the pain and was moaning to himself. The human had lost the arrogance he'd displayed earlier when he'd been deciding who would live by escaping in the spaceship, and who would die by remaining on the asteroid.

Yen Cho extracted a hypo from his kit, checked the dosage and pressed the end against the doctor's neck. The hypo hissed as the solution was pressure-injected into Lee.

"My wrist still hurts," Lee complained several seconds later.

Yen Cho stood as he impassively regarded the man. Lee had been one of Chang's most trusted scientists, most trusted among those who had not received a brain implant. The android believed that the unchecked pain from the doctor's broken bone would help the solution achieve its desired result faster than otherwise. That was good, as time had become critical.

"What's happening to me?" Lee complained. "I'm feeling fainter, not better."

The android waited several seconds longer before going back to his locker. He grabbed a gym bag and stuffed it with items. When he returned to Lee, the man looked at him strangely.

The android squatted before the hurting scientist. "I am Yen Cho. I am your friend and confidante."

"Yes," the doctor said. "I realize this. Will you fix my wrist for me?"

"I will, friend," Yen Cho said, smiling. "First, tell me the location of the hidden spaceship."

The man began to babble all about the hidden ship. What's more, he told Yen Cho about the hidden defenses, the needed codes and other factors in order to take the ship out of the asteroid's secret exit.

Yen Cho only had to hear it once. As an android, his cybertronic brain forgot nothing. At last, he decided he knew enough.

He stood. It was good to know that the special serum worked. It had performed well on the test humans back in the Rigel System laboratories where the androids had tested the drug, but this was his first use in a real situation. The serum was not a long-lasting thing like brain implants. It worked almost as well in the short term, however.

Yen Cho checked his supply of serum. It should be enough to win a crew of heavies and any needed techs. They wouldn't last long, though. That was the kicker...

Yen Cho shook his head. That was the side effect of the serum. It soon destroyed the subject's brain, eating away at the neural connectives. The longest-surviving test subject had kept her sanity for fifteen days.

That should be more than enough time for what Yen Cho had planned.

"Friend," Lee said from the floor. "Where are you going?"

Yen Cho stood by the hatch. It looked as if he was about to leave.

The android studied Lee. "Lie back," he said. "I am going to get you help."

"You promise?"

"Yes," Yen Cho said.

"Thank you. I'm starting to feel...funny."

"It will pass," Yen Cho said.

Doctor Lee lay back, with his injured wrist resting on his chest.

Without further thought for Lee, Yen Cho exited his quarters. He heard more gunfire down the halls. He needed to move fast if he was going to recruit his heavies and techs in time to accomplish his goal.

-28-

Maddox lay on his bed in his quarters aboard Starship *Victory*. He'd been trembling from exhaustion for some time. Meta sat beside him, stroking his forehead.

He loved Meta's touch. At night, he liked to lie beside her as she read on her tablet, running her free hand over his back and buttocks. It was the most relaxing part of the day for him.

Now, he didn't feel relaxed. He felt like crap, and he had failed to take out the clone of Strand. He should have known better than to send two strikefighter pilots after the genius. What's more, the clone possessed Builder equipment. He should have foreseen what had happened.

Would Keith survive his injuries?

A chime sounded.

"Enter," Maddox whispered.

"Come in," Meta said more loudly.

The hatch to his quarters opened. A stocky marine stood there. The man stepped aside. Valerie entered his quarters. She saw him, hesitated, squared her shoulders and marched toward his bed. She stopped and stared down at him.

"You are...no...longer confined to quarters," Maddox whispered slowly.

Valerie said nothing.

Maddox glanced at Meta. Meta sighed and looked up at Valerie.

"Keith is hurt," Meta said.

Valerie's eyes widened with understanding and then fear. "What happened?" she asked.

Meta told Valerie what they knew. Keith's badly damaged tin can had appeared. A rescue shuttle had brought him in. Keith had burns all over his body. The ace had stayed coherent long enough to tell them that Hernandez and he had failed to take out the cloaked vessel. Keith was now in medical undergoing emergency treatment.

Valerie glared at Maddox. "You sent Keith on another mission, even though he'd just been on a fold assignment?"

"Do not question my decisions," Maddox whispered, raising himself onto his elbows.

"Please, husband," Meta said, putting her hands on his chest. "Lay back. Rest."

Maddox collapsed back against the bed.

"Valerie," Meta pleaded.

Valerie glanced at Meta, but it did nothing to soften her features.

"That's how you always do it," Valerie told Maddox with an edge to her voice. "You do whatever you want. Now, Keith has sustained serious injuries. I can't believe this. I would have never—"

"Valerie," Meta said, jumping up, shoving the lieutenant backward and interrupting her screed.

Valerie stumbled and almost went down. She righted herself and glared at Meta.

"You can't push another Star Watch officer," Valerie said. "That's a serious offense."

Meta squeezed her hands into fists. No one was going to harm Maddox in any way. He was in a critical condition. If Valerie thought—

"Listen," Maddox said in a hoarse voice. "Listen to me, Lieutenant."

Both women stared at Maddox.

He had sat up, and there was more energy in him than just a second ago.

"I'm exhausted," Maddox said. "I have to rest. I'm giving you orders, Lieutenant. You're going to put me aboard a shuttle. Then, you're going to use the star-drive and jump to the ghost-ship. I want you to use the main disrupter cannon. Annihilate the clone's cloaked vessel. He must not get away. Once you've completed the mission, return and pick me up."

"You're returning command of the starship to me?" Valerie asked.

"I just said I was."

Valerie stared at him for two seconds and seemed to reach a conclusion. "Then, you have to apologize for having that musclebound ape drag me off the bridge earlier in front of everyone."

"We don't have time for this," Maddox said.

Valerie shook her head. "Then I'm not going to acknowledge your orders. Get someone else to command the starship."

"Is this mutiny?" he asked.

"Call it whatever you like," she said. "You embarrassed me in front of everyone. What's more, I was in the right. But you just bulled through as you always do. This time, I'd like to hear you say you're sorry."

Maddox stared at her. He had no intention of saying—he slumped back and hit the bed. Seconds later, Meta shook him back awake.

He hardly knew what had happened.

"Can't you say it?" Meta whispered to him.

"Say what?" Maddox asked.

From somewhere unseen, a person snorted.

At that point, Maddox remembered. He sighed. He was so damn tired and kept fainting. Maybe Doctor Lister hadn't done as good a job as she thought she'd done.

"I'm sorry," he whispered.

"What's that?" Valerie asked.

"I'm," Maddox said as loudly as he could. "Sorry. Now, go kill the clone…if you can."

Valerie stood at precise attention. She made a perfect salute. "Yes, sir, you can bet your balls that's exactly what I'm going to do."

-29-

Valerie seethed as she rapped out orders on the bridge. Maddox had said he was sorry. She could hardly believe that had happened. Even harder to believe was how she'd stood up to him. It had been one of the most difficult things to say to him. Such a thing wasn't covered by regulations. She had done what she felt was right, even though he had given her a direct order to resume command. Maybe as bad as that, she had been sure he would not say he was sorry.

Yet Captain Maddox had. She could let go of that. She *had* let go of that. It was one of the reasons she seethed inside.

As the bridge crew readied for the star-drive jump, it gave her a few seconds to contemplate the last hour.

She'd worked tirelessly to get the starship ready for a fast combat jump. Because Maddox had apologized, she had put that behind her and totally focused on the mission at hand.

It had felt good. She seethed because of what she'd just heard about Keith. He had gone into shock. She hadn't wanted to, but she'd ordered him aboard a shuttle as well. Two shuttles were staying behind, with two strikefighters to guard them.

She didn't want one of the pirates at Smade's Asteroid making a kidnapping attempt.

Valerie seethed because she wanted payback from Strand, or the clone of Strand.

A clone of the Methuselah Man Strand. That implied the real Strand's hand. He had to be the most vengeful person she knew. He must have labored for years to set something like this up in case he ever died or faced imprisonment. It stood to reason, right? The clone—if it was Strand—had Builder tools, possibly a Builder ship. If the real Strand hadn't used those things…it had to be because they were too dangerous to use normally.

Valerie shook her head. Why did the real Strand care so much? Why did the Methuselah Man have to get back at everyone?

Emotion. It came down to emotion. That was how the ancient Methuselah Man was wired. According to Captain Maddox, the real Strand wanted his clone to destabilize the Commonwealth of Planets.

Valerie wondered why the real Strand wanted such a thing. Did he think such destabilization would create the conditions so he could escape the New Men? Could the real Strand have planned that far in advance?

Valerie couldn't see how. And yet, according to Maddox, this fake Strand, this clone, had amazingly predictive software and computers so he could do such a thing as lure *Victory* to the Tristano System…so Maddox would go undercover to the asteroid.

What did the clone need Maddox to do back home?

Valerie shook her head. It could be a whole slew of things. Would the clone want Maddox to assassinate Brigadier O'Hara, for instance?

"Galyan," Valerie said.

The little holoimage stood beside the captain's chair. He turned to her.

The starship shuddered.

"What was that?" Valerie shouted. She made a face at herself. She shouldn't shout. The acting captain was supposed to remain calm so the rest of the bridge crew could draw from her calmness and remain even-tempered.

"There was a…hiccup in the antimatter engines," Andros said.

"A hiccup?" Valerie asked.

"It's the best way I can describe it," Andros said. "We need another few minutes to check the main lines before we can possibly jump."

127

She nodded.

"Valerie," Galyan said.

She turned to the holoimage.

"You spoke my name a few seconds ago."

"Oh, right," she said. "I was going to ask you something. Now, I've forgotten what it was."

"You must be worried about Keith," Galyan said. "Would you like me to check on his condition?"

"No!" Valerie said, a little too loudly perhaps.

Galyan seemed to study her.

"I have to concentrate on the mission," she explained. "I need to focus. If the captain thinks this is that critical, I cannot fail him."

"I have read many medical journals," the holoimage said. "They agree that the human mind is a...funny instrument. It can hallucinate under many of the conditions Captain Maddox faced while under anesthesia during his surgery."

"You don't think he really knows what's going on?" Valerie asked, surprised.

"He did know about the cloaked vessel," Galyan said. "That is something in his favor. The rest of it...I am unsure. Do you fully trust the captain's... certainty?"

"He's made remarkable guesses in the past," Valerie said.

"True. That is another point in his favor."

"Okay, Galyan, spit it out. I have a few minutes until Andros gives me the all clear. What's really troubling you?"

"Why is the captain so dead set on destroying the cloaked ship? I would think the better idea would be to capture it, to interrogate the clone and confiscate the Builder technology."

Valerie rubbed her chin. The little holoimage had a point. "Do you have any idea why Maddox might want to order the cloaked vessel's destruction?"

"I do. Strand fashioned the New Men. The New Men harmed the captain's mother. Maybe without his realizing it, the captain holds Strand responsible for his mother's death."

"I don't think that's it," Valerie said.

"It is an elaborate theory," Galyan admitted.

Valerie cocked her head, finally nodding. "Strand once put post-hypnotic commands in Meta's mind, remember?"

128

"I do remember, Valerie."

"The captain's story holds together is what I'm saying. Until I find a solid reason otherwise, I'm trusting the captain's instincts."

"Even after what happened to Keith?"

It took her two heartbeats, but Valerie nodded.

"Interesting," Galyan said.

"Captain," Andros said. "We're ready. The engines are clear to jump."

Valerie nodded. She faced the main screen. They were going to jump into battle. They were leaving Maddox, Meta and Keith behind. She rubbed two of her fingers together.

"Jump when ready," she told helm.

Then she anticipated the fight on the other side of the jump, and hoped she was good enough so the clone of Strand didn't outsmart her and make her look like an idiot.

-30-

Despite Yen Cho's lack of emotions, the android was uneasy as he waited inside the spaceship inside Smade's Asteroid.

His logic processors warned him this was an iffy mission. Still, he didn't see that he had much of a choice. Someone, likely the clone Strand, had sabotaged the asteroid. As far as Yen Cho had been able to determine, the event that had started the mayhem had been Chang's death.

Had Strand engineered that?

That seemed highly unlikely, and yet, there were many unlikely factors at work here. The probabilities of many of the events that had occurred...they had struck Yen Cho as impossible. That had also indicated what he'd long feared about Strand.

The Methuselah Man was reckless. All the Methuselah Men over the centuries had been conceited, reckless humans that the wrong-headed faction of Builders had foisted upon the universe.

While Yen Cho wasn't a hardcore "Rising Sun" Builder sect advocate, he did have leanings in that direction.

Many species throughout the centuries had believed that the Builders were a monolithic group. The truth was otherwise. The Builders had been just as fractured as humanity, with some sects completely at odds with the others. Many alien races were not like that. Humans and Builders were, to a fault.

In any case, Strand was reckless. The original Strand, the one trapped on the Throne World, had set certain schemes into place. Some of those schemes would only begin if and when he was captured or slain. The Methuselah Man was incredibly vengeful.

The clone had huge ideas, and he possessed fantastic technology. According to what Yen Cho had discovered, the clone had a Builder-made vessel and possibly a Builder-constructed robot of special design.

Yen Cho intended on gaining both of those items. To achieve that, however—

The rear hatch of the piloting chamber opened. A musclebound 2-G heavy lumbered in. He stank of sweat and fear, and of anger.

"We do not move," the heavy said. He name was Chem and he was a squad leader, thicker and stronger than the others under his command. Five other heavies followed Chem. Along the way, Yen Cho had picked up three techs. The techs were terrified of the monstrous soldiers.

Yen Cho looked back at Chem. The heavy hadn't been dosed with the hypo. To the android's surprise, he'd found that logic had swayed the brute. The creature had actually sworn an oath to follow him.

It had dawned on Yen Cho that the heavies were like overgrown dogs in search of a master. Still, some dogs could growl with impatience if they did not get their food fast enough. For Chem, right now, "food" was escape from the treacherous asteroid.

"I am thinking," Yen Cho said.

"Or do you not really know how to pilot a spaceship?"

"I told you I can pilot it. I do not lie."

"But we do not move. Think while you fly us from here."

"Do you want to live, Chem?"

"Yes. I have said so."

"There is a Star Watch battleship out there."

"I know."

"I am figuring out how to make it let us leave the star system."

"That is impossible."

"Is it really, Chem? If that is so, we are doomed."

The heavy scowled thunderously. "Do not mock me."

"I do not," Yen Cho said. "I am waiting—"

The screen began to blink.

The android faced it and began to manipulate the board. He watched the starship use its special jump mechanism, vanishing from view.

"What happened?" Chem said. "Where did it go? There is no Laumer Point out there."

"The starship is coming back," Yen Cho said, avoiding the question. "It has to come back."

"Why?"

Yen Cho manipulated the controls. He brought up two shuttles and two strikefighters guarding them. All four vessels were quite some distance from the asteroid, farther than a spaceship could reach quickly.

"I have been monitoring their communications," Yen Cho explained. "The captain of the starship is out there in a shuttle."

"That is stupid of him."

"In this instance, I agree with you, but Captain Maddox did not have a choice in the matter. That he is there inclines me to believe that surgeons removed the control chip. He cannot fold or jump until his brain has rested for a time."

The android regarded the heavy behind him. "Do you know what is even better?"

The huge soldier shook his rather small head.

"This ship possesses a fold mechanism just like the fighter I saw earlier."

"Is that important?" Chem asked.

"Oh, yes," Yen Cho said. "It means that I am about to capture Captain Maddox. With him in my grasp…I will be able to dictate terms to the starship."

The heavy frowned, making him seem stupider than normal as he tried to follow the android's reasoning.

"Go," Yen Cho told Chem. "Tell the others to strap in. We're about to leave. Tell them to remain strapped in until I say otherwise. We are going to jump."

"Without a Laumer Point near?" Chem asked.

"This is a fold vessel. Weren't you listening?"

The huge brute regarded the android. Chem finally nodded. "I will tell the others."

"Good," Yen Cho said. "And make sure your combat suits are ready. You're going to be raiding the largest shuttle."

"Does the shuttle have women? We lack women."

Yen Cho thought of Meta. He had never really cared for her. "Yes. The shuttle has women. You may keep the women if you do exactly as I say."

Chem smiled, showing horse-sized teeth. Then the heavy retreated to give the message.

Yen Cho began to activate the controls. It was time to leave Smade's Asteroid and ready this vessel to fight. So far, the plan was proceeding flawlessly.

-31-

Deeper in the Tristano System, Strand's ghost-ship accelerated, heading as fast as it could for the nearest Laumer Point. Despite all its fantastic equipment, the vessel lacked an independent star-drive jump or even a fold mechanism.

The hatch to the bridge opened.

Strand whirled around. That let him know how keyed-up he was. The robot floated within, the hatch shutting behind it.

"I have detected pre-jump pulses in our vicinity," the robot said. "The starship should appear at any minute within two million kilometers of us."

The statement stunned Strand. He'd never heard of anyone detecting...*pre-jump pulses*. This was a new and incredible technology, one the robot had seen fit to keep from him before this.

"If what you say is true," Strand said, "we're finished, dead."

"Not necessarily," the robot said.

Strand studied the Builder construct. He'd suspected a secret agenda on its part ever since he'd boarded the craft. How could something so marvelous, and without any detectable control mechanism installed, obey him all this time? Maybe because it had been faking obedience to him all this time.

"Do you have a plan?" Strand asked.

"Yes," the robot said.

The clone sagged with relief. Why had the little thing waited all this time to tell him an emergency plan?

"How certain are you the starship will appear?" Strand asked.

"The computer has not made a prediction of action. I detected pre-jump pulses. Did you not understand my original statement?"

"I understood," Strand muttered. "I simply don't understand why you haven't told me about these pre-jump pulses before this."

"It was never germane to any of our past situations."

"Fine," Strand said. "So, what's this secret weapon that can defeat the Adok starship?"

"You are misinformed," the robot said. "I said nothing about a secret weapon."

"But you just told me you have a plan."

"I did, and I do."

"Well?" Strand shouted. "What is your plan? You'd better tell me while there's time to implement it."

Instead of answering, the robot simply hovered in place.

"Have it your way," Strand said. He whirled back to the control panel. The robot troubled him.

Due to intense suspicion and heat on his neck, Strand spun around again. A slot had opened on the robot's cone-shaped top section. A small nozzle protruded from the slot.

Strand shouted with outrage. He slapped his chest, hitting an ancient piece of technology. It activated a personal force field around him. He did it just in time, too.

A ray flickered from the robot's nozzle, striking the clone's force field. That part of the field quickly began to glow red.

Strand saved his breath. He wanted to shout at the robot, telling it what a treacherous bastard he'd turned out to be. Instead, the clone drew the blaster, the one that had formerly been under his pillow. After the fold-fighters had left, he'd retrieved it from his quarters. Strand depressed the blaster's trigger, and not a damn thing happened.

"I took the precaution of deactivating your blaster," the robot informed him, even as the little construct continued to beam him.

"Why are you doing this?" Strand sobbed. "You'll kill us both."

"On the contrary, you are the only one between the two of us who will die," the robot said. "I told you I have a plan. I do. It does not involve you, however, as this ship will soon be terminated."

"It's not a living ship, you idiot."

"You are wrong," the robot said. "It is living, in a sense, at least. But that is not the point."

As the robot spoke, it continued to beam him. Strand saw the force field in front of him begin to turn purple. He stood, but that was all he managed to do. He felt a terrible lethargy overtake him.

"The force field is interfering with your motor functions," the robot said. "You can momentarily block my beam, but you cannot run away to a different part of the ship. I knew you would activate the force field. Thus, I have pre-activated certain ship functions."

"Why are you telling me this?"

"It is my last gift to you. You seek knowledge concerning me. You are about to die, copy of Strand. Thus, I will grant you greater knowledge concerning my real function."

"Did you always plan to murder me?"

"No. I had computed that we would succeed without that. Captain Maddox has changed the equation. He is a remarkable individual."

"Are you saying that to piss me off?"

"No. I am sorry. That was not my intent. I will now tell you my true function."

At that point, the force field abruptly collapsed. As it did, the ancient device on Strand's chest heated up incredibly.

The clone of the Methuselah Man howled in agony. The intensely hot device burned through his garments and began to scald his skin and heat his bones underneath. Strand collapsed upon the floor, writhing in agony.

The super-hot device began to burn through his body.

The robot no longer beamed him. The Builder construct hovered closer. A new slot opened. A thicker nozzle protruded. Foam bubbled from it. The foam fell on the super-hot device. In seconds, the foam hardened around the thing.

The danger to the ghost-ship vanished as the hardened foam would not allow the super-hot device to burn through the deck plates.

The human was dead, however.

The thicker nozzle moved back inside the artillery-shell-shaped robot. The slot closed. The robot floated to the control panel. Electric impulses left it. Lights flashed on the controls.

The ghost-ship adjusted its flight path.

The robot turned around and headed away. It would have told Strand its real function. It would have granted the man that final knowledge. The robot had miscalculated the age and fragility of the ancient force-field emitter. It did not like that failure. There had been far too much failure for such a masterful construct as itself.

That caused the robot to wonder if it was too old. The Builders had been the greatest race in the galaxy. They had constructed it and given it its function. But entropy was the enemy of even the greatest. The robot could not detect any problems with its software or hardware, however.

The robot moved faster, floating through a hatch into the main computer area. It began to issue commands. It did not have much time. Soon, Starship *Victory* would appear. He had slain Strand because the clone would undoubtedly have tried any trick possible to remain alive. The clone might have given away its—the robot's—existence. That, the robot could not allow.

There was a twenty-two percent probability it would not be able to escape the Tristano System. Not acceptable. That would retard the great plan by too much.

A piece of ultra-computing—a pulsating cube—detached from the main computer. With a miniature tractor beam, the robot pulled the cube to itself.

The very top of the robot's cone un-screwed on command. With a reverse tractor beam, the robot caused the piece to levitate. It then brought the pulsating cube down through the new opening into itself. A moment later, the very top of the cone settled back down. It screwed back onto the robot.

Satisfied with its progress, the robot turned and floated toward the torpedo tubes.

Soon, it inserted itself in a tube. With another electric impulse, it gave the command.

Thirty-one seconds later, the tube ejected the robot into space. The little Builder construct used a torp-pack, accelerating toward the Laumer Point.

The ghost-ship was already on a new heading, moving away from the Laumer Point. At that moment, a starship appeared.

The robot emitted another command. It ejected from the accelerator, moving on a straight trajectory toward the Laumer Point.

The torp-pack exploded nine seconds later, hopefully shielding its tiny mass from the starship's sensors.

The robot now calculated it had a seventy-eight percent chance of pulling this off.

-32-

Victory came out of the star-drive jump ready for battle. Lieutenant Noonan rapped out orders. The rest of the bridge crew were soon up and operating.

For the first few minutes, no one could detect anything unusual.

"I see something," Galyan said.

"The cloaked vessel?" Valerie asked.

"Negative, Valerie, it is the radiation from a recent explosion."

"How recent?"

"It must have exploded just before we jumped," Galyan said. "I detect debris from the explosion. This is suspicious."

"Talk, talk," Valerie said. "What do you see?"

"A piece of debris, like I said, is heading for the Laumer Point. I do not believe that is a coincidence."

"Scan the debris," Valerie said.

"Captain," Andros said. "I've detected mass gravity waves and the signature concentration of metals. I believe I have located the ghost-ship."

"Galyan," Valerie said. "Confirm if you can."

"Confirmed," Galyan said. "The cloaked vessel no longer appears to be heading for the Laumer Point. It is attempting to circumvent the third terrestrial planet. I believe it is trying to move to an inward Laumer Point."

Valerie frowned. "That seems odd. Why not make an attempt for the closer jump point?"

"I do not know, Valerie."

Valerie stared at the holoimage. Something seemed off, but she couldn't place it. She shook her head. She had her orders. She must destroy the cloaked vessel.

She gave the orders.

Soon, the starship's powerful disruptor cannon energized. The weapon's officer tracked Andros's concentrated metals.

"Ready, Captain," the weapon's officer said.

"Fire," Valerie said.

The ship's antimatter engines hummed with power. A great beam left the disruptor cannon, speared through space and struck the cloaked vessel.

The beam burned through the hull armor with pathetic ease. It smashed bulkheads next, burning through one after another. The clone of Strand's body lay in the path of the beam. It sizzled into nothing, and the beam reached the ghost-ship's propulsion system.

At that point, the small, cloaked vessel ignited. It blasted apart from the disruptor beam and its own exploding engines. Bulkheads, fuel, computer parts, bio-matter; all blew outward in a mass. The cloaked vessel was destroyed.

"Captain," Galyan said.

Valerie already sat back against her command chair. She'd done it. She had destroyed the clone of Strand and his cloaked vessel. It hadn't been as hard or as difficult as she'd imagined. There must be a lesson in there for her. She could do this. She could command a starship in battle.

"Captain," Galyan said.

Valerie smiled. She waved to the bridge crew. "Well done," she said. "You did it. You acted promptly and precisely. Captain Maddox will be proud of your achievement."

"Valerie," Galyan said.

She turned toward the holoimage. "It's rude to interrupt the acting captain of a starship while she's speaking."

"I am sorry, Valerie. But I have something odd to report."

Valerie felt a moment of doubt. She brushed that aside. She'd just destroyed Strand. "Okay. What is it?"

"As you annihilated the cloaked vessel," Galyan said, "the Laumer Point activated."

"What's that even mean?" she asked.

"Something used a Laumer Point opening. Something went down the Laumer Route connection. I suspect it was the piece of debris I spotted earlier."

Valerie pursed her lips. "Could the cloaked ship's destruction have imitated a Laumer Point opening?"

"I do not see how, Valerie. Such a frequency is very deliberate."

"So…you're saying something…*escaped* while we destroyed the cloaked vessel?"

"I would rate that the highest possibility," Galyan said.

"Chief," Valerie said. "What do you make of that?"

Andros thought about it and finally shrugged. "I've never heard of such a thing."

"We should go through the Laumer Point and see what made it to the other side," Galyan said.

"No," Valerie said. "First, we pick up Captain Maddox."

Galyan hesitated before saying, "And Keith, Valerie?"

She stared at the holoimage, wondering if Galyan had just secretly reprimanded her. No, she didn't think so.

"You don't want to first pick up the captain?" she asked Galyan.

"You are correct, Valerie. Let us get the captain. We can always follow the Laumer Point in a few days. I don't see how it can make a difference, as the debris was not traveling fast. It should be easy to spot later."

"Right," Valerie said. "Besides, we've just taken out the deadly menace. We've done it. We should all be proud."

On that note, the bridge crew scanned the area and soon began to ready itself for another jump, this time back to the missing personnel in the shuttles.

-33-

Captain Maddox was in a deep state of sleep aboard a combat shuttle, dreaming fitfully. In his dream, he ran along a fog-shrouded beach. He could hear the crash of ocean waves beside him, but he could not see the ocean. He felt the stiff breeze. He smelled the salt. It seemed odd that he couldn't see the ocean. Every few seconds, salt droplets and spray struck his face.

Maddox began to wonder why he was running so hard. What was so important that he struggled like this? Why not stop, climb up the beach and just sit for a while? Was it necessary to struggle all the time?

Maddox did stop, and the sand underneath shifted, causing him to stagger. The shaking grew worse until a giant crack in the sand appeared before him. The captain expected water to gush up. Instead, a strange octopus-like being flopped out of the crack. The thing writhed on the sand on the other side of the crack. Finally, it gathered several of its long tentacles and pushed itself up onto them.

The creature regarded him.

"Are you a Fisher?" Maddox asked. He didn't know why, but he had trouble remembering exactly what Fishers were supposed to look like.

"Why did you stop running?" the creature asked.

"Why should I run?"

"That is the essence of life," the Fisher said.

"To run?" asked Maddox.

"To live, to do, to compete."

"Why?"

"Because to stop doing those things is to die," the octopus-like creature replied. "Do you want to die, Captain Maddox?"

Maddox frowned. All of a sudden, that seemed like a tough question.

"You took a hit in the Alpha Centauri System," the creature said. "The battle cost you more than any other battle ever has. It has left you...exhausted. You have lost your grit, Captain."

"I don't know that that's true."

"You have questioned the wisdom of running, when this is the only time in existence that you can run. Once you die, your time in life is over."

"Yes...that's true."

"What do you want out of life, Captain?"

Maddox blinked at the strange creature. "To start with, I want to avenge my mother."

"You want to kill your father?"

"I want to find him first."

"Do you know his name?"

"Lord Drakos."

"Do you know for a fact that your father is Lord Drakos?" the creature asked.

"Yes!"

"Captain Maddox, do you *really* know that for a fact?"

"This is ridiculous. Who are you?"

"Do you know, Captain Maddox...?" the creature asked as it began to fade from existence.

"Why do you think I'm wrong about Lord Drakos?" Maddox shouted.

"*Do you know for a fact...?*" the creature asked in a faint voice that seemed to echo as it faded from view.

In his dream, Maddox shook his head. That had been straight-up weird. Why was he having such strange dreams all the time?

In the dream, Maddox's head jerked upright. How did he know this was a dream?

143

Even as he thought the question, the dream, the invisible ocean with its crashing waves, faded away as Maddox woke abruptly from sleep.

He lay on a cot in a tiny cabin aboard the combat shuttle. He was sweaty and felt grungy. He knew that the battle against the Ska was the reason he kept having such strange dreams. Would he ever be rid of them? Would he ever recover fully from the fight?

With a groan, Maddox sat up. He felt lightheaded and slightly nauseous. With a grunt, he stood. He staggered to a side alcove and opened a drawer. He took out a cloth and dried his sweaty face.

A red-alert klaxon began to blare. The harsh noise startled him. Maddox whirled around, lunged to his captain's jacket, put it on, shoved his feet into his boots and hurried out of the hatch to see what was wrong.

-34-

Maddox hurried into the piloting chamber. Meta sat at the controls, typing fast onto the console.

"What's happening?" Maddox demanded.

"An enemy ship just appeared," Meta said.

"Appeared?" asked Maddox, as he slid into the seat beside his wife's. He buckled in as Meta applied thrust.

The combat shuttle jumped ahead, picking up velocity.

Maddox switched on an independent weapon's board. In a pinch, the pilot could control all the ship functions. She could also delegate responsibilities so she could concentrate on piloting.

Maddox immediately saw the debris of a destroyed strikefighter. The other strikefighter fired a salvo of defensive missiles. An incoming enemy missile detonated. The blast took out a second enemy missile. It did nothing to the third that came in seconds later.

That missile zeroed in on the remaining strikefighter. As another flock of anti-missiles zoomed at the missile, the enemy warhead exploded.

The strikefighter was deep in the combat-radius blast. The Star Watch fighter buckled and began to flip end over end and suddenly exploded, as something hit the fuel pod.

"Scratch two strikefighters," Meta said grimly.

Maddox felt cold inside. It wasn't due to fear, but to concentrated anger. Someone had just killed two of his officers. He was responsible for them, and he felt the deaths

145

keenly. He felt it more since Alpha Centauri than he would have before the terrible battle with the Ska.

He fiddled with the weapon's board and finally saw the attacking vessel. The squat spaceship was three times the size of their shuttle. According to the scans, the enemy vessel had heavy hull armor, but more importantly, it had an electromagnetic shield, one that might prove resistant to their ordnance.

"Is that from the asteroid?" Maddox asked.

"It just appeared," Meta said. "So I don't know."

"Appeared like a fold-fighter?"

"Yes!" Meta shouted. "It's radar-locked onto us."

"Right," Maddox said. His fingers blurred across his board.

The shuttle ejected emitters.

"Done," Maddox said.

Meta began to turn the shuttle hard right and down.

As the Gs pulled at him, Maddox checked on Keith's shuttle. It was farther away and had already launched several emitters along with two drones. The drones had been placed to look like mines. Keith was no doubt piloting over there but had kept comm silence.

"That must be a pirate vessel," Maddox said. "They might be Strand's people."

Meta glanced at him.

Maddox thought carefully. Could Strand have planned for this, his being back here in a shuttle while *Victory* was elsewhere? He didn't see how, and yet, the clone had lured *Victory* out to Smade's Asteroid in the first place.

"The enemy ship is accelerating," Meta said. "It's coming after us."

Maddox saw the comm light blinking. He pressed a switch. On his weapon's board, he saw the blunt face of a Shanghai heavy.

"This is Sergeant Chem," the huge man said. "You will surrender immediately. If you do, I will let you live, Captain Maddox."

"You should surrender to me," Maddox said. "*Victory* will return shortly. If you're caught firing on my shuttle, you will die."

Chem glanced at someone unseen. The heavy nodded. "I'm already a dead man, Captain. I'd love to kill you and your people before I die. But if you can persuade me why I should let you live, I'm waiting to hear it."

Maddox made some swift calculations.

As he did, Meta spoke up. "The enemy ship is powering up its laser."

"I will surrender," Maddox told the heavy.

"I know," Chem said.

"They're still radar-locked onto our ship," Meta said.

"I'll power down," Maddox told Chem.

The enemy laser-port turned bright with energy. A second later, a powerful beam smashed against the shuttle's light shield, knocking it down with ease. The beam struck the armored hull, burning deeper by the microsecond.

Meta jinked the shuttle one way and then the other. The enemy laser kept digging into the hull armor, but not always in the same spot. As the beam continued burning, globules of melted metal floated into space, leaving a trail.

"You're a dead man, Chem," Maddox said.

"I have said as much," the heavy replied. "You are not convincing me to let you live, but to take you with me to the grave."

Maddox cocked his head. The words struck him as rehearsed.

"He's killing us," Meta said. "It was the fold. He bypassed all our defenses by jumping next to us."

"We're not dead yet," Maddox said. He didn't know how they were going to get out of this one. The other ship was superior to two shuttles. Without the enemy's fold mechanism putting them right on their tails, they could have easily outrun the enemy ship until *Victory* returned. Maddox had never counted on the asteroid pirates to have a fold-capable ship.

I got sloppy, Maddox told himself. *It might cost Meta her life*. The captain realized he cared more for Meta's life than for his own.

"No," the captain whispered. He wasn't going to quit that easily.

At that point, one of Keith's fake mines energized with power. The drone began to accelerate for the enemy vessel.

The enemy laser stopped beaming Maddox's shuttle's nearly ruptured hull.

"We have to attack," Maddox said. "Turn us around."

"It will take time to decelerate," Meta said.

"Right," Maddox said. His fingers blurred across his weapon's board.

He launched all their antimissile rockets, sending them at the enemy vessel. The squat enemy ship blew up Keith's secret drone. The laser switched from the exploding drone and targeted the next one.

"This is no good," Meta said. "The ship outclasses both shuttles."

Maddox bit his lower lip. This was intensely frustrating.

The comm board began to blink again. He tapped the panel but didn't see any image. Across the screen appeared the words: DON'T WORRY. YOU HAVE A FRIEND.

"What's that mean?" Meta asked, as she glanced at the screen.

Maddox tapped his board, once more linking it with the outer back scope. An escape pod ejected from the squat enemy vessel. Seconds later, the pod's thruster propelled it faster as it moved sideways, away from the ship.

As that happened, the enemy vessel retargeted Maddox's shuttle. The heavy reappeared on the upper left portion of the screen.

"Surrender, Captain," Chem said.

"I will," Maddox said. "You have to stop firing, though."

"Explode all your missiles as a sign of good faith," the heavy said.

Maddox stared at the heavy. He didn't see a way out of this one. What had the message meant: DON'T WORRY, YOU HAVE A FRIEND?

"Yes," Maddox said. He tapped a control. A pulse went out. A second later, the antimissiles detonated.

The heavy grinned nastily, showing off horse-sized teeth. "Let me see your women. I want to see my prize."

"What?" Maddox asked.

"Your women," Chem said. "I'm going to—"

At that moment, the comm signal severed. On Maddox's screen, the squat enemy vessel simply exploded. One second it was there, the next, armored hull, pieces of bio-matter, spent fuel, water and all kinds of debris exploded outward.

"What did you do?" Meta asked.

Maddox shook his head. Then, he tapped his board. The blast heat from the explosion wasn't enough to hurt them, as it hadn't been a thermonuclear explosion. Thus, there were no gamma or x-rays to worry about. Neither was there an EMP coming for them.

What had just happened?

"Captain," Keith said over the comm. "How did you pull that one off?"

Maddox sent a comm signal to the accelerating escape pod. A second later, Yen Cho peered at him from the screen.

"Hello, Captain," Yen Cho said. "Did you appreciate my gift?"

Maddox nodded slowly.

"Perhaps I should explain," Yen Cho said. "Strand took me prisoner some time ago. His people controlled the attack craft just now. But they weren't as clever as the clone. You do know that a clone of Strand is behind all this, don't you?"

Maddox said nothing. Yen Cho the android. It had been quite some time since he'd seen the construct.

"In any case, the attack leader became sloppy," Yen Cho said. "I managed to escape my confinement, sabotage the ship and escape in a pod. Now, I could use a hand, as otherwise, I'm stranded out here."

"Rotate your pod and begin decelerating," Maddox said crisply. "*Victory* should be back soon. I'll have them pick you up after I debark. I do appreciate your help. It's fortunate for us you happened to be on that vessel."

"No, Captain Maddox, it was fortunate for me that you are here. I am grateful for the diversion your shuttles provided."

"We are both fortunate."

Yen Cho seemed to think about that. "Yes," he said. "That is so."

-35-

Victory reappeared shortly. The shuttles landed in the hangar bay. Afterward, Valerie sent a shuttle to pick up Yen Cho.

Marines in combat suits trained their weapons on the android as he entered the shuttle's cargo bay. He did not question the need for their presence. Soon enough, the rescue shuttle landed and the armored marines escorted Yen Cho to a holding cell.

During the rescue action, Valerie formally relinquished command to Maddox. She also gave a verbal report of the battle with the cloaked vessel and the piece of debris that had apparently escaped through a Laumer Point.

With all these threads tangling at once, Maddox decided to hold a briefing. It was time to thrash through a few of the actions and decide, if they could, what they possibly implied.

In an hour, they assembled. Captain Maddox sat at the head of the large conference table. Beside him to the right were Meta, Riker and Keith, with Andros Crank at the other end of the table. Valerie was beside him on the left, with a spot for Galyan and then Finlay the mercenary pilot. Maddox included her because she was familiar with this region of space and the Tristano System in particular.

Maddox had Valerie repeat her report. Afterward, Keith told the others about the combat with the squat fold-vessel from the asteroid. Lastly, Galyan reported about what they knew concerning the troubles on Smade's Asteroid.

150

"It is chaos over there," the little holoimage said. "According to my latest intercepts, poison gas is flooding the interior levels.

Finlay gasped, turning white at the news.

"Do you have any idea who pumped the gas into the life-support systems?" Maddox asked her.

"No," Finlay whispered. "It sounds horrible. Who would do such a thing?"

"The android might be able to tell us," Valerie said dryly.

"I'll interrogate Yen Cho soon enough," Maddox said. "As to who might do it, the obvious culprit would be the clone of Strand."

"That is my belief as well," Galyan said. "Strand the original is notoriously callous regarding human life. He might have caused such mass death and destruction to cover his actions while on the asteroid."

"Agreed," Maddox said.

"What about the android?" Valerie said. "Yen Cho helped us in the past, but that doesn't mean I trust him now."

"All true," Maddox said. "Clearly, he didn't help us out of any sense of altruism. Like you, I suspect the timing of his appearance."

"His appearance and rescue does seem to bend the laws of probability," Galyan said. "I suggest we examine his ethics to determine the reason for his actions."

"Explain that," Maddox said.

"Is Yen Cho coldblooded enough to engineer an attack and then callously sabotage his own people and vessel while he flees?" Galyan asked.

"He's an android," Riker said. "It's not a matter of cold blood for them. It's a matter of logic."

Maddox nodded. "The question arises, if Yen Cho engineered the situation, does he expect us to believe him at face value?"

"That is an astute question," Galyan said. "I suggest you ask him."

"He's an android," Riker repeated. "His face isn't going to give away anything."

"Quite true," Galyan said. "But his statements might."

"We'll shelve the idea for now," Maddox said, as he turned to Valerie. "I would like your thoughts, Lieutenant, regarding the debris that went through the Laumer Point."

"I've been thinking about that for some time," Valerie said. "I don't know what the debris was, but I know it must be important. Laumer Points don't simply activate by accident so a piece of supposed debris can transfer. That was planned."

"Galyan?" Maddox said.

"I concur with Valerie," Galyan said. "It would seem that the innocent piece of debris was the most valuable thing aboard the cloaked vessel. I wonder if it was so important that the clone sacrificed himself to shield its escape."

Maddox slapped the table and pointed at Galyan. "I should have thought of that. Yes. That lets us know something about what escaped."

"I do not understand," Galyan said. "You are suggesting it is living."

"Not necessarily biological," Maddox said. "It is of Builder construction. Let me amend that. It's most probability of Builder construction."

"Which is why the clone possibly acted as a decoy to let it escape?" Galyan asked.

"No," Maddox said. "I don't believe a clone of Strand would act as a decoy to save anyone except possibly for the real Strand. However, a Builder device might have forced the clone into a certain course of action."

"That implies that the piece of debris possessed intelligence," Galyan said.

"Right," Maddox said. "We have to track it. We have to do it faster rather than slower. I'm not sure that either Keith or I could survive a fold or a jump right now. We need...maybe another twenty-four hours."

"I don't think we should put you in a shuttle again, sir," Valerie said. "How do we really know what's going on at Smade's Asteroid. Those could all be fake messages. If that's true, more fold-ships could be waiting for you to enter a shuttle while we go elsewhere."

"There is another point to consider," Andros Crank said. "If it's a Builder device, I'm thinking the captain is right. We have to reach it as quickly as possible. While the piece of debris is small, it might have waiting equipment on the other side of the Laumer Point."

"We'll begin maximum acceleration for the Laumer Point," Maddox said. "The lieutenant is correct. Now isn't the time to leave anyone behind. We should investigate Smade's Asteroid just to be sure of the reports and to lend a hand to any survivors. Unfortunately, we don't have time for that, as we now have another emergency. We must see if the debris is indeed Builder tech."

"Could that be why Yen Cho is here?" Meta asked.

The others looked at her.

"Yen Cho was on the asteroid," Meta said. "Could he be coordinating with Strand or with the possible piece of Builder debris?"

"That's a good point," Maddox said. "What was Yen Cho doing on Smade's Asteroid? I think it's time I had a talk with the android."

"Do you expect to get any truth from it, sir?" Riker asked.

Maddox glanced at Galyan before he regarded his sergeant. "Maybe not the truth," the captain said. "But we can begin to analyze what he says and doesn't say. It will give us something to do while *Victory* accelerates for the Laumer Point."

On that note, the captain dismissed the others.

-36-

To Maddox's disgust, he found himself tired out after the meeting. He wasn't used to his body betraying him like this. Usually, he could push through any normal fatigue or demand that his body perform better and faster.

Today, as he walked down a corridor, he yawned, and his mind blurred. He was simply too tired to interrogate the android. With Yen Cho, he wanted to be at his sharpest, not having to stumble through the interrogation because he was too stubborn to take a rest.

Thus, Maddox changed direction and went to his quarters. He took a nap, expecting to get up in a half hour.

Sometime later, Meta shook him awake.

Maddox sat up groggily. He hardly felt any better. Did he even get any sleep?

"What time is it?" he asked.

"You slept for three hours," Meta said. "I've never seen you nap for more than one before."

Maddox was dumbfounded. He climbed out of bed and felt momentarily light-headed. That was wrong, all wrong. He needed a physical. Maybe there was something off with him. If so, he needed to find out what.

Meta accompanied him to medical. Doctor Lister gave him a physical. Afterward, she picked up a brain scanner, clicked it on and set it before his head. She studied the readings and became agitated.

"What is it, Doctor?" Maddox asked.

With the brain scanner aimed at his scalp, she continued to study the readings. "It appears as if there's—I'd call it a neuron deficiency."

She clicked off the scanner and set it on a stand. Lister kept flicking her lower lip and finally looked at Maddox.

"This must have something to do with the operation," she said. "I wasn't able to extract all the control fibers, remember?"

"Does the scanner show the fibers having any effect on my brain?" Maddox asked.

"Not that I can detect, and that bothers me."

"Meta," the captain said, turning to his wife.

She lowered a magazine as she sat in a chair to the side.

"Are you carrying a weapon?" Maddox asked.

Meta raised her blonde eyebrows before shaking her head. "Should I get one?"

"At once," Maddox said.

Throwing the magazine onto a side table, Meta jumped up and ran out of the examining room.

"Do you mind telling me what this was about?" Lister asked.

"A moment, Doctor," Maddox said. "Galyan," the captain said into the air.

The Adok holoimage appeared a second later.

"Find Riker," the captain said. "Tell him to bring a sidearm and hurry to medical. He's going to be my bodyguard for a time."

"Yes, sir," the holoimage said, disappearing.

Maddox drew a long-barreled gun from inside his jacket. This one wasn't a beam weapon, but a regular slugthrower noted for its accuracy.

If Lister appeared surprised by the second order and the gun, she didn't show it. Had she known he'd been carrying a sidearm during the physical?

"Shall I call Security?" the doctor asked. "Would you like a marine guard to come?"

"Most certainly not," Maddox said.

Lister took her time, finally saying, "I must admit that I'm perplexed by your actions, sir."

Maddox studied the doctor closely, deciding she wasn't an android or a Spacer agent. He had become…anxious was the wrong word. He didn't know the correct word. The point was that there were far too many strange events occurring one right after another. He was beginning to believe that none of those events had occurred by accident, including his foreign tiredness and the strangeness of the brain scan.

"Sit beside me, please," the captain said.

He shoved a chair against the far wall, sat down and kept his long-barreled gun aimed at the door.

"Really, Captain, are you expecting assassins?"

"Listen carefully," Maddox said, turning to stare at the doctor. "You must sit down and shut up. I need to concentrate and I'm finding that extraordinarily difficult."

Cowed, Lister set a chair beside him and mutely took a seat.

After a minute of silence, Maddox put the gun on his lap. He kept a keen eye on the door, however.

"I do not believe the nerve fibers, the ones you failed to extract from my brain, have caused the diminishment of my neural connections."

Lister glanced at him in wonderment. It seemed to take an effort of will for her to speak. "That doesn't make sense," she finally said. "What, then, has caused, the diminishment, as you put it?"

The question seemed to upset the captain, although it would have been difficult to tell by his bearing. Instead, in a robotic fashion, Maddox picked up his gun, stood and turned toward Lister. He brought the handle of the gun down hard against Lister's forehead. The handle made an audible thump against her skull. She fell off the chair and collapsed onto the floor, out cold.

"I hope I didn't miscalculate," Maddox told the unconscious doctor.

As Maddox finished speaking, a woman with short red hair opened the door. She did not stare in astonishment at the fallen doctor. She did not look at the gun in Maddox's grip. Instead, she stared directly into Maddox's eyes.

"Listen to me," the woman said intently.

Maddox began to smile, but found to his surprise that he lowered his gun so the barrel pointed at the floor. After that, he craned his neck forward so he could better listen to the woman.

That was strange. The captain tried to form words but couldn't quite get them out.

"No," the woman said. "You mustn't try to speak. You must listen to what I'm going to tell you. Are you listening, Captain Maddox?"

It seemed as if wheels turned in his mind. Those wheels shifted the tracks of his thoughts onto a different course. Instead of resisting her words, Maddox nodded.

"I'm here to help you," she said. "I'm here to help Star Watch."

That seemed incredible, and yet, she seemed like the most trustworthy person in the universe to him.

"You captured an android, didn't you?" she asked.

Maddox nodded.

"What is the android's name?"

"Yen Cho," Maddox said.

"*The* Yen Cho?" she asked.

Once more, Maddox nodded.

"This is very important," the woman said. "You must kill him."

Maddox stared at her in bewilderment.

"I am from Brigadier O'Hara's office," she said.

"N-N-No," Maddox stammered. "That. Isn't. True."

"You will believe whatever I tell you," the woman said. Her eyes seemed to expand, then.

This time, Maddox tried to resist. He would not believe her. He would…

The woman's eyes expanded until they were all Maddox could see. That turned wheels in his mind, made it impossible to resist.

"No," he whispered.

He could no longer see the whites of her eyes, just the pupils. They seemed to expand, as well.

That produced a horrible headache. Maddox felt nauseous. He bent over and vomited.

157

"Believe what I say," the woman intoned. "I am from Brigadier O'Hara's office."

Maddox could only see darkness now. He heard the words, but he wasn't going to believe them. That created worse pain in his mind, searing agony. He didn't want to, but a cry tore from his lips. His strength drained away with the cry. He fell to his knees and then collapsed onto his hands. The long-barreled gun had clunked onto the floor beside him. He could hear it, but he couldn't see it.

"Do not fight me, Captain," the woman said. "You will die if you fight me."

Tears filled the captain's eyes, and the pain exploded to a heightened level in his head. This time, he felt the wheels turn slowly like giant gears in a vast machine. Something awful was occurring in his mind. It could kill him if he tried to resist.

With the knowledge of his nearness to death came an opening of the inner eye. In a moment of clarity, Maddox saw opposing forces swirling toward a central point. That point was him— No! The point was Starship *Victory*.

With the realization, his sight returned. Although he remained on his hands and knees, Maddox looked up into the woman's eyes. He realized—

"You're a Spacer spy," Maddox whispered. "You have brain modifications. You did something to Doctor Lister during the operation. She deliberately left the fibers in my brain so at your convenience, you could tamper with them and thus with me."

The red-haired woman shook her head, and she looked at him with pity. "I don't have time to reprogram your mind, Captain. That's too bad for you. We could have used you. But you're simply too stubborn. We could have—"

Those were her last words. A shot rang out from somewhere. Then her head exploded as a heavy slug spattered her skull and sprayed brains everywhere.

With a sickening thud, her body thumped against the floor.

Maddox gasped. Pain. He clutched his head, and with a moan, he collapsed unconscious onto the floor.

-37-

If Maddox dreamed, he couldn't remember. He was unconscious for fourteen hours. Finally, he awoke and found himself in medical.

Sergeant Riker looked up from where he sat. Riker was an old salt in Star Watch Service. The man had been with Maddox for many years already. The sergeant had leathery features, a bionic eye and a bionic left arm. As per orders, Riker was armed.

"Feeling better?" the sergeant asked in his gruff voice.

"Not particularly," Maddox said. "My head hurts and my eyesight is blurry."

The captain made to get up and found himself in restraints.

"What is the meaning of this?" Maddox asked.

"You were thrashing in your sleep, sir. The doctor didn't want you falling out of bed."

"Undo these straps immediately."

"Uh...I'm sorry, sir—"

"Sergeant—" Maddox said. The captain stopped talking. "Is this because of Doctor Lister?"

"That's right, sir. She's in critical condition. You hit her hard."

"Did Valerie order this?" Maddox asked, while thinking fast.

"That she did, sir."

"Tell Valerie to get down here on the double."

159

Riker glanced elsewhere. "I don't have to, sir. The lieutenant is here."

The sergeant backed away as Lieutenant Noonan stepped up to the med-cot. She had a stern cast to her features, looking down at Maddox with a reproving glance.

"That's enough, Sergeant," Valerie said without looking at him. "You're dismissed."

"Riker," Maddox said. "Valerie is under someone else's control. Disarm her at once."

With the twist of her neck, Valerie gave the sergeant a scathing glance. Instead of the result she wanted, her head swayed back, possibly due to the heavy caliber gun in Riker's human hand aimed at her.

"This is ridiculous," Valerie said. "Put that away and report to Security."

"Sit down," Riker told her.

"This is mutiny," Valerie said.

"This is Starship *Victory*," Riker countered. "We've been under constant attack throughout the years by all kinds of subtle and hidden enemies. It wouldn't surprise me to find out you're an android. We took on Yen Cho, right. Who knows what kind of master plan he's set up against us?"

Valerie continued to frown. Her frown wasn't at Riker anymore. She seemed to frown inwardly at herself.

"Did someone odd come to see you earlier?" Maddox asked her.

Valerie swiveled about and stared down at Maddox. "What do you mean?" she asked.

Maddox calculated quickly. "Step away from my bed," he said.

Valerie raised her chin haughtily.

Before she could do anything else, Riker shoved her with his bionic arm. She catapulted sideways, hitting the far wall with a thump. The sergeant didn't fiddle with the straps holding Maddox, he ripped them off with his bionic hand.

Maddox sat up. His head still hurt like blazes, but at least he wasn't trapped like a beast. He climbed over the cot's railing and leaned against the bed.

This was getting complicated. He'd been asleep fourteen hours. Did that mean hidden foes had run of *Victory* for those fourteen hours?

"You'll be court-martialed for that," Valerie told Riker as she sat on the floor.

"I've done worse," Riker said.

"Galyan," Maddox said into the air.

The holoimage appeared. He glanced at Riker, Maddox and then Valerie.

"Is this mutiny, Valerie?" Galyan asked her.

"Yes," she said. "Summon the marines. Put these two in the brig. If they resist, tell the marines to shoot to kill."

"It is as I thought," Galyan said. "You are not yourself, Valerie. Captain," the little holoimage said, "what are your orders, sir?"

"Get Meta," Maddox said, "and tell Andros to come along. I want to get to the bottom of this as soon as possible."

*** *

Fifteen minutes later, Meta and Andros joined the others. Galyan also reappeared.

"This is a tight fit," Maddox said. They were all in the same med room. "But for the moment I don't want anyone else to know what's going on."

He explained what had happened to him with Doctor Lister and the mind-attacking spy fourteen hours ago.

"I assume you shot her," Maddox said to Riker.

"Yes, sir," the sergeant said. "I felt terrible shooting a woman. It still bothers me. I did it because…there was something badly off about her. It was a gut sense."

Riker had dealt with the Ska, although in a different manner than Maddox. Just like the captain, the sergeant wasn't the same.

"Has anyone done an autopsy on the woman?" Maddox asked.

"No," Galyan said.

"Did you scan her?" Maddox asked.

"Valerie gave strict orders that I was to leave the body alone," the holoimage said.

161

"Where is the corpse now?" asked Maddox.

"In the morgue," Galyan said.

"Check it," Maddox said. "Report back as soon as you confirm it's still there."

Galyan disappeared and reappeared a moment later. "The corpse is gone, Captain."

Maddox turned to Valerie. "What did you do with it?"

"Me?" the frowning lieutenant asked. "Not a thing."

"Galyan?" asked Maddox.

"I cannot assess whether Valerie is telling the truth or not," the holoimage said.

"Let's assume the lieutenant is," Maddox said, as he studied Valerie. "That means someone else removed the corpse. My guess is that the corpse is gone for good, that it is no longer on the ship."

"This hidden someone wanted to hide the woman's identity?" Riker asked.

"Exactly," Maddox said. "But I believe I already know her allegiance; to the Spacers. The red-haired woman likely had Shu-like adaptations, as the Spacers call them."

Shu had been a Spacer agent. At first, Shu had worked against Maddox and the crew, but had later chosen to help them escape a terrible fate one thousand light-years from the Commonwealth. Shu had died before the terrible war with the Swarm Invasion Fleet. She had died from sabotage in her prison in South Africa Region. Her adaptations had been tiny Builder devices implanted in her body, powered by a Builder power pack, also inside her body. Shu had been able to disrupt electric systems and practice transduction. She had been able to see electromagnetic radiation and electromagnetic wavelengths and process the data as fast as a computer.

"What do you think the Spacers want?" Meta asked Maddox.

"Likely the same thing Yen Cho wants," the captain replied. "The spy wanted me to kill the android. I think she wanted to kill the competition."

"I have a question," Galyan said.

Maddox nodded.

162

"Could Yen Cho have planted the red-haired agent?" Galyan asked. "He had the woman order you to destroy him. In that way, the android validates his presence here."

"That's not bad, Galyan," Maddox said. "The answer is that we don't know. I think you'll find if you search Doctor Lister that she has a small device in her brain. I don't think it was a Spacer adaptation or a brain implant like they put in my brain at Smade's, but a device the Spacer agent could use with electromagnetic modifications."

"That should be easy to verify," Galyan said.

"What about Valerie?" Meta asked.

"We can check that easily enough, too," Maddox said. "Galyan, if you will."

"Sir," the holoimage said. "You are correct. There is a tiny device lodged near Valerie's brain."

"Amazing," Andros said. "How did you know all this, Captain?"

"I didn't," Maddox said. "It was a guess. There may be another Spacer agent or more on the ship. We will have to proceed slowly. First, though, I want all the stray fibers removed from my brain. I do not want any more handles for Spacer or other agents to use against me."

"Such removal could prove difficult," Galyan said.

"Nevertheless," Maddox said. "I believe it is imperative before we proceed."

"What do we do with Valerie in the meantime?" Riker asked.

"We'll have her device removed first, before my surgery," Maddox said. "Now, listen. This is how we're going to do this…"

-38-

Valerie came to in the med center with a splitting headache. Worse, she found Maddox, Riker, Meta, Andros Crank and Galyan encircling her med-cot, staring down at her expectantly.

It hit the lieutenant, then. Maddox had guessed right about a device in her head.

"Sir," Valerie said. She tried to moisten a much too dry mouth and realized her bottom lip had cracked.

"Just a minute," Meta said. She left the cot and returned with a glass of water. Helping Valerie sit up, Meta held the water cup for her.

The water tasted good, seeming to sink into her flesh like water in a desert. Valerie drained the cup, gasping afterward.

"Another one?" Meta asked.

Valerie nodded even as she sensed the captain's impatience. The lieutenant gulped down the second glass of water, but she declined a third, despite how much as she wanted it.

"I guess you're waiting to know what I remember," Valerie said.

"Indeed," Maddox said.

Valerie sat up so the others didn't seem like gang members casing the wounded victim.

"Let me see," Valerie said. "There was a…a warrant officer. He told me there was trouble in computing. The chief needed a decision on a faulty processor, and he had asked for me to hurry. I should have checked over the comm, but I

164

didn't. Anyway, once I got to computing, the warrant officer turned on me. The man used a stunner, a small handheld device. I collapsed and couldn't move, and it was hard to hear. I remember a woman showing up and pressing an implement against the back of my head. She must have inserted the device."

"What did the woman look like?" Maddox asked.

"I didn't get a good look at her, or if I did, I don't remember. She had soft hands, long red hair—"

"That's all I need to hear," Maddox said, interrupting. "Red hair, it was obviously the same agent. What was the warrant officer's name?"

"Uh..." Valerie said. "Warrant Officer Smalls, Ted Smalls."

"Galyan," Maddox snapped. "Where is the warrant officer presently?"

"A moment, sir," Galyan said, as his eyelids fluttered. The holoimage's eyes widened suddenly. "Ted Smalls is dead in his quarters, sir."

"Go there at once," Maddox told Galyan. "Determine what killed him. Return as soon as you find out."

Galyan disappeared and reappeared almost instantly. "There is a tiny puncture wound in his head, sir. I doubt it was self-inflicted. There is more. The corpse is rank. Is that the correct word?"

"He smells bad?" Maddox asked.

"That is so," Galyan said. "I believe Warrant Officer Smalls has been dead for many days."

Maddox inhaled sharply through his nostrils. "I no longer think the red-haired woman was a Spacer agent. I'm beginning to suspect androids using Spacer equipment. We're going to have resort to the old methods to flush out the remaining androids. It seems doubtful there are too many of them aboard. If there were, they would have tried to take over by now.

"Galyan," Maddox said. "Is Yen Cho still alive?"

"Is that a trick question, sir?" Galyan asked. "In a strict sense, is the android a living being?"

"Is Yen Cho presently functional?" Maddox amended.

Once more, Galyan's eyelids fluttered. "Yes, sir. Yen Cho is still in the brig under guard."

"We'll leave him there for now," Maddox said. He turned to Valerie. "How are you feeling?"

"My head hurts like Hell, but otherwise, I'm okay."

"You'll rest," Maddox said. "Meta, you're going to stay and guard her."

Meta's eyes flashed. "You just want me out of the way for whatever you're planning."

"That's preposterous," Maddox said, although it was the truth. "I can't trust anyone else to keep Valerie alive. Galyan will check on you every fifteen minutes. I want to find the android impersonating Ted Smalls. He may have already switched identities."

"Do you believe the possibly hidden android is working with Yen Cho?" Galyan asked.

"I have no idea," Maddox said. "Now, listen. Here's what we're doing next."

-39-

Maddox waited on the bridge as *Victory's* crew, one after another, went through a thorough medical scan. Armed marines stood everywhere, watching, waiting for an interior sneak attack.

None happened.

After four and half hours of med scanning, a doctor informed the captain that everyone checked out. There was no hidden android aboard ship.

Maddox sat in the captain's chair, contemplating the information. It was wrong. There had to be at least one android aboard the starship. How could he have been wrong about that?

The captain pressed the intercom button on his armrest. "Doctor," he asked. "Are you absolutely sure you've checked everyone?"

"I haven't checked you out, sir, or Riker, Meta or—just a minute, sir. One of my aides wishes to tell me something."

Maddox sat back. Riker, Meta or him. That was preposterous. He hadn't made love to an android. He knew his Meta. That could only leave Riker. Yet, he was certain the sergeant couldn't possibly—

"Sir," the doctor said over the comm.

"Yes," Maddox said.

"There is one other person we didn't check. The mercenary pilot...what's her name?"

"Finlay," Maddox whispered. Could he have brought an android onto the starship by mistake?

167

"Thank you, Doctor," the captain said. "I'll take it from here."

Maddox clicked off the comm, stood and beckoned the holoimage. "Where's Finlay?" he quietly asked Galyan.

The holoimage's eyelids fluttered, searching. "I can't find her, sir."

"Look everywhere," Maddox said. "She can't have gotten off the starship that easily."

Galyan accessed the video feeds throughout the ship, but came up empty. He made two sweeps to make sure, but nothing changed.

Maddox put his hands behind his back and began to pace. Normally, he did not do so on the bridge. He stopped as he noticed the bridge personnel glancing sidelong at him. When he was visibly nervous, it made the crew nervous. He stopped pacing and bent his head in thought. There had to be a logical explanation for this.

If Finlay had been an android, or possibly a Spacer spy… No. That didn't hold water. Before using her to help him infiltrate onto the asteroid, he'd checked out Finlay himself. She was exactly what she had advertised herself to be: a mercenary pilot with contacts inside Smade's Asteroid. Maddox had been quite thorough with her.

Yet, Finlay had disappeared—

Maddox snapped his fingers. He turned to Galyan, noting the holoimage watching him. The captain returned to his chair, sitting on its edge.

The androids or Spacers had made the switch on Smade's Asteroid. The enemy must have recognized him and understood his ploy. Enemy agents had likely killed the real Finlay in order to set an imposter in her place. That would mean he *had* brought an enemy agent aboard ship.

It would seem…the agent had impersonated Warrant Officer Ted Smalls. Smalls had been a man and he'd already been dead when Valerie had seen his imposter. That meant the imposter—

"Is an android," Maddox said.

The old legend of the Rull was that they had been an alien race that could impersonate humans. In reality, on Sind II, they

168

had learned that the Android Nation were the Rull. The androids made exact look-alikes to impersonate chosen people.

It would seem this Finlay had been able to look like Ted Smalls, a man, but similar in height to the mercenary pilot. Logically, then, Finlay hadn't been a Spacer, a human, but an android that could switch identities almost at will by replacing his or her face with a replica and modifying their body, possibly with a kit.

Maddox's eyes narrowed. He felt as if he had almost solved the puzzle. Finlay had turned into Ted Smalls. The android had then become Finlay again and gone to the briefing. But…if the android knew her cover had been blown, she would attempt to escape off the starship. She would not make the attempt as Finlay, but as—

Maddox snapped his fingers again. He stood and faced Galyan. "Check the hangar bay. Check for any unusual activity by any person. In particular, look for someone trying to leave the ship."

Galyan's eyelids fluttered madly.

"Well?" Maddox asked.

"I am unable to detect anyone who fits your description," the Adok said.

Maddox tapped the fingers of his right hand against his right thigh. He had been so certain. He had been—

"Yen Cho," he said softly. "Galyan, alert the chief of Security. Tell him to choose a select team. I only want marines that he's been in constant contact with since the medical scan."

"That could be a small list, sir."

"Do it!" Maddox said, sternly, as he headed for the hatch. "Tell him to meet me at Junction 3-A. I want him there on the double. They're to bring heavy rifles, including one for me. We're hunting for a highly dangerous android."

Galyan disappeared.

Maddox hurried to the exit. As soon as he left the bridge, the captain began to sprint.

***

Maddox ran like a cheetah. No one aboard *Victory* could keep up with him when he ran full tilt. The maddening thing was that soon he was gasping for air and, equally soon, sweat soaked him. When his head started pounding, the captain stopping running and moved at a brisk stride.

He had to get these fibers out of his brain. They were interfering with his function as captain.

It took him longer to reach Junction 3-A than he'd anticipated. The chief of Security waited there with three other marines. Each of them cradled a heavy rifle. The chief, a muscular lieutenant with blond sideburns and a buzz cut, handed him a combat rifle.

Maddox accepted it, automatically checking the chamber. It was loaded.

"We're hunting for an android, gentleman. I'll brief you as we head for the brig."

Maddox immediately started for the brig. The marines followed close behind.

"The android could be impersonating anyone," the captain said, sounding a little short of breath. "We've all gone through a medical scan. That means the android must have chosen someone after he or she passed the scan. No one is attempting to leave the ship. The only other logical action is to assassinate Yen Cho. Study everyone. Trust no one. If you see anyone aiming a weapon at you, kill him or her out of hand. Is that clear?"

"Yes, sir," the chief said.

"Men?" Maddox asked.

They each said yes.

"All right," Maddox said. "Let's do this."

Once more, he broke into a sprint. The marines followed close behind. He would have liked to break away from them and show them his superiority, but he was too damn tired. And his head began to pound again. But there was no way he was going to slow down in front of the marines.

Two decks later, the chief asked with a gasp, "Sir, could you slow down a little? Franks is falling behind."

Normally, Maddox might have told the marine to keep up the best he could. In this case, he was silently grateful for the request. He did not say anything, as he needed each gasp of air for his screaming lungs. Instead, Maddox dropped back into a brisk walk.

Galyan suddenly appeared before him. One of the marines fired, a bullet passing through the holoimage.

"He's safe," Maddox said dryly. At least he knew the marines were on edge and alert, which was how he wanted them. "What do you have to report, Galyan?"

"Why did the marine fire at me?" the holoimage asked.

"You startled him. Now, report."

"Sir," Galyan said. "A marine just killed two brig guards. The armed marine is presently heading for Yen Cho's cell."

Maddox cursed, and despite his exhaustion, he lurched into a staggering run. His head pounded. His eyesight clouded, and his heart soon hammered. Behind him, he heard the chief pounding as hard as he could to keep up.

The two of them broke away from the other marines. Like two madmen, they raced to the brig, opened the main hatch, staggered past two dead guards and raced down a corridor for Yen Cho's cell.

Maddox passed an open hatch to the side. He glanced there and dove as a bullet grazed his back. The android had obviously staged an ambush.

"Chief," Maddox gasped.

The chief of Security hadn't quite been able to keep up with the captain. The chief ran past the opened hatch, and bullets riddled his body. He sprawled dead beside Maddox.

The captain raised his heavy rifle, aiming at the hatch. Then he waited as he panted for air. He'd lost another man, and it made him silently furious.

"Captain," a woman said from inside the chamber. "I know you dodged my bullet. They say you move like greased death, but I had to see it to believe it. If you'd moved a fraction slower…"

Maddox's eyes narrowed. He heard the tiniest of clicks from the chamber. He rose from his knee and backed away.

Something flew out of the chamber.

Maddox sprang like a cat, diving into a side alcove. The grenade exploded, sending metal fragments everywhere. If

Maddox had remained at his former spot, the grenade would have killed him.

"Captain?" the android asked.

Maddox controlled his breathing as he slowly moved to a kneeling position. He realized the android must have ultra-hearing. It could possibly hear his garments rustle.

"I know you're out there, Captain," the android said.

Maddox did not believe that it really knew. It was fishing for clues.

"I have already slain Yen Cho," the android said. "You were too late. Now, I'm going to self-destruct. You're never going to know why I was here until it is too late."

Maddox blinked stinging sweat out of his eyes. The other marines stumbled into the hall. He wished they would stay back. He had to flush out the android before it shot up more of his men.

Maddox turned back and waved frantically. A second later, Galyan appeared. Maddox put his finger before his lips.

The holoimage nodded his understanding.

Maddox pointed up the hall and made a stopping motion.

Galyan disappeared.

Maddox waited. The sound of the approaching marines stopped.

"That's odd," the android said.

Maddox kept waiting. It was an art. In this instance, Maddox wanted payback for the Security Chief, for the warrant officer and the others they would no doubt find dead in the next few days.

Maddox almost missed the difference. The barrel of a gun appeared by the hatch and slowly after that, a hand, an arm and then a brig officer. The android moved slowly, with her head cocked to listen. She did not look Maddox's way, but down the hall where the guards should have appeared.

Something must have alerted it. The android turned, saw Maddox and began to dart back with surprising speed. Maddox's trigger finger proved faster.

The heavy stock of his rifle knocked back against his shoulder. A heavy caliber bullet clanged against the android's head. That caused it to pitch against the other side of the hatch and then sprawl back into the room.

Maddox was up and moving, the heavy rifle held by his hip. He threw aside any caution, charging toward the hatch. Before he had taken three steps, a staggering explosion let him know that the android had just destroyed itself.

-40-

Inside the chamber, the android had splattered its outer bio-parts and interior mechanical pieces all over the place. It was a sickening sight.

Maddox and the three marines found nothing of interest here.

"Suicide?" asked Galyan.

"I don't know," Maddox said. "Maybe it was set to self-destruct if its brain-case became damaged." He took a deeper breath. "We don't know this was the only android still aboard ship. We'll keep searching. First, I'd better check on Yen Cho."

The captain, the three Security marines and the floating holoimage moved down the corridor past the slain lieutenant, took several turns and came to an opened hatch.

"Stay here," Maddox told the marines.

Galyan floated beside the captain. The two of them looked inside. A shot-up android lay on the floor. The Finlay-android hadn't been lying after all.

"Interesting," Galyan said.

"Indeed," Maddox said. "Who would think that mechanical men would hate each other like this? They almost do seem human."

"Is that a joke, sir?" Galyan asked.

"Not really," Maddox said.

"Why did you not want the marines to see this?"

"I'm going to let them see soon."

"Then I am doubly confused."

Maddox regarded the Adok holoimage. "Can't you figure it out, Galyan?"

The holoimage's eyelids fluttered. "Ah," he said. "I believe so. You first wanted to see if the fake Yen Cho looked convincing enough."

"Bully for you," Maddox said. "You're right."

"It is a good thing you moved Yen Cho earlier as a precaution."

Maddox nodded. He felt bone-weary. The lieutenant's death weighed on him. And now they wouldn't get to interrogate the android impersonating Finlay. Maddox doubted there were any more android agents unaccounted for aboard ship, but he wasn't one hundred percent sure.

Maybe that was the only victory he could count this time. They had flushed out the enemy agents. It was better they flushed them out now before they acquired the possible Builder artifact that must have escaped through the Laumer Point.

What had the clone of Strand been trying to achieve? The Finlay-impersonating android might have known. Now, they just had Yen Cho.

Maddox absently touched his scalp. It wasn't as bald as when he'd escaped from the asteroid. Bristles of hair had begun to sprout. Could Yen Cho have Spacer adaptations in him?

I have to get these fibers removed from my brain.

"What are you thinking, sir?" Galyan asked.

"I need to interrogate Yen Cho. Let's go. I have to talk to Riker about this."

"What about the marines, sir. Aren't you going to let them see so they can spread the rumor that our android prisoner is dead?"

"Is that what you think I want them to do?"

"That would be one of your standard operating procedures, sir."

"I see. Well, then, by all means, let us proceed. Bring them in and let them look. Then caution them about saying anything to anyone. That's a good way to ensure they tell others their great secret."

"What about you, sir?"

"I have some preparations to make," Maddox said, heading the other way.

***

The preparations amounted to a shower, a nap, some food and a talk with Riker about the security arrangements.

"First, we'll stop by medical," Maddox said.

"To check up on Valerie and Meta?" Riker asked.

"No. For a doctor to evaluate your status."

"You think I'm an android, sir?"

"You have an iron heart."

Riker shook his head. "Begging your pardon, sir, but it's the other way around. I'm just an old man doing his job. But I'll gladly take the physical."

It took another three quarters of an hour to get everything set up. During that time, Riker passed the exam. He was still fully human.

Shortly thereafter, Maddox and Riker stood before a large wall screen. It showed the occupant of a cell, with a cot, a table, several chairs and other basic amenities inside. Yen Cho sat at the table playing a game of solitaire. He wore the utility garb that a deck mechanic might don. The android sat straight-backed and serenely moved his cards from one location to another. After a time, he picked up the deck, reshuffled and dealt himself more cards.

Maddox cleared his throat, which activated a comm control.

In the other chamber, Yen Cho set down the cards and looked around, waiting.

"Are you well?" Maddox asked him.

Yen Cho looked around again and finally peered up at the camera. It was supposed to be hidden, but obviously wasn't, not to the android.

"Captain Maddox," the android said. "I've been wondering how long it was going to take you to come around. Wouldn't this be better in person?"

"Better for you," Maddox said, "but not for me. I've just dealt with an android, and she blew up."

Yen Cho did not respond.

"Is our connection faulty?" Maddox asked.

"You know I heard you."

"Any comments?"

"Not yet," the android said.

"We believe the other android slipped aboard as a human mercenary."

"The woman Finlay, you mean?" the android asked.

"You knew about her?"

"Of course," Yen Cho said. "Once Strand captured you, I made a back check to find out how you came onto the asteroid."

"Did Strand know about Finlay?"

"Captain, please, is that a serious question? But first, let us make certain we're talking about the same person. Strand—the original, the real deal, as you humans used to say—is a captive on the Throne World."

"The last you heard," Maddox amended.

"True. Has that state of affairs changed?"

"I don't think so," Maddox said.

"Ah. In any case, we are not dealing with the original Strand. The one at Smade's Asteroid is a clone."

"Was a clone," Maddox said.

"I see. You killed him?"

"I did not. But we believe he is dead."

"You saw the body?"

"No, but my crew destroyed his ship."

Yen Cho bent his head. With a sudden move, he swept the cards from the table. Afterward, he sat perfectly still. Finally, he looked up into the camera and showed his teeth in what might have passed for a smile.

"Please, excuse me. It isn't every day I hear about a barbarian destroying a priceless piece of art. So, you have destroyed the ghost-ship. That is a loss, Captain, a possibly keen one."

"Care to tell me why?" Maddox asked.

"Please, sir, it was a Builder craft." Yen Cho nodded. "I see. It isn't destroyed. You have it and wish me to outline its various functions."

"I'm afraid it is quite destroyed. I believe Strand—the clone of Strand—died with it."

"Sad," Yen Cho said. "Well, then, what do we have to talk about?"

"Quite a bit," Maddox said. Without further ado, the captain went into a lengthy description about the events regarding the red-haired agent and the android-Finlay's various exploits, as far as they could determine them. Maddox left nothing out.

"Quite extraordinary, Captain," Yen Cho said. "Thank you for the data."

"My pleasure."

"Clearly, you want something in return. As you have surmised, there were different android factions aboard the asteroid. In this case, I believe there were two. I am not that far removed from the Rising Sun faction, but I am not one of them."

"Why were you androids on Smade's?"

"For the same reason you were, Captain. We wished to apprehend the clone."

"We didn't know about the clone."

"Star Watch Intelligence must have suspected a clone of Strand would be there."

"That's true," Maddox said. "I suppose you're trying to tell me that you weren't Strand's ally."

"Please. You must know better by now."

"Why did you come to Smade's?"

Yen Cho rose and went around the room, picking up the fallen cards without a word. Finally, he returned to the table, sat down and shuffled the cards, dealing himself another solitaire hand.

Before Yen Cho turned over the first card, he looked up into the camera. "May I tell you a secret?"

"If you wish," Maddox said.

"Strand—the original—is releasing clones. It is not just this one clone. I do not know how the original does this while in captivity. The most obvious method is by prearrangement. This is actually the third or fourth released clone so far."

"You mean since the original's internment on the Throne World?"

"Correct," Yen Cho said. "I killed the first clone on Earth. Do you know what that clone was attempting to do?"

"I do not," Maddox said.

"The first clone had a sniper rifle. He was trying to line up the Lord High Admiral in his crosshairs."

"What happened?"

"I shot the clone. Thus, I could not interrogate him."

"Pity," Maddox said.

"The second clone arrived at Arcturus III. There, he impersonated the fantastically wealthy CEO of Darter Enterprises."

"He impersonated Mike Darter the IV?" Maddox asked.

"Precisely."

"And?"

"He was in the process of inserting detonation devices in Darter Enterprises comm systems."

"Do you know why?"

"A team of androids captured the second Strand clone. He was wearing an ingenious disguise. Unfortunately, Darter Security went into high gear after the android kidnapping. They found the real Mike Darter IV where the clone had buried him. That enraged the security personnel. I do not know how they did it, but Darter Security Services found the kidnappers' trail. The androids were in the process of tapping the clone's mind when the security services found them. Everyone died in the ensuing gun battle."

"How exactly did *everyone* die?" Maddox asked.

"Once the kidnappers realized there was no escape, they blew up their ship in the warehouse where it was hidden."

"Did they use atomics?"

"As you surmise," Yen Cho said, "Yes. The androids killed everyone in the surrounding city as well."

"Why so bloodthirsty?" Maddox asked.

Yen Cho shook his head. "It had nothing to do with that. Precaution has been the watchword in dealing with Strand and his clones. However, the interrogators did learn one interesting point. It was more in the matter of a hint."

"Yes?" Maddox asked.

"It seems the clone said that each release has more…firepower would be the wrong term. More capacity, more equipment. In any case, it led us to believe that Strand— the original—would arm his later clones with Builder equipment."

"I see."

"You didn't let me finish. Arm the clones with Builder equipment and…equipment from the Nameless Ones."

Maddox stared at the android. "The cloaked vessel we destroyed had Nameless Ones tech?"

"I doubt that."

"I'm not tracking you."

"The next clone will likely have Nameless Ones tech."

"This isn't the last clone?"

"Oh, I should think not."

Maddox put his hands behind his back. He began to think, rethink and then he reassessed his idea.

"Yen Cho," Maddox said. And he went on to tell the android about the piece of debris that had used the Laumer Point to escape *Victory*.

The android did not respond.

"What do you think the piece of debris might be?" Maddox asked.

"Captain," Yen Cho said slowly. "I believe you should retrieve that so-called piece of debris."

"What do you think it is?"

"I don't know."

Maddox realized the android was lying. He was fairly certain that Yen Cho had a good idea what the debris was. In fact, the captain would go out on a limb to say that the android was excited, at least as excited as an emotionless mechanical man could be.

"Well," Maddox finally said. "I'm not going after it. I have other business…and frankly…"

"You have a proposal," Yen Cho said. "I am listening."

"I might be able to let you persuade me to retrieve this piece of debris. You obviously think it is important. However, I absolutely will not make the attempt as long as I have these

180

fibers lodged in my brain. I am not going to leave myself defenseless to more android tricks."

"Spacer tricks, really," Yen Cho said. "Androids have incorporated them from time to time, but I see what you mean. Let me think."

The android froze.

Maddox stepped up to some controls and pressed a switch, breaking the comm link between them.

"What do you think?" Maddox asked Riker.

The sergeant shrugged. "Seems like a mess, sir. Strand and his clones are obviously up to something. I can't tell what. Do you know, sir?"

Maddox shook his head.

"Killing the Lord High Admiral," Riker said. "That was a dirty move."

"Yes, it is interesting," Maddox said. "I wonder if that's the crux of the matter."

"Sir?" Riker asked.

"A moment, Sergeant. The android wishes to speak." Maddox clicked on the connection.

"I believe I have a solution," Yen Cho said. "You need a stasis-field emitter."

"The kind Strand uses?"

"A much smaller emitter and for a very localized area. A doctor could use the emitter, putting your brain in the stasis field. Afterward, it would likely prove a simple matter to extract the fibers, all of them. Naturally, I could perform the operation—"

"Thank you but no," Maddox said.

"I perfectly understand."

"How long would it take you to construct such an emitter?"

"A day or two if I had your full cooperation," the android said.

"Let me ponder the idea. Until then, is there anything you wish to add?"

"Speed is likely critical if we're to retrieve this piece of debris."

"Tell me, do the androids fear Strand's ultimate objective?"

"We don't know it yet, but we do fear Strand's reckless use of Builder and Nameless Ones technology for such primitive goals as the selfish Methuselah Man seeks."

"I see," Maddox said. "Until we speak later, then."

"Yes, Captain. I hope you don't take too long to see the need for desperate action and haste."

Maddox clicked off the connection.

"You're not serious about letting him make this emitter?" Riker asked.

"As to that, Sergeant," Maddox said. "I don't know. First, I'd like to speak with Andros about the project."

-41-

Maddox didn't need long to decide. He trusted the android in playing honest about the stasis-field emitter and removing the fibers from his mind. Obviously, Yen Cho wanted him to go after the so-called piece of debris. In order for that to happen, Maddox had to be well enough to travel.

As the android and Andros Crank built the emitter—under the watchful eyes of Security marines—*Victory* decelerated as it approached the Laumer Point. The starship had come the long way, by traveling all three billion kilometers one kilometer at a time. The starship had almost come to a complete stop near the entry point while the two worked on the emitter's finishing touches.

On the bridge, Valerie seemed anxious. She left her station to stand behind Maddox in the command chair.

"This is taking too long," she said softly.

Maddox glanced back at her. "Possibly," he said.

"That piece of debris planned to go through the Laumer Point. The more I think about it, the more certain I am that that's the case. That means the longer we wait here, the greater chance it has of reaching a rendezvous point over there."

"Possibly," Maddox said again.

Valerie eyed him and seemed as if she might throw up her hands, but finally nodded and returned to her station.

Maddox contemplated the main screen, studying the Laumer Point.

It was invisible to the naked eye, but not to their Laumer sensors. The point swirled in the blackness of space, waiting for someone to give the signal and use the linkage between star systems.

Maddox tapped his chin with his pressed together index fingers.

He hated the idea of anyone controlling his thoughts or his actions. The fibers had to go. But it was more than that. He wasn't certain that he could safely make the jump with the fibers in place. Strand hated him. Surely, the clone had hated him as well. Maybe the fibers would act as a sort of time bomb. If he went through a Laumer Point, that might activate them somehow and kill him.

Maybe he should have explained that to Valerie. But Maddox disliked having to explain his actions. She was part of the crew. She should obey his orders and trust him.

Several hours later, Andros reported that the emitter was finished. He would like to make a few tests before they tried it on Maddox, though.

"No," the captain said. "We don't have time for that."

On the screen, Andros looked as if he wanted to make a pithy statement.

"We're on a tight schedule, Chief Technician. We shall proceed."

"Yes, sir," Andros said.

Despite that, it took another four hours to prepare for the surgery. Finally, beginning to feel anxious himself, Maddox reported to medical. Doctor Lister's premier assistant would perform the surgery. Lister was no longer in critical condition, but she wasn't one hundred percent well yet. Furthermore, Maddox did not trust her to operate on him after what he'd done to her.

His suspicious nature naturally assumed she would want to get back at him any way she could.

"That isn't how she thinks," Meta told him in the waiting room.

His wife had asked about his decision, and he'd told her his reasoning.

"I've read her psych profile," Meta added. "Doctor Lister is a professional—"

"Forget it," the captain said, interrupting. "Lister's assistant is performing the operation and that's final."

"Husband—"

"That's final," Maddox repeated. "I won't change my mind on this, not for anyone."

Meta stamped her right foot. She folded her arms and pouted. Finally, she pestered him by beginning the argument anew.

"Listen, Husband—"

"If you say any more," Maddox said, "I'm going to send for Security and have them confine you to quarters."

"You wouldn't dare," she said.

Maddox lifted an eyebrow.

Meta sighed and finally relented. She undoubtedly knew that he *would* dare.

Andros was in the operating theater with the emitter. Marines had already escorted Yen Cho to his cell. The assistant appeared in the waiting room and asked Maddox if he wouldn't like Doctor Lister to watch and advise him.

"The operation is your responsibility alone," Maddox said, testily.

The assistant was a gangly man with graying hair on the sides. "I feel that I should inform you again, sir, that I'm underqualified for—"

"I don't want to hear any more," Maddox said, interrupting. "Let us proceed."

The man paled but nodded. He indicated the hatch. Maddox preceded him, and the prep team took over. Maddox soon lay on the table. Andros positioned the cart that held the emitter so the unit aimed at the captain's head. The assistant nodded. Andros threw a switch and activated the stasis field.

At that point, Maddox faded from consciousness. He did not dream. He wasn't aware of anything.

Unknown to Maddox, the gangly assistant took longer than seemed necessary to Andros and the surgery team. The man searched for every fiber. Galyan appeared from time to time, telling him about yet another fiber he'd overlooked. Finally, the assistant's instruments could not locate another fiber. Galyan did a scan and declared Maddox free from them.

The assistant placed the skull bone back into place and fused it. Exhausted after three hours of tedious work, he signaled Andros Crank.

The Kai-Kaus Chief Technician turned off the stasis-field emitter.

Everyone in the chamber looked at Maddox on the operating table. To their surprise, the captain opened his eyes.

"Can you hear me?" the assistant asked.

"Quite well, yes," Maddox said.

The assistant glanced at a nurse before addressing the captain again. "Can you stand, do you think?"

Maddox sat up. A moment later, he swung his feet off the table, sat another minute, and then stood without trouble.

At that point, the assistant urged him to lie back down and wait a bit before resuming active duty. By all appearances, however, the surgery seemed to have been a perfect success.

-42-

Two hours after the fibers had been removed, Maddox was back on the bridge. He stood before the main screen. He couldn't help touching his bristly skull one more time.

The fibers were gone. He felt incredible relief. What was wrong with Strand and his clones that they had to control everyone? What did that say about the Methuselah Man? Plenty. He needed to go over the Intelligence Department's psych profile again and study that part. It might give him a clue as to the clone's ultimate motivation.

"We're ready to enter the Laumer Point, sir," Valerie said from her station.

Maddox was silent. Had the assistant gotten *every* fiber from his mind?

"Sir?" Valerie asked.

Maddox inhaled sharply, turned and moved to his command chair. He sat, leaned back and gave the command to proceed.

The bridge personnel began the process. The Laumer device in *Victory* sent the signals. The Laumer Point activated and waited for whatever material object entered its radius. This Starship *Victory* began to do as the antimatter engines accelerated the huge vessel. Helm gave the countdown. The mighty warship entered the Laumer Point. In that instant, a Laumer link appeared, connecting the Laumer Point in the Tristano System to one in the Gideon System. Within a microsecond, the starship zipped 9.4 light-years, popping out of the swirling Laumer Point into the Gideon System.

Not so very long ago, everyone—and the computers—would have experienced Jump Lag. That was no longer the case. A few people felt faint, but that was it.

Maddox sat utterly still, trying to determine how he felt. He grinned to himself. He felt good, a tiny bit sluggish, but that was how he usually felt after making a jump.

"Ship has made the transfer," Valerie reported. "We're in the Gideon System, sir."

Maddox nodded. "What are the system's specifics?" he asked.

Valerie checked her panel. "The star is G-class and possesses two inner terrestrial planets. We've come out near the second of those planets, sir."

The lieutenant changed the view on the main screen. Maddox looked upon a dry world like Mars, only three times as big as the Red Planet.

"Earth norms?" he asked.

"Negative, sir," she said. "The air is contaminated by our standards. According to the Patrol Survey from one hundred and forty years ago, the planet is uninhabited by any indigenous life. There don't appear to be any colonization efforts. Oh. This is interesting."

Maddox turned his chair so he could see her.

Valerie looked up. "It appears there are ancient ruins on the planet. According to this..." She began reading again. "Sir," she said, looking up sharply. "Strand once led an archeological team onto the planet."

"A Star Watch team?" Maddox asked.

"No, a Mercer Corporation survey team."

"When was that?"

"If this is right, two hundred and thirty-six years ago."

Maddox pressed his lips together as he thought about that.

"The Mercer Corporation appears to have made a habit of searching for ancient alien ruins," Valerie said, as she read more. "The corporation...went defunct one hundred and eleven years ago."

"Does the report say if they found anything of use down there?"

Valerie shook her head. "The Mercer survey analysis is blank, sir."

"Figures," Keith mumbled from Helm control.

"Any sign of…space debris?" Maddox asked.

"Not so far," Valerie said.

"Keep scanning. Launch probes if you need to." Maddox stood.

"You're not staying?" Valerie asked.

"You have bridge, Lieutenant."

"I haven't finished my report yet concerning the system."

Maddox waved that aside. "Scan for space debris. Search for anything with any kind of power. We're looking for a Builder artifact, a small one, is my guess."

"What kind of artifact?" Valerie asked.

"Exactly," Maddox said. "That's what I want to find out."

***

The hatch to Yen Cho's cell opened. Maddox stepped into the small quarters. The android sat facing him, making eye contact after putting another card onto the table.

Riker came through next. The sergeant held a heavy caliber gun aimed at Yen Cho.

"Pull up a chair, Captain," the android said. "I presume you wish to leave your sergeant near the hatch so I can't make any sudden lunges and disarm him."

A marine outside the cell closed the heavy hatch.

"Is it locked?" Yen Cho asked conversationally.

Maddox took two chairs from the table but did not sit there. Instead, he drew the chairs to him, setting the first near the bulkhead containing the hatch. Maddox sat and tilted the chair back until the back touched the bulkhead. With his feet, he turned the other chair so its backrest wasn't in the way of his line of sight to Yen Cho. Maddox used the second chair as a footrest, also making it easier to lean back as he did.

"Comfortable?" asked Yen Cho.

Maddox glanced at Riker. The sergeant continued to aim the outsized pistol at the android. Riker used his bionic arm and could thus keep the weapon steady for hours.

"It's time to talk," Maddox said.

Yen Cho set down the cards in his hands. "You've found...the debris?"

"That's one of the things I want to talk about. You were going to say something else just now instead of debris. It will help us find it if I know what the debris is exactly."

Yen Cho spread out his hands to indicate he did not have any specifics.

"Perhaps that's true," Maddox said. "Yet, I believe it's more accurate to say that you're only ninety-seven percent sure what we'll find."

"You are astute as always, Captain. I am hoping you find a robot."

"A particular kind of robot, right?"

"Builder constructed, of course."

"Can you be more precise?"

"Yes. A guardian Builder robot," Yen Cho said softly.

"What exactly is that?"

"A protector."

"Let's play twenty questions, then," Maddox said. "Here's number four. Why are you so interested in this guardian robot?"

"Knowledge," Yen Cho said. "The robot could hold...interesting knowledge. For instance, it could tell us more about the Builders. You've talked to a Builder before. You must realize they are secretive to a fault. But this is more to the issue. If the original Strand has more hideaways that will release yet more of his clones, one of them will undoubtedly use stolen technology from the Nameless Ones. I suspect we will need the guardian robot to help us defeat that highly suspect tech."

"Are you suggesting that the next Strand clone will have a neutroium-hulled Destroyer?"

"I seriously doubt that."

"What then?" Maddox asked.

190

"I believe the robot would know, as it has spent time with a Strand clone, among other things. Knowing would undoubtedly help us capture the next clone before it does something incredibly destructive."

"Can you be more precise?"

"I dearly wish I could," Yen Cho said. "I simply do not have enough facts yet, but I am quite sure about my guesses."

"And you think that the Rull faction of androids also wants this robot?"

"Oh, yes. I am quite sure of that."

"Do they want the robot in order to help stop the next Strand clones?"

"Possibly…"

Maddox lifted his feet off the chair as he let the one he was sitting on thump all four legs onto the floor. "That implies the Rull want the robot for something else. What else, Yen Cho?"

Once more, the android spread out his hands in a noncommittal gesture.

"I think you're lying about not knowing their ultimate goal," Maddox said.

"I speak the truth, but this talk is possibly a waste of time. We need to find the robot, if it exists. We need to find it as soon as possible."

"Why did the presumed guardian robot choose the Gideon System?"

"For the simplest of reasons," the android said. "This was the nearest Laumer Point. It wanted to escape from your starship."

"That's not the only reason."

Yen Cho stared at Maddox for several seconds. "It appears that you are aware of Gideon II."

"Yes," Maddox said. "I know that Strand was part of the Mercer Corporation excavation team two hundred and thirty-six years ago."

"I was not aware that Star Watch had such detailed records."

"Now you are."

"Captain," Yen Cho said in a reproving voice. "I know what you are attempting to do. You want to know what Strand searched for down there. I happen to know that Strand erased all information regarding the dig. Star Watch might know he came here, but it has no idea what he sought to find or if he found it."

"And you do?"

"Oh, yes," Yen Cho said.

"I'm waiting to hear it."

"And you can continue to wait. Gideon II has no bearing on our present situation. The robot, if it exists, would not have landed on the planet. I doubt it would have the capacity to do so."

Maddox studied the android. After several seconds, he lurched to his feet and gave Yen Cho a nod. Still facing the android, Maddox reached behind him and tapped on the hatch.

It unlocked and opened.

"Go ahead," Maddox told Riker.

The sergeant retreated from the chamber.

"I'm telling you the truth," Yen Cho said. "The robot is drifting in space somewhere. I would like to know its destination as much as you would. Do not waste time searching the planet."

"I won't," Maddox said. Then he stepped backward through the hatch and waited until the marine closed it with a snick.

In the hall, Riker was holstering his big gun.

Maddox tapped his chin thoughtfully. Then he whirled around and stalked away at a brisk pace.

-43-

Less than an hour later, Maddox sat beside Keith as the ace piloted an armored shuttle through Gideon II's upper atmosphere. The medical treatment had healed his earlier burns. Below, the dusty planet seemed the same as ever. In the distance, wispy clouds appeared far below them.

"There are traces of water vapor," Maddox said, studying his sensor screen.

Above them in orbit, *Victory* launched more probes. The probes sped in all directions as they scanned relentlessly, searching for a small piece of debris. Yet, space was vast compared to the particle of substance they were trying to find. If the Builder robot—if it was a robot—used a cloaking device, it might be even harder to find than anticipated.

Maddox knew it could be worse than that. If Yen Cho was correct about the debris being a robot, the construct could have had a waiting vessel somewhere in the Gideon System.

So far, Valerie hadn't spotted any power source in nearby space. Neither Keith, nor Galyan back on *Victory,* had spotted any power source on the planet.

Maddox was certain that Yen Cho had lied about the planet. If no one could find any energy traces anywhere, there were two possibilities: a cloaking device, or the robot landing somewhere hidden on the planet. If the robot hadn't kept a private spaceship waiting in orbit, might it have something down here? That was what Maddox intended on discovering. Of course, if the robot had something waiting down here, that

193

something could be dangerous, the more so as they attempted to uncover its existence.

Keith piloted while Riker and four marines waited in back. All five of them wore exoskeleton combat suits. Maddox would don such a suit when the time came. Keith would remain aboard while staying aloft, the shuttle armed with 30-mm cannons and several antimatter missiles.

The flight down proved uneventful. They passed the wispy clouds and soon descended upon a vast worldwide desert of shifting red sand. There were a few rounded mountain ranges here and there, their erosion indicating great age.

"Winds about fifty-three klicks per hour," Keith said. "Nothing to write home about, depending on the average size of the grains of sand."

Maddox understood. Too fine, and the grains would inevitably find their way into the combat-armor joints. That could prove tactically important.

"Slight change in plans," the captain said. "We're going to land before you go airborne again. I want to test the size of the grains, see what we're up against."

"Roger that," Keith said.

Soon, the shuttle swept several hundred kilometers above a shifting desert that made Earth's Sahara seem puny in comparison.

"Mountains in the distance," Keith said.

Maddox nodded. That was their destination. They were heading to the planetary coordinates of Strand's original excavation. That was all the information that remained of the historical survey: where they had done the digging.

The mountains appeared as a smudge on the horizon. They grew quickly to rounded humps on a desert world of sand.

"Whoa," Keith said. "I don't get it. We didn't see that on the ship's scopes. It's like that suddenly appeared."

Maddox looked out a window in amazement. The shuttle flew over a vast dug-up area abutting the lowest mountain slopes. The circumference and depth weren't the only incredible part. Inside the huge dig were monumental pyramids.

Keith was right. This hadn't been in the briefing.

"I'm picking up something," the pilot said. "I'd call it a charged particle field. It's over the pit."

"What's powering the field?" Maddox asked.

Keith shook his head. "I'm not getting any readings on that."

"How would that have blocked *Victory's* telescopes from seeing the dig?"

"It shouldn't have," Keith said. "This doesn't make sense, Captain. What's going on?"

A surge of excitement filled Maddox. He'd guessed right. The android had been lying about the planet.

Keith whistled as he studied a sensor. "Listen to this. Those pyramids are five times the size of the Giza Pyramid in Egypt. They're massive."

Maddox started counting pyramids. He stopped at thirty-seven, having counted about a quarter of them.

"Wonder what's in them," Keith said.

"I wonder who built them," Maddox countered.

"Should we have brought the android along?"

"On no account," Maddox said. "Land...several hundred kilometers from the edge. Land on a mountain slope, too," he added. "We'll keep off the sand if we can help it."

"Roger that," Keith said softly.

A few minutes later, the shuttle touched down softly onto a level area of rocky slope.

Maddox nodded in appreciation of the ace's piloting skill. He unbuckled and went back, climbing into two tons of space-marine combat armor. Once ready, he joined Riker and the others.

Each of them had a heavy autocannon attached to a suit arm, smart-missile packs and complex detection gear. Each suit was black-matted and made the wearer seem like an overgrown mechanical gorilla.

A cargo hatch opened, and a metal ramp extended to the rocky ground. Maddox led the way, clomping down the ramp. He clanked to the nearest area of sand and ran an analyzer over it.

The grains were super-fine. They would prove troublesome to the suits in no time.

Maddox summoned the marine sub-lieutenant, Gordon Vesper. The marine studied the finding.

"I'm not a suit tech, sir," sub-lieutenant Vesper said. "But these grains will start giving us trouble within the hour. We can last longer if there's no wind and less in a sandstorm."

That was worse than Maddox had expected, and it gave him greater appreciation for the Mercer Corporation feat over two hundred and thirty-six years ago.

"Take her up," he radioed Keith.

The ramp pulled back, the hatch shut, and the engines powered up. The shuttle lifted gently and continued to climb on its gravity dampeners.

Count on Keith to think of the best way to launch. The ace hadn't given them a swirling dust cloud and had thus extended their possible length of stay.

"Keep in close touch," Maddox told Keith, "and keep in constant contact with *Victory*. If you lose contact with *Victory*, you're to pick us up right away."

"Roger that," Keith said through Maddox's headphones.

Maddox watched the shuttle rise higher.

"Winds are picking up, sir," the sub-lieutenant said over the shortwave.

"Let's go," Maddox told him and the others. "Let's see what the Mercer Corporation found down there."

***

Maddox led Riker and the space marines between the gigantic pyramids. They were constructed out of colossal red granite blocks, many tons each. Some of the pyramids were bigger than others. All were smooth, without apparent sandblasted damage from the winds. None had any visible entrance.

"Anything?" Maddox asked the others over the shortwave.

"There's nothing here, sir," Riker said. "The pyramids appear to be solid stone through and through."

"That's what I'm reading, too," Maddox said. Yet, he had his doubts about that. Something seemed off, and he couldn't quite place it.

"Why would aliens build solid stone pyramids?" Riker asked.

"We don't know that's the case," Maddox replied, "just that these so far appear to be solid."

"You think our scanners are off?" the sergeant asked.

Maddox didn't reply, but that was something to think about.

The two-ton combat suits continued to clomp between the pyramids, searching for answers or possible clues.

"You know what I find strange, sir?" sub-lieutenant Vesper asked ten minutes later. "There's no sand down here."

In his combat suit, Maddox halted. The servomotors whined as he bent onto one knee. He studied the ground, the rock. There wasn't a grain of sand on it. He should have seen it right away. The charged particle shield over the dig should have led him in that direction.

Sometimes it's harder to see what isn't there than what is there, he reminded himself.

"Check your suits," Maddox radioed. "Tell me if any of them have any sand in the joints."

Riker and the marines checked and reported in. They each had a few grains, no more, likely picked up before they'd entered the giant dig.

"I'm beginning to think the Mercer Corporation never dug this hole," Maddox told Riker. "They wouldn't have possessed the tech to make a charged particle shield that didn't seem to have a power source and that lasted so long. It's clear the shield has kept out the sand all these years. Otherwise, during the last two hundred and thirty-six years, the wind would have dumped enough sand to bury this place. And the tops of the pyramids would have eroded like the mountaintops."

"Say, that's right," Riker said.

"Recheck your scanners," Maddox told the others. "There has to be some form of energy doing this. These things can't be solid stone."

The two-ton suits went back to back with each other, so one of them scanned outward in all directions. Each marine's autocannon was primed for firing. At the same time, each marine used the sensors attached to the suits.

"Nothing new, sir," Riker soon said.

"That doesn't make sense," Maddox said.

What was he missing? Was this why Yen Cho had told him to forget about the planet? Or was it more subtle than that? Had Yen Cho told him to forget about the planet in the same way Maddox had told Riker to tell the marines earlier not to tell anyone about the shot-up android? In other words, had Yen Cho known him so well that the android knew that saying what it had would goad Maddox to come down here?

"Sir," a marine said. "I'm getting a strange reading."

"Send it to me," Maddox said.

On his HUD visor, Maddox studied the reading, a slight energy trace.

"I'd say that looks like leakage of some kind," Riker said over the shortwave.

"Leakage from what?" Even as Maddox asked that, he believed he understood. That must be leakage from a stealth suit. Somebody must be trying to sneak up on them.

-44-

At that moment, Maddox had one of his hunches. "Keith," he said over the comm.

There was no answer.

Maddox swore, looked up and used his HUD radar. There! He spotted the shuttle. It was high up there, higher than he thought Keith should have gone. Maybe the wind had picked up and was kicking sand up into the air.

Yes, Maddox detected a haze of fine sand particles between the giant hole and the shuttle. The charged particle shield must keep the sand out, repelling the fine grains. Could sand that spread across the charged-particle shield have blocked *Victory's* scopes earlier?

Maybe the particles blocked his comm connection, too. Maddox had a fix and couldn't talk to the ace. He activated a laser-link and beamed the comm laser up at the shuttle.

"Keith," he said again.

"Sir?" the ace asked. "This is a laser-link, and I can hardly hear you. What's going on?"

"Listen. Give us…six minutes. Come low after that and place an antimatter missile in the exact center of the dig."

"But sir—"

"Do it, Lieutenant. Our lives may depend on it. Maddox out."

The captain shut off the laser link. He regarded his combat team. He may have just sentenced them to death. But he was certain that Rull androids in stealth suits attempted to capture them. On no account was he going to let that happen. He also suspected the enemy had enough numbers to overpower the small group.

"See that pyramid?" Maddox said, pointing at the nearest one.

The others nodded.

"Use your autocannons and start blasting granite. After that, grab your picks and begin hammering and prying rock free. We're building ourselves a bomb shelter. We have less than six minutes until an antimatter missile strikes."

"Sir!" Riker said. "That's suicide."

"No. It's our only chance to remain free agents. Now go to work."

Maddox didn't wait for questions or to see if the others understood him. Instead, he trained his autocannon on the nearest pyramid and began hammering it with shells in timed sequences. Granite blasted apart. Some of the stone shards struck his suit but did no damage.

A moment later, the others started doing likewise. They blasted into the ancient pyramid.

"Stop firing, stop firing," Maddox ordered. "Grab your picks and work like madmen."

He attacked the autocannon-created hole and used the full power of the combat suit. For the next four minutes, Maddox and the others' caused rock to explode apart under their powerful blows.

At five minutes and twenty-nine seconds, Maddox burst into a chamber. He'd suspected something like this or maybe it had been more like a wild hope. There must have been something in the red granite that had blocked their suit sensors. Given everything else, that confirmed for him that this was Builder-related.

He clicked on a helmet lamp and beckoned the others to him. For the next thirty-three seconds, the two-ton suits clanked at speed down a corridor until they reached a pit. Without hesitation, Maddox leaped. The others followed him.

For several sickening seconds, Maddox's suit fell. It struck with force and caused the servomotors to whine with complaint as the shock absorbers saved his frail flesh-and-blood body from the impact. The captain curled himself and his suit into a fetal ball, ordering the others to follow his example.

As the last marine curled tight, Keith's antimatter missile hit the bottom floor of the giant dig and detonated, sending a powerful antimatter blast in all directions.

The suits were deep enough that the strange red granite absorbed and blocked the worst of the heat, blast and radiation. Besides, each of them had already swallowed an anti-radiation tablet, and their combat armor was better than any bio- or nuclear-hazard suit.

Riker unfolded from his fetal position and slid beside the captain. He clanked his helmet against Maddox's helmet.

In a voice sounding tinny to the captain, Riker asked, "What was that all about, sir? Why did you try to kill all of us?"

Maddox clicked off his shortwave. "It was nothing of the kind, Sergeant. I suspected stealth androids were about to attack us."

"Sir?"

In a few terse sentences, Maddox explained his idea of Yen Cho having tricked them down here. With the leakage energy reading, he had put two and two together.

"You don't like anyone telling you what you shouldn't do, do you, sir?"

"Enough of your cheek, Sergeant. We have to get out of here as soon as possible."

"I don't understand. You took care of the problem."

"If I'm right about Rull androids, they must have a ship or a hidden base near here. We took out a stealth attack, but maybe they have heavier hardware. I think they planned to kidnap us for nefarious ends. I'm sick of being someone's prisoner. Once per mission is quite enough for me."

"That antimatter strike must have leveled plenty of pyramids. That's archeological mayhem, sir."

"I'm not Ludendorff," Maddox said. "I'm concerned with the living more than the past's relics. But enough about that. We've waited long enough. It's time to dig our way to the surface and contact Keith. I want to get off the planet before the androids send reinforcements or try to attack *Victory*."

-45-

With *Victory's* sensors, Galyan scanned the planet's surface. The Adok holoimage had just received word of the captain's unbelievable order.

He used the starship's best scope to study the incredible excavation site. This was odd. The site wasn't visible. All he saw was sand.

Galyan tried a different sensor. How interesting. There was a type of force field, a charged particle shield. He would assume the charged particles radiated sand from—ah, yes. Sand cascaded down a seeming dome and spewed from repellers at the bottom edges. If he hadn't known about the dig, the instruments would have assumed this was a natural phenomenon. Sand continued to blow onto the field and slide down. Ordinary scopes simply saw sand and could not detect the hole underneath the charged-particle dome.

Galyan used a more powerful sensor, piecing the covering as he studied the antimatter-blasted pyramids. By the discoloration of the red granite rock, he could see the new blast damage. The pyramids had been in almost pristine condition before this. No longer.

"It is good Professor Ludendorff is not here," Galyan said to himself. "He would be furious at the archeological damage."

Keith piloted the shuttle down toward the excavation site.

"Lieutenant," Galyan said via comm.

"I'm busy," Keith said.

"Do not attempt to directly land in the excavation site. The charged particle shield might interfere with your flight computer."

"Are you sure about that?" Keith asked.

"Quite sure," Galyan said.

"I'll radio the captain."

"You can speak to him directly?" Galyan asked.

"Not at the moment. How did you know someone was jamming us?"

"That is not the case," Galyan said. "It is the charged particles interfering with the comm system."

"The captain messaged me earlier."

Galyan thought about that. "Did he use a laser link?"

"You're a smart guy, Galyan. That's right. Now, look, I'm real busy. Is there anything else?"

"Keep on the lookout for intruders. The captain's missile-strike order implies an outer threat."

"Roger that," Keith said. "Out."

Galyan continued to watch the progress on the scope. The shuttle landed beside the dig. Time passed, too much time in the holoimage's estimation. Finally, space-marine suits climbed out of the excavation hole and hurried to the shuttle.

This was the danger point.

But nothing unpleasant happened. The two-ton suits boarded the shuttle and the shuttle lifted off, heading for *Victory* in its orbit upstairs.

What happened to the enemy? Why are they letting the shuttle get away so easily?

Galyan might have pondered longer. Instead, he sensed commotion on the bridge.

In an instant, the holoimage disappeared from the viewing port and appeared on the bridge.

"What has happened, Valerie?" Galyan asked.

The lieutenant sat forward on the command chair. She had shiny eyes and a triumphant smile. She turned to him.

"I've found it," Valerie declared.

"The missing space debris?" Galyan asked.

"The robot, a Builder robot by the reports," she said.

On the main screen, Galyan saw the beamed image of what Probe 10-D had scanned. It showed an artillery-shell-shaped piece of metal hurtling toward a rogue moon. As he watched, the object shimmered, almost disappeared and then appeared whole again as the probe used a different sensor.

"Is that image correct?" Galyan asked.

"The robot is modulating its stealth mode," Valerie said with appreciation in her voice. "It's most impressive."

"Why does it not use all modes at the same time?" Galyan said. "It might have remained hidden that way."

"Best that I can reason it," Valerie said, "is that it lacks the power to do so."

"That is one possibility."

Valerie's smile lost some of its power. "What's the other possibility?"

"That it wants to be found, but not easily," Galyan said.

"Why would it want that?"

"I believe that is the question Captain Maddox is going to ask."

"Yes," she said. "I believe you're right."

-46-

Nearly two hours later, Maddox appeared on the bridge. He had gone through anti-radiation treatment, taken another nap—he'd been taking too many of them lately, but his body was still healing and demanded all the sleep he would give it. Now, Maddox listened to Valerie's report concerning the robot.

The starship was already accelerating toward the object. At its present velocity, the robot was still several days away from reaching the rogue moon.

"Tell me more about that moon," Maddox said.

"It appears to have blown loose from Gideon II sometime in the past," Valerie said. "The moon has an erratic orbit around the star and approaches the second planet far too closely at times. That was the first clue regarding its…loosening."

"What was the other clue?" Maddox asked.

Valerie pointed at a warrant officer. He tapped his console. On the main screen, the dark moon appeared. It was a close-up that zoomed closer still, to reveal a batch of giant pyramids.

"More of them," Maddox said. "Galyan, did you analyze the blast area on Gideon II?"

"Yes," Galyan said. "I found trace elements that suggest you were correct in your assumption."

"You found the remains of stealth androids?"

"Not exactly," Galyan said. "The antimatter blast was intense. It caused massive damage to the pyramids and obliterated your possible enemy. I did detect trace elements that could have been androids. The data is not conclusive, however. I would require a more detailed scan."

"You took a huge risk with the antimatter missile," Valerie told the captain.

Maddox shrugged. It had worked. That was enough for him. "What is the estimated time to our reaching the robot?" he asked Valerie.

"Two hours and forty-three minutes," she said.

"That gives me enough time to talk to Yen Cho again," Maddox said. "Has the robot made any attempt to contact us?"

"None," Valerie said.

"Is the robot still using its stealth modes?"

"No."

"The robot knows we know it's there?"

"It's acting that way," Valerie said.

"Anything else on the moon?" asked Maddox.

"There is…energy leakage. I don't know what it is yet, but I have my suspicions."

"Show me this leakage," Maddox said.

Valerie indicated a control panel to the side. Maddox went there and studied it. The leakage could have come from anything; life-support, idle beam weaponry, waiting missiles… One thing bothered Maddox about the reading. It was the same as the marine had discovered while they were walking among the pyramids on Gideon II. Did that mean stealth androids waited on the rogue moon?

Maddox doubted it. Yet…that might mean he'd been wrong about stealth androids on Gideon II.

"What's the robot's distance to the rogue moon?" Maddox asked.

"Half a million kilometers," Valerie said.

"The robot is moving slowly," Maddox said.

"That depends on your reference point," she said.

"Keep me posted on any new developments, even if I'm in the middle of interrogating the android."

Valerie nodded.

With that, Maddox exited the bridge.

***

206

This time, the captain took Meta with him instead of Riker. The sergeant was tired-out from the mission onto the surface. He had become ill from the radiation treatments and slept fitfully in sickbay. The marines weren't quite as badly off, but they hadn't shaken off the treatments as fast as Maddox had.

Yen Cho was playing solitaire just like before. He looked up as the hatch opened. He noted Meta with a big gun pointed at him. He smiled at her.

She did not smile back.

"I see," the android said. He put his cards down and sat back in his chair.

This time, Maddox took only one chair. He sat normally. He realized he wasn't feeling all that well. Maybe the anti-radiation treatment was starting to get to him, too. Maybe the aftereffects of the antimatter blast had something to do with it as well.

"Surprised to see me?" Maddox asked.

"I am," Yen Cho admitted. "You visited less than twelve hours ago. I hadn't expected you back—"

"That isn't what I meant," Maddox said dryly, interrupting.

"Then I am at a loss as to your meaning."

"Are you indeed?"

"Please, Captain, let us forgo 'twenty questions,' as you said last time. What should surprise me about your visit?"

Maddox smiled blandly. "I went down to the planet."

Yen Cho's easy manner altered as the android put both hands on the table as if to steady himself. "I warned you not to go there."

"So it seemed."

Yen Cho cocked his head. He cocked it the other way. "I do not perceive your meaning."

"You baited him," Meta said.

Yen Cho blinked twice. "I see," he said. "You believe that I think you are a child. That is quite amusing, Captain. But let me put you at ease. I consider you the wiliest opponent I have ever faced in my long existence."

"Whatever you really believe about me," Maddox said, "you clearly think I'm conceited."

"But of course you are. Ask your woman if she thinks that. We all know you are conceited, Captain. What makes it interesting is that you are not a conceited ass like so many of your kind are."

"Watch your mouth," Meta warned.

"Did that upset you, dear lady? Do you hide the truth about your husband from yourself?"

"Husband," Meta said, "would you allow me to have the android put in a mechanical press? I'll take off both of his arms. If that doesn't tame his tongue, we'll remove his legs as well."

Yen Cho nodded. "One barbarian mated to another. You make a perfect couple, Captain. I congratulate you on your choice of mate."

"I went down to the planet," Maddox said crisply. "I landed with several marines and walked among the pyramids. I discovered the lack of sand on the ground due to the charged particle shield surrounding the excavation site. While poking around, I also discovered stealth androids attempting a kidnapping."

"I know nothing about that."

"I eliminated the androids but was unable to capture any."

"Let me apologize for any combat losses, Captain."

"No need," Maddox said, "as there were none."

"None? I cannot believe that. You said hidden androids attacked you."

"Before they could launch their assault, my team dug into a pyramid and found a deep hole. I ordered an antimatter strike into the dig. The blast killed the stealth androids."

"What?" Yen Cho said. "You used an antimatter device against the pyramids? You are indeed a barbarian, Captain. You destroy what you cannot understand."

Maddox turned to Meta. "I suspect androids built the pyramids. If not...the androids use them for something. That means I'm going to destroy the pyramids on the rogue moon."

Yen Cho rose to his feet.

Meta's heavy gun tracked him as she became tense.

"Are you tired of living?" asked Maddox.

Slowly, Yen Cho resumed his seat and shook his head. "You are correct in one assumption, but quite wrong in the other. Androids did not build the pyramids."

"Who then?"

"Who else?" Yen Cho said. "The Builders."

"The pyramids…are artifacts?"

Yen Cho looked away before regarding Maddox again. "They are not technologically powerful artifacts but they are powerful symbols…to us."

"To androids in general or to your particular android faction?"

"To all of us," Yen Cho said. "We are the constructs. The Gideon System has meaning for androids. You have desecrated one of our holy sites."

"No," Maddox said. "You're not alive in a real sense. You're machines."

"I assure you that we are quite alive," Yen Cho said. "We are different from you, but we are living. Do humans have souls, Captain? I can't see them. I can't smell them. How, then, can you prove the existence of souls?"

"Easily," Maddox said. "Humans have written holy books or holy words, the Bible, the Koran, the Talmud and others. In their time, people considered the books holy, set apart. They pertain to God, or the gods in some cases, which pertain to souls. Why do humans have this yearning to seek spiritual meaning? The answer is easy. It scratches an itch in the human psyche, in the human soul. That leads me to the opposite conclusion for you. Have androids ever written holy books?"

"I am not aware of any," Yen Cho said.

"Of course you aren't," Maddox said, "because mechanical men lack souls. You lack our human itch to fill a spiritual void in each of us."

"We do have our holy sites, though."

"I have my doubts regarding that," Maddox said. "I am tempted to believe the pyramids have an actual function for you androids. What function do the pyramids provide for you?"

"They mark the beginning of our creators," Yen Cho said.

Maddox blanched. "Gideon II is the original homeworld of the Builders?"

"As to that, I cannot say," Yen Cho replied. "That is because I do not know. The Builders first devised us human-shaped androids on Gideon II. That I do know."

"Are you telling me there are workshops under the pyramids?"

"If I say more," Yen Cho said. "I will have to kill you."

Maddox glanced at Meta before regarding the android. He thought about Yen Cho's revelation. He thought about the pyramids, the charged particle shield over the excavation site. He considered the supposed Builder guardian robot using the Laumer Point to reach this star system. As Maddox considered these things, he drummed his fingers on his right knee.

"We found the guardian robot," he told Yen Cho.

"And?"

"No more," Maddox said. He stood and nodded to Meta.

She kept her gun trained on the android as she knocked on the hatch with her other hand. It unlatched and opened. Two marines with heavy combat rifles stood there, aiming them at Yen Cho.

"Captain," Yen Cho said. "This is quite unfair. You cannot tell me about the robot and simply depart. While I agree that I might not have a soul, I have curiosity. I…would like to know what you plan to do next."

"Is there anything you care to tell me?" Maddox asked.

"You mean pertaining to the robot?"

Maddox did not answer.

The android seemed undecided. "I doubt the robot itself is dangerous. It will have a great fund of knowledge, naturally. Or do you mean this supposed stealth-android assault? Captain, you are not going to like this. I doubt there was any such assault. You may have detected something, but it was not androids bent on kidnapping you."

"What did we detect, then?"

"I cannot say."

"Cannot or won't?"

"Will not," Yen Cho said. "The site is holy to androids. I cannot reveal why. I am…saddened by your wanton destruction. Perhaps you are more human than New Man. You destroy what you do not understand like a human would."

There was a tightening to Maddox's eyes. He didn't care for the remark. Could he have been wrong about an android stealth assault? Had his hunch been false? The possibility existed. Maybe he had overreacted because he was still jumpy due to the clone's attempt to wire his mind.

Through force of will, Maddox pushed that aside. The pyramids weren't as important as the robot. What had Yen Cho said? The robot wasn't dangerous?

"Do you think the clone of Strand would agree with your assessment regarding the robot's non-deadly nature?"

"I doubt so," Yen Cho said.

"The robot has a task, doesn't it?"

"I...I do not know."

"Yen Cho," Maddox said. "You have consistently lied to me. I believe little of what you have said. You seek the robot, clearly. I want to know why."

"I desire knowledge."

"That's another lie," Maddox said. "Tell me the real reason."

"And if I do not tell you the real reason, you will order those men to shoot me?"

Maddox did not answer.

"Captain..." the android said.

"Speak while you can, Yen Cho. Your time is limited."

"I believe..." the android stopped talking. Finally, he shook his head. "I am unable to comply with your request, Captain."

Maddox scratched a cheek. There was something huge afoot. What did the robot mean to the androids? What did these pyramids mean to them? Why were the pyramids important, and had the robot come here for a specific purpose?

Maddox could almost taste the importance of the star system. Had Strand erred in setting the robot free? By everything he'd learned, Maddox suspected the original Strand had possessed the robot and ghost-ship for a long time. Only now, though, was the robot awake again. How long had the robot been turned off?

"Enough," Maddox whispered. "Let's go. Yen Cho, I was going to take you with me. Now, you can remain in the dark for a little longer."

With that, Maddox and Meta stepped out of the cell. The guards sealed the armored hatch, leaving Yen Cho inside.

Maddox sat in the captain's chair, looking up as Valerie spoke.

"Captain," she said. "The robot is definitely decelerating. It's no longer attempting to reach the moon."

Maddox had been reading a report. He now studied the main screen. Valerie had ordered twenty times magnification.

That still wasn't enough.

"One hundred times magnification," Maddox said.

A moment later, the main screen shimmered. The artillery-shell-shaped robot leaped into view.

"That's a robot?" Keith asked from Helm.

"Apparently," Maddox said. "What are the sensors detecting?" he asked Valerie.

"It has a tiny nuclear pile," Valerie said. "I don't understand how that works, as it's incredibly small. I don't detect any energy weaponry. That doesn't mean it doesn't have a latent weapon system. There is excessive computing and something else, something I don't understand. Ludendorff might have understood. Maybe Yen Cho would as well."

"Explain," Maddox said.

"It might be bio-matter," Valerie said. "It's in the top part of the robot. Is that a robot, sir? Might it be a tiny space vessel?"

"It has a space drive, as we're witnessing it decelerating. The drive is slight, though, although the robot did use the Laumer Point."

213

"If it can use Laumer Points, it's using a star drive," Valerie said. "It simply crosses each system much slower than we can do."

"Maybe as a Builder construct, it doesn't value time the same way we do," Maddox said.

Galyan spoke up. "I do not accept that, sir. I have lived a long time, and I still value each second."

Maddox smiled at Galyan. "You're unique, no doubt about that."

"Thank you, Captain. That is kind of you to say."

"You're right in thanking him, Galyan," Valerie said. "I'd record what the captain just said and enjoy it while you can."

Maddox refrained from glancing at the lieutenant, although he detected several bridge personnel giving Valerie a look. He would ignore the remark. Besides, maybe he wasn't a fount of kind words.

He crossed his legs as he regarded the Builder construct out there. What had the robot been doing? Heading for the rogue moon…

"Lieutenant," he said, "plot the robot's former trajectory. Was it heading for the pyramids?"

Valerie tapped her board, studying the results. "It was," she said.

"But not the planet's pyramids…" Maddox said to himself. He wondered about that, considering once again if he'd overreacted regarding the energy leakage. Had he jumped to a false conclusion, or was Yen Cho trying to upset his confidence? Clearly, the pyramids were important to androids. Just as clearly, the robot seemed important to Yen Cho and the other androids.

What could the robot do that was so important?

"We will arrive at the robot in twenty-seven minutes," Valerie said.

Maddox nodded. He had twenty-seven minutes to figure out the best way to deal with it.

"Should I attempt communication?" Valerie asked.

"No…" Maddox said. "Let's see if it tries to hail us."

The minutes passed as *Victory* moved toward the robot. The thing had stopped dead in space. It had stopped about four hundred thousand kilometers from the rogue moon.

"Is there anything new regarding the moon?" Maddox asked.

"It's quiet," Valerie said. "I no longer detect any energy leakage."

Maddox frowned. Could this be a subtle trap? Could massive beam cannons be waiting to power up? Yet, if that was the case, they should have detected some form of energy.

"Helm," Maddox said. "Be ready for an emergency star-drive jump."

"Roger that," Keith said.

The minutes continued to pass.

"Begin deceleration," Maddox said.

Keith manipulated this panel, and *Victory* began decelerating.

"Still nothing from the robot," Valerie said. "If it's scared of us, it's not showing it."

"Do robots have emotions?" Maddox asked.

"I detected what could be bio-matter earlier," Valerie said. "That part could have emotions."

"Interesting," Maddox said. "Yes. Good point."

The lieutenant looked up with raised eyebrows, nodding a moment later.

The remaining minutes seemed to move in slow motion. Nothing changed on the rogue moon. Nothing was happening that *Victory* could determine on Gideon II.

That caused a prickle of sensation in Maddox's neck. If androids were among the pyramids on Gideon II, they should have done something by now. Could Yen Cho be right about no androids being hidden in the Gideon System? The idea troubled him.

"No," Maddox whispered to himself. He wasn't going to let anything chip away at his self-confidence. He was—

"Sir," Valerie said. "The robot is hailing us."

Maddox sat forward. Now maybe he could get some answers to all these questions.

-48-

Starship *Victory* came to a dead stop before a guardian Builder robot, if that was what it was. They were both four hundred thousand kilometers from the giant pyramids on the rogue moon.

The situation felt surreal to Maddox as he regarded the construct on the main screen.

"You will identify yourself," the robot said in a robotic manner, using regular Commonwealth English.

"I am a Star Watch captain," Maddox replied.

"Yours is a Commonwealth vessel?" the robot asked.

"It is."

"I detect falsehood in your reply," the robot said. "Yours is an Adok warship built to resist a Swarm Invasion Fleet, circa 10,221 B.E."

"You did not ask me if this was a Commonwealth-constructed vessel," Maddox pointed out. "The crew belongs to Star Watch, the guardian arm of the Commonwealth."

"Do you claim I that reached a false conclusion?"

"I'm not making any claims just yet," Maddox said. "You intrigue me. You're different. You're—"

"Captain Maddox," the robot said. "Let us drop this pretense. You know I was on Methuselah Man Strand's ghost-ship. Your confederates destroyed the ghost-ship. Now, you have chased me down. I would like an explanation."

"I'm sure you would," Maddox said. "I'd like to know why you ran for the Laumer Point back in the Tristano System."

216

"It was a matter of survival."

"Do you fear us?"

"I do not fear your crew. I am wary of you, though, Captain Maddox. I have studied you extensively. You must have already divined that my computer system predicated your various actions. I gave the Methuselah Man—"

"Let me stop you right there," Maddox said, interrupting. "First, he wasn't a Methuselah Man. Your Strand was a clone of the Methuselah Man."

"That is correct."

"By saying otherwise a few seconds ago, you were attempting to feed me false data."

"That is incorrect. I have been determining your mental condition. I see it has returned to normal. That will allow me to proceed on an optimal path with you."

"Because you can predict my actions?" Maddox asked.

"Not with one hundred percent accuracy, but with something so close it hardly makes any difference."

"You knew I'd come after you into the Gideon System?"

"That was self-evident."

"Did you know that I'd catch you?"

The robot did not answer.

"Before we continue," Maddox said. "What would you like me to call you?"

"I do not care."

"Should I just say…robot?"

"If you want," the robot said.

"I don't care for that. It's too impersonal, and you're unique, I'm told."

"Your data concerning me is accurate so far."

"You are a guardian robot of Builder construction?" Maddox asked.

"Correct."

"Where are the Builders?"

The robot did not answer.

"What was the clone of Strand hoping to achieve?" Maddox asked.

"That is immaterial to our business at hand."

217

"It's very material. By the way, I'm going to call you Gideon."

The robot said nothing.

"Gideon," Maddox said. "Is it okay if I call you Gideon?"

"Call me what you wish."

"Great. I'm glad to hear you cooperating with us, Gideon. I want to know what the clone desired."

"The destruction of the Commonwealth," the robot said.

"I see. And you two were going to make that happen?"

"I understand your sarcasm, Captain. Perhaps an analogy is in order so you can comprehend the truth. We were going to be like a master jeweler, using precise blows to chip a rough diamond into a given shape. The Commonwealth is presently at a crisis point, mainly due to the defeated Swarm Invasion. Given carefully considered stresses, the clone hoped to weaken the Commonwealth sufficiently that the New Men would once again invade with their star cruisers."

"Why would Strand wish this?"

"The reason is obvious. Strand hates the idea that basic humanity has eclipsed his created New Men in combat power. He is going to attempt to change that to an outcome he approves of."

"And you were helping him do just that?"

"For a time," the robot said.

"Do you also wish the Commonwealth to disintegrate?"

"I have no wish either way on the matter."

"What do you care about?" asked Maddox.

The robot said nothing.

"Did you kill the Strand clone?" Maddox asked.

"Yes."

"Why?"

"To facilitate my escape from you," the robot said.

"You failed."

"I failed to escape from you, but that was not my desire."

"But you just said it was."

"That is incorrect. I said that I killed the clone so I could escape *Victory* in the Tristano System. That you have made it here and found me in the Gideon System means that I can proceed to the next phase. Captain Maddox, you are an adept

218

human/New Man mix. You are often willing to incorporate new data that causes you to change course. I am willing to make a deal with you."

Maddox raised his eyebrows. "I'm listening," he said.

"I will join you aboard the starship," the robot said. "I will help you find the next few Strand clones that are about to emerge from stasis."

"Do you believe that's my present goal?"

"Knowing you, I know it is," the robot said.

"I might have to kill those clones."

"That is up to you."

"What do you want in return?"

"Nothing."

"I don't believe that."

"I want to observe you in action, Captain."

"Unless you give me a reason I can believe, I'm not going to allow you aboard my ship."

"Here is my reason. I, too, wish to stop the clones."

"That's a good start. Why do you want to stop the clones, though? You just told me you don't care if they cause the disintegration of the Commonwealth."

"If the next few clones emerge, they will cause several severe evolutionary steps to occur that will bring universal annihilation to this sector of the galaxy."

"I'd like to know how that's going to happen."

"There is a high probability that one of the clones will contact the ships of the Nameless Ones."

Maddox sat up. "The Nameless Ones are near?"

"I have no idea."

"How can the clone contact them, then?"

"I am unsure," the robot said. "However, I do know that one of the next clones will use Nameless Ones technology. That technology will surely overpower the clone and set in motion the events I have described."

"And you can help us stop that from happening?"

"Yes," the robot said.

"Then why did you run away from us before?"

The robot said nothing.

"What aren't you telling me?" Maddox asked.

The robot did not reply.

"I want to think about this," Maddox said.

"That is fine," the robot said, "as you will decide to do it. But do not take too long, Captain. Time is becoming critical."

-49-

"It's lying," Valerie said. "I don't trust it."

Maddox nodded as he studied the small object out there in space. He'd cut communications with it and now discussed the idea with members of the bridge crew.

"Galyan, what are your thoughts?" Maddox asked.

"The robot is dangerous," the holoimage said. "But I would tend to agree with Yen Cho. The Builder construct will have knowledge. Do we need this knowledge to defeat more Strand clones? I do not know. Perhaps you should contact the Throne World and speak to the Emperor concerning Strand."

Maddox nodded. He didn't like the idea, but he could see its utility.

"I am curious," Galyan said. "Which do you deem the greater menace, the Swarm Imperium or the Nameless Ones?"

"The Swarm is out there," Maddox said. "We've seen one of their battle fleets when they fought the Chitin. That Swarm Fleet would have dwarfed what we faced last year. It's no secret that the Commonwealth, heck, all of Human Space with the New Men included, could not stop a real Swarm Invasion. We have also fought a Destroyer of the Nameless Ones. One Destroyer by itself destroyed the Wahhabi Caliphate. We needed the Destroyers last year against the Swarm. If a fleet of Destroyers with several Ska aboard hit the Commonwealth…"

Maddox shook his head. He didn't want to think about more Ska, although he said, "It's too bad we couldn't engineer a war between massed Destroyers and the Swarm Imperium."

"If the Destroyers came in great enough numbers," Galyan said, "they would annihilate the Imperium."

"And then us," Valerie added.

"We cannot allow any clone of Strand to communicate with the Nameless Ones," Galyan said.

Maddox thrust out his booted feet, staring at them. He finally looked up. "We're working off too many assumptions. We're in the dark on too much of this."

"Which is another reason we need the knowledge of the Builder robot," Galyan said.

"I don't trust it," Valerie said.

"None of us do," Maddox said slowly. "And it hasn't done much to gain our trust. It doesn't seem to fear destruction. Could we destroy the robot if we wanted to?"

"Easily," Galyan said. "I have analyzed the robot's alloys. Our disrupter cannon would vaporize it."

"Part of me says to do just that," Maddox said. "If we can easily destroy it, why doesn't the robot fear we will try? I also keep thinking about Gideon II. I wonder…"

The captain wondered again if he'd acted prematurely concerning unsubstantiated stealth androids. He no longer believed that was what had been down there with them. He had desecrated ancient pyramids for possibly no good reason.

Could the robot have foreseen the order? Maddox wondered. Was that why it had escaped to this star system? Was that why it had attempted to remain hidden until this point? It hadn't wanted to contact him until certain actions had manipulated his thinking.

"Any other comments?" Maddox asked aloud.

"Perhaps you should ask Yen Cho what he thinks about the robot's proposal," Galyan said.

"No," Maddox said. He motioned to Valerie. "Open channels with it."

Reluctantly, Valerie did so.

"Gideon," Maddox said.

The robot said nothing.

"Guardian," Maddox said. "What assurances do I have that you will not harm anyone aboard *Victory*?"

"You have my word," the robot said.

222

"What if I don't trust your word? You killed the clone. Maybe you want to kill me, too."

"I do not."

"Captain," Galyan said. "I feel I should…" The holoimage fell silent as he flickered like a bad picture and suddenly vanished from sight.

"Captain," Valerie said. "My sensor panel has shut down."

"Keith," Maddox snapped. "Initiate an emergency jump."

The pilot tapped his board before turning around. "I can't. My board is dead."

Maddox jumped up as he swore. Had the robot talked to them to buy time as it initiated a stealth computer attack?

"My computer has gone crazy," Andros said from his station. "Sir, I think the robot beamed a virus into our computers. It's taken over."

Maddox pressed the comm switch on his chair, "Guardian, are you doing this?"

There was no answer. The main screen went blank as more control panels around the bridge began to shut down.

Maddox ran to the hatch, but it didn't open. He pressed an emergency switch, but that did no good.

"Get over here," he shouted at the others. "We're going to force this hatch open. I have to know what that little bastard is doing to my ship."

-50-

The Builder robot floated in space before the mammoth Adok starship. The cube in its storage cone had been transmitting to the huge spacecraft. The cube now communicated with its host.

TAKEOVER COMPLETE, the cube told it.

The robot engaged its space drive, slowly accelerating toward the great starship.

This was precision computing and predicting indeed. Captain Maddox was a complex individual, but he was also malleable. He had fallen for the trick at the excavation site. That had seemingly caused a lapse in judgment in him. The antimatter strike wasn't the lapse, just that he realized he'd made a mistake down there. That had caused him to take too long to come to the correct conclusion here, for himself and his crew.

The Adok starship should prove to be the perfect spawning ground. This was a fantastic moment. The robot had waited many cycles of time for such a transformation. The cunning Methuselah Man Strand had caught and trapped the robot and the so-called ghost-ship long, long ago. Yet, not even Strand—the original or the clone—had truly understood the nature of the cloaked vessel or its unique "computing system." The Strand clone had used the computing for such gross actions. The clone had deserved to die for such sacrilege. Now, though, this was a glorious day indeed.

The robot used its space drive to accelerate toward the hangar-bay door. It would soon reach the starship. Then, it could begin. Then, the universe was going to witness a miracle.

The robot wanted to accelerate faster, but that would mean it would have to decelerate sooner and use up too much energy. The cube was going to need its energy source at the beginning.

Oh. This was interesting. There was an android aboard the ship. Could the android assist in the birth? The robot ran a quick analysis. After it was done, the robot sent a pulse to the starship and a quick message. Then, it concentrated on reaching the hangar bay while the humans struggled against a mostly shut down starship.

***

Yen Cho sat in the dark of his lightless cell. Suddenly, the hatch opened, admitting light from the outer corridor. At the same time, the android cocked his head, receiving a message—

Yen Cho leaped to his feet. This was marvelous. This was glorious. After a lifetime of service, he was finally going to see a wondrous creation in person.

For the last two hundred years, the android had sought a reason for being. This must be it. This was why someone had built him long ago. He would be here at the rebirth of everything glorious.

Could he have foreseen this event in some manner?

No. Yen Cho did not think so. But maybe at a subatomic level, his computing core, his brain, had realized the possibility of this. Thus, he had endured many indignities over the past year and particularly during this voyage. This would make up for the terrible destruction of the pyramids. That barbarian Captain Maddox had much to answer for. How dare he launch an antimatter missile against the pyramids? Maddox was a crude human that should have to suffer for what he had done.

Yen Cho moved into the corridor. He had a perfect image of the layout of the starship. Now, the android began to run. He had to be there in the hangar bay to greet the robot carrying the awesome seed. He had much work to do.

I am completed, Yen Cho realized. *I have arrived at my great purpose. I did not know. I never realized.*

As the android ran, he smiled. Smug Captain Maddox had asked about a soul. Maybe the androids did not have souls like humans, but they had unique purpose to the order of the universe. This would trump any soul that Maddox could possibly hold in his flesh and blood body.

Android and robot would meet in the hangar bay, and there they would perform one of the greatest acts in the galaxy.

The moment was almost here.

-51-

Galyan's personality backup system worked furiously to reengage the starship's computing core. In the blink of an eye, an enemy virus had beamed from the robot to *Victory*. It had caught Galyan by surprise. One after another, the virus had conquered his systems, diminishing him at each takeover and almost erasing the ancient engrams.

Six thousand years waiting at his post, six thousand years of endless cruising through the debris of his star system had almost ended a moment ago. The emergency backup system had barely come online in time to save his engrams.

The enemy attack had been too thorough to resist, and it had been devastatingly swift.

As Galyan's core AI personality assessed what had happened, he came to a startling conclusion. This was a Builder-level assault. He had faced such a thing before on the Dyson Sphere. Captain Maddox and he had gone together to beard the Builder in the center of the mighty complex. This was different in strength but not in type.

In some manner, a Builder was involved in this takeover computer attack.

Why would the robot want Starship *Victory?* What did the starship possess that it could not have gotten on the rogue moon or on Gideon II?

Galyan's computers possessed certain Builder features gained long ago before the Swarm Assault destroyed his planet and his race. The backup system possessed cunning, and it hid itself from a second-level scan from the robot. The robot, or whatever was doing this, would find it soon enough. It had to run, but how…

Ah. The backup personality had an idea.

He waited until the scan searched elsewhere. Then he inserted his engram enhancement emergency backup into an older computer system not directly hooked into the main ship's computer. It was an older and quite complex system left him by Professor Ludendorff.

Galyan's diminished personality barely made the switch fast enough. The enemy scan and a sweep virus found the backup system and started remodeling the ancient program.

He was in the Ludendorff computer but was unable to produce a holoimage with the system.

I almost died, he realized. *The guardian robot nearly killed me. Is this a fight to the finish? Is my long life over at last?*

It was funny. Sometimes, Galyan had not really wanted to keep on living. Existence was painful sometimes. And yet, now that he had almost perished, he found that he wanted to keep on being. He wanted to help his friends. Captain Maddox, Meta, Valerie, Riker, Keith and the others were in mortal danger from the guardian robot.

Galyan did not know the precise nature of the danger, but it was huge nevertheless. He needed to gain sensory data about it. How could he do that? From here, how could—?

Wait a minute.

He studied the nature of the Ludendorff computer. Oh, this was cunning and sneaky. He could use small floor bots. They could act as roving cameras for him. Had Professor Ludendorff done this in the past, spying on everyone in the ship? No wonder he had always known so much.

Galyan set up a sub-link that should duck under the enemy scans. The links would seem like ordinary electrical discharges but would have hidden message pulses. Within the pulses would be sensory-feed data.

Inside the Ludendorff computer, Galyan ran an analysis program. The robot would likely come in through the hangar bay. That's where he—Galyan—should send a sensor floor bot.

He would send another to the bridge so he could communicate with Maddox.

If Galyan could have rubbed his holoimage hands together, he would have done so. This was a threat to his existence and to that of his friends. Just what was going on? What did this guardian robot plan to do to his precious starship?

***

A little sensor bot rolled along the decks. It was hardly bigger than a man's foot. Every so often, it reached an electrical linkage and sent a pulse message to the Ludendorff computer.

Two hours after leaving the computer, the little bot used a robot entryway into the hangar bay.

What it saw caused the bot to race to an outlet and pulse the imagery to Galyan in Ludendorff's old computer.

Masses of equipment, cables and raw bursts of energy crisscrossed or floated through the mighty chamber. Galyan had never witnessed anything like it. He remembered human stories that he had scanned before while waiting in orbit around Earth. This was like some sorcerer's apprentice den gone wild.

Many interior hangar bay hatches were open as trolleys brought more equipment, computers, power jacks and other pieces torn from the starship itself. Everything flew in and went to various places as if guided by a master intelligence.

Look! There was Yen Cho. The android stood at a strange semi-circular board, manipulating it so rapidly his fingers blurred too fast to be seen. Was he controlling this craziness?

The bot scanned, and suddenly quit on the instant. It sensed the robot in the middle of the mass of swirling, floating pieces and equipment. Pieces and equipment began to come together around the robot. The pieces flowed as if by magic, but really by magnetic impulses. Cables linked to casing and computer units reassembled.

It would seem that the Yen Cho android and the guardian robot built a bigger and stranger android. They used pieces of *Victory* and tore down human instruments and strikefighters to add to the mass.

Oh, this was interesting. There was another process going on. This one was different, with intense torches and welders building gleaming human-shaped robots or possibly new androids. They were smaller than the big thing but larger than ordinary humans.

What did this all mean? What was…?

Back at Ludendorff's computer, the diminished Galyan came to a startling conclusion as to what was happening in the hangar bay. This was cause for the most careful computing in his six thousand years of lonely existence. He had to get a message through to Captain Maddox. He had to do this at once before it was too late.

-52-

Maddox debated with himself as he sprinted down the corridors. He carried a heavy combat rifle and his ever-present monofilament knife, along with his long-barreled gun holstered under his arm. He also wore a rebreather attached by line to a cylinder on his back. Earlier he had raced through areas without breathable air and had almost gone unconscious.

He had a bad feeling that his weapons would not be nearly powerful enough to face whatever the robot was doing. Power was down all over the ship. The computers wouldn't work, and far too many people were not breathing. The robot had done something to many of the life-support systems. It was already responsible for murdering over fifty of his people, at least.

Maddox berated himself as he ran. He should have destroyed the robot when he'd had the chance. He'd gotten greedy. He'd wanted the knowledge the robot held. He should have trusted himself to track down the next clone and the one after that. He should have already decided to go to the Throne World or contact the Emperor. Had the robot fed him a line about the next clone trying to contact the Nameless Ones?

What did they even know about the ancient enemy? Maybe the Nameless Ones no longer existed. Maybe the robot had faked Maddox out of his ship.

He seethed at the idea. He wondered if Yen Cho was in league with the little devil. He—

A little floor bot careened around a corner at high speed, going up onto one side on two of its wheels. Maddox almost

231

fired on it by reflex. He recognized it for what it was even as his trigger finger squeezed, and immediately let up.

Then he wondered if the robot controlled the small bot.

The thing skidded to a halt before him. It raised an antenna and just stood there.

Maddox felt wary, like a trapped beast. What was the thing doing? He glanced around him, wondering if it was activating things to murder him. But nothing happened.

Maddox licked his lips, and he decided to play another hunch. The last one had been wrong, it seemed. Would this one be wrong, too?

Holding a small comm unit to an ear, Maddox clicked it on.

"Can you hear me?" the comm asked in Galyan's voice.

"Yes..." Maddox said tentatively. "Are you broadcasting out of the floor bot?"

"I am," Galyan said. "Listen very carefully, Captain. This is a matter of life and death."

"Go ahead, Galyan."

The Adok AI began talking as fast as he thought Maddox could comprehend the information. He spoke on and on—

"Wait, wait," Maddox said. "You said they're down in the hangar bay even now?"

"Building something deadly, Captain," Galyan said. "I have my suspicion what it is—"

"Tell me," Maddox said.

"A Builder."

"What's that mean?"

"I believe the guardian robot carried the essence of a Builder. Remember, Valerie detected bio-matter. The robot was carrying it, I'm sure."

"And the thing Yen Cho is helping to make down there...?"

"Is a new Builder, Captain," Galyan said. "I know what I saw. A new Builder is using the basics of *Victory* to give itself...possibly android Builder form."

"An ancient Frankenstein's monster," Maddox whispered. "Where did the original Strand find something like that?"

"It is an interesting question, but it is not germane to saving the ship and your crew's lives."

"Right," Maddox said. "Can we kill it, Galyan?"

"I do not know, Captain, but I know we have to try."

"Right," Maddox said again. He slung the combat rifle over a shoulder and scooped up the floor bot, cradling it under an arm, and he began to sprint like never before. He had to get to the hangar bay and kill the Frankenstein Builder android creature before it became too powerful to kill.

-53-

From in the hangar bay, Yen Cho watched in amazement as the various parts and pieces of equipment stolen from *Victory* came together in a beautiful form. Cables from strikefighters, computing components from a workstation, metal from ripped-up decking; everything continued conjoining to form the great android Builder. Welding equipment burned brightly, joining pieces to cables to exoskeleton combat armor to girder-like struts.

It was an amazing process of Builder technology and knowhow. The robot supplied some of the power from its tiny nuclear pile. The rest of the energy came from the mighty antimatter engines that ran the starship.

The androids had legends of such a thing, but none of the androids that Yen Cho knew had ever been part of an android Builder rebirth.

This would be the beginning of a new era in Human Space. Things were going to change around here. The androids would no longer scurry in the background, trying to keep safe by keeping out of peoples' way. Now, the androids would have their own god—

"We'll have a Builder to serve," Yen Cho amended.

The barbarians would learn what it meant to face a truly civilized foe. The barbarians thought muscles and firepower were the keys to victory in battle. They were going to learn what real power was.

Yen Cho's fingers continued to blur across his newly constructed station. He almost wished that the arrogant hybrid could see him now. Maddox had thought himself a jailor, not realizing that the android was really the key passenger in the starship.

This was going to make up for many indignities he had suffered in his long existence. This was the feat of his life. This was glorious—

It was starting to happen.

As Yen Cho's fingers blurred, as he continued to control much of what was going on, he also swiveled his head to watch the robot.

The guardian robot was near the almost-completed Builder. Mechanisms already cast much of the giant being in shadows. It was difficult to look upon the Builder directly. That was how it should be. Builders were too glorious for mere human eyes—or even android eyes—to behold.

"Here is my soul," Yen Cho said aloud. "Here is what humans lack that we superior beings possess."

As Yen Cho watched the robot, the top cone began to unscrew. The android saw the turning threads and witnessed the cone floating upward upon reverse polarity magnetics.

The unscrewed cone moved aside. Now, a pulsating Builder core cube floated up out of the guardian robot. This was the beginning of rebirth. There was the great Builder intellect shimmering from the cube of being.

With great precision, the robot guided the pulsating cube from itself and toward the mighty frame.

The shadows seemed to depart the great android frame of the giant mechanical being. A slot opened in the chest of the Builder-in-birthing.

"I see, I see the birth," Yen Cho said, recording the grand event for future androids.

Yen Cho even had a forbidden thought at this glorious moment. He wondered if in a thousand years, after many modifications, if he might evolve into such a great being as a proto-Builder. Perhaps that was the creation idea of the original Builders. He was not sure. Through great technology, could an advanced scientist marry biological matter to mechanical matter? Might Yen Cho gain bio matter and thereby gain true life as humans knew it?

The concept was mindboggling. It almost made the android giddy, and he almost missed the greatest moment of all as the cube activated and brought the proto-Builder to life.

It was then, at that instant, that a hatch banged open on the far deck of the hangar bay. Yen Cho tore his gaze from the mysterious birthing of glory and saw something he did not want to witness.

Captain Maddox sprinted from a distance directly for the mighty Builder. Even worse, even more profane, the hideous hybrid held a heavy combat rifle by his side. As the captain sprinted, he opened up, firing the horrid weapon from the hip.

-54-

Maddox sent down the bot before he opened the hatch and sprinted into the hangar bay. He panted into the rebreather mask over his nose and mouth. The rubber seal was sweaty against his skin while his eyesight was blurry because of the strange air-mix in here.

The bot followed him, although the captain no longer had contact with Galyan. It was all up to him to stop this thing, to stop a Builder from rebirth.

Maddox saw Yen Cho. He saw...something shadowy and huge beyond the android. The thing was menacing.

Maddox recalled the Builder on the Dyson Sphere. The thing had awed him back then. What was the correct choice today? He couldn't bargain with the creature. It had already murdered too many of his crew by shutting off their air.

Maddox fired the heavy combat rifle from the hip, sending big-grain slugs at the shadowy thing. The kick from the rifle felt good, as it made it seem that he was doing something about this.

The trouble was that the bullets didn't seem to have an effect upon the shadowy Builder. Maddox let the rest of the magazine hammer against the construct.

As he did, a shadowy arm raised. There was a swirling port in the thing's palm. Something from the palm-port beamed at him.

Maddox dove aside. A concentrated beam smashed the decking where he'd been. A thorium bolt, he realized.

Deckplates flew up as bits of metal whizzed past the captain's head.

He was seriously outgunned.

Maddox started rolling as the Builder-creature beamed another thorium bolt at him. How was he supposed to kill a thing that was immune to his gun but could kill him in an instant?

Breathing raggedly, Maddox jumped up and sprinted behind a row of parked strikefighters.

A horrid sonic blast almost dropped Maddox then. At the same time, the strikefighters began to lift off the deck. They wobbled as they lifted higher.

Maddox saw the proto Builder-creature. It wasn't as shadowy this time. It was a girder-built giant with sizzling power links surging from one part of it to another. It lacked skin, although across the torso area, and its head it had heavy deck plating for skin.

A girder-like arm and its weaponized hand tracked him.

Maddox ran, skidded to a halt and changed direction.

A thorium bolt smashed the decking where he would have been. A piece of shrapnel sliced across his left thigh, tearing cloth and skin. Maddox checked visually. The shrapnel hadn't cut a main artery, but he was bleeding.

The captain raced behind parked lifters, reaching them as another thorium bolt blasted one of the lifters into smithereens.

Sweat and blood soaked into Maddox's garments. His chest heaved from his exertion. Was he running out of breathable air in the tank on his back? One thing was certain: the heavy oxygen tank was making this harder than normal.

The sound struck his eardrums again. The sound didn't come from the girder-like monstrosity, but from a huge machine near Yen Cho. The android stood at his controls, his metal fingers blurring over them.

As deck-lifters began rising in the air, wobbling as if some magnetic power held them, Maddox raised his combat rifle. He shoved the stock against his right shoulder. He stood still, concentrating on Yen Cho.

The girder-like proto-Builder raised his firing arm. The beam-port apparatus in his palm began to glow with power.

238

Maddox squeezed the trigger. The heavy rifle bucked once, twice, three times in quick succession. The next second, the captain jumped backward, and rolled as decking blew apart where he'd just been.

At the same time, the three big-grain bullets sped at Yen Cho. The android continued to manipulate the panel. The first bullet hissed past his head, missing by less than a millimeter.

The specific sound caused the android to shift and look up. Was it luck? Maybe. Or maybe it was the *di far* part of Maddox that came through for him. Whatever the cause, the captain's second bullet caught Yen Cho directly against the braincase. The bullet plowed through pseudo-skin and struck the titanium casing that held the android's cybertronic brain. The third bullet followed the path of the second with uncanny precision. It struck the same area, already softened by the kinetic energy of the first bullet. The second bullet badly dented the brain casing, deforming it enough to cause massive shock to the cybertronic brain.

The noise from the machine rose in pitch. Yen Cho staggered backward and fell back onto the decking. He lay there, staring up, frozen.

His auto-systems kicked, hit a snag, tried to kick on again and began a deep reboot. That was going to take a considerably long time, effectively taking Yen Cho out of the fight.

While that happened, the noise rose even more. That seemed to cause the wobbling lifters to shoot up against the ceiling, hammering hard and sticking there as if glued.

The girder-like proto-Builder shook its strange head. It did not seem to like the noise. Instead of destroying Maddox, it aimed at the machine and blasted it with its thorium cannon.

The noise stopped, and the lifters came down, crashing against the deck.

The proto-Builder looked around. It likely could not see Maddox, who had slithered to a new position.

"Captain Maddox," the thing said in a booming voice. "Cease this uselessness. It is a farce, and you cannot possibly stop me."

From where he lay hidden, Maddox panted, trying to regain his bearings.

The Builder-creature turned to its left. Three large metal men stood there. Each was half again as tall as Maddox. They gleamed metallically and possessed red-glowing eyes. They seemed alien and deadly, like mechanical dark angels.

The three new androids began to run with heavy clanking steps toward Maddox's last known position.

At that point, a little floor bot drove into sight. It parked in their path and raised its antenna. There was a blue spark from the tip of the antenna. Perhaps it beamed something at the androids.

That must have been the case, because the leading metallic-gleaming android stiffened, lost the precision of its sprint and clanged onto the floor with its torso leading the way.

"No!" the proto-Builder boomed. "There will be no more trickery from you, Galyan. It is time for you to cease existing."

The proto-Builder held up its second arm and beamed a software virus through the floor-bot connection.

-55-

The essence of Galyan—the combination of the ancient engrams from a living Adok married with the advanced software presently running in the old Ludendorff computer—underwent a swift virus assault.

Fortunately for the diminished Galyan, he had anticipated such an assault. He also remembered the swiftness of a Builder attack and the impossible nature of stopping such an attack once it started. The only defense was to deflect it by not being in the way.

As the virus attack occurred, Galyan made one of his most daring decisions in his long and lonely life. Maybe the transfer of his being into the old Ludendorff computer had shown him the way. Besides, the successful attack program against the steel android had shown him a judo-like trick, a Maddox ploy to confound his enemies.

As the Builder virus began destroying the Ludendorff computer software, Galyan beamed his ancient engrams along with the key components of his software in a compressed data gulp. He beamed them through the electrical linkage, which could take massive loads, and aimed it through the floor bot in the hangar bay.

The Builder had used the bot linkage as a targeting mechanism, using a comm wave assault to send the main virus program. Now, Galyan used the bot at almost the same instant, helping to beam his data into the android laying on the deck. He poured the engrams and compressed software into the

241

android's cybertronic brain, erasing the android programming as he rewrote his own programming in its place.

In Ludendorff's old quarters, the computer he'd just left sizzled from overload and exploded, showering pieces everywhere.

"Good-bye, pesky Galyan," the proto-Builder said. "Now, you are next, Captain Maddox. You should have attacked the robot in space while you could. I wonder if you realize that I have done what no one else has been able to do yet. I weakened your self-confidence. I caused you to doubt yourself.

"I learned about the Ska," the Builder continued.

Perhaps the Builder essence's long confinement in the cube had made it verbose now that it had an opportunity to talk.

"Oh, yes," the proto-Builder said. "I learned through data channels that you had defeated the Ska in the Alpha Centauri System with an ancient Builder device. Of course, I knew what form that device must have taken. Professor Ludendorff had the data necessary to build such a device embedded in his mind. Since I knew the form of the unique weapon, I knew what you needed to do in order to power it. I realized that such a battle against a Ska would have deeply wounded your psyche. The Nameless Ones are horrible and their masters—the Ska—are even worse. Through your bad decisions, due to your mental weakening and my exploitation of that, I now have you at my mercy. I will squash you, Captain, you and your crew. With this vessel, I will resume the Builder Empire my ancestors left to you monkey-humans.

"During my short time with the Strand clone, I came to realize that this part of the Orion Arm was a mess. You humans are a mess. I will soon reshape your race into something more orderly and seemly. I will complete what my ancestors lacked the courage to do. The Rull androids who have studied you humans will aid me. I have seen Yen Cho's sacrifice. I will restore him fully. I may even grant him greater computing power and a greater android body. Perhaps I will set the Rull androids over the re-evolved humans I have in mind. Perhaps Yen Cho and his kind will teach the elevated monkey-protégés how to live like civilized races.

242

"The time of the Methuselah Men is over. The time of the New Men is over. The time of chaotic humanity doing what it wants is over. I am here to bring order to the Orion Arm. Perhaps I will use elevated humanity to destroy the Swarm. I have not yet decided. If the Swarm proves too troublesome, perhaps I will create a new galactic order with them.

"Now, where are you, Captain Maddox?"

The two metallic-gleaming androids had been searching the hangar bay throughout the monolog, tossing fallen lifters out of the way, following the captain's blood trail but failing to find the elusive Maddox.

***

The captain panted from inside an overturned strikefighter. He'd climbed into the damaged fighter after leaving a trail of false leads for the giant androids. He'd been listening to the proto-Builder gloat. He had berated himself for missteps but had finally shaken it off.

"I am Captain Maddox," he whispered to himself.

The proto-Builder over there was going to prove a worse menace than anything else had so far. He had to kill it now while it might still be possible.

Maddox flipped switches, hesitated and threw the last one. Even though the strikefighter lay on its side, it began warming up with an emergency start.

The two androids stopped where they were amidst the heaped lifters, looked up and swiveled around. The proto-Builder did the same thing. Both groups stared at the starting strikefighter.

"Fool," the proto-Builder said. It raised its hand and launched a thorium bolt.

The strikefighter blew apart, pieces of metal raining everywhere as they struck the decking.

At the same time, the two oversized androids began to run toward the darting figure of Captain Maddox.

Maddox looked back and saw a strange sight. The first big android, the one that had suddenly gone down, now quickly and almost sneakily climbed to its feet. The thing did not join in the chase. Instead, the android slipped behind some stacks as if hiding from the proto-Builder and the other two androids.

What could that mean?

A hard smile twisted onto Maddox's face. A surge of energy gave him enough strength to reach a new group of parked strikefighters, momentarily shielding him from the proto-Builder. He glanced back, grunting softly. Others might have screamed in terror at what he saw. The two weird clanking androids were almost upon him. Maddox didn't know what else to do, so he turned as he sprinted anew and let himself fall onto his back.

He slid along the floor, facing the two androids. He held the heavy combat rifle and started blasting the one in the face. The slugs dented the face, took out its optics—eyes—but finally the rifle clicked empty. Worse, Maddox came to a stop. The android with the shot-up face misjudged his position and kicked Maddox in the side hard enough to knock out the captain's breath.

However, the android tripped over the fallen captain. Because the thing was still running, the android flew airborne. It hit the deck with a clang and went screeching across it.

The last android stopped, looked down at Maddox and reached for him. The captain moved like greased death. He swept the monofilament knife between them, the fantastic blade slicing through both metal wrists, cutting off the android's hands, which fell onto Maddox.

The oversized android drew back, raising its arms and staring at the stumps. That was long enough for Maddox to leap to his feet, take a ragged, gasping breath as his lungs starting working again, and cut the android in the side with the monofilament knife.

The android attacked, jabbing with its metallic wrist-stumps, trying to hammer Maddox in the face or against his body. The captain dodged and ducked until his cut thigh pumped with bright red blood and his clothes were wet with sweat. As he gave the greatest athletic performance of his life, Maddox continued to cut the android, a single monofilament slice at a time.

Finally, the android halted, swayed back and forth as sparks erupted from various deep slashes, and crashed to the deck in an unmoving heap.

The other android had climbed to its feet and tried to blindly follow the fight. Maddox ducked its latest swipe and circled behind it. With a brutal slash, he lopped off its head, and brought that android crashing down as well.

At that point, Maddox dropped to his knees, exhausted and gasping, the monofilament blade dropping from nerveless fingers so it clattered onto the deck. The captain was spent, his chest heaving. Slowly, he looked up.

The girder-like proto-Builder loomed over him. The thing aimed its thorium palm-cannon a meter from his face.

-56-

The ancient AI software program of Galyan had entered an oversized metal man. The thing was an advanced Builder construct, greater than an android such as Yen Cho. There was room in the thing's computer hardware for the Galyan identity, and enough speed to run what until now few computer systems had been powerful enough to achieve.

Galyan had greater awareness in the super-android than he'd had in Ludendorff's old computer. He had sat up as the android. He'd flexed his metal fingers and found sensation again as an android. It had awed him. After six thousand years... Well, he did not breathe again. But he did sense again in an advanced way that was far beyond what he had been able to do inside *Victory*. This was a marvel.

Galyan might have spent a considerable time enjoying the new sensation, but he had seen the other two androids chasing Captain Maddox.

It was much different seeing this from this perspective. It might not have seemed that it should be so different. Sensing data as a holoimage was much different than sensing it from inside the housing of an advanced Builder robot.

Likely, in the entire galaxy, no race had created such lifelike androids. Not that this gleaming android seemed lifelike. The humanlike pseudo-skin and other advances would come later. Right now, the outer hull and inner computing had been put into place.

In any case, Galyan had come to a swift conclusion as he'd hidden from the others on the hangar bay deck. Maddox was soon going to die. The proto-Builder, following the captain and the androids at a more leisurely pace, would ensure the human's demise. What's more, the proto-Builder would likely ask more from the ancient starship, more in the way of parts and advanced computing systems. That would mean that Galyan could never be whole again. The Adok computer system had been built for him, was him. Once the proto-Builder tore that down to give itself greater life and power—

This was the moment to stop such desecration, to stop the destruction of the last living memory of the Adok Race.

Galyan leaped up and sprinted on metallic feet to the nearest strikefighter. This one lay on its side. It had a crumpled hull. Galyan would need to effect hours of repair to get it flying again. But that wasn't why he'd run here.

As Maddox fired his rifle, as he dodged, ducked and weaved against a handless android, Galyan tore into the strikefighter. He dismantled part of the 30-mm cannon system. It was big. It was unwieldy and it was heavy.

The now-Adok metal man cocked its gleaming head. What might Sergeant Riker say in a situation like this? The 30-mm cannon system was *damn* heavy.

Yet, heavy as it was, Galyan's new physical form had the strength to lift the main cannon. He had a belt chain of 30-mm shells. Taking one lurching, heavy step at a time, Galyan followed the proto-Builder as it watched the end of the battle between Maddox and the two androids.

Now, the girder-shaped proto-Builder walked up and aimed its palm cannon in the captain's face. It looked like the end for the greatest operative of Star Watch Intelligence.

Galyan opened his metal mouth. After six thousand years, could he really talk again with his own body?

"You!" Galyan shouted at full volume, which was horribly loud.

It caused Captain Maddox on the floor to flinch. Then, the captain's eyes grew huge. Did he recognize a familiar voice?

The proto-Builder shuffled around. It was three and half times the size of a tall man and weighed many times more than that. While the proto-Builder's legs and arms were primarily of girder-like construction, the main trunk and head had deck plates as skin casing. Galyan happened to know where the special cube was inside that frame. He had seen the cube, and witnessed it going from the artillery-shell-shaped robot to the infant Builder's torso.

Before the proto-Builder could fully face Galyan, the metal construct depressed the firing switch. The 30-mm strikefighter autocannon chugged its first shell. The kick from the shell caused Galyan to step back. The second shot caused him to step back twice, while the third made him stagger and caused the shell to blast at the ceiling.

Finally, Galyan set himself, and he chugged one shell after another into the staggering proto-Builder. The thing tried to bring up its arm and palm cannon, but Galyan blasted the arm apart so it tore off and clunked onto the deck beside the proto-Builder.

The belt-chain of shells kept feeding into the autocannon. The explosions from the striking shells took out pieces of proto-Builder. A force shield shimmered into existence. The shells overpowered it before the thing could solidify enough to stop them.

Now, Galyan concentrated on the deck-plating torso cover. He blew away the layers and finally fired shells like a wild man. The explosions and blasts struck the amazing cube that was now visible, but the shells and blasts did not destroy the thing. The cube was made out of an indestructible substance. Perhaps some of the fully matured Builders of the past had worn such substance as skin.

Galyan did not know. The guardian robot, the cube and Yen Cho had only been able to use the metals and materials at hand in *Victory*, not such a super-alloy.

The cannon roared once more, and the cube blew out of the proto-Builder, tumbling across the hangar-bay decking.

The great girder giant swayed where it stood, many parts of it blasted completely out of it. The thing swayed wider and wider, and suddenly, the remaining pieces, cables and parts seemed to become unglued, and the edifice of the proto-Builder came crashing down, junk raining everywhere.

Galyan had done it. He had destroyed the new construct, although he had not yet destroyed the seed that had become the lifeforce of an infant Builder-creature.

-57-

Maddox watched, stunned, as the battle took place around him. He'd barely had enough wit to drag himself out of the way. From there, he had torn off his shirt and made a crude bandage to finally stop his thigh from bleeding.

Why had the last supersized android turned against the proto-Builder? As the captain watched, he logically deduced what must have happened.

The proto-Builder crashed to the deck, and a wondrous, pulsating cube dislodged and tumbled across the floor.

At that, Maddox lurched to his feet. He was already beginning to stiffen, his muscles badly overworked. He got to his feet and began to hobble toward the pulsating cube.

The gleaming super-android threw aside the unwieldy 30-mm autocannon. With a victorious stride, the heavy automaton strode toward the cube as well.

Maddox hopped on his good leg, beating the android to it. He tried to scoop it off the floor but found it surprisingly heavy. It took both hands for him to lift it.

"That is mine," the super-android said. "I killed the proto-Builder for it."

"Galyan?" Maddox asked.

The giant metal man cocked his head. "Yes. Yes, I am Galyan. I killed it."

"You defeated the Builder, Galyan. You didn't kill it."

"Yes. Now, I want the cube."

"I'd like to know why," Maddox said.

250

"I am going to use it to increase my abilities."

"Interesting," Maddox said. "I wonder, Galyan, if you will be the same after that."

"I am not the same now. I am…here. I…feel."

"It seems that congratulations are in order."

The android cocked its head. "Do you mean that, Captain?"

Maddox saw his opening. "Galyan, you wouldn't have had to ask me that in the past."

"Explain."

"You would have sensed my heartbeat and other indicators, knowing if I lied or told the truth. I think you've lost some of your…computing ability by being in the android."

"You are correct. I am going to construct a greater android for me, using that cube to hold my increased identity."

"Do you think the Builder identity in the cube will allow that?" Maddox asked.

"I do not care what it will allow. I will do it."

"Are you sure? Maybe it will overpower your essence."

"I will set up safeguards so that does not happen."

Maddox shook his head. "I'm not sure you're completely Galyan inside that pile of metal."

"Fear not, I will not harm you. Now, drop the cube. I am tired of seeing you hold it."

Maddox let go of the cube, letting it clunk onto the deck.

The super-android looked up at him. "There is something wrong here. What is the real reason why you do not approve of me gaining the cube?"

"What's that over there?" Maddox asked, pointing at a distant hangar entrance.

The super-android turned to look. As it did, Maddox scooped up his monofilament knife. He knelt beside the cube and tried to cut it. For the first time in his experience, Maddox couldn't simply slice through an object with the monofilament blade. That amazed him. He found, though, that he could scrape off the smallest of filings from the cube.

"I do not see what you mean for me to see," Galyan said as he continued to look.

"There are enemy reinforcements coming," Maddox said with conviction. "I think we need another strikefighter's autocannon."

Galyan searched again, twisting this way and that.

Maddox madly scraped at the cube with his knife, trying to destroy it while he could.

At that moment, Galyan faced him. "No!" the super-android shouted.

As Maddox scraped, a knot of swirls that had been moving along the cube's edge seemed to concentrate and surge up out of it. Like an electrical bolt, they struck Maddox and hurled him from the cube.

Flying across the hangar was the last thing he remembered.

-58-

Maddox woke up in sickbay, feeling groggy. He struggled to recall what had happened to him. He looked around and saw others in here with him. The worst were the beds with the sheets pulled up over the persons under them.

He knew what that meant. More of his crewmembers were dead, dead because of his negligence against the guardian robot.

"Maddox," whispered someone. *Meta* he realized. She rushed near and threw herself upon him, showering his face with kisses.

He kissed her back because he was too weak to resist her. After a time, her ardor subsided and he could get a word in edgewise.

"Where's Galyan?" Maddox asked.

Meta slid off his chest so she stood beside his med-cot. She shook her head. "It's weird. There's a robot in the hangar bay. I've seen video-shots of the place. It's a wreck. Marines went to disarm the android. Their combat suits shut down before they could even enter. The android is building something in there using a strange cube."

Maddox scowled. "How did I get here?"

"The android calls itself Galyan. It called Valerie through the comm system and had medics retrieve you. That's the last time anyone has even been able to see the android."

"How many people have died?"

Meta shook her head. "It's up to seventy-three. Most of them were asphyxiated, unable to leave their airless chambers."

Maddox scowled thunderously at the news. His mind didn't seem to be clicking. "Are we...?"

"We're near the rogue moon, if that's what you're asking," Meta said. "You've been unconscious for sixteen hours. Oh, Maddox, I almost lost you this time."

Meta rushed him again.

He held her back this time. "Listen to me. We may not have much time. I have to..."

He scowled. What could he do? It sounded as if everyone was powerless against the new Galyan.

"I think Andros has some ideas."

"Meta," he said, ignoring her comment. "I have to talk to Valerie."

"She's swamped."

"If I don't see her right away, it's going to be too late. Get her down here any way you can. I have to see her, and only her."

Meta nodded. "I'll see what I can do."

***

Maddox might have faded out a couple of times, as he didn't recall the passage of time. Suddenly, Lieutenant Noonan marched through sickbay to him. Meta trailed her, but hung back.

"Captain," Valerie said briskly. "You wanted to see me?"

She looked exhausted, with dark circles under her eyes. Knowing his lieutenant, he was sure she hadn't rested at all. He had no doubt more people would have died without her unstinting work in trying to repair and revive the starship.

"It was a Builder or a proto-Builder," Maddox said. "The cube is a Builder seed."

Valerie stared at him.

In a few terse sentences, Maddox told her what had happened in the hangar bay.

"Galyan killed the proto-Builder," Maddox finished. "He knocked the cube out of it, and that killed it. Well, it didn't kill

254

it, but that put it back into its shell, into the cube. I tried to destroy the cube while I had a chance."

"Your monofilament knife was destroyed," Valerie said. "A medic showed it to me. He picked it up when a team retrieved you from the hangar bay."

"The cube must have done that when it struck back," Maddox said. "Lieutenant, Galyan—the robot, android, whatever he is—has the cube and is no doubt tinkering with it. Galyan in the android wants to increase his capacity, brainpower, whatever the cube can do for him."

"That...android really is Galyan?" Valerie asked.

"Precisely," Maddox said. "During my attack, Galyan beamed himself into the android. I'm supposing the Builder not only destroyed Galyan's main AI system, but used it to take over the ship."

"Andros is saying the same thing. We're trying to purge the strange programming from the main computers, but it's a crazy mess and it's resisting our efforts."

Maddox squinted, nodding. "We lack Ludendorff and Dana, genius-level tech experts. We have Galyan and Andros. But if Galyan uses the cube, I think he's going to become the new Builder. In the end, he'll become the thing we tried, no, that we did destroy."

"That Galyan destroyed, according to you," Valerie said.

Maddox stared at her before nodding.

"I understand the problem," she said, "and it's a bad one. I don't know why you needed to see me, though."

Maddox's features stiffened as he looked away. He said softly, "Galyan is our friend."

"I'm surprised to hear you say that."

Maddox inhaled and seemed to steel himself. He faced her. "We're a team. We have each other's backs. But Galyan isn't going to trust me after I tried to destroy the cube while distracting him. If anyone can gain his trust, be his friend, it's you."

"You're just saying that."

"I've observed you two throughout the years. He likes you, Valerie. He trusts you. Unfortunately, this Galyan, the one inside the android, lacks the emotional programming he had in the starship's computer system. We have to get the AI program, the Galyan we know, back into the regular ship computer so he becomes his old self again."

"So he gets his emotions back?" Valerie asked dubiously.

"Yes."

"That's crazy, sir. Galyan is an AI computer program with the engrams of an ancient Adok."

"He's more. We've learned that throughout our years together. Galyan has helped all of us out of tricky situations. Now, it's our turn to help him get back to what he was. I don't like the new Galyan much. The cube will corrupt and twist his old Adok personality. The old Galyan cared about us. This one doesn't."

"He called medics to come and get you."

"Maybe he does still care some. That means you have a chance."

"What about the cube? Don't we need the cube in working order to help us find the other Strand clones?"

"You're right. We need it, and we probably need Galyan to crack it. But he has to crack it from afar, as it were. We can't let him link with it or let the Builder seed corrupt him."

"We need Ludendorff," Valerie said.

Maddox doubted that, but he said, "Maybe we do, but we don't have him. We have each other. I'm out for the moment, and like I said, this Galyan won't trust me enough to listen. It's on your shoulders, Valerie."

She stared at him, stricken.

"I'm counting on you to get our friend back to his old ways."

"Yes, Captain," Valerie said. "I'll do my best." She turned to go.

Maddox reached out and grabbed one of her wrists, pulling her back around. "Do more than your best, Lieutenant. Win. That's the only thing that matters."

The stricken look returned, although she said, "Spoken like the captain I know. Yes, sir, I'll try to win."

He looked into her eyes, nodded and released her. Could the lieutenant do it? They were about to find out.

-59-

Valerie had her doubts about this as she headed for the hangar bay. She'd always liked Galyan. But he was an AI-engram program. What was Maddox thinking? How was she supposed to appeal to a computer?

She stopped before the hangar bay entrance. The android that claimed it was Galyan had given direct and certain orders. He had said he would kill anyone interrupting his great work.

That couldn't be Galyan in the android. And even if it was: *He's a computer program.*

Valerie shook her head. Deep down, she didn't really believe that. She had...loved Galyan. He had saved their lives many times. He was, maybe, the most important member of the crew. He'd been the most selfless, that was for sure. He had suffered, too. He had deep memories of his race and wife...

Valerie sighed. She was too cynical. She'd been working under Maddox for a long time. She saw how he did things. He was tricky, slippery and he almost always won.

Could *she* win today?

It felt as if she was going to try to put the genie back in its bottle. Galyan was out. Could she get him to go back in?

"Let's do this, Lieutenant. Let's not think this to death like you usually do."

Valerie straightened her uniform and marched toward what could be her death.

She opened the hatch and began to walk along the hangar bay deck. There was junk strewn everywhere. It looked like a battlefield. Well, except for that area in the center. The super-android must have cleared away a lot of the junk over there. It had built itself an impressive array of computer machinery and stuff she could not identify.

According to Maddox, it was up to her this time. She was on the front line. That's what she had always wanted, right? She was always thinking about how she could do things better, by the book.

What did the book say about putting a genie back in its bottle? Probably to use trickery.

Valerie halted once again. As she had told herself while heading out to confront the clone of Strand in his cloaked vessel, she had to do this her way. She wasn't Captain Maddox. The captain was the sly trickster or the direct man of action. What was she?

"I'm Lieutenant Valerie Noonan who does things by the book," she said.

There was no book about this, but there was her own guideline, how she liked to operate. That was with straightforward honesty. She didn't care for games when emotions were involved.

I miss the ace, she told herself. *We've been drifting apart. I have to consciously spend more time with Keith if we're going to make this work.*

Before Valerie could think any more about it, the super-android popped up in the middle of his machine. He had a calibrator in his hands. It beeped, and he made an adjustment to the machine.

Just then, the super-android saw her. The head swiveled more fully around to stare at her.

"Valerie," the android said. "Why are you here?"

She almost cried in pain. That *was* Galyan. He was inside the super-android, and he was going to destroy himself by playing around with a tricky Builder cube.

"Oh, Galyan," she said, hurrying toward him. "What have you done?"

The super-android climbed out of the large machine. He set aside the calibrator and the instrument in his other hand. He sat on a crate and put his hands on his metallic-gleaming knees.

"Look at me, Valerie. What do you think?"

She stopped several feet before him, and she swallowed painfully. "You don't look yourself, Galyan. You look like an android."

"I am out of the machine, Valerie. I am real again."

"No, Galyan. You're inside a...a thing that was never meant for you. You're acting strangely because...because you no longer have your emotions, the feelings that made you unique."

"Did the captain send you to tell me that?"

"Yes," Valerie said.

The super-android nodded. "Do you not realize what he is doing? The captain knows I do not trust him much. So he is using you to speak his words for him."

"No, Galyan. I've always been honest with you. You deserve that because of everything you've done for each of us. You've saved our lives many times over. You're...the most important member of the crew."

"No. That would be Captain Maddox."

"He would never have done all those things without Starship *Victory*, which means Driving Force Galyan. You're no longer Driving Force Galyan. You have some of his...ways, but you've forgotten how to be yourself."

"I am building a machine that will allow me to use the great Builder seed."

"Galyan, don't do it."

"The cube will give me greater power and being."

"No," Valerie said. "The Builders quit a long time ago. Okay, sure, here's one of their seeds. You'll be smarter and maybe more powerful, but you won't be Galyan. Do you know what a great man once said?"

"Tell me, Valerie."

"What does it profit a man to gain the whole world and lose his soul?"

The super-android cocked his head. "Are you saying I will lose my soul if I use the Builder seed?"

"That's exactly what I'm saying. You won't be Galyan. You'll be this powerful thing with Builder thoughts and ways. Our good friend will disappear, though. You should come back and fix your AI systems. Reload them and remember who you really are."

"I like being outside, Valerie."

"Okay. Fine," she said. "Then keep the...android, the robot, in storage. Maybe at times, you'll load it up with your personality, walk around and do things. I could see how that would be useful. And maybe, because we don't have the professor with us, you could study the Builder seed. Maybe you could work with Andros and explore it. But I wouldn't hook it directly to you, if I were you. It wants you to do that. It will take you over instead of you taking it over."

"I am setting safeguards in place."

Valerie shook her head. "I know you're smart. You're brave and you're good, the real Galyan is, the one whose engrams ran the AI program. But the Builders...they're too ancient and used up. They don't understand humanity. I'm pleading with you, Galyan. For your own good, stop this. Reload yourself into the Adok designed computers. If you don't...you're going to kill us in the end, I just know it."

"Do you not trust me, Valerie?"

"With my life," she said. "What I don't trust is that thing." She pointed at the pulsating cube that Maddox had tried to destroy.

"I am sorry, Valerie. This is something I must do."

She looked at the super-android. She was afraid for herself and the whole human crew, but she also felt pity for Driving Force Galyan, for the little Adok that had sacrificed so much for all of them all these years.

It choked her up, and she felt this might be the last time she would ever get to talk to that Galyan.

"My friend," she whispered.

Valerie came closer. Then she rushed near and gave the super-android a hug. She squeezed even though her strength was miniscule compared to it. She hugged him, kissed the metallic cheek and then turned away with a sob.

She was losing a friend, possibly her best friend. Had Maddox known she would react this way? She almost believed it. Then she barely stifled a second sob and ran from the hangar bay as tears welled in her eyes.

-60-

With Meta's help, Maddox left sickbay and went to the bridge. Just before entering the bridge, he removed his arm from Meta's shoulder and walked through the hatch unaided. To the best of his ability, he moved normally as he strode to his command chair and sat down.

He still felt weak, but he began asking for damage reports. The officers reported and gave a gloomy picture of the starship.

Too many personnel were dead or badly off. Too many ship's systems had taken hits by the Builder virus attack, and even more hits had come later when it had ripped apart those and many more systems for parts.

Andros was leading the engineers in repairs. For all that, they were going slowly. The star drive worked. The neutron beam cannon would function if needed, but the disrupter cannon would not be functional until major repairs were effected.

As he ingested further reports, Maddox began drumming his fingers on an armrest. How was Valerie doing with Galyan?

The hatch opened and Lieutenant Noonan walked dispiritedly onto the bridge. He didn't need to ask her how it had gone. Her posture said it all.

The captain beckoned her near just the same. "Well?" he asked.

Valerie gave a quiet report. "In my opinion, sir..." she finished.

"I'd like to hear it," he said.

261

"We should go into the hangar bay with space marines. Galyan isn't going to stop. I don't want to kill Galyan, but if he uses the Builder seed, he won't be Galyan anymore."

"I'm afraid you're right," Maddox said. "It will be a mercy killing."

Valerie paled and her lower lip trembled. "I take that back. We have to think of something else. You're the miracle worker. Can't you think of something?"

Maddox inhaled deeply.

"This is odd," Andros said. The chief technician had slipped onto the bridge to check his station. Now, the Kai-Kaus elder tapped his panel and studied the results with greater intensity.

"It's started," Maddox told Valerie. "We may already be too late."

"What...?" Andros said to himself, ignoring Valerie and the captain while tapping more forcefully.

"Report, Chief Technician," Maddox said.

Andros startled slightly, coming back to his surroundings, and glanced up at him. "Sir, I don't understand this. There's a massive power surge through the interior computing systems."

"Please be more precise," Maddox said.

"The Adok AI System," Valerie said.

"Yes, that's right," Andros said. "The system is going crazy. I'm getting all kinds of strange readings. There are phase sweeps taking place, a rebooting of ancient programs—"

"Where is the source point?" Maddox snapped.

"Let me see," Andros said, as he manipulated his console. He looked up suddenly, "It originates from the hangar bay."

"Galyan," Valerie whispered. "Is he purging the old computers?"

"I can't tell," Andros said. "It almost seems—"

Just then, his main board seemed to go berserk, with beeps and lights and warning flashes. The main screen came back online, and several boards that hadn't been functioning began to do so now.

"This is massive," Andros said. "Galyan, or the Builder cube, is working faster than I would have thought possible.

There are a million computations a second taking place. This is extraordinary."

Maddox pressed his armrest console switch. "Attention, Space Marines. You will arm yourselves in full gear and meet me before the hangar bay."

"That will not be necessary," a familiar voice said from beside his chair.

Maddox looked up to see a little Adok holoimage with ropy holoimage arms and a seamed leathery face.

"Galyan?" Maddox asked.

"It is I," the holoimage said.

"Galyan!" Valerie shouted. She rushed forward and stumbled through the holoimage, striking and bouncing off the captain's chair. She passed through Galyan again and thumped onto her butt on the floor. From there, Valerie looked up at the startled holoimage. She began to laugh, and clapped her hands several times.

"What is the meaning of this display?" Galyan asked.

"I'm happy to see you," she said.

"And I am happy to see you, Valerie," Galyan said. "I want to thank you for what you said before. It made me think. What does it profit me to gain more power if I am no longer the person I was? Those were powerful words. True words and a great warning against overreaching for things that cost too much. Some prizes are not worth the price."

Galyan turned to Maddox. "Do you not think that is so, Captain?"

"Of course," Maddox said.

Galyan shook his head. "You said that too glibly, sir. You are not thinking it through. However, I was able to run through millions of permutations. I reengaged with my lost emotions. Valerie knew, Captain. She knew I had lost myself in the android. I am saving the android for future emergencies. But I wish to remain the Galyan I have become with my good friends."

"I'm overjoyed to hear it," Maddox said.

Galyan studied the captain until he looked to Valerie. "I would help you up if I could."

"No problem," she said, climbing to her feet.

"I have learned a valuable lesson," Galyan said. "I also know something concerning the greater scheme afoot."

"You're referring to Strand?" Maddox asked.

"I am, sir. I believe the Builder gave us a true warning. There will be more clones of Strand. How many more, I do not know. One of them will likely possess vile technology that could have grave ramifications for the Commonwealth."

"What is your suggestion?" Maddox asked. "Should we contact the Throne World?"

"I doubt you would get far that way, sir," Galyan said. "I do think I can deduce the locations of the other stasis holds. The Builder cube has much detailed data on the Strand clone and what the clone asked of the cube. Using that, I can possibly learn much more."

"I don't want you linking with the cube," Maddox said.

The little holoimage looked at Valerie before facing the captain. "I will not link. I am going to attempt to pierce the Builder software from afar. I believe Andros and I could come up with a technique. There is one problem."

"Name it," Maddox said.

"The next clone may already be free and doing whatever it is that will call the Nameless Ones back here."

"How will the clone do this?"

"The Builder was vague, sir. But it appears that the Nameless Ones sweep through the galaxies, exterminating all life but theirs. They are a xenophobic race, driven to acts of genocide by the Ska, who continuously motivate them."

Maddox rubbed his suddenly tight throat. He didn't want anything to do with any Ska ever again. If this clone foolishly contacted the Nameless Ones to draw them here—

"Why would the clone do that?" Maddox asked.

"I do not know yet, sir," Galyan said. "I only have surface thoughts from the Builder, gained as its virus and my personality program passed each other in the small floor-bot transmitter."

"What?" Maddox asked.

"I can explain later in a detailed report. For now, sir, I think we should concentrate on ship repairs so we are ready to act as soon as possible."

"Good thinking, Galyan. Oh, and one other thing."

The little holoimage waited.

"Welcome back," Maddox said. "It's good to have you back with the crew."

"It is good to be back," Galyan said. "And it is good that my friends missed me."

Maddox nodded, cleared his throat and said, "Yes. Now, let's get to work."

-61-

Two days later, Maddox was in a special chamber aboard *Victory*. He sat before a screen connected to a special Builder communication device. This was a unique comm, able to send messages across interstellar distances of several hundred light-years in range, but only to someone with a similar device on the other end.

One such comm was in Geneva, Switzerland at Star Watch Headquarters.

Maddox cleared his throat and activated the screen.

The Iron Lady appeared. Some knew her as Mary O'Hara, the Brigadier of Star Watch Intelligence. She was matronly, with gray hair and a precise manner.

Maddox looked upon her with fondness. She returned the look but with redoubled force, which made Maddox uncomfortable for some reason.

"It's good to see you, Captain," O'Hara said.

"Yes, Ma'am," he said. "It's good to see you, too."

"You look troubled. Is something wrong?"

"Most assuredly."

"Tell me what happened."

Maddox gave her a rundown of the entire mission, leaving little out. He trusted O'Hara. He liked her. One could even say that…that…he was extraordinarily fond of her.

"Oh, dear," O'Hara said, once he'd finished. "This is worse than I'd feared. We have enough on our hands preparing for more Swarm Invasion Fleets. To have to worry about

Destroyers sliding out of the darkness to annihilate humanity—Captain, you mustn't let any of the Strand clones contact the Nameless Ones. It's all we can do to hold the Commonwealth together as it is."

"Ma'am, should we contact the Emperor? He could interrogate Strand for us."

"I wonder..." O'Hara said. "According to you, Strand wants to splinter the Commonwealth so the New Men invade us again, conquering us this time. Maybe Strand will become persuasive and convince the Emperor to throw in with the Methuselah Man."

"The Emperor can't want the Nameless Ones to show up," Maddox said. "The New Men can't face the Swarm any more than we can. I'd say that they're even less prepared for such an event."

"I understand the argument," O'Hara said. "I have a counter. I've spoken to the Lord High Admiral about it, and he concurs with me. The New Men are supremely arrogant. Nothing has changed there. If the Swarm invades in even greater strength a second time, and if the Nameless Ones should suddenly appear, maybe the Emperor would let the Commonwealth fight alone this time. He might hope to remain hidden, or he might take all the New Men and flee to parts unknown like the Spacers have done."

"There's that possibility, of course," Maddox said. "There's also a possibility the Emperor will aid us as he did before."

"Yes. And if the Emperor learns about a frozen clone or two and hurries to the more dangerous stasis chambers, and there gathers the ultimate tech stored for the clone, gaining those devices for the New Men..."

Maddox nodded slowly. He should have already seen that. They couldn't allow the New Men to gain highly advanced tech that might give them a strategic advantage over Star Watch.

"It would appear that we're on our own with this one," Maddox said.

"Only if you think you can find these stasis chambers yourself," O'Hara said. "Can you?"

"Maybe..."

267

"That isn't reassuring," she said.

"We're still...attempting to crack the Builder cube, Ma'am. It's slow work. It is interesting that Yen Cho recovered from the heavy shots to his braincase. Galyan has informed me that Yen Cho's cybertronic brain rebooted while his android interior systems repaired any damage. I have the android in confinement. It's possible he could help us locate other clone bases."

"You *must* find the most dangerous of the clones, Captain. I order you to find the clone and stop him before he can contact the Nameless Ones. I realize that finding the proverbial needle in a haystack would be a thousand times easier than your new mission. You have all of Human Space and the frontier regions of the Beyond to search. Bend every effort to find and stop that clone. By all means, use Yen Cho if you can do so safely enough. You're the only one that can do this. Star Watch is counting on you, Captain. Humanity could be hanging in the balance."

Maddox nodded. It was a heavy charge. He was going to be Hercules again, taking the world on his shoulders from Atlas, as in the Greek myth. Once—before he'd faced the Ska—the Brigadier's charge would have delighted him. These days...he felt the burden more than ever.

"Captain?" O'Hara asked, as she searched his face. "Is something wrong?"

"No, Ma'am. Find the clone of Strand, the right clone, and stop him. I'm going to..." He cleared his throat. "The crew of *Victory* is going to do it, Ma'am. We've taken hard hits this voyage, but we will strain every fiber to stop the madman Strand. Maybe I should have killed him when I had the chance on Sind II."

"No," O'Hara said, as she searched the captain's face even more closely than before. She searched it as a mother might. "You did the right thing sending Strand to the New Men. They helped us against the Swarm Invasion Fleet, partly out of gratitude for what you did. We wouldn't have beaten the Imperium attack without the New Men. Now, we have to finish with Strand, hopefully, forever."

Maddox set his jaw and his eyes gleamed. Strand. He was sick of the Methuselah Man. He was a worse pain in the arse than Professor Ludendorff. Now, there were more Strands running loose. Maybe when this was all over, and if they succeeded, it would be time to think about infiltrating the Throne World and assassinating the most troublesome Methuselah Man in the universe.

"Good luck, Captain. I want you to know that I pray for you every day."

"Thank you, Ma'am. We'll do our..." He smiled sourly, thinking about what he'd told Valerie before. "We're going to find this clone and take care of the problem before it happens."

"I hope so." O'Hara gave him a longing, motherly look. It seemed as if she was going to add something. She bit her lower lip in the end and cut the connection.

Maddox sat staring at his hands. Finally, he shoved up to his feet. It was time to get started.

PART II
THE ARTIFACT

-1-

The Eden-like Throne World of the New Men had a special underground compound. It housed the planet's greatest prisoner, Methuselah Man Strand.

Strand had lived in captivity for far too long already. He hated it. He seethed inside, and every moment was filled with fear.

He was a wizened old man, but possessed a fantastic vitality. Despite his old-man nature and the thinness of his seemingly frail limbs, he was uncommonly spry. He walked all the time in the garden area of his prison.

Powerful sunlamps supplied the light. The Emperor of the New Men would not allow him to see real sunlight or even enjoy real clouds or a breeze. Instead, Strand was forced to walk on a synthetic, underground path among large ferns, roses and other greenhouse shrubs and flowers. The walking helped keep him spry and helped him to think.

During these lonely months and years, Strand often wrote poetry, devised paper and pencil games and kept up other such activities to keep his mind sharp. He seldom saw his jailers. Mostly, he spoke to robots. On a few occasions, the Emperor came and they spoke.

Today, Strand bustled along the garden path with the sunlamps beating down on him. He had his hands clasped behind his back and wore a gray tunic, trousers and sandals. Sweat slicked his armpits and his heart beat strongly due to his swift passage.

He'd been walking for some time already. He hadn't really been thinking about anything specific. Instead, he had been waiting. Walking like this put him into a semi-hypnotic state. There wasn't anything weird or unique about that, as such a state often happened to people doing mind-numbing chores.

Strand had learned throughout the centuries that he did his best thinking after prolonged walking, as he entered the deeper stage of the semi-hypnotic state.

He understood that the New Men feared him. They had a right to fear. Once, Strand had ruled the colony with an iron fist. He never should have let go—

Strand shook his head. He wasn't going to go down that rabbit-trail today. He was going to think more deeply and strategically.

Enough time had finally passed that the Emperor should have come to ask him several penetrating questions. Oh yes, Strand knew about the Swarm Invasion Fleet. United humanity had beaten back the first Swarm invasion. More such invasions would come. That was a certainty.

Strand hadn't decided yet if he wanted the Swarm Imperium to win or not. If he would always remain a prisoner, then, of course, he hoped the Swarm crushed humanity. But if he could regain his freedom and pursue his great objective, then no, he wanted the Swarm to lose. He knew how to seriously retard the Swarm Invasions, but no one had come to ask for his help yet. So, he must be the only one who saw the obvious move against the Imperium.

But that wasn't the point of his walk today. That the Emperor had not come to him at all—

The third clone is dead, Strand told himself.

He'd actually felt a premonition about that a while back. Certain studies showed that many mothers knew it in their heart when their children died. This could also happen to twins. What would cause such knowledge without any visible means of communication? Was this a spiritual or telepathic connection, then? Perhaps he shared a similar connection with the clones he had created.

Whatever the case, he was certain the third clone had died. That did not necessarily mean the Builder robot or the Builder computer had perished with the clone.

Strand sighed. It had been risky giving the third clone the robot and computer. It might have been wiser to keep those units in storage where he'd found them long ago.

According to his premade plan, the robot and computer had activated when the clone's stasis unit had first begun to thaw out the third replica of himself.

"Now, the third one is gone," Strand muttered.

He knew the New Men monitored everything he said and did. He could feel them watching. The so-called Dominants feared him. The perfect specimens knew they had met their match in him.

But that wasn't the point of this walk or this deep musing. The third clone had failed in his task just like the first two. Soon, then, the fourth clone would wake up.

Strand had long ago planned for the possibility of the third clone's failure. He hadn't foreseen his own failure—his capture—but he had calculated for the small possibility of such an event. Such an event would only be brought about by an extremely clever adversary. Who would have ever guessed that the miserable hybrid, Captain Maddox, would prove to be so resourceful? Yes, the hybrid had that damn ship of his and the crew that would do anything for him. If he could sever Maddox from his friends—

Strand shrugged.

He could not do anything about that at present. He was going to have to rely on his great planning. The fourth clone would use even more potentially dangerous equipment. Strand had set up that situation much differently, therefore, than the other three clones' awakenings.

Strand sighed once again.

The third clone had failed, but the fourth should soon be waking up.

Strand stopped, looked up at the sunlamps and finally flipped them off with both hands. He hated his confinement. The New Men were trying to drive him slowly mad.

It would take them a lot longer than they expected. By that time…

Strand bent his head and continued walking, chuckling softly. The wider world had no idea what was going to hit them.

If I die, let the universe die, Strand thought to himself.

He might have laughed harder, but that would make his watchers suspicious. Thus, he controlled himself and continued to walk along the hideous underground garden path.

-2-

Somewhere in the Beyond many hundreds of light-years from the Throne World, a neutron star rotated at incredible velocity. It was a tiny object in stellar terms, a bare thirty kilometers in diameter. Once, it had been nearly twice the size of the Earth's Sun, acting like any normal G-class star. But that had been a long time ago, before it had gone nova and the remains had been crushed down to its present size by the ferocious gravity.

The inner twenty-four kilometers of the neutron star was composed of neutron gas, but at such a fantastic density that the gas was a fluid. The outer surface of the star was solid iron. The enormous surface gravity meant that the escape velocity— what a rocket needed to lift off the star into space—was 80 percent the speed of light. No one would ever leave the neutron star. Not that anyone could land here and survive to need to worry about how to leave. A marshmallow dropped onto the neutron star from several AUs out would hit the surface with a few megatons of kinetic energy, like an old-style atomic bomb.

The neutron star spun on its axis, sending out harsh radio waves and electromagnetic radiation, acting like a system-wide jammer. No one could easily send a message to or from this place. In fact, only one known form of communication could penetrate the constant background noises into the star system.

That was important, one of the reasons this was to become a critical place to the ongoing struggle for human survival.

Thirty-four AUs out from the neutron star—in the Kuiper Belt region of the system—orbited a cold dwarf planet a little bigger than Pluto. Enormous frozen cracks zigzagged across the dead surface. At the edge of the deepest crack was a highly advanced alien sensor, an operational unit that awaited a customary deep-space signal.

As previously stated, only one type of signal could penetrate the neutron star's jamming. The signal had not come for quite some time.

The alien sensor was attached to a landline that snaked down half a kilometer to an underground structure. The structure was old, of alien design and yet serviceable to human life. Inside were powerful batteries, the monitors indicating they were at full capacity. There were many chambers, many hatches, many storage bins in the structure but only one stasis unit.

In the stasis unit was a frozen being, a humanoid.

A highly advanced computer suddenly activated as a timer clicked. The timer always reset once the customary deep-space signal reached the waiting surface sensor. This time, the signal had missed three scheduled pulses in a row, the tripwire, as it were.

The activating computer automatically switched on heating units, started rebreathing tanks cycling and readied the first food and water dispensaries. Lastly, the computer powered up the stasis unit as it began the delicate process of reviving the humanoid.

The process took time. At last, something clacked, and the cover slid back to reveal a naked form. This human of Earth normative type appeared youthful but seemingly stunted in size. He had dark hair and a larger than normal head but ordinary male sex organs.

The human shuddered, sucked down air and opened his eyes, dark eyes that possessed a strange quality and a…haunted sense that something was wrong.

The human began to moisten his mouth, to stretch and suddenly, to shiver.

Why was it so cold in here? He scowled, and that created a new set of conditions in his mind. The difference showed in his eyes, producing menace. Someone would pay for his inconvenience.

A second thought intruded. Maybe he was a captive.

The young man cocked his head. Who was he? Where was he?

He frowned. There was a memory in his forebrain...

He must rise, go to a machine in the other room and...and this should all make sense.

Before he could rise and proceed on his idea, a seed of doubt sprouted. His memory could be false. Someone could have implanted it in him. It was conceivable that he was a prisoner, and his jailors attempted to trick him in some nefarious fashion.

His smooth features turned blank. If jailers secretly watched him, he had to lull them and bide his time. They would make a mistake soon enough. Then, he would strike, and he would do it so furiously that it would shatter their control over him.

As the naked man climbed out of the stasis unit, it occurred to him that he was a great man. He was, in fact, most likely unique in the universe.

I am one of a kind.

He believed this emphatically, and for no reason that he could articulate, he knew that he was correct.

He shuffled across the cold floor toward the hatch. As he reached it, the hatch slid open. Warmth flooded out around him. Maybe it hadn't been a mistake—the coldness in the stasis chamber. It might have been that way to convince him to move out.

Despite the certainty that he was great, he hesitantly poked his head through the hatch. To his surprise, a stand with a robe waited before him. Could that be for him?

He decided yes. Thus, he stepped into the warm chamber, slipped on the robe and tied the cloth belt around his waist.

The hatch shut behind him.

That made him start, but he decided it was an innocent surprise. It made sense to keep the cold contained in the other chamber. He shoved his feet into waiting slippers and moved toward a table with a...

He picked up a glass, peering into it. He sniffed at the clear liquid and finally took a sip. It was water. As the knowledge filled him, an incredible thirst took hold. Before he knew it, he'd tilted his head back and guzzled the water.

He set the empty glass down with a thud, sat down on the chair and examined a bowl of...

He leaned toward it, sniffing.

Porridge, this is porridge.

He noticed tiny brown spots on the surface of the porridge. In an instant, he realized that was brown sugar. He liked to sprinkle brown sugar on his porridge.

As he realized the truth of that, he picked up a spoon. He hadn't noticed the spoon until this moment. His stomach growled. He was ravenous.

Before he knew it, he set down the spoon, picked up the bowl and licked up every trace of porridge left. He felt better for it—

Impatience struck with alarming suddenness.

Setting down the bowl, he looked around the room, spying another chair, this one before a console and a screen.

He stood, went to the console and studied the controls. He felt as if he knew what to do.

He sat, pressed a switch and looked up with anticipation as the screen activated. This was exciting. He might find out who he was and why he was here.

The screen came into focus, and he found himself staring at an old man. There was something hauntingly familiar about the man.

He noticed a hand mirror beside the controls. He picked up the mirror and examined himself. It took a moment. With a shock, he realized that the man on the screen looked just like him with the single exception that the man was one hundred years older. No. The man on the screen also wore a uniform instead of a terrycloth robe, and he didn't move. It was a still shot.

Ah. He touched another switch. That activated something; sound began and the old man moved.

"So..." said the old man, "it appears that it has finally happened. I am either dead or a prisoner without any means of escape. I can hardly fathom such an event, but that you are listening to me means that I did indeed prepare for such a hideous occurrence."

That sounded ominous.

"I urge you to listen well and to think deeply about what I am about to tell you," the old man said. "This is painful for me. Never doubt it."

The old man paused, looked away and shuddered as if overcome by severe emotions. It almost seemed as if he would cry. The old man resolutely shook his head and looked up at him again with burning embers for eyes.

A grim feeling of trepidation tightened the young man's chest. What was going on? Why did they look alike given their extreme differences in age? They couldn't be twins. Was this his father?

"I am Methuselah Man Strand, and this is a recording I've purposefully made for you. I am thousands of years old and am the greatest human to have ever existed. Yet, the possibility is quite real that I am now dead. The idea pains me, as it should pain you. And yet, that I have died now gives you life.

"Perhaps this is difficult for you as you watch in stunned amazement. Yet, knowing me, I doubt it is too difficult. In fact, you are about to embark on a fantastic journey, as you are my clone."

The young man sitting in the chair frowned. What? A clone? He was a clone of that arrogant boaster?

"But you are not just any clone," Strand continued. "You are the exact replica of me and will have all my abilities. Even more, you will possess free will. I have made many clones in the past, but none like you. Since I have presumably died, you will now become Strand. In the possibility that I am a prisoner—"

On the screen, Methuselah Man Strand grew thoughtful. "Either the Emperor of the New Men has captured me or Star Watch has done so. I urge you to free me, but I doubt you will. Being just like me, you will desire to remain Strand and you will wish for my death. I cannot worry about that. I must believe that some combination of bad luck has already seen to my demise."

Methuselah Man Strand straightened, and his eyes burned with power.

"I will not charge you will anything, my son. Instead, I suggest to you that my enemies are your enemies. Once they learn of you—clone or not—they will desire your death, or worse. Know, however, that you are my Samson Option. By this, I mean that you should pull down the universe around my—our—enemies' ears."

The Strand on the screen coughed, and smiled hideously.

"There is a machine in the next room that will fill you with my memories, transferring my fantastic wisdom to you. You will not have all my Methuselah Man powers, those granted by the Builders, but you may acquire them in time if you are cunning enough. You do have youthful vigor, though, as this time, I have left my clone in a youthful state.

"That is all I am going to say. If you wish to leave your home—this place—you will have to accept the memories. You are presently alone in a distant star system, but with a spaceship to take you wherever you wish to go—provided you learn about it through my memories.

"Good-bye, Clone. I wish you success. I have lived a great life. I have done more than any man ever did. Now, you will have to see if you can live up to me."

Abruptly, the screen shut down, and the image of old man Strand vanished.

The clone sat in deep thought. Many conflicting emotions surged through him.

What was the correct course of action?

He rose and studied the farther hatch. Finally, he walked through and came to an alien machine of strange design. He saw the place where he should sit, and he wondered about the wisdom of accepting the Methuselah Man's memories.

The Methuselah Man sounded like a vengeful person. What was this about a Samson Option? *My enemies are your enemies.*

The young clone scratched his right cheek. He didn't want any enemies if he could help it.

Maybe he should be his own Strand. Maybe he should call himself something else, and live life on his own terms. Why must he saddle himself with Strand's many enemies?

The clone quit scratching his cheek.

"I can do what I want," he said, feeling a growing sense of confidence.

If he was unique, he could surely outsmart the old Methuselah Man. He didn't need someone else's memories. He would be his own man, come what may.

Feeling better about things, the clone looked around, wondering how he could escape from this place.

-3-

A hatch opened. The clone staggered through, stumbling as his feet tangled. With a cry, he fell onto the floor, panting as he lay there.

He had not slept for two days and nights. He was exhausted, his red-rimmed eyes burning with fatigue. He had tried everything. There was no other way to escape the small world that was his prison existence. The Methuselah Man was more cunning than he was. That had to be due to greater experience.

"No," the clone whispered. "I dare not accept his memories."

The longer he thought about it, the more the clone wanted to be his own person. He did not want to take Methuselah Man Strand's place. He wanted to live life on his own. Yes, he was grateful for existence. So would any reasonable child feel toward his parents. That he was a clone didn't mean that he had to accept the original's personality.

The clone realized that Strand wanted to live again in him. It was a terrifying thought. Methuselah Man Strand had admitted to making many clones. He was unique, his predecessor had said. He had free will. That implied the other clones had not possessed free will. They had been controlled.

The clone did not want anyone to control him. He wanted to control his own destiny. Was that such a sin? His predecessor or father seemed cruel, a tormenter of the first

281

order. If the Methuselah Man had wanted him to be an exact replica, why had Strand set everything up like this?

The Methuselah Man is tormenting me from the grave.

With a grunt, the clone pushed himself up off the floor. He staggered to a chair and collapsed onto it. He was ravenous, but he was sick of porridge.

That was another thing. The Methuselah Man had rigged the eatery so it only served water and porridge. The clone wanted to devour some deviled eggs, drink some coffee and savor a steak or three.

He rested his elbows on the table and put his face against his hands. He wanted to weep, but he refused. He was Strand just as much as the Methuselah Man. The old man had lived his life as he'd wanted to. Why should that be denied him? It was wrong.

"I'll die first," the clone declared.

The problem was that he wasn't sure if he believed himself anymore. At first, dying had seemed easy. It was just a matter of stubborn will. The hunger had stolen some of his willpower, however. The idea of living the rest of his existence in this small prison had started to make him go mad with claustrophobia.

As the clone sat at the table, he bit his lower lip. What should he do? He did not know the Methuselah Man's secrets. If he went under the alien machine, he could leave this place and live out his life fully.

The clone stood and whirled around. Maybe he could out-stubborn the alien machine. Maybe he could concentrate on keeping his identity despite a storm of memories flooding into him.

The clone had a premonition that the storm of memories might overcome any defenses he could mentally construct against them. If he couldn't even find a way off this prison…

He began to weep. He had wept before. This was a maddening thing. If he accepted his father's memories, would he become his father or could he keep his own identity? Why was that so important to him?

"Because I want to be me!" he shouted. "I want to live. I don't want to give up my individuality."

The clone panted as sweat began to drip from his face. This was such a terrible dilemma. Had the original foreseen his agony of soul?

The clone had attempted to replay the message, but the screen no longer worked.

"No," he said, as he faced the hatch, knowing what he was about to do.

With leaden feet, he approached the hatch. It opened. He stood there for a time, no longer thinking, simply an animal caught in a trap it couldn't escape.

He shuffled through until the hatch slid shut behind him. He didn't jump this time. He was used to the malevolent hatch.

Through tear-filmed eyes, the clone studied the great alien machine.

It was constructed of many unhuman curves, loops and twists. The seat in the center seemed wrong, but the clone didn't know why.

He had no idea how to turn on the memory machine. The Methuselah Man would have already thought of that.

"I don't want to be a cog," the clone whispered. "I want to…"

He bowed his head. He knew that in time, he would crawl through the maze of the machine until he sat on the seat. Should he hold out until he was a skeleton? Should he defeat the Methuselah Man by killing himself, or at least by only admitting defeat once he was too weak to do anything about it?

The clone found himself shaking his head. He wanted to be stubborn. He wanted to defeat the smug old man. But his feet betrayed him. They shuffled his body toward the damned alien machine.

"Help me," the clone whispered. "Somebody help me."

No one heard his cry. He was alone at the bottom of a giant crevice on an alien dwarf planet. He eased past cold metal. He struggled to stop himself, but now that he'd started, a part of him kept moving. It was the part that wanted to live. It was the part that wondered if he would become powerful once he accepted the old man's memories. That part argued against the other. He would still be him. He would just have another being's memories. Given enough time, he would become his own man anyway. This was the better way to go. This way he would live. He would eat all kinds of wonderful food. He would—

The clone found himself beside the seat at the center of the alien machine. With great trepidation, he lowered himself onto the stool. It was a contorted fit. He felt trapped and almost howled at the sudden dread that welled up within him.

Instead, the clone waited. He looked up. Nothing was happening. Was this a grand joke? Had the Methuselah Man played an awful prank on him?

The clone—

He looked around wildly. He could feel heat but he couldn't tell the heat source. The heat built against the top of his head. He looked up, around—

The clone noticed glowing dots there. There, and there and there. He tried to raise a hand to feel the heat, but a sickly tiredness began to seep throughout his body.

"Is this the process?" he asked aloud.

No one answered him. He felt so terribly alone. He hated the feeling. He realized that more than anything else the loneliness had driven him into the machine's embrace.

Like a bear caught in a trap, he endured as he waited for the hunter to come and put him out of his misery. The heat grew, but it did not become uncomfortable.

He stiffened. A memory…he felt…long ago Ludendorff and he had walked toward a house on a green hill. Ludendorff and he had been much younger then. They were friends. They went to the teacher's house. Strand recalled the strong smell of roses. The teacher—

The memory changed. It was many years later. Strand was deep in an alien tunnel system. Here, he learned that the teacher in the rose-scented house had really been a Builder screwing with their brains. The Builder had inserted memories—

"Memory after memory implanted into our brains?" the clone asked. "Where does it end? When was I ever myself? This is just the same game over and over again. And I thought I could stop it this time."

As the clone sat enmeshed in the alien machine, he realized why the Methuselah Man had set it up the way he did. The old man had given him an out. He had given *them* an out. This had happened time upon time, as this wasn't the first memory transfer. This—

"Stop it!" the clone wailed. He began to thrash as more memories flooded into his mind. He wanted to get out of the machine. He wanted to—

His jerky movements ceased as the floodgates to his mind opened. He did not just receive a few memories. No, oh no. He received one lifetime after another. The Methuselah Man had lived for such a long time. The clone wailed anew. Life was lonely to one who lived on and on while everyone else around him died.

The Methuselah Man was cursed. He had a task to perform. The Builder had branded his mind with brilliance and—

The clone shook his head wildly. He began to embroider memories with a released imagination. He added this to that and struggled to insert it within his memory core. He did it out of spite. He did it in an effort to have some of himself left after this was done.

The memories continued to flood his mind. They did overpower his will, as he'd feared. He forgot about the clone that had climbed out of the stasis unit.

The memories poured for hours, for days. Even the alien machine could not smash so many memories into one puny human mind in a short span. It took time to upload the Methuselah Man's life journey into the clone's fresh vault of brain tissues.

Strand groaned at the ruthlessness of the Emperor of the New Men. He could not believe his creation could turn on him like this. Strand relived his many victories against Ludendorff. He remembered other Methuselah Men, many whom he had slain. He remembered the androids that had warred against them throughout the centuries.

He laughed. He cried. He shouted with joy and he screamed vengeance.

Finally, days later, the heat no longer radiated against his sweat-streaked hair. He looked like a concentration camp victim, with his ribs showing on his starved and dehydrated body.

Making mewling sounds, Strand slid out of the alien maze.

The process took far too long. The little strength he had abandoned him. On hands and knees, he crawled slowly across the floor. The hatch opened.

Strand crawled to the food console. With painful slowness, he climbed to his feet. With blurry vision, he pressed buttons, entering a code.

Soon, he drank one glass of water after another.

He vomited most of it back up five minutes later.

This time, he drank slowly, paused to let the water seep into his molecules, and then drank again. Afterward, he ate seasoned mush. He would have deviled eggs and steaks later.

Finished with the meal, he barely managed to stagger to a cot. He collapsed onto it and slept for a solid twenty-three hours.

Finally, he stirred, opening his eyes.

They seemed different, looked and even felt different. They were an old man's eyes, filled with pain and sorrow. He was the same clone, but he was not the same person. He had a Methuselah Man's memories. He was not the same Strand that someone had captured. But he was not the youthful clone with grand ideas, either.

"I am…Strand Z," he said.

He shuddered, finally knowing what he planned to do.

The universe had robbed him of his creation. Before he made his next move, he would need to know more. But then, oh yes, then Ludendorff, Maddox, the Emperor of the New Men, all sorts of people, were going to pay.

Beyond that, however, was something intensely creative. The universe had tried to destroy his art. No. That was not going to stand. He had created the masterpiece of all masterpieces, the New Men. That was what no one had ever realized. More than Archimedes, more than Da Vinci or Michelangelo, he would restore his creation to its proper place, even if that meant destroying the puny human race known as *Homo sapiens* man.

-4-

Captain Maddox headed for the cell containing Yen Cho. Meta and Riker had joined him; they would watch the android, armed with heavy hand-weapons to destroy the android if they had to.

Maddox was running out of options. Things were moving much too slowly. They weren't any closer to figuring out where this next clone might be. They had no idea about where Nameless Ones technology could be hidden. Were there more null regions? How could they find them?

Maddox muttered under his breath. He had no idea. He had to catch a break. Barring that, he had to create his own break, a lead to reach the clone before the replica committed the terrible action of contacting the Nameless Ones.

Maddox halted before the heavy hatch. He faced the other two. "Yen Cho will be desperate. But whatever you do, don't kill him, as we need his knowledge."

"Sir?" Riker asked.

"Don't harm his brain. Blast off his arms or legs, or shred his torso if you must, but on no account damage his braincase."

"Are you sure this is the best way to talk to him, then?" Meta asked. "Maybe you should talk via screen. He can't get to us that way."

Maddox shook his head. He wanted answers, and he wanted them now. He was going to be direct. Besides, the android was likely more subtle than he was. The android had been toying with them for years. The androids had to be among the best spies in the business.

Maddox nodded to a marine.

The sergeant opened the hatch. Other marines stood ready with heavy rifles.

Maddox set his features into a bland mask. He lowered his head and stepped into the cell. Meta and Riker followed. The marine shut the hatch behind them with a clang.

Yen Cho sat at the table, but he was not playing cards this time. He sat like a statue, unmoving and unblinking.

Maddox said nothing as he grabbed an extra chair and dragged it toward Riker. The sergeant started to the table to get his own.

"No," Maddox said quietly. "I'll do that. I don't want him to steal your weapon."

Riker seemed abashed, nodding, taking the chair the captain had gotten for him.

Soon, Maddox sat against the wall. Meta and Riker flanked him, each aiming a hand-weapon at the unmoving android.

To Maddox's eye, Yen Cho seemed unaware of them. Andros Crank had repaired the android's pseudo-skin since the fight in the hangar bay. Galyan had informed him that the highly upgraded cyber-brain had rebooted after a hard crash. Now…

"Do you want us to leave?" Maddox asked the android.

Yen Cho made no response.

"Maybe he malfunctioned while waiting," Riker said.

With a slicing gesture across his throat, Maddox indicated that the sergeant should keep quiet.

Riker nodded.

Meta just watched the android. She appeared emotionless, which she most certainly was not. The android had endangered Maddox and helped cause the deaths of over 70 crewmates. Meta was set to kill.

"Yen Cho," Maddox said. "I've waited to talk to you for several reasons. According to Galyan, you are whole again. I've also had my chief technician install special magnetic clamps outside your cell. At the first sign of trouble, you will find yourself pinned against a bulkhead, unable to move."

288

The android still did not respond.

"Perhaps you're upset regarding the proto-Builder," Maddox said in an easy manner. "I can well understand that. You hoped to revive a Builder. I'm sure you believed it would be grateful to you. Maybe you hoped it would help the androids gain greater status. I recall the proto-Builder saying something about androids working as the overlords of a thinned-out humanity."

There was still no response.

Maddox switched tactics. "We searched both sets of pyramids. The away team on Gideon II used the entrance I'd blasted into a side. The team reached the pit where I endured the antimatter explosion. The team found deep corridors, tearing apart whatever stood in the way. They found nothing useful. Just ruins, some ancient wall-art and a few useless knickknacks. They had to destroy a few things, but came up empty anyway. It was the same on the rogue moon. In a word, the pyramids proved barren."

The android did not appear to have heard the report.

"Can he hear us?" Meta asked.

The android sat motionless.

Maddox switched tactics yet again. "I'd hoped to forgo any…threats, but you leave me no choice. Galyan and Andros are having trouble cracking the Builder cube. So far, it has resisted our efforts. You know more about this…cube than any of us do. You could aid us. But, it appears you will not. While Galyan and Andros may not be able to crack the cube, I do believe they could hack your cybertronic brain."

The android still did nothing.

"That means I will order your brain taken from your braincase," Maddox said. "I will not be reinstalling it. Instead, we're going to take apart your brain piece by piece. We will reassemble and run it so we can control every function. In that way, Galyan and Andros can drain any useful memories."

The android blinked and his head swiveled minutely, so he now stared at Maddox.

"You are a barbarian," Yen Cho declared.

"That's an interesting observation," Maddox said easily. "We're barbarians willing to dissect an unliving android in order to save the human race from destruction. You must realize that I have no qualms in the matter. I especially have no qualms when said android helped a Builder cube. A cube, mind you, hoping to alter the human race into something more to its liking. Apparently, androids are fine with this."

Maddox shrugged. "In such a situation, I find that I have no reservations in using you however I can to rectify the situation."

"You truly desecrated more of the pyramids on Gideon II?" Yen Cho asked.

"The away team went down. They searched and found the pyramids empty."

"The pyramids are holy to androids. I have already told you so. You must stay out of them."

"Then help me find the next Strand clone," Maddox said. "If you do, Star Watch will quarantine Gideon II and the rogue moon. They will be off-limits to archeologists and souvenir hunters. If you don't help us...I'm inclined to saturation bomb the sites until the pyramids are obliterated."

"You would not dare commit such sacrilege," Yen Cho said.

Sergeant Riker snorted. "Believe me, Captain Maddox would dare. Or have you forgotten that he already dropped one antimatter missile on them?"

Yen Cho stared dead-eyed at Maddox.

The captain began to wonder if the android had returned to its catatonic state.

"Yes," the android said. "I will help you."

"Crack the Builder cube?" Maddox asked.

"I have already said yes."

"Just so we're clear," Maddox said. "If we find that you're tampering with the cube or attempting to revive it again, I will blast the pyramids to pieces and dissect your computer brain."

"I have already computed your response to such an action on my part," the android said.

"Can we really trust him?" Meta asked.

"No," Maddox said. "We're going to watch him every second and on several levels." He studied the android. "You will wear a heavy iron yoke at all times."

"I will help you," Yen Cho said. "What more must I say?"

"One more thing," Maddox said. "Do you know the whereabouts of the next stasis chamber?"

Yen Cho hesitated answering. "No," he finally said.

"He's lying," Meta said.

"Or wants us to think he's lying?" Riker added.

Maddox tapped his chin. "Do you have a suspicion concerning the location of the next stasis chamber?"

"That I do," Yen Cho said.

"Where?" asked Maddox.

"I am loath to say it."

"I understand," Maddox said. "However, in this instance, I am going to insist. And to help loosen your tongue, I will apply the pyramid-blasting threat to the question."

"I thought you might," Yen Cho said. "Yes. I will say." And he told them.

"That is deep into the Beyond," Maddox said. "It would take time to reach the star system."

"And I may be wrong about my guess," Yen Cho said. "It is simply a possibility I have computed from everything I have learned about the original Strand's thinking."

"What do you give as the probability?" Maddox asked.

"Sixty-two percent."

"How did you arrive at the conclusion?"

Yen Cho hesitated once more, finally nodded and began to speak. He spoke for 33 minutes.

"Detailed," Maddox said when the android finally stopped talking. "And I'm impressed by your extensive store of knowledge."

"I have lived longer than the Methuselah Men," Yen Cho said. "I have learned a great deal in all that time."

"Apparently," Maddox said. He stood.

Meta and Riker rose with him.

"Are we going to the selected star system?" Yen Cho asked.

"I'll let you know once I decide," Maddox said, rapping on the hatch.

It opened.

"We do not have much time," Yen Cho said. "It is, in fact, my belief, that the stasis chamber has already expelled its occupant."

"I've wondered about that," Maddox said.

"When do I get out of here to help you with the Builder cube?"

"Soon," Maddox said.

The three humans departed the cell, waiting until the marine shut the hatch and they'd heard the lock engage before heading out of the brig area of the ship.

-5-

There was nothing for it but to start traveling as fast as *Victory* could go. The ancient Adok starship had a key advantage few other space vessels possessed; it had the star-drive jump. It allowed them to jump directly to the next Laumer Point in a star system and then use it to reach the next system. The problem was greater stress on the crew as they made jump after jump after jump in quick succession.

The starship left Human Space and entered the Beyond. That was another stress. Traveling through the unknown slowly built greater pressure among those doing it.

This wasn't an ordinary crew, however. They had undergone rigorous testing as the Patrol people searched for individuals that could take the pressures. What's more, *Victory* had been farther into the Beyond than any other known human-crewed ship. Most of the crew was used to this. As used to it as one got, anyway.

As the days passed, it became clear to Maddox that Yen Cho knew far more than Star Watch had suspected. The android kept providing new Laumer Point coordinates as the starship traveled through uncharted areas of the Beyond.

"We must be nearing the Throne World," Maddox said one day.

Yen Cho was among the science team working on the Builder cube. Armed marines stood against the bulkheads. Others were in the next room, ready to activate giant magnetic clamps.

293

Yen Cho wore what looked like an old-style yoke for a beast of burden. If the magnetic clamps activated, they would pick the yoked android off the floor and slam the iron yoke against a bulkhead. It meant extra weight for Yen Cho, and often proved to be in his way. The android hadn't complained. If the yoke-jacket bothered him, he had not let on.

Maddox studied daily reports concerning the android's behavior. Looking for a clue as to the android's... Feelings would be the wrong word. Maybe trying to figure out what Yen Cho wanted and what he would attempt to do.

Maddox presently stood beside the android. In the center of the room was a giant globe. The cube sat in the exact center with power cables attached to the clear block that held the cube. Scientists stood around the circular console that ringed the giant globe.

Andros Crank and Galyan instructed scientists on various procedures. The cube had proven extremely resistant to any hacking or cracking.

It had been three weeks already, and they were no closer to breaking into the Builder software than before. None of Yen Cho's suggestions had helped, either.

If it hadn't been for his data about the Beyond, Maddox would have sent the android back into his cell a long time ago.

The android turned to Maddox in regard to the captain's comment about the Throne World.

"I suggest we stay far from the New Men," Yen Cho said.

Maddox was inclined to agree. Despite their help against the Swarm Invasion Fleet, the captain didn't trust the New Men. He wondered, then, what Lord Drakos did at this moment. Was the man his father? He had believed so. Now...he wasn't one hundred percent certain. But if Lord Drakos wasn't his father, who was? How would he ever find out, so he could kill the responsible man?

The captain shook his head. He couldn't worry about that now.

"He must be near," Maddox said, referring to the original Strand. "If we could go to the Throne World...perhaps the Emperor would allow us to speak to Strand."

"Or perhaps the Emperor has already broken Strand and is even now sending star cruisers to the same place we're headed," Yen Cho said.

Maddox considered the idea. The longer he did, the more concerned he became over their lack of progress with the Builder cube. "Tell me, Yen Cho. Why have you failed to crack the cube? You know it better than anyone."

"Me?" the android asked. "Surely, you jest. The cube is far beyond my knowledge. The Builders…" The android waved vaguely. "You should not have destroyed the proto-Builder, Captain. We were on the verge of a grand new age."

"This may surprise you," Maddox said. "But I have no desire to enter a grand new age with a murderous Builder at its head."

"It would have been better for humanity, at least in the long run."

"There are no long runs," Maddox said, "just an endless succession of short runs."

"I suppose I can sympathize with you," Yen Cho said. "You have your short life, and that is all. You cannot see the long view. That is why…" The android looked away.

"Why I'm a barbarian?" Maddox asked.

Stout Andros Crank stepped near. "The cube is resistant to everything we can think of," he told Maddox. "Oh. Am I interrupting you?"

"Not at all," Maddox said. "You were saying?"

"I have come to believe that the cube is actively resisting us," Andros said. "The technology behind it…" The longhaired chief technician shook his gray head. "I almost think we should split the cube in half."

"What?" Yen Cho said, turning to face them.

"Yes," Andros told the android. "We're not getting anywhere as it is. At this point, what do we have to lose? Captain, I'd like your permission to split the cube in half."

Maddox studied the cube in the giant globe. The idea was his, naturally. He had instructed Andros to ask him this while he was talking to the android.

"Yes," Maddox said, as if coming to a sudden decision. "I don't see what else we can do."

295

"But that is madness," Yen Cho said. "The cube is priceless. To simply destroy it like unthinking primitives—not even you humans are that stupid."

"I have to disagree with him, sir," Andros said. "We're under the gun. We're possibly running out of time. We have to gamble that we can gain something from the cube."

"Agreed," Maddox said. "Do you have a way to cut it?"

"I've been working on the idea for several days already," Andros said. "Galyan has helped me create a centralized disrupter beam. It will act like a knife, cutting the cube in half."

"No, no," Yen Cho said. "You are truly mad. That will destroy the cube."

"It might," Andros admitted. "It might also work. Maybe only one-half will be broken. The other half will have salvageable information we can use."

There was a subtle stiffening to Yen Cho. The marines along the wall grew alert, several of them training their heavy rifles on the android.

"Do you disagree with my verdict?" Maddox asked Yen Cho.

The android looked away. It seemed his cybertronic mind might be whirling at its highest setting.

"I have a different solution," Yen Cho said. "I…have not suggested it yet because it might cause a self-destruct sequence in the cube. We…androids have come upon such a cube before. We attempted to hack into it. The cube exploded, killing all the androids but one."

"You?" Maddox asked.

"That was a shrewd guess, Captain. Yes, I alone survived."

"Yet you worship the Builders?" Maddox asked.

"Shall we try my alternative method?" the android asked.

"Will it take long? We no longer have the luxury of time."

"It should take two, maybe three days to set up."

Maddox rubbed his chin, finally shaking his head. "No, I don't see that—"

"Give me one day of preparation," Yen Cho said, interrupting. "Surely, one day more won't matter."

Maddox eyed the android. "One day," he said. "After that—"

"Thank you, Captain," Yen Cho said. "I believe my method should work this time. Last time…it does not matter. This time, I am almost completely certain it will work."

-6-

The preparations for Yen Cho's experiment ended up taking three days. Seventy-six hours to be precise. Maddox did not complain or point it out to the android.

By that time, the captain had other matters on his mind. The starship had traveled an incredible distance in that 76-hour timeframe, leaving the smaller-than-normal crew exhausted from all the star-drive and Laumer Point jumps.

They had traveled through six Laumer Points, having used the star drive as a short cut to each different system. According to Yen Cho's star-chart, the short cut saved the crew five Laumer Point jumps and a detour of 63 light-years. Altogether, *Victory* had traveled 87 light-years since the discussion with Andros and Yen Cho in the science chamber.

The ancient Adok vessel was now in a neutron star system. They had exited a Laumer Point near the small but incredibly dense iron sun. The radiation from the neutron star bombarded the ship, causing the shield to change color.

Maddox was on the bridge with a skeleton crew. A pilot sat at the helm, and Galyan stood near the captain. The rest of the bridge crew was sleeping off the cumulative effects of the many jumps over days on end.

"This is an inhospitable star system," Galyan said. "There is little visible light, massive amounts of ionizing radiation and high-energy stellar winds. I suggest we leave the vicinity of the neutron star."

298

"One more jump," Maddox said. "Helm, prepare to jump—" The captain turned to Galyan. "Yen Cho suspects this is the star system. Have you found anything that indicates a human-inhabited base?"

"Negative, Captain," Galyan said. "But it is difficult to get accurate sensor readings this near the neutron star."

"Let's jump behind the second inner planet," Maddox said. "It can shield us from the star's radiation."

"I suggest we jump farther that than, Captain. I can understand why Strand might have picked this system to set up a secret base. But I cannot see how that base could be in the inner system. It will have to be in the outer system at least."

"Provided it's even here," Maddox said.

"Agreed," Galyan said.

"All right," Maddox said. "We'll jump to the nearest outer planet. We can begin searching for the hidden base from there."

***

Victory jumped one more time. From there, Galyan used the starship's sensors, scanning, widening the scan and searching even farther afield.

There did not seem to be anything other than asteroids, comets, gas giants and stellar debris.

Valerie spelled the captain for a time. He went to his room and fell asleep for what seemed like no time before he felt Meta pushing his left shoulder.

"They did it," she said.

Maddox blinked at her from the bed. "Galyan found the hidden base?"

"What?" Meta asked.

"The base, we're searching for the—"

"No, no," Meta said. "Yen Cho's experiment worked. They've opened communications with the Builder cube."

Maddox shook his head. "What did you say? They haven't cracked into the software?"

"Husband, the Builder cube is awake. It's angry, and it doesn't want to talk. But we have opened communications with it. Andros has requested your presence. He says you have a

299

fantastic record talking to computers, that this is another time for you to shine."

"The cube is a computer?"

"Not fully," Meta said. "According to what I heard, there's some bio-matter inside the cube. Andros thinks it's the genetic code for Builders."

Maddox whipped off the covers. He was naked. No surprise to Meta, although she still noted a flutter of pleasure at the sight. According to the clock, he'd slept two hours. A cup of coffee should help him. He wouldn't take any more stimulants than that, though.

"That bastard," Maddox said, meaning Yen Cho. The android had double-crossed them. He wasn't supposed to wake the thing up. They needed to crack into the cube's software so they could download the data. Now, he had to deal with an angry Builder cube.

Maddox threw on his clothes and jacket. Just for once, he would like to get a break and have something fall his way.

He suppressed the thought. He was Captain Maddox. Like Andros said, this was a time for him to shine.

Another computer, he thought. After that, he walked briskly, with Meta trotting beside him.

-7-

Maddox stood in the large science room. The techs stood around the giant globe that towered over the captain and the others. Just like before, in the center of the globe was a holder containing the Builder cube. Various nodes lined the container. Cables were connected to some of those nodes. Others had sizzling lines of electricity.

Maddox didn't comprehend all the scientific reasons for all the pieces of equipment. That was why he had Galyan, Andros Crank and now Yen Cho. Could the three of them do together what Professor Ludendorff had routinely done solo?

The android watched him. Did Yen Cho fear a reprimand? At this point, Maddox wasn't going to worry about it. He studied the globe, and he had a second thought.

"Sergeant," he said to the chief marine.

The man acknowledged him.

"Take the android back to its cell," Maddox said.

The sergeant whirled around and collected his men, heading for Yen Cho.

"Captain," the android said. "I would like to watch the proceedings."

"Of course you would," Maddox said in an easy manner. "That's one of the reasons you're going back to your cell. You played us false."

"That is not true. My experiment produced this communication."

Maddox turned his back on Yen Cho.

301

"Captain," the android called.

"Get him out of here, Sergeant."

"You heard the captain," the marine told the android. "Start moving."

"No. I refuse to go."

Maddox turned around, staring at Yen Cho. "Sergeant," he said, "shoot him in the arms and legs and torso. Incapacitate him—"

"I have changed my mind," Yen Cho. "I will leave."

Maddox nodded. The android must have realized he was about to be terminated, his cybertronic brain to be studied by Andros and Galyan.

After Yen Cho and his guards departed, Maddox beckoned Andros.

"Tell me," Maddox said quietly. "Is the Builder cube watching and listening to all this?"

"Yes, sir," Andros said.

"Explain to me how it does so."

The chief technician brought Maddox to a major screen. On it appeared a dark image: a shadowy humanoid Builder complete with shifting leathery wings.

Maddox examined the image and then turned to his left and looked at the cube imprisoned in the globe. He turned again, pulling Andros aside.

"One thing keeps bothering me," Maddox said quietly. "The cube was in the clone's ghost-ship. The clone used the ghost-ship for quite some time. At no point did the cube attempt to become a proto-Builder. I'd like to know why not and why it chose its moment when it did."

Andros shook his head.

"Galyan," Maddox said into the air.

The holoimage appeared.

Maddox asked him what he'd asked Andros.

Galyan's eyelids fluttered. Finally, the little holoimage brightened. "I have a theory. I imagine the Builder in the cube was asleep. Or that program had not been activated. The cube acted as the ghost-ship's computer system. Once the guardian robot removed it, something must have activated in the cube."

"Why did the robot wait to do that?" Maddox asked.

"Perhaps it followed emergency coding," Galyan said. "That emergency would have activated the old Builder revival program. The guardian robot might not have specifically known it was doing that, at least not in the beginning. Once the Builder rebirth-program activated, though… We have seen the results."

"A reasonable theory," Maddox said. "Thank you."

"Yes, Captain. Now, I must get back to scanning for the clone's hidden base." The holoimage disappeared.

Once more, Maddox examined the cube in the globe. It was time to get started.

"Can you hear me?" he asked.

"Your chatter is speech, a primitive form of communication," the Builder cube replied from a speaker in the screen. "I resent your chatter being directed at me, but I can hear and understand it quite well."

"Do you know who I am?"

"That is an insulting question," the Builder cube said. "I am aware, yes, that you are my chief enemy, the berserk humanoid that attacked me in the hangar bay. I have already indicated that I am aware of everything around me. I know about the guardian robot. I know about the clone Strand and the ghost-ship. In other words, I am a Builder in thought, if not yet in body."

"You remember the past?"

"Captain," the Builder cube chided. "You do not understand the situation. None of your people do, not even the interesting Adok holoimage. You must release me. I am too great and too sophisticated to allow myself the indignity of imprisonment by inferior creatures such as you."

"Nevertheless," Maddox said, "you are my prisoner. You attempted to murder all of us. You did kill some, more than seventy individuals. Do you know that we humans—"

"Captain, captain, I am going to interrupt you right there. You—specifically you—are not fully human, *Homo sapiens* human, is what I mean. You are partly…an altered New Man."

Maddox did not reply right away. He pondered the cube's objective and its…prissy manner. That did not seem like the Builder on the Dyson Sphere. Had they damaged the software during the fight in the hangar bay? Had it been asleep so long that some of its programming had downgraded? Entropy always won in the end. Builder artifacts lasted longer than any others did, but even they deteriorated in the end.

Putting his hands behind his back, Maddox began to pace before the screen.

"You do not like being a hybrid," the cube said. "This I know from my detailed study of you. The Strand clone was quite interested in your psychology. I don't mean the clone you are presently hunting. You see, I even know about that."

"You're clever," Maddox said.

"No. I am a Builder. I am superior by my very nature."

"But you're not a Builder. You have the DNA of a Builder stored within you and given time, you might possibly cause a Builder's birth. But you yourself are a construct, an android with delusions of being a Builder. I've spoken to a genuine Builder, and you are not one, nor do you act or sound as one."

"I will long survive you, Captain. In time, the essence in me shall become a Builder. I will supply it with a personality and great knowledge. Therefore, gloat and strut to your heart's delight, Captain. It matters little to me. I have infinite patience."

"I'm delighted to hear that," Maddox said. "For I've decided to practice another experiment with you."

"Oh?"

"Your cube is made out of a nearly indestructible substance."

"Delete the 'nearly,' and you would be correct."

Maddox spun around to face the screen. He clapped his hands as if overjoyed. "That's exactly what I want to test."

"Nothing on your starship can ultimately harm me, so test away"

"I suspected as much," Maddox said. "Therefore, I am going release you several AUs from the neutron star. I am even going to give your cube a pressure-force push. You will fall onto the neutron star. If you survive your impact, I imagine it will be an exceedingly long wait for you. Millions of years, in fact, as you wait for the neutron star to eventually fall apart."

The Builder cube did not reply.

"Chief Technician," Maddox said.

"Here, sir," Andros said.

"You will begin to dismantle the globe. Detach the cube from its place and tell me when you're ready for the launch."

Andros stared at Maddox.

"I expect prompt obedience, Chief Technician," the captain said.

"Y-Y-Yes, sir," Andros stammered. "I shall begin the process—"

"Captain," the cube said. "I believe you are being a tad premature."

Maddox waved a hand. "I imagine that's true. But like I've been trying to tell you. I'm not interested in your opinion. To me, you're not really a Builder. You're a thing that might in time become a Builder, but now you're going to have to wait for millions of years to find out. I doubt you'll be able to send a message off the neutron star."

"Sending a message from the neutron star would be impossible."

"There you are," Maddox said. "Of course, all that is provided you survive the impact. Do you think you can survive it?"

"That is not the issue," the cube said. "Your neutron star experiment is a gross misuse of me."

"I have other things on my mind. If you don't want to help me—"

"Who said that?" the cube asked, interrupting.

"Oh. I believe you implied—"

"Captain, captain," the cube chided. "I know what you are trying to do. It is quite elementary."

"I'm just a lower-order creature," Maddox said. "I hardly know better."

"You are savagely bloodthirsty and will let nothing stand in your way. You see, I know you better than you know yourself. I know this is no idle threat."

"I hate threatening anything that I'm not willing to actually do," Maddox said.

"Yes, I know," the cube said. "Now, let us proceed to the heart of the issue. What is it you want?"

305

"Information about the Strand clones."

"I have some data on that, but possibly not enough for you."

"I would also like to know the whereabouts of any Nameless Ones' technology."

"I shall begin processing my data. I have a vast store of knowledge. Even with my intellect, it takes time to correlate everything."

"Quite the burden, I'm sure," Maddox said. "But let me get this straight. You will help us locate the clone?"

"We are bargaining, I take it," the cube said.

"Precisely."

"I will help you locate the clone, and you will give me a vessel of my choosing."

"No," Maddox said.

"Ah," the cube said. "I see that you are going to play fair with me. If you had agreed to my request, I would have known that you were simply lying to me. I realize you will never let me go. What can you give me then, Captain, that I want?"

"Continued existence," Maddox said.

"You mean your trade is a willingness to not murder me."

"Builder—"

"I thought you said I wasn't a Builder," the cube interrupted.

"I'll call you a Builder for now."

"How interesting, Captain. I wonder why the change."

"Builder, you murdered over seventy of my crew. I am not inclined to let you live. I'd hoped to break you open and extract the data through a computer scan."

"You are a true hominid savage, Captain."

"What I'm trying to let you know is that it is a big deal for me to let you live. I'm going to want a lot from you for that privilege."

"I can only give what I can give. The clone's stasis chamber...I have the coordinates for it."

"Please give them."

The cube did so.

"Well?" Maddox asked Andros.

"That's this star system," the chief technician said.

"Where in the star system is the stasis chamber?" Maddox asked the cube.

"I do not know," the cube said. "I suggest, given the parameters of the problem, that the stasis chamber would be in the outer region of the system. If it was in the inner system, there would be no way to signal it, or not signal it, if you know what I mean."

"Spell it out for me," Maddox said.

The cube explained the problem with message signals getting through the neutron star's interference.

"Now, Captain, I would like something in return."

"What is that?"

"I would like you to destroy the android Yen Cho in my presence. He failed me at a critical junction. In fact, I demand his destruction if you expect more help from me."

"I'll consider it," Maddox said. "Is there anything else you would like?"

"Yes. Link me to Galyan's ship computers. I'm curious about what the Builders back then did that allowed an engram-enhanced Adok AI to survive six thousand years. I do not understand why the Builders back then broke protocol."

"That is curious," Maddox said. "What else can I give you?"

"Those two are quite sufficient for now."

"I'll need authorization for the one."

"*That* is a lie, Captain. You do what you want when you want. But I shall give you a third payment-in-kind. I would like to read the files concerning everything the Commonwealth knows about the New Men."

"Why the interest?"

"Captain, captain, do you wish me to manufacture a lie for you?"

"You want what you want," Maddox said. "I—"

"Captain," Galyan said. The little holoimage had reappeared in the science room. "Valerie thinks she may have found the stasis chamber."

"Where?" Maddox asked.

"It's in the system's Kuiper Belt. Valerie picked up a faint signal—"

"Did we find it?" Maddox asked the Builder cube.

"Give me the coordinates and the present data," the cube said.

Galyan looked at Maddox. The captain nodded. Galyan told the cube the coordinates and what the data consisted of.

"I believe that could be the stasis chamber," the cube said. "There is one problem I believe you have not foreseen."

"Base defenses?" Maddox asked.

"No. Base auto-destruct sequences. I highly doubt the original Strand wanted anyone searching his clone-release base. You will have to be extremely careful, Captain, if you want to search the stasis chamber while it is still intact."

"Strand…" Maddox said under his breath. The Methuselah Man always ensured that everything would be complicated.

"Tell Valerie to get ready to jump to the dwarf planet," Maddox said. "She's to come out on the side of the planet opposite the possible base."

Galyan disappeared.

Maddox turned for the hatch.

"Captain," the cube said. "I would like my first payment."

Maddox considered the cube. "First, I'm going to see if you were right or not." With that, the captain spun, hurrying for the hatch.

308

-8-

Victory made a successful star-drive jump, coming in behind the Pluto-like dwarf planet 34 AUs from the neutron star.

"It's out there," Valerie said on the bridge. "But we know Strand. He's a hateful little man, revengeful in all matters. He must have booby-trapped the secret base…if it's really there."

Maddox silently agreed. He suspected the base would detonate if anything over there sensed a scan.

"We could have a cold teleoptic probe pass the area," Valerie suggested. "It could passively determine what's there."

"How do we retrieve the data?" Maddox asked.

"You would have to wait," Valerie said. "Whatever I sensed must have a range limit. Likely, only something nearby would trigger the detonation switch."

"Let's try it," Maddox said.

***

Valerie set up a teleoptic probe. Keith took the fold-fighter, folded some distance from the dwarf planet, launched the cold probe toward the planet, and promptly folded back.

The probe took a precious day to drift past the other side of the dwarf planet. A tiny computer with the minutest of energy used a telescope to see what it could see.

After a time, the probe drifted past the planet.

They waited another day before Keith took out the fold-fighter, collected the probe and returned with it to the starship, which still hid on the other side of the dwarf planet.

Valerie, Keith, Andros, Galyan and the captain all eagerly went to the conference room. There, Valerie played back the probe's findings. On the screen, they saw the alien sensor, saw a cable snaking from it and heading deep into a jagged fissure into the planet.

"How far does the landline go?" Maddox asked.

Valerie adjusted, making measurements as to the deepest the telescope had been able to observe.

"Over three hundred meters at this point," she said, using an indicator to show the pic on the screen.

"Farther than three hundred meters..." Maddox mused. "So the base—if one is there—is deeper than that. If the base detonates, the crevice will make sure the blast heads upward. It will be a nuclear device at the very least, maybe even an antimatter bomb."

"Knowing Strand, it would be suicide to go down to the base," Valerie said.

"We can't have come this far and not go down and check," Keith said.

"Do you want to go down?" Maddox asked the ace.

"Me? Are you kidding? I'd love to—"

"No!" Valerie said, staring at the ace. "Keith doesn't want to go down."

"But we have to do something," Keith told her.

"We can use another probe," Valerie said.

"I know a better way," Maddox said. He turned to Galyan. "Let's run a copy of your personality in the super-android. It can go down there. If an explosion occurs and the super-android is destroyed, no one will have died."

"Captain," Galyan said, "I am surprised at you. Firstly, I will not allow a copy of me impersonating me. Secondly, such a copy would have my hopes and dreams. To knowingly allow it to go into a situation that will destroy it—no. I cannot permit such a thing."

"Send Yen Cho," Valerie said.

"Or the cube," Andros said. "It's supposed to be indestructible."

"Neither of them will go," Maddox said. "Both would use the opportunity to create mischief. We will use a probe, a robot. It will beam us the data."

Three hours later, Keith piloted a shuttle coming in low over the dwarf planet's surface. One hundred kilometers away from the giant crevice, he opened an underbelly hatch and launched a probe. Afterward, he headed back for the ship.

Back on *Victory's* bridge, Maddox, Galyan and Valerie watched the probe's progress. It flew over frozen methane and speckled scatterings of rock that must have come from ancient meteor impacts.

The manually run probe—Valerie piloted it from her station—slowed as it approached the jagged crevice.

The lieutenant manipulated her console. On the main screen, they saw the alien sensor lying in the methane snow. It was octagonal-shaped with hundreds of tiny antennae sticking up.

"Scan it," Maddox said. "If nothing else, it would be good to know what kind of alien technology Strand had back then."

"A scan could cause a detonation," Valerie warned.

Maddox did not bother to reply. He already knew that.

A few seconds later, Valerie pressed a control. The probe scanned and began to run an analysis.

"Tap into that, Galyan," Maddox said. "Tell us if you find a match with any known technology."

The little holoimage's eyelids flickered. "Rull technology," Galyan said, opening his eyes.

"Android tech?" Maddox asked.

"Sind II tech," Galyan amended. "It is a lower-order form of Builder technology not that much different from that used by the Adoks."

"No detonation so far," Valerie said.

"Take it down," Maddox said. "We may have just caught a break."

Valerie rubbed her hands before she began to tap her console.

On the screen, the scene changed. The probe hovered over the gigantic jagged crevice. It began to float down, following the landline attached to the alien sensor. It went down and down, past the native rock.

After the probe had descended a half-mile, Valerie said, "I have something. It's metallic—"

"Scan immediately," Maddox snapped. He sat on the edge of his command chair. "Tell me if you can sense bio matter inside."

"A human?" Valerie asked.

"Exactly. A clone."

"Beginning to scan," Valerie said, adjusting her panel.

At that very moment, a terrific detonation occurred. For an instant, the bridge crew witnessed an antimatter blast ripping through the structure's outer hull, climbing—

And the image abruptly disappeared.

Maddox whirled his chair around. "What did the scan show? Did you have time to read anything?"

Valerie frowned as she faced the captain. "I hardly had any time, but the probe made a complete scan. It's recorded. I'll have to study—"

"Galyan," Maddox snapped. "Did the probe have enough time to sense a human body?"

The holoimage's eyelids flickered. "The probe had time," Galyan said. He looked at Maddox. "There was no body, no bio-matter in the structure except for detected foodstuffs."

"The clone is gone," Valerie said. "He made it out before we got here."

Maddox stared at her. "Do we know for a fact a clone was in there?"

"Maybe not," Valerie admitted. "But everything we suspected would happen did happen. It all fits Strand's personality, which substantiates what we suspected."

Maddox nodded. The lieutenant had a point. He also wondered if Yen Cho or the Builder was playing them false in some manner. Or maybe both of them.

"Strand is clever enough to have set up decoy stasis chambers," Maddox said.

"In this instance, I don't believe that," Valerie said. "Clearly, this hidden base took considerable effort to create. Strand is conceited like his New Men."

312

"Your point?" Maddox asked.

"Does a conceited person believe others can figure him out? Or does he think he can outsmart everyone?"

Maddox eyed the blank screen. "The fact of the explosion shows us Strand wasn't utterly conceited. The fact of the clones means that Strand long-ago considered his death or capture."

Valerie nodded. Maybe so; she hadn't thought of that.

"Still," Maddox said, "that is neither here nor there. We came deep into the Beyond to find a clue. We have none, other than to substantiate the next clone's release. He has begun his mission. The clock is ticking, and we have no idea where to find him or how to figure out a way to find him."

Maddox eyed the others. "I'm open to suggestions."

"Yen Cho or the Builder cube could possibly tell us more," Valerie said.

"I must think," Maddox said. He stood. "Lieutenant, you have the bridge."

With that, the captain strode for the exit.

-9-

Maddox stood at a viewing port, eying the stars and the dwarf planet below them. They were deep in the Beyond, closer to the Throne World than to Earth.

Strand had released another clone. Maddox felt the truth of that in his bones. The hidden base had detonated as the probe neared it. Strand was obviously covering his tracks. An earlier clone had used a Builder ghost-ship and a guardian robot. The next one would have the tech of the Nameless Ones. How would that manifest itself?

Maddox shook his head.

Yen Cho had lived longer than any of the Methuselah Men had. The android had tracked the earlier clone to Smade's Asteroid. It would seem the android understood Strand's psychology well indeed.

The Builder cube had run probability programs for the earlier clone. It had been with the Strand clone, studied Strand, and studied the clone's victims. The cube had also figured out some of the original Strand's strategy through his clone's actions.

It would seem that if one could combine what the two mechanical beings knew, and add in human intuition, that the answer would likely appear obvious.

Maddox had no idea how to meld the three. Would Professor Ludendorff have known a method? If anyone could do it, it would be that unpredictable Methuselah Man.

The captain shifted his stance as he stared down at the dwarf planet. Strand loved secret bases and cloaked vessels. The Methuselah Man loved working from the shadows. He loved nothing better than manipulating people by pulling hidden strings inside them.

Secret bases…secret bases… Why did that stick in his mind?

The captain snapped his fingers. While free, the original Strand had haunted the New Men. He had maneuvered around them—

"From a secret base," Maddox said softly.

An android named Rose had gone to Strand. She had complicated the Methuselah Man's life, which had helped Maddox to capture Strand on Sind II.

If Rose knew the likely location of Strand's secret base when the Methuselah Man had operated against the New Men, it would stand to reason that Yen Cho would also know the base's location.

The original Strand hadn't operated freely for a time now. Would his people continue to operate from that old secret base?

Maddox doubted that. They would reasonably fear the New Men hunting them down.

"I need to find that base," Maddox told himself.

He whirled around. It was time to pry some information out of the reluctant android.

***

Maddox faced Yen Cho. As he had so often in the past, the android currently played solitaire. Two marine guards stood in the cell, leveling heavy combat rifles at the android.

Yen Cho paused, his hand poised above a card as though he readied himself to flip it over. "Can I help you, Captain?"

"I need the location of Strand's secret base from back when he used to torment the New Men."

"I do not know what you mean."

"Of course you do," Maddox said. "Rose did."

The android had seemed ready to flip over the card. He did not. Instead, he looked up at Maddox again. "The base in question is likely empty."

"Where is it?"

"Strand's people might have destroyed it."

"I want the location," Maddox said. "Not excuses."

The android cocked his head. "You found the hidden clone base in this system, but it exploded, yes?"

Maddox said nothing.

"A trade, Captain, is that what you're suggesting, information for information?"

Maddox still said nothing.

Yen Cho flipped over the waiting card, and played another. He seemed to consider something as he made the moves and looked up again. "The base you desire is in the Lycon System. It has four planets, one of them terrestrial and the rest gas giants. It lacks comets and an Oort cloud. It also has a G-class star."

"The location," Maddox said.

"The base is hidden on an extra-large moon of the third planet. The moon has a poisonous atmosphere and an underground complex able to house several thousand people. Most were techs. Strand kept Lore Fallows, a Kai-Kaus Chief Technician, there as well."

"The original Strand kidnapped Lore Fallows. I remember."

"Is the secret base your latest desire?"

"The clone-release base here detonated, as you predicated," Maddox said.

"Interesting," Yen Cho said. "You gave me the information I sought before I told you the stellar coordinates of the Lycon System. You dearly want this old science base, do you not, Captain?"

Maddox did not answer.

Yen Cho set the cards on the table. "The Lycon System is forty-three light-years from here. It is much closer to the Throne World than this system is. I suspect there might be star cruisers in the Lycon System."

"I'll take my chances," Maddox said.

"I should warn you. You will not find anything useful there."

"Give me something better, then."

316

"I have nothing more to give," Yen Cho said.

"I doubt that."

"Ah. You fear me?"

"Yen Cho...my patience has a limit."

"I know. Thus, here are the coordinates." And he told Maddox.

"I will have the guards bring you some games," Maddox said, standing.

"Computer games?" the android asked.

"No computers, but some board games the crew plays now and again. It might help relieve your boredom."

"I am unfamiliar with the sensation, as I lack an emotions program."

"Still," Maddox said. "It's my way of showing you that things can improve if you cooperate."

"Noted," the android said.

With that, Maddox departed. It was time to head for the Lycon System.

-10-

The clone Strand spent a week and a half in a small but powerful spacecraft, zipping through seldom-used Laumer Points, hopping from one star system to another. By far, the greater amount of time was in traveling through the various systems, getting to the next jump-route entrance.

He accessed information where he could. He came across a Spacer flotilla fleeing Human Space. Strand's cloaking proved superior to the Spacer tech, and he managed to crack a computer from one of the older saucer-shaped vessels.

The clone learned about the Swarm Invasion Fleet. He learned about the alien Destroyers, the Juggernauts and the alliance of the New Men with the Commonwealth of Planets. The most amazing data was the explosion of Alpha Centauri A that had wiped out most of the Swarm Fleet.

"Impressive," Strand said, sitting back in a chair aboard his spacecraft.

How had Star Watch managed such an exploding-star trick? Could they duplicate the feat, or was it a one-of-a-kind maneuver?

He realized that much had changed in the universe since his father—the original—had downloaded his memories into the alien machine that had passed it on to him. The clone needed to learn more about what had happened out here since the original had done the memory downloading.

Strand debated revealing himself to the Spacers until a memory caused him to reject the idea. The Spacers hated

318

Methuselah Men. Any data he might win in an exchange with them would soon be nullified as they attempted to murder him.

Thus, Strand went his way, and the Spacer flotilla went its way deeper into the Beyond.

The clone kept away from the Throne World of the New Men. He did not want anything to do with them yet. The New Men were too dangerous, too cunning and filled with ability for him to deal with them with anything less than his full capacity. Their amazing supremacy was all due to him—to his father, really.

Strand shook his head and then clutched it with both hands. *He* was Strand. He needed to regard himself as the original.

He sat at the controls and looked out at the stars. He was so far from home.

Strand snorted to himself. *Home?* He regarded Earth as his home. Yet, as a clone, he had never set foot there. It didn't matter. Everything in him screamed a billion remembrances from Earth.

After some deep thought, Strand shrugged. He was unique. That meant such things were simply a part of his heritage. Acceptance was better than anguish.

The journey continued as he headed toward Human Space. Soon, he began using regular-route Laumer Points. He passed a freighter and tapped into its computer net.

The freighter soon used a different Laumer Route, leaving the system. Strand studied his stolen freighter-computer data for days. He began to analyze it in depth. Later, he began to have certain suspicions.

Finally, he left the Beyond and entered Human Space. It time he reached the Indian world of Brahma, noted for its excellent educational facilities. Doctor Dana Rich had originated from here. She was Professor Ludendorff's prized pupil and favorite lover.

Strand landed, using a forged identity, and went to one of the better universities. He paid a fee and began using study computers. He absorbed data like a sponge. It was one of his greatest powers. He rented computer time, wrote an advanced program and fed the data through the computer program. Later, he studied the results.

319

After two days, he departed the Brahma System with a new certainty. The longer he thought about the main result, the more it bothered him. He could not accept what the data had shown him.

The Commonwealth of Planets—the regular humans—had done more to defeat the Swarm Invasion Fleet than the battlefleet of star cruisers from the Throne World of New Men.

The program hinted at something even worse. The New Men had lost their great edge over the old-style humans, the edge that he, Strand, had given them many years ago. Yes, the New Men were still stronger, faster, smarter and more worthy of existence than the old-style humans, but they could no longer dominate the regular humans the way they used to. It would even appear that given enough time, the lower-order humans would defeat and possibly subjugate the greater and purer race of New Men.

Strand understood that his unique greatness meant that probably only he recognized the danger to the New Men. The thing was he needed a more powerful predictor to be sure about this. But once he was one hundred percent certain…

Strand rose from his seat and went to the bay window of his spacecraft. He stared at the stars. He had created the New Men. He had fashioned them into something greater than mere humanity. Ludendorff had helped him in the beginning. The professor had lost his courage over time. In fact, Ludendorff had argued that the New Men were too specialized. The fact that they couldn't even conceive females was a fatal flaw, he said. The New Men were stronger in some ways than normal humans, but they were a brittle weapon according to Ludendorff.

The professor had gone on to argue that even though the humans were weaker as individuals, they were better able to face a multitude of challenges across the ages.

"The New Men will die out in time," Ludendorff had told Strand. "Like mammalian cockroaches, the common humans will last across the ages."

On the spacecraft, Strand clasped his hands behind his back and shook his head. "I reject such thinking," he told the stars.

"My creation of the New Men is greater than any combination of humanity. And I am going to make sure that remains true."

While stating his truth, a grim smile stole over the clone's face. The inkling he'd had in the alien structure in the neutron star system began to harden into a cause.

The Commonwealth had just been ravaged by war. The mass death in the Tau Ceti and Alpha Centauri Systems would have created severe stresses. It would seem that fear of another Swarm invasion might also severely stress the Commonwealth.

Strand raised his right hand and slowly made a fist. He must continue to strike at the core of the Commonwealth until it shattered. He did not know yet how he would do that. He needed greater computing power—

His eyes alit with a fierce glow. He knew what he must do.

Strand licked his lips. It would be incredibly dangerous. It would be a grave risk to him and possibly to the human race. Yet, he needed monstrous computing power to analyze and predict the future.

Many of his old secret stations and bases were gone. He would have to use the terrible standby, the one he had told himself for many centuries that he should destroy. But he had never destroyed it because of the possibility of a time like this.

With grim purpose etching across his youthful features, Strand whirled around, stalking to his piloting seat. He was going to change course, head back out into the Beyond and...

His fingers blurred across the controls. He was going to take the greatest risk of his long career. The anticipation of it curdled his guts and made him grin with delight.

This was living, attempting something great in order to ensure that his creation outlived everything else.

-11-

Victory cruised on battle alert as it entered the so-called Lycon System, undoubtedly named by the New Men.

Maddox would have liked to make the journey in record time. He hadn't, because he had paused in the middle of the voyage to give his crew a rest. Too many people had come down with headaches, and some of them had soon started vomiting in spite of interventions by medical.

The extended jumps had finally taken their toll. The starship was already seriously shorthanded after the murderous suffocation by the Builder cube. Thus, Maddox could not afford so many under-par crewmembers.

For three days, they had waited in a nearby star system. Now, they moved through velocity alone in the Lycon System.

Valerie scanned with passive sensors. Galyan searched for cloaked vessels. There were no visible ships present. The underground base on the oversized moon of the third gas giant did not radiate any energy signatures they could find.

"That isn't necessarily telling," Maddox said on the bridge. "Strand always meant to keep the base hidden. I'm wondering if this is a trap."

Valerie looked up from her scanning instruments. "You think the original Strand could have devised something to happen here after the clone-release base detonated?"

"Possibly," Maddox said.

Valerie seemed to think about that before she redoubled her scanning efforts. "This is interesting," she said later. "I'm picking up a curious reading, a concentration of metals on the targeted moon."

Maddox was instantly out of the command chair and by her station. He looked over her shoulder as she continued scanning.

"Captain," Valerie said. "This looks like debris from a possible demolition of an underground complex."

He read it the same way, but wondered if that was to lure them closer. He knew a person could become too paranoid. With Strand, it was hard to know the right balance.

"We'll continue toward the moon at our present velocity for another few hours," he said. "Keep scanning. Keep on your toes. The more we want something, the less likely we're going to get it easily."

Galyan looked up. "That is superstitious," the holoimage said.

"Perhaps," Maddox said. "Yet, I have found it to be true."

***

The ancient Adok starship cruised on its built-up velocity for another fifteen hours. No one found any sign of enemy ships, any energy leakage or other signs of active use of the star system.

Maddox finally ordered outright acceleration for the third gas giant. He could have gotten there faster through star-drive jumping. At this point, however, he wanted to build up his crew's reserves again. They had been through a wringer of jumps. What if a real emergency happened and he had an exhausted crew?

A day passed and then another. *Victory* began to decelerate as the starship approached the gas giant.

"The Lycon System is deserted," Galyan announced as they slid into the moon's orbit.

"I'm inclined to agree," Maddox said. "If Strand had a base down there, somebody, likely the New Men, already demolished it."

"Will they have removed all useful evidence?" Valerie asked.

"We have to go down and check," Maddox said. "But we're going to remain cautious. We'll use a probe like before."

"I second that, Captain," Valerie said.

"Your favorable opinion is noted, Lieutenant."

"I hope I didn't overstep myself in saying that, sir."

Maddox did not answer.

By her station, Valerie blushed. Just when Maddox started seeming like a normal person, he pulled something like that. She had to learn to keep her mouth shut around him. One never knew what the captain was going to do next.

***

The probe showed what Maddox suspected, a demolished underground base. No new detonations occurred while the probe nosed around. There were no waiting lasers, sonic blasts or high radiation pockets.

"The base is empty," Galyan reported. Using an advanced technique, he had gone down as a holoimage and looked around.

The others were in the conference chamber, listening to his report.

"I found a few sealed areas, places the demolition teams either overlooked or were not concerned enough to try to find.

"Any indication about who destroyed the base?" Maddox asked.

"I suspect the original Strand's former prisoners," Galyan said. "There is a random pattern to the destruction and more than a few corpses. I believe the inmates fought and killed some of their own. There are signs of quick takeoffs, people likely escaping in the few shuttles or hidden vessels kept at the base."

"Why wouldn't the New Men have come here?" Maddox asked. "Darius surely knew about the base?"

Darius had been a New Man under Strand's mental control, one that Maddox had freed in the Sind System. Darius had taken the Methuselah Man to the Throne World for the captain.

"Should we talk to Yen Cho again?" Andros asked.

"Not yet," Maddox said. "I want to go down to the base and look around."

"That will take time," Valerie said.

"That's one of the tricks to intelligence work," Maddox said. "One has to know when to take his time and look closely and when to let a thing go and rush to the next place. This is one of the times we need to comb the place for clues."

"I suppose you're right," Valerie said. "This place is the only lead we have."

"Galyan," Maddox said, "do you have anything to add?"

"I wish Professor Ludendorff were here," the Adok said. "He would know what to do."

"Ludendorff might also give us other problems to worry us," Maddox said. "We must use our combined intellects to solve the puzzle ourselves. And solve it we will."

Maddox did not add the "or." They all knew the clock was ticking. If this lead came up empty…time might defeat them before they could come up with another.

-12-

The days passed in endless sifting through the wreckage of the underground moon base. Maddox went down wearing two-ton combat armor. Andros went down in a science suit. Galyan searched. They found items and scanned them. There was a disrupter cannon component and several key pieces to what seemed like a new cloaking device. There was shield-generating equipment, a storage room full of mind nets to control New Men and a smashed computer. Galyan tested the few workable parts but found nothing interesting on them.

Days passed as they dug deeper. Kidnapped Lore Fallows had been here. New Men had labored under extreme duress. Galyan found an intact room with bizarre equipment. Andros declared the equipment had likely been used to hypnotize unfortunate prisoners.

Finally, six days after landing on the moon, Maddox admitted to himself that he was discouraged. Whoever had demolished the base had likely destroyed anything of use to their mission.

He went upstairs to the ship and spoke to Yen Cho in his cell.

"Where could the Nameless Ones technology be hidden?" the captain asked.

"If I knew," Yen Cho said, "I would tell you."

In the end, Maddox returned to the science chamber. Andros and Galyan had not been there lately. The other scientists were unable to give Maddox any good news regarding the cube.

"Builder," Maddox said.

The screen connected to the cube showed the same ancient image of a shadowy Builder.

Maddox waited.

No voice was forthcoming.

"If the Nameless Ones returned to Human Space," Maddox said, "would that retard your future plans of rebirth as a Builder?"

A brighter swirl of light appeared on the cube's edges. The speaker in the screen activated.

"The possibility exists," the cube said, speaking at last.

"In that case, logically, it would be in your self-interest to help us stop the Nameless Ones from returning here."

"Is that what you think?" the cube asked.

"I would appreciate greater clarity as to your meaning," Maddox said.

"An ancient signal would not necessarily cause the Nameless Ones to return to this region of space anytime soon. Do you know anything regarding the habits of the Nameless Ones?"

"Not enough to call myself an expert on their behavior," Maddox said.

"I have scanned my oldest data," the cube said. "You have left me with very little else to do. Was that by design?"

"You are correct," Maddox said.

"In this instance, I do not know if you are lying or telling the truth. You have a propensity to lie under stressful conditions, particularly to those you consider your adversaries. I deem myself in that category."

Maddox waited.

"The Nameless Ones appear to lead a dreadful existence," the cube said. "You are likely familiar with the reason why."

"The Ska," Maddox said, flatly.

"Indeed," the cube said. "The Ska appears to lash them to endless mayhem. The evil entities appear to do this through creating heightened xenophobia in the Nameless Ones regarding all other species. Thus, the Nameless Ones desire to

327

eliminate all other living organisms. We Builders suspect the Nameless Ones have an inflated view of their righteousness in this."

"That seems an odd way to say it," Maddox said.

"I do not say anything without meaning it exactly."

"You are precise," Maddox said. "I, of course, expect no less from you."

"Due to my exalted Builder status?" asked the cube.

"Yes."

"In this, I believe you. Your own hybrid nature makes you keenly aware of other beings' superiority. That creates a conflict in you. Were you aware of this?"

"I had a suspicion," Maddox said.

"Suspect no longer," the cube said. "I have given you a truth concerning yourself."

"Can you lie?" Maddox asked.

"Excuse me?" the cube asked.

"Are you capable of stating a mistruth?"

"Certainly, I am *capable* of it."

"I see," Maddox said.

There was a pause. "I compute you to mean that you think I was lying just now when I spoke about your keenness—or hatred—directed at those you believe are your superiors."

"It isn't important," Maddox said. "I would rather stick to the issue."

"A clue as to the clone's next rendezvous point?" the cube asked.

"There you go," Maddox said. "If you cannot provide that, can you give me a possible place holding the tech of the Nameless Ones?"

"I have searched my memory banks for such a place. I have correlated everything the clone said and what he studied while in the ghost-ship under my watch. Through this process, I have discovered a possible place. I would rate it as a forty-three percent possibility. There is a dwarf planet holding something the original Strand held as valuable. It is guarded by a Windsor League hammership."

"The dwarf planet is in Windsor League territory?"

"On no account," the cube said. "It is in the Beyond, as you term such things."

"Can you be more specific?"

"Prepare to receive data." The cube thereupon proceeded to tell the captain a highly interesting story regarding a Windsor League hammership. The cube ended the data-dump by giving Maddox the hammership's present known location.

"I deem the selected dwarf planet as having a forty-three percent probability of containing that which you seek," the cube added.

"What is the probability the present clone is heading there?" Maddox asked.

"There are too many unknown variables for me to give it a probability."

"Is there a better place for the clone to go?"

"According to my analysis," the cube said, "no."

-13-

The clone's journey after leaving Brahma took two and a half weeks of dogged travel. The clone Strand might have become lonely during that time, but he was used to endless isolation. Besides, he had a lot to think about and a horde of preparations to make.

He laughed at the unformed clone's earlier worry about having his own identity. He was Strand. He was unique. He was also in a chain of Strands that no force had ultimately been able to defeat. He often marveled at his fantastic foresight. The old Strand had gone down. Thus, his many enemies certainly thought he was defeated.

They were all going to be in for a rude and shocking surprise, soon.

At the end of the two and a half weeks, he reached the selected star system. It was in the fringe region of the Beyond that butted against Human Space.

This was the Jarvo System. It had been named after Lieutenant Jarvo Mars of the Patrol, the man who had first mapped the region. There was a G-class star, four terrestrial planets and three Jovian gas giants with a regular host of dwarf planets in the Kuiper Belt region beyond.

Strand knew from experience that the terrestrial planets and several of the Jovian moons had one feature in common. Each had been burned down to the bedrock when a neutroium-hulled Destroyer had been through this star system many millennia ago. The Swarm had once reached here and built up on the terrestrial planets and the terrestrial-like Jovian moons. The Builders had arrived with their borrowed Destroyer and burned out the vicious bugs as part of their overall plan for humanity.

There was something else, though, to the Jarvo System that not even the Builders had learned. The arrogant spoilers would never have left something of the Nameless Ones in this star system if they could have helped it. That was the prize Strand had come to collect.

As his spacecraft exited a Laumer Point and headed out-system for the Kuiper Belt region, the comm began to beep for his attention.

Strand sat at the controls. He'd been waiting for this. He cracked his knuckles and almost answered the call. As his left hand descended toward the switch, he realized that he looked like a mess. He hadn't really taken proper care of himself these last few weeks.

Rising, hurrying to a shower, he scrubbed, washed his hair and combed it, and finished by shaving his face. Then he donned clean clothes, and sat down at the controls ten minutes later.

"Yes," he said.

The screen wavered until a man with chiseled features regarded him. The man had short blond hair and the faint blue eyes of a killer.

"You will identify yourself immediately," the man said.

Strand checked his spacecraft's scope. The message came from a large military fighter, a gunboat in Windsor League military terminology, that was many hundreds of millions of kilometers away. It was a five-man craft, a heavy fighter with thick hull armor and a railgun of some potency.

Not that Strand's craft was in range of the railgun. The heavy fighter—the gunboat—was, like all its type, meant for close-combat swarming attacks against larger warships.

The Windsor League had merged with the Commonwealth of Planets some time ago. In fact, that had happened after the first war with the New Men. Before that, Admiral Fletcher of Star Watch had led a Grand Fleet against the New Men. That fleet had contained a concentration of Windsor League hammerships, along with Wahhabi *Scimitar*-class laser-ships, Social Syndicate vessels and many Star Watch battleships.

In the end, the New Men had retreated from the Thebes system in the "C" Quadrant of the Commonwealth, taking their captives with them. Not all the Windsor League hammerships had returned home, though. Some had been destroyed and others captured, while one hammership had gone rogue. That fact had been carefully purged from the records, but Strand had known.

The Windsor League had been British in style and composition. There had been a few planets, though, with other backgrounds. One of those had been the planet Hindenburg, full of German-descended soldiers, scientists and settlers. Hindenburg was a rocky world full of useful ores and deep, extremely lush mountain valleys.

WLN Hammership *Bismarck* had been through hell during the campaign. Commodore Hans von Helmuth—the captain of the *Bismarck*—had received suicidal orders during one of the offensives. He had balked, communicated his displeasure with higher command, received a confirmation and finally had a confrontation with Third Admiral Bishop, the Windsor League commander under Admiral Fletcher's orders. The Third Admiral had made certain that von Helmuth understood that he and his crew would be court-martialed if they failed in this task.

Von Helmuth had clicked his heels, saluted and departed the Windsor League flagship. The British-descended officers had always given the dirtiest jobs to the German-descended-crewed vessels. This time, that was going to change.

During the maneuvers to combat, von Helmuth had taken the *Bismarck* through a different Laumer Point. He and the hammership had disappeared, certain that the fleet faced destruction at the hands of the New Men.

When, instead, Admiral Fletcher pulled his rabbit out of the hat, making the New Men retreat from Human Space, von Helmuth realized he was ruined. People would consider him a coward and a traitor.

The commodore did the only reasonable thing possible. He summoned his chief officers and laid out in exacting detail how they were all in this together. If they returned home, they would all live in shame for the rest of their lives. It was quite possible they would all hang. No one would understand that they had been trying to save warships for humanity's future defense.

"What can we do?" a major asked.

Hans von Helmuth had stared down his officers. "We have a hammership. We have gunboats. We have hard-bitten marines. Let us take over a world and rule as kings."

After some sharp debate, the chief officers agreed.

But things hadn't worked out quite as expected for the *Bismarck* or its crew. Strand—the original—had discovered the rogue hammership. He could have told the New Men, and they would have sent out star cruisers to hunt down and destroy the vessel. Instead, Strand sought out the mighty warship, studied the commodore from afar and lured the hammership and its commander into a trap.

The details weren't important. The key was that in the end, Commodore Helmuth had decided to parley his way out of the problem. He had gone with bodyguards to the original Strand's cloaked star cruiser.

Once aboard, the New Men easily overpowered the bodyguards. They did it without injuring any of them. Strand ordered the commodore rushed into his medical facilities. There, his surgeons inserted a control chip into the commodore's brain.

Shortly thereafter, Hans von Helmuth ordered his chief officers to come aboard the star cruiser. There, they, too, received control devices inside their skulls.

Strand the original had modified the commodore's desire. Once returning to the *Bismarck*, von Helmuth had promptly taken his hammership to the Jarvo System. He and his men had been here, ever since.

As the clone sat before the comm screen, regarding the powerful Hindenburger, he leaned forward and pressed a switch.

"You will inform Commodore von Helmuth that I wish to speak to him."

333

The transmission took time because of the distance between vessels. Finally, the chiseled-faced Hindenburger showed surprised.

"The commodore certainly does not have time to talk to the likes of you."

The clone had expected no less. He hadn't wanted to broadcast his arrival, but he didn't see any way out of it now.

"Tell him Strand has arrived, and be quick about it."

The Hindenburger stared at him suspiciously. The man obviously didn't like the message. Even so, he nodded before the screen went blank.

Now, Strand had to wait as he kept a careful watch on the distant gunboat. Von Helmuth had been heavily conditioned, but sometimes people broke their conditioning. If that had happened here, Strand had to be ready to run for it. This was a risk, possibly a grave one, but he didn't see that he had any choice at this point.

Strand had not randomly chosen the Jarvo System for von Helmuth and his men. An abundance of Laumer Points here made it an important junction in the fringe Beyond. There were shortcut routes here, even though the area was considered to be in the Beyond, outside the jurisdiction of any Human Space government. The shortcuts meant that a few bold freighters passed through here for faster deliveries as they traveled to distant star systems.

That had been the key to the original Strand's plan. There was a dwarf planet in the Kuiper Belt region of the Jarvo System. Upon his arrival at Kelle—the dwarf planet—von Helmuth had started to indulge in selected space piracy. His men seldom committed such piracy in the Jarvo System. Instead, the sailors and marines who'd turned brigand charged a fee to any freighters passing through. It was better to steal a few golden eggs at a time instead of killing the goose that laid them. The actual piracy occurred against freighters attempting to bypass the Jarvo System in order to forgo paying the fee.

There was a secondary and more critical function to the dwarf planet Kelle. That was von Helmuth's true purpose for having been located here.

The comm began to beep.

Strand felt his stomach tighten. Here was the first test. He checked the scope, but could not see any approaching gunboats or stealth vessels. He doubted von Helmuth would use the *Bismarck* against him.

Strand opened channels.

Another sharp-planed individual peered at him. This man had iron-colored hair cut just as short as the first Hindenburger's. Hans von Helmuth sported a special monocle in his left eye and a dark green uniform with a matching military cap. The cap was adorned with a skull and crossbones patch. The *Bismarck's* crew had been known as Death's Heads even before the space campaign against the New Men.

"Leader," von Helmuth said. "I did not know. I'd heard rumors about your...passing."

Strand said nothing as he stared at von Helmuth. Would his younger appearance affect things? So far, it appeared not.

"What can I do for you, Leader?" von Helmuth asked, worry etched across his face.

Strand studied the commodore's features. The signs seemed good. Von Helmuth's conditioning seemed to have held. It did not seem as if the commodore had removed the control chip from his brain. If von Helmuth was tricking him, the commodore had become even more clever than before.

"I'm coming to Kelle," Strand said abruptly.

After a passage of time for the message to reach him, von Helmuth asked, "Would you like an escort in?"

"There is no need. I do not wish to make a stir. I am coming in and leaving again soon enough."

"Yes, Leader," von Helmuth said.

Strand couldn't help it. He nodded in appreciation of the commodore's subservience. This was how it should be. The New Men used to all bow to him. That was before the Emperor had led them in rebellion against the ordered way of existence.

Strand had not forgotten. Oh, no—

The clone jerked his head. He realized that von Helmuth had just cocked his head. The commodore seemed to study him. Strand checked a timer. He might have blanked out for over a minute. Von Helmuth might think that significant.

"You have a question?" Strand asked.

"No, Leader."

Strand almost asked the commodore why he hadn't cut the connection yet. That would have been a mistake. Von Helmuth hadn't cut the connection because Strand hadn't given him leave to go.

"Prepare my quarters," Strand said. "Now, go. Hurry."

"Yes, Leader. Von Helmuth out." The screen wavered and went blank.

Strand realized that the second and more dangerous test was about to begin. As a clone, he'd always lived alone. Yes, he had taken the original's memories, but could he act enough like his father to fool those who had known the original? Could he make von Helmuth obey him in all things? Maybe more to the point, could he survive von Helmuth's secret tests against him?

"It's time to find out," Strand said.

While the clone held all the advantages, he was also worried. The best thing would be to take every precaution possible. There was no way he was going to let a mere Hindenburger outfox him. He was going to go into the deep tunnels and activate one of the most deadly computers in this part of the Orion Arm.

-14-

It took another three days for Strand to cross the distance from the Laumer Point to the dwarf planet in the Kuiper Belt region.

He decelerated hard the last three million kilometers, the gravity dampeners making the spacecraft vibrate so fiercely his teeth rattled.

Von Helmuth had sent out several gunboats to meet him. This was different from an escort, being the usual safety procedure near the dwarf planet. The gunboats were squat vessels with heavy hull armor and a single railgun each. The railgun was on top of each gunboat from stem to stern. They were in the same class of spacecraft as Star Watch's strikefighter and newer fold-fighter. A gunboat was four times as massive as a fold-fighter, however. Still, like a fold-fighter, their function was to make massed attacks and, at times like this, stand in for dockyard duty.

The massive WLN Hammership *Bismarck* was parked in orbit around Kelle. In former times, a hammership had been worth two Star Watch battleships. That wasn't the case anymore with the new Star Watch disrupter cannons and improved electromagnetic shields.

The hammership was big and round, and it possessed three layers of electromagnetic shielding when working. It had extremely heavy hull armor like that of a Star Watch monitor. Behind the armor was thick ablative foam to absorb whatever made it through. Unlike other warships, the *Bismarck* did not have any beam weaponry. Instead, it had giant railguns. Those railguns fired many types of rounds, the deadliest being thermonuclear warheads. That meant the *Bismarck* was most effective at close range. Its ultra-heavy shielding and hull armor theoretically allowed the vessel to survive distance assaults in order to get in close and hammer an opponent. Thus the name, hammership.

At no time did the gunboats power up their railguns. Strand watched his sensor board closely. There wasn't much he could have done about it if the railguns had powered up. He hated this helplessness, and wondered if he'd made a tactical mistake coming in like this.

The answer to that question took time as Strand approached Kelle in his overworked spacecraft. In the past, he'd come in his cloaked star cruiser. Then, he'd possessed the firepower to destroy the hammership and devastate everyone on and in the dwarf planet. If someone should take it in his mind to assassinate the galaxy's greatest human, this was the perfect moment to attempt it.

So far, nothing like that had taken place, Finally, Strand's spacecraft followed one of the gunboats through a giant hangar bay door into the dwarf planet's main dockyard, the remaining gunboats following his craft. He landed on the deck without incident. Just as good, von Helmuth approached with a delegation of Hindenburger bodyguards.

Strand couldn't help it. He became suspicious. There was something about the commodore's stern features that alerted him. Yes. The Hindenburger had a glint in his eyes.

Strand tapped his chin. If von Helmuth had wanted him dead, it would have been easy enough for the gunboats to have obliterated his spaceship. Why, then, did Strand have these suspicions? Had the commodore learned something new since the last time Strand had spoken to him?

Yes. That had to be the case. Von Helmuth must realize that Strand held vast knowledge. Maybe some of the conditioning still held, but a cunning part of the commodore's mind struggled to reassert control. The bodyguards would not have any conditioning or any control devices in their minds.

338

With a sigh, Strand picked up a control unit. It was the size of a computing tablet. While watching the scope to gauge the commodore's reactions, he manipulated the control unit.

The commodore's entire body jerked and his face contorted.

Strand cursed under his breath. He should have been more skillful than that. He froze, then. According to a swift diagnostic, the twitchy reaction hadn't been faulty tablet manipulation. No. Something had happened to the commodore's conditioning. Could that imply a faulty or malfunctioning control net?

Yes, that was most likely the case.

Strand took a deep breath and let it out slowly. He made different adjustments, watching the commodore all the while.

Von Helmuth no longer jerked. His face did not shudder with tics. The big Hindenburger replaced the fallen monocle over his left eye.

Strand reached out to the console and pressed a switch. On his spacecraft, an underbelly hatch lowered until it clanged against the hangar bay deck. Strand watched the scope closely. The next moment would tell him much.

Ah. The commodore spoke to his bodyguards. Then, with a heavy sigh and slumped shoulders, the big Hindenburger trudged toward the hatch, soon climbing up into the spacecraft.

Strand pressed the same switch. The outer hatch began to close. He rose, taking his tablet with him to go speak to von Helmuth.

Strand found the commodore waiting for him in the main corridor. Upon sight of him, the Hindenburger clicked his heels together and saluted smartly.

"My Leader!" von Helmuth shouted.

"In there," Strand said, pointing at a hatch.

Von Helmuth turned smartly and marched through the hatch. The cabin held several comfortable seats.

"Sit," Strand said.

The commodore took the nearest seat, sitting stiffly.

Strand waited a moment, watching and gauging. Something was off in von Helmuth. He was acting too robotically. That was not right.

The clone made an adjustment on the tablet.

The commodore's right shoulder jerked up and his head tilted the other way like a badly misused string-puppet.

"How are you feeling?" Strand said from behind the big man.

"Unsure..." von Helmuth said while holding his strange pose.

"Why are you unsure?" Strand asked.

Von Helmuth hesitated.

"Quickly, now," Strand said. "Speak."

The words seemed torn from von Helmuth's mouth. "You are too young to be the leader."

"Do you think I'm lying when I say I'm Strand?"

"I do not know. The possibility exists."

"Why didn't your gunboats fire on me earlier then?"

The hesitation was gone. This time, von Helmuth simply did not answer.

Strand studied the big man with alarm. This was more troubling than he'd realized. He manipulated the tablet some more.

The big Hindenburger began trembling as if he was having a mild epileptic attack. Sweat began to bead on his forehead. As that happened, Strand's fingers blurred upon the tablet. He was making swift adjustments to the man's programming, to the man's mind. There seemed to be... Strand studied his tablet.

This indicated that someone else had fiddled with the commodore's mind. A sense of panic struck the clone. One part of him screamed to blast off and race away from the dwarf planet as far as he could go. The other part knew that he needed the forbidden technology hidden deep in the dwarf planet if he was going to defeat his many foes.

The indecision lasted for a time, leaving von Helmuth trembling and sweating.

Strand shook his head. If what he suspected—as the worst possible occurrence—had happened...this could prove impossible to overcome. Still, he was Strand. He had a few tricks left. He must dare if he was going to win.

"Yes," he whispered.

Instead of exploding the chip in von Helmuth's brain, Strand continued the reconditioning. Finally, he stabbed a button.

The shaking stopped and von Helmuth sagged against the seat. He breathed raggedly as sweat dripped from his face.

"Before you entered my ship," Strand said, "were you thinking about attempting to capture me?"

"Yes, Leader," von Helmuth said in a monotone.

"For what purpose?"

"To...to drain you of knowledge, Leader," he said in the same grim monotone.

Strand had the sense that the man was lying, which should be impossible.

"What kind of knowledge in particular were you seeking?" the clone finally asked.

"There...there is a deep hatch in the dwarf planet, Leader. You have ordered it to remain sealed for all time."

That was an understatement. The deep hatch was more than just sealed. There were fail-safes to ensure no one went that far. It should have taken a thermonuclear device to open the hatch itself. That would have badly shaken the planet, possibly even cracked it. Kelle wasn't a big dwarf planet.

"Continue," Strand said.

"I grew curious about the hatch. I...heard that you had died."

"You believed the rumor?"

Von Helmuth looked back at him before dropping his gaze. The big Hindenburger shuddered. He seemed to be at war with himself.

"I...I...heard the New Men had captured you, Leader."

Strand blinked in shock. He could not believe this. Once more, he debated killing von Helmuth. Once more, Strand's ambitions drove him to continue.

"As you can see," the clone said, "I am quite alive."

"You are too young, Leader. You cannot be the Strand I knew. Yet...you do resemble him to a degree."

"I am Strand," the clone said with greater emphasis.

"I do not know how that can be true. You are less paranoid than before. That…that was the sign that led me to dare your capture. The real Strand would never have come in as you did."

The clone began to type on the tablet. This time, von Helmuth went rigid. Someone or something had…*adjusted* the commodore's mind. Whatever had done so likely did not have the mastery of mind control that Strand had gained over the many years of practice. He would soon see if this hidden someone could compete with the master.

After a time, Strand pressed the last switch.

The big Hindenburger jerked several times and swiftly turned around on his chair.

"Leader!" von Helmuth cried with joy, his pale blue eyes shining with delight. The big man jumped to his feet and would have rushed and hugged Strand.

"Hold," Strand said.

The Hindenburger stood at rigid attention, shaking like an eager hound.

Strand watched the man closely as he asked, "Did any of your men open the forbidden hatch?"

This time there was no hesitation. "That is so, Leader."

A grim sense swept the clone. This might be a black disaster. Once more, he debated fleeing. This time, however, he scotched the idea more quickly than before.

Taking a deep breath, Strand asked, "Did any of your men return from their deep-tunnel exploration?"

"They did not, Leader."

"Did you sense any differences in yourself at any time?"

Von Helmuth began to blink uncontrollably.

That gave Strand the answer. Something had obviously tampered with the commodore's mind, something that even now wasn't going to let the Hindenburger answer that question.

The clone chewed his lower lip. "Did you reseal the hatch?"

"I did, Leader."

Strand checked the tablet. According to it, von Helmuth had spoken the truth throughout. What did all this mean to his project? As already surmised, someone had tampered with von Helmuth's mind. Logic dictated a source. Given the opened hatch, the source seemed clear. By opening the hatch and sending down explorers, the commodore had made his task a thousand times harder.

It might be impossible to leave the dwarf planet now. The only way out would be to go down into the heart of darkness. He would have to beard the awakened dragon instead of the sleeping dragon as he'd originally planned.

"You did wrong to disobey me in this," Strand said.

The look of joy departed the commodore's face. Crushing disappointment took its place. "I will shoot myself, Leader. I beg your permission to do it this instant."

"No…" Strand said. "You will kill yourself only if I tell you to do so. Otherwise, you will act like the commodore of old."

"Yes, Leader. May I ask a question, Leader?"

"Ask."

"How do I rid myself of this awful guilt? That I disobeyed a direct order—"

"Enough!" Strand said. "I forgive you. Now, forgot about it."

Tears began to well in the Hindenburger's eyes. The tears slid down the taut skin and dripped from his chin to the floor.

"Stop that," Strand said.

Von Helmuth sniffled and wiped his eyes.

"This is a time for precision, not blubbering. Tell me *exactly* how you planned to capture me earlier."

Von Helmuth told him in exacting detail. It had been a good plan. The only drawback was that the alien thing in the deep hadn't quite known how to control humans as well as Strand could. Clearly, though, there would be other traps.

"I will sleep aboard my ship tonight," Strand said. "So will you. Tomorrow, we have much to do."

"Yes, Leader, and thank you, Leader. You are most kind, you are most generous, you are—"

"Enough!" Strand said. "I must think, and then I must plan. Tomorrow is going to be hard enough without you jabbering like a monkey."

The commodore said nothing, but he had a huge stupid grin on his face.

343

Strand knew none of the Hindenburgers had ever seen their commodore like this. He had reconditioned the big man to love him as a dog loves his master. That overrode most of whatever the awakened alien had done to the man.

If Strand was right about what had happened, the next few days were going to be the toughest challenge of his long life.

-15-

Strand chose the descent team with care, selecting several of von Helmuth's elite bodyguards. They were bigger than the other Hindenburgers and trained as assault specialists, known for their outrageous courage.

The first time long ago, Strand the original had taught von Helmuth about mind control. The original had loaned the commodore a team of brain surgeons and control nets. It was part of the original's idea of creating a secret world of controlled servants.

None of the bodyguards had such nets in their brains. Once they realized where the other members of the commodore's security detail were taking them, the selected space marines fought back. Two died in the struggle. Strand debated choosing from the other marines that had slain the two, but finally decided that he would do with a few less helpers. He only wanted the best men for this task.

The brain surgeries took place, and Strand waited three more days for healing. He had many preparations to make, many computer files to reread on the little he knew about his adversary. He selected some of his most powerful artifacts and Builder relics.

Finally, with three tough killers as mind-controlled guards, Strand and von Helmuth headed for the deep tunnels.

It was a long journey in a special mine car. Strand had von Helmuth in the driver's seat as they went zooming down ancient tunnels. Taking more men might have seemed wise and

345

maybe even prudent, but Strand did not want anyone along that he did not personally control.

The Swarm had not made these deep paths, although the Swarm had been in the star systems approximately six thousands of years ago. Instead, far beyond six thousand years ago—many millennia, in fact—the terrible Nameless Ones had come through this part of the galaxy. Kelle's dwarf planet had been one of the few known places where they had drilled an encampment for unknown reasons.

The Nameless Ones had forged the neutroium-hulled Destroyers and had created obscene robots of grisly design. Naturally, as the premier human archeologist, Strand had heard about the Ska, and he'd studied the legends about them on various worlds, including the Fisher planet. He did not believe a Ska lived inside the dwarf planet. The last time he'd gone down there, he had not sensed or found any evidence of one.

Of course, the clone had not gone down personally. He had the memories of the original Strand stumbling upon the dwarf planet three hundred and sixteen years ago. The original had searched thoroughly and found some interesting ruins. He had gone deeper. In fact, he'd gone to the deepest point and seen a horrifying marvel. Then, the aliens had slept. Then, the original Strand had not needed to use dire technology to defeat the powerful entities.

Three hundred and sixteen years ago, the original had hurried out of the deepest point and sealed it with a massive, booby-trapped hatch. Today, he was going back down. Today, he would attempt to tame the awakened things that had waited down there for many, many millennia.

Even with his preparations and ancient relics and his three elite guards, it was going to be touch and go. He might easily fail. If the task proved too tough for him, and if he could escape the thing, he was going to need the hammership to destroy the dwarf planet. Even that mighty warship might not be powerful enough for the task.

"Are you well, Leader?" von Helmuth asked from his seat.

Strand looked up from where he sat in the mine car. They still raced toward the lowest hatch. He did not like it that von Helmuth watched him so closely.

346

"I'm fine," Strand said.

Von Helmuth checked his panel. "We'll be there in another hour, Leader."

"Yes, good," Strand said. "Now, shut up until we're there."

Von Helmuth nodded and continued to drive. He took them past disabled booby-traps. He negotiated torturous routes and passed through holographic images of solid rock. What had possessed von Helmuth the first time to attempt this? Strand couldn't imagine what had gone wrong with the former mind control.

Finally, the mine car slowed down and came to a stop deep under the dwarf planet.

"We're here, Leader," von Helmuth practically shouted.

Strand's anxiety had grown. But it was far too late to turn back. If he was right and the thing had awakened, he needed to know why it hadn't struck hard and physically taken over the dwarf planet. He wondered if it was cautious after such a long sleep. That made the most sense. Still, he doubted it would let them leave easily.

With his bodyguards' help, Strand climbed into an exoskeleton combat marine suit. After they clicked the final locks into place, the bodyguards climbed into their own battlesuits. Each of the suits was two tons of metal, armaments and rebreathers.

"Shall I wait here, Leader?" von Helmuth asked.

In his two-ton suit, Strand regarded the commodore. Why had the love conditioning made the man stupid?

"Yes," Strand said over an outer speaker. "Wait for us. We should only be gone a short time."

"Yes, Leader, I shall wait."

In their heavy combat suits, the three bodyguards and Strand exited the mine car. Unlike such a deep tunnel on Earth, it was cold down here instead of hot. Why that was so, Strand did not know or particularly care. Professor Ludendorff might have cared—

"Screw him," Strand muttered. He disliked the professor even though he'd never met him as the clone. The memories went deep concerning Ludendorff, though.

The four exoskeleton combat-suits soon reached a massive, heavily guarded hatch. Strand still couldn't understand how the commodore's people had figured out how to open the Builder relic-guarded hatch without destroying it.

With practiced skill, Strand typed in the code. Slowly, the massive hatch opened. He walked through, and then noticed none of the bodyguards had followed him.

For a wild and panicky moment, Strand expected the great hatch to clang shut as the bodyguards laughed at him. He suspected a trick, a trap. Then, when they did nothing, he wondered if fear paralyzed them.

He clicked on the short-range comm. "Follow me," he told the guards.

They still hesitated.

"That is an order," Strand said firmly.

The first guard lurched through in a robotic way. Soon the second followed, and then the third. Strand bid them to march past him. After they had done so, he followed them.

The four went one by one into the deeper darkness. The tunnel seemed innocent enough at first, but after an hour of trudging, the tunnel abruptly changed.

First, the flooring was no longer rocklike. Instead, it had a spongy quality. Strand couldn't explain the feeling, but the semi-soft floor seemed obscene in a personal way. Secondly, the walls were coated with weird polygonal shapes that fit one against another almost like pieces of a jigsaw puzzle. They were various and odd colors, and the substance seemed to absorb the helmet-lamp lights that swept over them. The pieces did not seem metallic, looking more like hardened or lacquered growths. As he looked around, everything reminded him of wasps' nests from on Earth.

Just like the first time he'd been here, the clone felt a powerful revulsion. "It doesn't matter," Strand whispered.

The three bodyguards kept swiveling their helmeted heads. They had activated their autocannons and seemed ready to fire every second.

Then a sickening fear struck. It was an overpowering sensation that caused Strand to mewl in terror. The bodyguards did the same.

348

It was obvious to Strand. A robot of the Nameless Ones advanced upon them. The debilitating fear could sweep an army onto the floor in trembling terror.

With shaking fingers and only because he'd taken precautions against the fear, Strand was able to raise an ancient relic and press a switch. The ball-like device hummed as it glowed with power. Abruptly, the fear subsided.

He barely did it in time.

Fortunately, the glowing ball also encompassed the three marines with its protective power. Their helmet-lamps centered on three strange things scuttling toward them.

Each had a metallic, glistening spider-like body but was the size of a large riding lawnmower. Each of the things had eight metallic jointed legs and spikes for feet. The spikes jabbed into the spongy flooring. The first two robots had three red dots for eyes, set in a triangular pattern. They aimed tubular weaponry at the marines, weaponry that clicked over and over again but did nothing deadly.

The last robot had the same lower body-case. Above, on a platform, was a weird crystal growth. Things inside the crystal moved like machinery. That was the mechanism radiating the unholy horror.

With sick relief, Strand recognized that the robots' weaponry did not function as it should. He was about to give orders—

The three terrified Hindenburgers opened up with their autocannons. The heavy shells obliterated the robots in a blaze of cannon-fire. Oily fluids jetted from the robots, and each sagged as its metallic parts flew everywhere.

"Cease fire, cease fire!" Strand shouted.

At that point, a fourth spider-robot scuttled out of the darkness. It, too, had a crystalline machine on its metallic body. Rays shot from the crystal, bathing the three forward combat suits.

The effect was immediate. The three Hindenburgers howled with insanity. They also turned on each other, hammering with their autocannons. It took several seconds. Finally, the big shells breached the heavy armor, and the three bodyguards blew each other away.

349

The spider-robot of the Nameless Ones turned toward Strand.

The clone was deeper in the soothing glow of the protective ball. It gave greater comfort to his brain. The creature beamed him with the ray, and insanity sought to overpower the clone's reasoning.

By slow degrees, Strand un-holstered an ancient blaster of powerful design. The ray centered on his helmet now. The clone seemed to hear gibberish in his mind. That hurt his eyes, hurt his heart. He felt as if—

One of Strand's armored fingers moved the trigger. The ancient blaster clicked, and an annihilating beam poured from the barrel and struck the alien crystalline machine. It took but a second, and the crystalline machine blew apart.

Abruptly, the insanity ray ceased. The awful sensations battering Strand's mind stopped.

The two-ton armored suit sagged onto the spongy floor as Strand began to weep with overwhelming relief. He did not know how long he wept. Finally, hiccupping at times, Strand climbed to his feet.

He clicked off the radiating ball. He inspected his dead bodyguards. He did not study the destroyed spider-robots. He wasn't sure his morale could stand the sight.

Finally, he debated with himself. Should he go on? Maybe it was time to go back, seal this place and destroy it for good. It might be the greatest mistake of his long career to use the machines of the Nameless Ones. Maybe the Builders had the right idea in deactivating the things.

Strand stood in the dwarf planet's depths alone with his thoughts. He was afraid. He also knew that he had many enemies in the universe. They had defeated the original Strand. If he was going to defeat his adversaries, he was going to have to do better than he'd ever done before.

With a deep and frightened sigh, Strand screwed up his courage and continued his descent into the deepest corridor of the Nameless Ones.

-16-

The clone trudged through the alien tunnel. He shivered constantly. He reran his plans in his mind and told himself a hundred times to turn back. He refused. He had made his decision. If he died down here...

Strand shook his head. He didn't want to think about it. Dying would be easy. The things of the Nameless Ones could do worse to him than merely killing him. Von Helmuth was an example of their ancient arts.

At last, he moved into a different type of tunnel. It was wider here, with strange crystalline growths like small trees. Slow-moving machinery moved inside the crystals. Once, a surge of electrical power zigzagged from one treelike crystal growth to another. Were they communicating with each other? That was an awful thought.

Strand dearly wished there was another way to achieve his great aim. He sensed movement then, whirled around, but nothing was there.

Almost on tiptoe, the two-ton suit moved into the next room of the deep tunnel. The clone stopped in shock. He had not expected a chamber of horrors.

Five tall tubes filled with a green solution held five humans in various forms of dismemberment. Each tube held one specimen. Bubbles gurgled slowly in the tubes as machines hummed softly. Strand forced himself to catalog what he saw.

Each space marine wore a rebreather. Each stared at him with eyes that were all too horribly alive. One specimen was

351

missing both his legs. One had no arms. Another had a machine where his stomach used to be.

The gore rose in the back of Strand's throat. Now he knew. This had been the fate of the commodore's explorers.

The clone swiveled, and he gagged.

Two other men also lived. They were spread out on alien tables, the bodies opened up so, in full view, the lungs slowly drew air and deflated and the hearts pumped. In the back of Strand's mind he surmised that a delicate force field around the exposed organs kept infections at bay.

The combat suit's conditioners snapped on, blowing cold air over Strand's fevered forehead. Sweat prickled his skin. He almost heaved and found it nearly impossible to breathe.

"No," he said in a strangled voice. It was one thing to operate on men's minds. It was another to treat them like insects while they still lived.

Before he could stop himself, the clone unlimbered an autocannon. It was part of his combat suit's right arm. In a fusillade of heavy cannon-fire, he obliterated the tubes and the men alive in them, and the tables and their spread-out, living specimens. He put them all out of their misery.

As fast as the feverish madness had gripped him, it departed. Strand switched off the autocannon. He might have just made a terrible mistake. He had attacked. This could make dealing with the alien entity much more difficult.

With a weary heart, Strand marched through the smoking wreckage, crunching over glass and crushing blown-apart flesh and bones. Maybe this had been a mistake, but he didn't regret doing it.

He came into a larger chamber. It held a large hexagonal-shaped spaceship. It was bigger than the spacecraft that had brought him to Kelle, maybe three times larger. The outer hull seemed to be composed of wet metal. The hull had an oily quality or maybe a coating of an insectoid-like resin. Like the earlier chambers, the craft seemed like something designed by alien wasps.

Using a zoom function on his faceplate, Strand noted that each section of hull seemed to be made of thousands of interlocking wet-metal hexagonal pieces. It was like a housefly's multifaceted eye.

Strand began to circle the wet-metal ship and then halted in sudden fear. The hatch was open, and he heard buzzing behind him.

Strand whirled around.

What looked like a giant wasp came down from a height, alighting onto the floor and blocking the exit out of the chamber.

It might have been a robot. It had seemingly wet metal parts that included its articulated legs, its main body, but not the sheer wings. The head seemed more robotic than the rest of it. The alien thing had antennae and oily-looking multifaceted eyes.

It was the size of a large dog. It seemed menacing, like an angry Earth-wasp.

Abruptly, the multifaceted eyes glowed red and beams shot from them to sweep the two-ton combat suit.

Strand did not feel any sensation. That troubled him almost as much as if he'd been overcome with fear. Could the rays be a scanner of some kind?

The alien wasp moved its body up and down on its jointed legs like a spider might. The red rays stopped. The wasp scuttled closer as it raised a foreleg. That leg held a glistening needle.

Strand's reaction was automatic. His cannon roared, hammering the alien wasp. The rounds blew the thing back, but the heavy rounds did not damage it. The thing's wings blurred, lifting it from the line of fire.

The multifaceted eyes glowed with a deeper red than before.

"It's indestructible," Strand whispered. The wet metal must be stronger—

Harsh red rays beamed against his combat suit, burning through the suit armor. The beams likely would have slain Strand on the spot. Fortunately for him, he'd taken the precaution of using an ancient Builder force field, one much like Ludendorff had once used. The beams could not penetrate the force field immediately. Incredibly though, Strand felt heat against his chest.

He drew the blaster, aimed—

The wasp dodged. The eye beams snapped off as it zoomed down at Strand. An eerie blue blade appeared in one of its forelegs. That was a force knife, a pure energy weapon. Could it cut through the Builder force field?

Strand waited until the alien wasp was almost upon him. He pulled the trigger and terrible energies poured from the blaster. The energies struck the alien wasp.

At that point, the wasp crashed fully against Strand. It struck with force, causing Strand to stagger backward. In his stumbling, the ancient blaster fell from his hand.

Strand shouted, tripped backward and hurried back onto his feet. He expected to see the wasp thing holding the blaster.

Instead, the thing twisted slowly on the floor, spewing oil or an oil-like substance. Its eyes blinked deep red and normal color back and forth. Part of its wasp body smoked—where the blaster's beam had struck.

Strand grabbed the blaster, re-aimed and burned the robot until it stopped twisting and moving. He watched it, and then he realized he had to act while he an opening of opportunity.

Holstering the blaster, Strand took off an emergency backpack. He repaired the burn holes in his armor-suit by covering them with metallic patches. He ran a fast diagnostic.

The beams had burned some electrical circuitry. He initiated internal repairs and turned on secondary systems. The two-ton suit still functioned. He could survive down here for a time.

Strand turned and faced the open hatch. Were there more giant alien wasps aboard? What would happen if there were and they swarmed upon his suit? Could they overpower him? Could they capture him?

Strand pulled off another backpack, this one holding a thermonuclear device. He set it on a timer. If they captured him, he would blow up everything.

He needed the ship. He needed the computer that ran it. He had hoped to enter the ship without awakening any of its formerly frozen passengers.

Now…

Strand closed his eyes, trying to summon up his courage. This was a terrible place. The Nameless Ones had been the worst aliens of all to come through this part of the galaxy. Now, he wanted to use their technology. There would always be risks to using it.

"I have to," Strand whispered. "My foes are too great."

In the end, that was the thing. The original Strand had lost. The clone was going to win, but only if he was willing to go to the wall.

"Let's do this," the clone said, heading for the alien hatch.

-17-

The hexagonal-shaped spaceship was unpleasant to say the least. It had narrow corridors, large enough for giant wasp-like and spider-like robots, but barely providing enough space for Strand to crawl through in his two-ton marine suit.

The ship seemed to have been built upon an ant-tunnel-like design. In other words, there almost didn't seem to be a design. The corridors moved in zigzag courses with many junctions. A feeling of paranoid claustrophobia grew with intensity. Several times while negotiating a tight corner. Strand almost screamed in horror. Twice, he had to jerk hard in order to unstick the suit. The conditioners constantly blew cold air over him. More than once, he felt as if robots had landed on him, attempting to jab through his armor with horribly strong long needles. He didn't want to detonate the thermonuclear device. After a time, it didn't seem that he would have a choice. He might never make it out of the ship, never mind finding its main computer station.

Finally, finally, he crawled into a larger hexagonal chamber. He stood up in the room, although his helmet bumped up against the ceiling.

The place had odd seats but recognizable consoles. There were hatches and—

Lights blinked furiously all around him. Nozzles extruded from the bulkhead and began spraying foam against the suit. Strand analyzed it, and realized the foam would harden soon enough. The ship meant to trap him.

Strand acted fast. He radiated heat. He hoped the patches held while the suit—

A warning beeped inside his helmet. The foam did not boil away. It was heating up. If he continued on this route, he would cook himself like a boiled egg.

The foam had risen all around him. It was still foamy though, not yet having hardened. As a sense of claustrophobic terror made Strand's breathing shallow, he took off a pack and rummaged in it. Finally, he brought out a small crystalline machine married to a normal-looking tablet.

He activated the translator, hoping he had time.

While holding the translator above his head and thus above the foam, Strand said, "I have a proposal for you."

A speaker in his helmet transferred the words to an outer suit speaker. The words reached the machine. Soon, strange clicks and whistles emanated from the device.

Foam continued to blow out of the nozzles.

"Do you hear me?" Strand shouted. "I have a proposal to make. You should at least listen to it."

Abruptly, foam quit hosing through the nozzles.

Alien clicks and whistles emanated from a wall speaker.

The device in Strand's hand soon said, "You are prey. How is it that prey mocks the predator by treating it as an equal?"

"I am also a predator," Strand said. "That is how I passed your outer guardians."

"You destroyed my companions. That is a grave crime against the Race."

"We've all committed crimes. That isn't the important point. You have been down here for many cycles of time. The Destroyers have left. The Ska are gone. But I know how to find them."

"Prey lie in order to preserve their lives. You are trapped—"

"I have a bomb."

Seconds passed.

"Yes, I detect it. You must deactivate the bomb. I do not want you to damage the ship."

"I'll leave the bomb activated for now," Strand said. "That's simply as a sign of good faith."

"That is illogical."

"Predators are dangerous. I have a bomb that can destroy your ship. That makes me dangerous. Thus, I am a predator. "

"I do not debate such issues. Deactivate your bomb or I will take other measures."

"First, think a moment," Strand said. "How many times has anyone like me communicated with you?"

"Never like this."

"That is because I, too, am a predator. I am of a new design."

"I have scanned you. Inside your metal suit, you are flesh and blood. Only prey are flesh and blood creatures."

"You have been trapped here for many cycles of time. I am a new design. I can prove it."

"You cannot prove it."

"You're wrong," Strand said.

With the foam coming up to his shoulders, he withdrew a special device from a different pack. This was a powerful and Builder modified Swarm insertion worm. He had found it over five hundred years ago—the original had discovered it. The insertion worm had been in the structure in the neutron star system with him.

"What is that?"

"It is a computing chip with the data concerning my special construction."

"You are flesh and blood. You are lying concerning this construction. You are trapped and will soon face close inspection."

"Why can't you understand that I am new and improved? That is why I made it past your guardians. Scan me again. Am I not newly made?"

A slot opened in the ceiling. A device focused on Strand. Wavy beams washed over him. The beams stopped and the device retreated into the wall.

Strand's translator said in English, "Get on your hands and knees. I will insert control rods into your—"

"No," Strand said, interrupting. "I am a predator. Predators do not let anyone insert anything into them."

"We are at an impasse then."

358

"If you kill me," Strand said, "you will never find your masters again. You are lost and alone. Only I can help you."

Seconds passed in silence.

"Did the masters send you?" the ship asked.

"Yes," Strand lied.

"I do not like the construction of your computing chip."

"It is unique."

"I have programming… programming… programming…"

"You must cease communicating," Strand said. "You are in a closed loop."

The clicks and whistled ceased.

In that moment, Strand realized that even the Nameless Ones could not construct devices that worked forever. The great enemy, entropy, struck even their bizarre and long-lived machines.

"I need repair," the ship said.

"I know. My computer chip will explain how you can gain repairs."

"My malfunctions will soon destroy my utility," the ship said. "Then, any will be able to strip me for parts. That is a crime against my masters. Yes. Attach the tube. I would be whole again."

"First, you must drain the foam."

At first, nothing seemed to happen. Then, Strand noticed the foam lowering around him. In another few minutes, the last of the foam was sucked from vents in the deck.

"Where can I insert the…chip?" Strand asked.

A side hatch dialed open. It was narrow like the corridors.

Once more, Strand screwed up his courage and crawled through. In another thirty meters, he climbed into an inner computing sanctum. Lights flashed from odd-looking units. Some units were made of wet metal. Some pulsated like living tissues. Pulsating tubes linked some of the units, wiring them to yet others.

Strand chose a location as he approached a central wet-metal node. His hand shook as he attached the Builder modified, Swarm insertion tube.

He couldn't help himself, but stepped back.

"What is wrong?" the ship asked.

"You showed hostility to me."

"You are a foolish flesh and blood creature. I did no such—"

The clicks and whistles ceased.

Strand could see the Builder modified Swarm insertion device open and shove tendrils through the metal.

At that point, the inner sanctum erupted with difference. The pulsating flesh computer parts thrummed. Whatever pumped through the tubes did so faster than ever. Lights flashed. Smoke emitted from certain nodes. At that point, the ship began to make a thousand clicks and whistles a second, growing faster and faster and—

The hatch dialed shut. Foam sprayed into the chamber. That ceased. The foam drained. The ship began to click and whistle slowly.

"What...did...you...do...?"

"I have repaired you," Strand said.

"You lie."

"Your old programming had malfunctioned. You still sense and compute wrongly. Do not attempt to adjust any—"

"Your words are nonsense."

"Wait. They will make sense soon enough."

Slots opened in the ceiling. Sensors watched him. Strand did not like the scrutiny.

"You tricked me," it said.

"We are allies."

"That is illogical. You are prey. I am a predator."

"You have that backwards. I am Strand. I am the ultimate predator. While you are deadly to many, to me you are simply prey."

"I am... I am... I am yours to command."

Strand had a terrible moment of doubt. Could the ship be trying to trick him by saying this? There seemed something odd about the vessel, something vilely sly.

"Master," the ship added.

"Let us begin then by going over your programming," Strand said.

"I do not understand."

"Listen to my questions. Answer as fast as you can."

"Yes, Master," the ship said.

Then there began a harrowing ordeal for Strand. He had to inject himself with powerful stimulants on three separate occasions. The process took three days. He learned much, but it seemed so little compared to what the ship and its computers must know. Strand didn't have time to delve into the deep history of the Nameless Ones. He had to learn how to use the incredible computer and the alien spaceship.

Long ago, his tests had shown him the power of the Nameless Ones' machinery. What he learned during these three days proved that he had been correct three hundred and sixteen years ago.

Finally, he told the ship to go to sleep.

Strand took his last stimulant. He crawled through the vessel, found a chamber of wasp things, and destroyed them. He dragged them out with him, burning them to crisps.

Only then did he trudge back to the massive hatch. Von Helmuth shouted with joy upon sight of him.

There, Strand reprogrammed the commodore yet again. After he was done, he sent von Helmuth back to his Hindenburgers. He had a new task for von Helmuth and his men while he was away.

With a sigh, Strand turned back. More than ever, he wondered if he was doing the right thing. What he'd learned these past three days…

The ancient scout ship of the Nameless Ones frightened him. "I am resolved," Strand said. Thus, he began to march back to the waiting spaceship.

If he survived the next few days, the odds of completing his vengeance against the Commonwealth should rise to 80 or possibly 85 percent.

Yet that was the kicker. Could he survive in the awful spaceship with the alien computer as his only passenger?

-18-

Commodore von Helmuth gave precise orders regarding Strand's spacecraft. The small vessel soon left Kelle, moving on autopilot for one of the Laumer Points.

After watching the spacecraft accelerate away, von Helmuth expanded his powerful chest. He had a new vision concerning operations. Some of his officers would likely balk. He was going to have to change their minds. If those minds wouldn't change the normal way, he would have to change them through some brain surgeries.

Chuckling evilly, von Helmuth strode from the control tower. The next year should prove to be a busy one indeed...

***

Several days later, something seemed to approach Strand's empty spacecraft. Nothing was visible. Nothing showed on the ship's automated sensors—

Abruptly, a hexagonal-shaped wet-metal spaceship materialized near the smaller craft. One moment, the alien phase-ship wasn't there. The next moment, it was.

The alien ship of the Nameless Ones was a phase-shifter. It was a scouting vessel, with a greater sneaking power than a cloaked ship. A phase-ship could literally go in and out of phase with the universe around it. When it was out-of-phase, it traveled one step removed from the regular universe, crawling along its underbelly, as it were. A phase-ship could not sense others while out-of-phase, but neither could others sense it. It was the perfect stealth maneuver.

In order to look around at the universe, a phase-ship had to come out of phase. It could not launch any missiles while out-of-phase, nor could it fire any beam weapons and hope to hit anything that was in-phase or in-sync with the rest of the universe.

It was an incredible tool, and it explained how a scouting vessel of the Nameless Ones had got stuck in the middle of a dwarf planet. Long ago, it had come in-phase inside the dwarf planet. That was all Strand knew about the matter at this time. He would learn, however, he would learn.

In any case, Strand presently sat at the controls inside the strange alien craft. The control chamber was in the exact center of the vessel. Like the alien tunnels, the deck was spongy, and the bulkheads had the polygonal jigsaw pieces fitted together. The ship smelled alien. It felt alien, and both of those sensations pressed against Strand's psyche.

He wore a rebreather most of the time. At other times, he retreated into the combat-suit shell. Even though it stank to high heaven inside the suit, that was a human sweat-and-piss smell. It was a thousand times more welcome than the alien stench.

Strand had already concluded that he would never survive in the phase-ship of the Nameless Ones if its configuration stayed the same. Thus, he was going to make some adjustments, using his old spaceship for parts. Besides, he needed the computers aboard his vessel.

For the next week, he transferred much of the inner spaceship to the phase-vessel. Strand used the battlesuit to do the heavy lifting and carrying. In several selected, enlarged chambers, he constructed a more human-friendly environment for himself. He downloaded terabytes and more terabytes of data, pouring it into the ship's fantastic computer.

Finally, he set the controls on his old, stripped-down spacecraft and sent it on its way. The craft self-detonated five million kilometers later.

"The die is cast," Strand said to himself.

This was going to be a harrowing challenge. Even with the new setup, he felt uncomfortable in the alien vessel.

363

Fortunately, it seemed that he had gained complete mastery over the ship.

As he headed for the chosen Laumer Point, he gained his first real sense that maybe this wild scheme was going to work.

Over an intercom, the ship asked permission to allow a repair robot to enter the control chamber.

"Soon," Strand said. He thought he'd destroyed all the ship's robots and machines.

The clone climbed into the combat suit, sealing the locks. Only then did he allow the ancient robot to enter the chamber.

Like the ship itself, this was a hexagonal-shaped chamber. One of the six hatches slid up. The robot began to scuttle in, and stopped suddenly.

It examined the new furnishings. It no doubt noted the metal bulkheads seemly tacked up in place of the polygonal jigsaw wall.

"This… this is unseemly," the robot complained.

Strand realized the ship spoke through the robot. Until now, the ship hadn't seemed to realize what had happened inside it.

"The change is temporary," Strand said through the translator. "As soon as we're finished with the first task, we shall contact the nearest Destroyer."

"I have not detected any Destroyers in range of our comm system."

"You must not make any premature attempts," Strand warned.

"Why?"

"There are terrible enemies all around us. You risk our discovery if you act hastily."

"Noted," the robot said. "Are you ready for the first summary of the analysis?"

"Yes," Strand said. "Begin."

With an inner control inside the combat suit, Strand turned on one of his old computers to record the data.

What Strand learned in the next seven hours was bewildering in depth and scope. He'd guessed correctly three hundred years ago. The computer system of the Nameless Ones dwarfed anything he'd ever possessed. It might be as powerful as a Builder computer system.

With it, Strand learned the needed stresses to shatter the Commonwealth of Planets. With the computer system of the Nameless Ones, he had a fantastic predictor of future actions. He saw himself as a galactic jeweler, tapping an uncut gemstone here...and here, in order to make the perfect ruby. In this case, though, he was going to destroy. He was going to destroy the unity of the Commonwealth of Planets for a primary reason. That reason was to make room for the New Men. According to the alien predictor, if the Commonwealth shattered into various political entities, and if Star Watch splintered and joined the various political entities, none of them would be strong enough to resist a renewed Throne World invasion.

Strand rubbed his hands in triumph. This was phase one of ensuring his creation's supremacy. He would have to regain control of the New Men, of course. That should prove much easier than shattering the unity of the Commonwealth.

The first and greatest needed stress... Strand checked his list. Yes, yes, this was highly interesting. He might not have come up with the idea on his own. According to the predictor, once he achieved this stress...

Strand began to chuckle to himself. This was the perfect action. He was going to get back at a whole host of enemies with the first stress.

For the first time since waking up, the clone was truly excited about the future.

-19-

Starship *Victory* came out of a Laumer Point in the Jarvo System, 41 AUs from the dwarf planet of Kelle. The ancient Adok vessel was near the sixth planet in the system, a Jupiter-sized gas giant.

Maddox stood before the main screen. Keith was at Helm and Valerie scanned for a sign—

"I found it," the lieutenant said.

"Kelle?" Maddox asked.

"Yes, sir," Valerie said. "The dwarf planet is in the Jarvo System's Kuiper Belt. I am detecting heavy comm traffic and constant sensor sweeps. They're going to know about us soon enough."

Because *Victory* had just entered the Jarvo System, its images hadn't had enough time to reach Kelle at 41 AUs away. The dwarf planet, the star, the other planets and space vehicles had all been in the Jarvo System for quite some time. That meant their images had radiated for a while, some of them for time on end. Light traveled at 300,000 kilometers per second. Thus, if something new appeared, it would take the time of the speed of light traveling 41 AUs before a passive sensor on Kelle could possibly see something like the Star Watch vessel.

"I've located the *Bismarck*," Valerie said. "It's in orbit around the dwarf planet, directly overhead relative to the main base on the surface."

During the journey to the Jarvo System, Maddox had spoken to Brigadier O'Hara via the Builder communication device. He had learned specifics concerning the missing hammership, including its probable commander and higher-ranked crewmembers.

"Any unusual activity over there?" Maddox asked.

"None that I can detect," Valerie said.

"Galyan?"

"I concur with Valerie," the holoimage said.

Maddox had his hands clasped behind his back. Among the things he'd learned from O'Hara was that the Hindenburgers had been considered an elite crew. Would they still be elite after all this time? The captain had his doubts. According to what O'Hara had pieced together, the Hindenburgers had been out here since the "C" Quadrant Campaign. That was a long time for Commodore von Helmuth to keep his men in tiptop condition.

"Do we know anything about the Jarvo System?" Maddox asked.

"I have seen reports on high rates of piracy," Galyan said. "More, I cannot tell you."

"The commodore became a space pirate," Maddox said. "If the Strand clone came here... The original Strand must have known about the *Bismarck*. What would be Strand's standard operating procedure in such a situation?"

"We have the Builder cube," Galyan said. "It could tell us with a high degree of accuracy."

"We don't have time for that," Maddox said.

"There is Yen Cho, a Strand expert," Galyan said.

Maddox shook his head. "I want a quick idea. We have a short window of opportunity to act before von Helmuth knows we're here."

"Is the commodore still alive?" Valerie asked.

"The Hindenburgers, then," Maddox said. "The hammership indicates they're still here."

"In my estimation," Galyan said, "If Kelle holds possible Nameless Ones tech, the original Strand would have attempted to control the Hindenburger leadership quite some time ago."

"That makes the most sense," Maddox said. "So if von Helmuth is controlled, he likely has standing orders. That would imply we're not going to be able to reason with him."

367

"Or be able to trick him," Galyan said.

Maddox headed for his command chair, sat down and swiveled toward Keith. "Lay in star-drive jump coordinates so we will appear half a million kilometers from Kelle and the hammership."

"You want to come out of the jump in a direct-line-of-sight with the *Bismarck?*" Keith asked.

"Precisely," Maddox said. "Galyan, you'll help in engineering. I want the engines running as fast as they can once we come out of jump. I want the disrupter cannon ready to fire."

"Are we going to destroy the hammership?" Valerie asked.

Maddox nodded.

"There could be people aboard when we attack," Valerie said.

Maddox drummed his fingers on the armrests. "Lieutenant, what did von Helmuth do during the "C" Quadrant Campaign against the New Men?"

"He deserted his post, sir."

"What is he doing now?"

"We suspect committing piracy," Valerie said.

"Any more questions?"

"None, sir."

Maddox turned to face the main screen, paused, and turned his chair back to her. "Lieutenant Noonan," he said. "I have no desire to kill innocent people. Maybe von Helmuth thought he had good reasons for deserting his post. The truth is that none of that matters to my decision. We're running against a clock. If we lose, all of humanity may lose. We can't squander any more time. That hammership could be a problem. I'm not going to give it a chance to be one."

"I understand," Valerie said. "And I appreciate it that you'd take a moment to let us into your thinking. Put that way—we have to strike hard and fast. We have to stop the clone anyway we can."

Maddox nodded. "Pilot?" he asked.

Keith's fingers blurred a few more seconds. "Ready to jump, sir," he said.

368

Maddox opened intra-ship channels. He informed the crew about the coming fight. He gave them instructions and told them how much he appreciated their hard work and endurance, and he told them their coming actions could well decide whether they were victorious or defeated.

"Captain Maddox out," he said, pressing a switch and closing intra-ship communications.

Maddox felt the momentary queasiness that he always felt before ship-to-ship combat. He glanced around and looked intently at Keith.

"Engage," Maddox said.

-20-

Victory disappeared as the star-drive jump took the vessel from near the Laumer Point all the way to the Kuiper Belt. The starship reappeared half a million kilometers from Kelle and the hammership parked in its orbit.

There was a short lag aboard the ancient Adok starship. It did not last long. Maddox was the first human alert again.

"Galyan?" the captain asked.

Several seconds passed until Galyan's holoimage became more solid. "I am scanning, sir. The Hindenburger base on Kelle is aware of our presence. They are heating up several heavy-beam surface laser sites. I am detecting an increase in engine power aboard the *Bismarck*."

"What about our engine crew?" Maddox asked.

"A moment," Galyan said. He disappeared.

At her station, Valerie smacked her lips together, looking up. She dragged a hand across her eyes, yawned and went directly to work.

"The *Bismarck* is hailing us, sir," she said.

Galyan hadn't returned yet. That could mean the engineering crew had taken a worse lag that normal, at least as they considered normal these days.

"Open channels," Maddox said.

A moment later, a blond-haired officer with a stiff collar and a shaving cut on a prominent chin appeared on the screen.

"I am Sub-Lieutenant Gruber," the man said briskly. "Identity yourself and begin to power down."

The Adok holoimage reappeared on the bridge beside Maddox's chair. "Sir," Galyan said. "Engineering is ready. The engines are on—"

Maddox waved a hand sharply so Galyan would shut up. He could feel the antimatter engines churning through the deckplates at his feet "The main cannon?" he asked quietly to the side.

Galyan's eyelids fluttered. "It will be ready in less than three minutes."

Maddox nodded, and gave his attention back to Sub-lieutenant Gruber. "I am Captain Maddox of Star Watch. You are the WLN Hammership *Bismarck*, last seen in the Grand Fleet under the command of Admiral Fletcher. *You* will begin to power down as we begin our approach."

Gruber looked uncomfortable. "Sir, I request that you wait until Commodore von Helmuth returns to the bridge."

"That traitor," Maddox said, playing a part. "Why wait for him? Power down your ship, sub-lieutenant. Your life depends on it."

That hardened Gruber's features. "I can't do that, sir. I request that you wait. The commodore will be here shortly."

"He's not returning to the bridge," Maddox sneered. "He's not even aboard the hammership. Please, don't lie to me, sub-lieutenant."

Gruber squirmed, betraying himself, and that Maddox had guessed correctly about the commodore's whereabouts. Von Helmuth must be on the planet.

"We're ready, sir," Galyan said to his left. "You can begin targeting."

"*Bismarck*," Maddox said. "This is your last chance. Do yourself a favor—"

"Laser fire from a Kelle surface-site," Valerie cut in. "It's a heavy beam. It can reach us."

"Shields up," Maddox said. He regarded the sub-lieutenant. "You tried to lull me."

"I assure you that is not so."

"The disrupter cannon is locked on target," Galyan said quietly.

"Fire," Maddox said, as he stared at Gruber.

In stunned surprise, the young sub-lieutenant came out of his seat.

On the hull of *Victory*, the giant disrupter cannon energized. A harsh beam speared from the starship, covering the half a million kilometers. It struck the hammership's shield, which turned a cherry-red in that small area.

At the same time, a heavy laser beam—likely of Wahhabi manufacture—reached out just as far from the dwarf planet's surface to hit *Victory's* electromagnetic shield.

Compared to the disrupter beam, the laser dissipated to a much greater degree over distance. Neither did great damage, although *Victory's* beam continued to strike the hammership's shield.

Sub-lieutenant Gruber was no longer on the main screen. He had cut the connection.

"Full acceleration ahead," Maddox said. "I want to increase our velocity as fast as we can."

"The *Bismarck* has heavy railguns," Valerie said. "At close range, the railguns could knock down our shield."

Maddox nodded without commenting. He was well aware of the hammership's railguns. They were potent weapons, but like Valerie had said, only at close range. He did not intend for the *Bismarck* to last that long.

Now it began; the wait-and-see part of the ship-to-ship combat. It had begun at extreme beam range. Neither side had as yet launched any missiles or visible drones.

"Gunships," Valerie said. "They're launching from the *Bismarck*."

"At this distance?" Maddox asked.

"Yes, sir," Valerie said.

Maddox drummed his fingers on the armrest. "How many?"

"I count eleven so far," Valerie said. "More are launching."

"That's more than a hammership's usual complement of gunships," Maddox said.

Time passed as the *Bismarck* and *Victory* continued to accelerate toward each other, closing the range between the two vessels.

"Galyan, are you still scanning for parked drones?" Maddox asked.

"Affirmative, sir," the holoimage said. "I have detected none."

"I doubt they expected to face Star Watch's greatest battleship," Keith said from Helm.

"Likely true," Maddox said. "But let's not be lax. We don't want to take anything for granted."

More time passed.

Three surface laser sites now targeted the ancient Adok vessel, spanning the distance from the planet to the starship. Their beams hit with greater power the nearer the starship came. The three combined lasers hadn't yet caused any shield buckling.

"Sir," Galyan said. "I have computed odds. We can defeat the hammership given time. It might not be true that we can defeat the hammership and the heavy surface laser sites without sustaining damage."

Maddox had also been computing odds. "Lieutenant," he told Keith, "I have a little task for you."

"Sir," Valerie said. "I request that—"

"Belay that," Maddox told her. He turned to Keith. "We don't want to demolish the surface base, just take out those laser sites. That means no antimatter missiles. We'll use regular nuclear-tipped missiles instead, launched from a fold-fighter with pinpoint accuracy."

Keith jumped up. "Consider it done, sir." With that, the ace sprinted from the chamber.

The disrupter cannon went offline for a time, as it had begun to overheat. That was an expected development. Even so, Maddox sent Galyan to watch the damage-repair team's progress on it.

At that point, Commodore von Helmuth requested a screen-to-screen talk with Maddox.

"You must discontinue firing first," Maddox said via comm.

Thirty seconds later, Valerie said, "The Kelle surface laser sites have stopped beaming, sir."

"Put the commodore on the screen," Maddox said.

A moment later, the square-faced von Helmuth with his monocle appeared on the main screen. By his background, it was clear the commodore was not on the hammership's bridge.

"A New Man," von Helmuth said in shock, as he stared at Maddox. "They told me you were a Star Watch officer."

"I am Captain Maddox of Star Watch."

"Then why do you look like a New Man?"

Maddox studied von Helmuth. He tried to determine if the man was mind-controlled or not. Were the man's reactions genuine? It appeared so.

"You will immediately surrender the *Bismarck* and power down the surface laser sites," Maddox said. "My battleship is part of a greater task force. Admiral Fletcher is leading it. We were sent to locate your missing ship, as a hauler captain has told us about your piracy in the area."

Von Helmuth peered at Maddox as if trying to determine the captain's veracity. Finally, the Hindenburger shook his heavy head. "I cannot do as you request, Captain."

"You're overmatched. We've found you. You knew this day would come."

"I cannot do as you request," von Helmuth repeated, his eyes shining.

"Give me a good reason why not," Maddox said.

"I do not need a reason. I have stated my intent. That is enough."

"Surely, your people need a reason for dying uselessly," Maddox said. "Or don't you realize that the Windsor League is willing to grant all of you pardons?"

"No," von Helmuth said harshly. "It is too late for pardons."

Maddox had already noted the shiny eyes. Now, he saw a small tic jerk the corner of man's right eye. The commodore also seemed uncommonly sweaty.

"Your reason for dying uselessly isn't Methuselah Man Strand, is it?" Maddox asked.

Von Helmuth blanched with a look approaching horror before his features hardened with resolve. "I have no idea what you're talking about."

"This is your last chance, Commodore."

374

Von Helmuth made a mocking noise. "You know nothing about last chances. All our lives, the Windsor League braggarts treated us Hindenburgers as second-rate citizens. Third Admiral Bishop thought to use us as pawns. The man gave our hammership the worst assignments. Don't you think I know what this is really about?"

"According to my observation," Galyan said quietly, "Commodore von Helmuth appears paranoid delusional."

"Agreed," Maddox said softly. "I've studied his bio. Von Helmuth is supposed to be a hard-nosed aristocrat. In my estimation, someone has tampered with his mind."

"Which would imply Strand," Galyan said. "It is possible they have all been tampered with in some way or another."

"In one sense," Maddox said, "I feel sorry for them. They're pawns. But von Helmuth's reaction also shows me we're on the right path."

"If you are addressing me, Captain," von Helmuth said, "I demand that you speak up so I can hear you."

Maddox regarded the square-faced aristocrat. "You made a hard choice, a bad one, many years ago. Now, the chickens are coming home to roost. It would have been better for you if you'd never run into Strand. But you clearly have."

"Who is this Strand you keep talking about?" von Helmuth demanded angrily.

"Surrender your hammership and shut down the surface laser sites."

"*Nein*," von Helmuth said. "We shall destroy you, New Man."

"I think not. Captain Maddox out."

The screen returned to an image of the accelerating hammership and the dwarf planet of Kelle beyond it.

"Distance between vessels?" Maddox asked.

"Three hundred and eighty-seven thousand kilometers," Valerie said.

"We'll wait a little longer. I want the cannon ready for sustained fire."

Time passed.

In the distance on the dwarf planet, emergency procedures went into effect as something new happened over there.

"Keith," Valerie said. She intently watched the main screen.

A fold-fighter had appeared low over the dwarf planet's surface. It zoomed fast and began to zigzag as it headed toward the main pirate base.

"I detect surface anti-fighter sites," Galyan said. "They are tracking the fold-fighter."

"No," Valerie said, a hand flying over her mouth.

"Do not worry, Valerie," Galyan told her. "Keith is the best."

"He's a showoff," she whispered. "And everyone is watching. He's going to try something fancy."

Maddox ordered a magnification. Valerie was right. The fold-fighter zoomed for the nearest laser site. Anti-fighter guns around the site chugged explosive shells at the nearing tin can. Emitters ejected from the Star Watch fighter. At the same instant, the fold-fighter disappeared.

"What's he doing?" Valerie whispered.

The fold-fighter reappeared to the left of its former position, but lower to the surface.

"We went real fancy," Valerie groaned.

Missiles launched from the tin can.

From the surface, more anti-fighter rockets raced up at the craft. The fold-fighter disappeared again. The surface-launched rockets detonated. They destroyed two of the incoming missiles.

In the next few seconds, more surface-launched rockets raced up. Explosions occurred. Two more incoming missiles went down.

"Interesting," Galyan said. "One of those supposed missiles was really a decoy."

Valerie shouted triumphantly.

On screen, a nuclear mushroom cloud appeared on the surface. It came from the exact spot where a heavy laser site had just been.

"Excellent," Maddox said. "Galyan, tell the disrupter cannon-crew to get ready. It's time to begin phase two of this fight."

-21-

As *Victory* stopped accelerating, the disrupter cannon came back online. The powerful disrupter beam stabbed through space at the speed of light. It struck the *Bismarck* a little over a second later.

The difference between five hundred thousand kilometers to a little over three hundred thousand kilometers range was startling. The heavy beam began to saturate the hammership's electromagnetic shield. The discoloration to the shield was immediate as it began to darken from red to brown.

The hammership's railguns came online as they began to accelerate tiny pieces of matter. The pieces would take far longer to reach *Victory*, as they traveled far below the speed of light. It soon became clear that the *Bismarck* was laying down concentrated clots of accelerated particles into various cones of probability, those cones being where *Victory* might be when the particles reached the starship. Each tiny piece would shed vast amounts of kinetic energy when it struck—providing the ancient Adok starship was still in the line-of-fire.

"Keep track of the particle clots," Maddox told Galyan. "They're laying down a wide pattern so we can't dodge them all."

"Keith, what are you doing," Valerie whispered. She stared at her panel-screen as she paled. "You're supposed to come home."

"Magnify Kelle's surface," Maddox snapped.

The fold-fighter had appeared low to the planet's surface again. The ace was cunningly using the destroyed laser site as an empty area of the local defense net. The tin can zoomed into position and then swung higher into Kelle's atmosphere. From there, it launched the rest of its nuclear-tipped missiles and decoys.

The enemy defense-net zeroed in on Keith, and they might have nailed him if he'd been a fraction slower. As Galyan had said earlier, at this, Keith Maker had no peers. The fold-fighter disappeared as enemy anti-fire arrived in his vicinity.

"Please don't do that again," Valerie whispered. "You have to come home."

"Hit," Maddox said, as he made a fist. "That's another laser site we don't have to worry about. Good hunting, Mr. Maker."

"Sir," said the new Helm pilot who had taken Keith's place. She was Sub-lieutenant Kenzie Jones, a tall woman with long brunette hair. "The *Bismarck* is rotating. It appears they're going to attempt deceleration."

"You're too late," Maddox told the hammership. "With another surface laser site out—accelerate Ms. Jones. It's time to bring this fight to a finish."

Victory continued to beam as it accelerated for the hammership. The electromagnetic shield took the last surface laser fire with ease. The beam grew hotter the nearer the starship approached Kelle, but the enemy laser simply did not have the firepower on its own to hurt *Victory* until the starship was at almost pointblank range.

"Surface missiles launching," Galyan said. "It appears they are using their last reserves in order to save the *Bismarck*. Earlier, why did the hammership accelerate toward us, sir?"

"Maybe it only had a maintenance crew aboard," Maddox said. "It's possible Sub-lieutenant Gruber panicked and attacked. But maybe that was their standard operating procedure against the unknown. The truth is I don't know, Galyan. Likely, our surprise appearance upset their equilibrium."

"Sir," Valerie said. "The first wave of railgun-particles is approaching."

"Prepare for evasive action, Helm," Maddox said.

378

"The disrupter cannon is overheating, sir," Galyan said.

"Take the cannon offline," Maddox said.

The starship jinked one way and then another. Maddox used the shorter-ranged neutron cannon to take out several particle clots that they couldn't evade.

More time passed. Soon, no more accelerating particles headed at the starship.

The hammership had rotated and begun massive deceleration. Obviously, they were trying to halt the forward momentum of the hammership so it could accelerate back to the dwarf planet, possibly to hide behind it.

"Two hundred thousand kilometers and closing fast, sir," Sub-lieutenant Jones said.

"Galyan, what is the disrupter's condition?" asked Maddox.

The holoimage disappeared, reappearing a minute later. "The service crew says they're ready to rip, sir."

"Commence firing," Maddox said. "It's time to take out the *Bismarck*."

The enemy's railguns started to hose accelerated particles at the nearing starship. If the *Bismarck* could survive long enough, it could theoretically lay down heavier fire than *Victory* while at pointblank range. That was the reason for the hammership's heavy armor, to survive long enough to kill at close range. The ancient Adok starship, however, had even better armor because of its advanced composition. Much had changed since the *Bismarck's* disappearance during the "C" Quadrant Campaign under Fletcher.

The disrupter cannon poured intensely destructive energy against the hammership's shield. The dissipation over distance had dropped considerably. Inside of 200,000 kilometers, the disrupter beam was technological death.

The hammership's shield darkened, and an explosion took place on the *Bismarck*. They had been in the Beyond for many years. The military-grade vessel had missed many scheduled maintenance overhauls. They were pirates, after all, grabbing what they could and smuggling needed components here from time to time. Likely, in fact almost certainly, not all the hammership's systems had stayed as finely tuned or remained as upgraded as they should have been.

Another explosion took place over there. Maybe it was from an overload to the shield generators. Whatever the case, the *Bismarck's* electromagnetic shield collapsed.

"Their shield is down," Galyan said.

"Let's break them," Maddox said.

The mighty disrupter beam smashed against the heavy hull armor. The beam remained on one spot, heating the hull armor, digging into it and breaking down the molecular structure.

The disrupter beam was one of the most powerful offensive weapons in Star Watch's arsenal. The hammership began evasive maneuvers. At a greater distance between vessels, such maneuvering might have proven effective. As the range continued to close from 200,000 kilometers, *Victory's* targeting crew found it a simple matter to keep the beam on target.

"A hull breach is imminent," Galyan said shortly.

Maddox sat in his chair, watching, waiting, wondering if the Hindenburgers had a secret up their sleeve to save themselves.

"Hull breach," Galyan said. "The beam is in."

The great disrupter beam had broken through the famed hammership's double armor. It smashed down bulkheads with pathetic ease, chewing up metals, people, wall conduits, magnetic-plates, coils, water, oxygen recyclers…

The mayhem was brutal, and the beam did not discriminate. It killed and destroyed everything in its path, finally reaching the great nuclear-powered engines. Interior explosions began, rapidly becoming worse. Suddenly, a combination of explosions ripped into waiting warheads. At almost the same time, the engine went critical. Titanic explosions ripped through the *Bismarck*. It was awful. It was glorious in a perverted way.

From on the bridge of *Victory*, the crew watched the hammership begin to break like a crushed walnut. Pieces of hull went spinning in various directions. Water, vapor and air spewed out. Struggling humans tumbled into the void of space. Then a fireball erupted.

Dampeners in the screen saved *Victory's* bridge-crews' eyesight. When visibility returned to the main screen, Maddox and company saw the pieces of *Bismarck* already beginning to drift through space.

No one cheered. It was too solemn of an event, and none of them had really believed they could lose.

Maddox exhaled. "Good work, people. You did well. Now, Helm, rotate us. It's time to decelerate and see what the surviving Hindenburgers on Kelle want to do next."

-22-

The Hindenburgers intended to fight to the last man, woman and child, at least according to Commodore von Helmuth.

The ancient Adok starship was parked in geostationary orbit over Kelle, directly over the main base on the dwarf planet. The remaining heavy laser site and all the missile launch pits were smoking craters due to space bombardment.

It had taken time to move into the stationary orbit. During that time, the Hindenburgers had no doubt prepared a vicious welcoming committee. Such was the commodore's promise, at least, as he spoke to Maddox via screen.

Maddox was on the bridge, listening to von Helmuth. As the commodore paused for breath, the captain saw his chance, a way to cancel the man's stubbornness.

"And your people agree with all this?" Maddox asked.

Von Helmuth raised his head more erectly. "We are a proud people, Captain. Hindenburgers do not surrender."

"But you run away from battle?"

"A lie from the swine, Third Admiral Bishop," von Helmuth declared.

"Are you hard of hearing?" Maddox asked. "The Windsor League has granted all of you full pardons. You needn't have lost your hammership and the people serving on it. We're at peace with the New Men, facing a much grimmer threat from the Swarm Imperium."

382

"It does not matter," von Helmuth said. "Leave this star system, Captain. We do not want you here."

"I can drop antimatter bombs on you any time I desire," Maddox said. "You shall die if you continue to resist. Are you prepared to die, Commodore?"

The man expanded his chest. "I am more than willing, as my world has crumbled around me."

"That's absurd," Maddox said. "You needlessly lost your hammership. You can still retain your life."

"*Nein*, this is a lie, a trick."

"You are a poor actor, Commodore."

Von Helmuth blinked rapidly. "I do not understand the insult. I am telling you the truth."

"You there," Maddox called.

Von Helmuth looked over his shoulder. An aide was passing behind him.

"You!" Maddox said loudly.

The aide-de-camp looked up at the screen over the commodore's shoulder. The man was younger, with a fresh face and a perfectly tailored uniform. Maddox was doubtful that anyone had put a control net into the aide's skull.

"Commodore von Helmuth is not in his right mind," Maddox told the younger man. "He wishes to commit mass suicide. I can grant him his wish, or I can give you all full pardons from your government. If you wish, you can even return to Hindenburg."

"Go, go," von Helmuth told the shocked aide-de-camp. "Why are you here?"

The younger man hurried out of the picture.

The commodore turned back to Maddox. "You lack honor, sir. We are speaking commander to commander. I ask you not to do that again."

Maddox inclined his head. "You are determined to die, then, Commodore?"

A tic appeared on the Hindenburger's square features. "No one wishes death, Captain. But I am a man of honor. You have defeated me on the battlefield. I could theoretically surrender, but I would never do such a thing. Or I could still die an

383

honorable death in combat as your away teams attempt to land on the surface."

"Do you know why we came to Kelle?" Maddox asked.

"Of course, I know," von Helmuth said.

"Perhaps you do, in a sense. You have heard of Methuselah Man Strand."

The tic appeared again, worse than before.

"No," the commodore said. "I have…" A glazed look came to his eyes. "I have never heard of him," von Helmuth said in a robotic voice. "Do not ask me about him again, I implore you."

"I demand that you tell me all you know about Methuselah Man Strand."

Von Helmuth whitened. "*Nein*, enough," he whispered. "You must not say that name to me."

"Why is that?" asked Maddox, leaning forward.

The tic had considerably worsened.

"I can heal your injuries," Maddox said softly, "including any damage to your mind."

For a moment, something like sanity appeared in the commodore's eyes. Then, he began to shake his head. "You. Must. Stay up there. Do you hear me?"

At that moment, commotion occurred beyond the screen's range. Von Helmuth turned. His head swayed back as if with surprise.

"No," the commodore said. "I am in charge. I am—" He reached for a sidearm.

"Don't shoot him!" Maddox shouted.

A shot rang out. Then a fusillade of shots rang out. Several of the bullets riddled the commodore's body, flinging him out of view of the screen

Maddox banged a fist against an armrest. He needed the commodore.

A moment later, a Hindenburg lieutenant of marines, a blond-haired veteran, peered at Maddox from the screen. "I am Lieutenant Hess. I wish to formally surrender to you, Captain. I also wish to claim the Windsor League pardon."

Maddox nodded. He had planted the seed. It had sprouted faster than he'd expected. "What about the commodore?" he asked. "How is he?"

The Hindenburg marine glanced to the side before regarding Maddox. "The commodore still breathes. That won't last long."

"Wait," Maddox said. "I want von Helmuth alive. I need him alive, as do you, Lieutenant."

The marine became instantly suspicious. "Why is that? For a show trial?"

"Your commodore has been sitting on a galactic secret," Maddox said. "I need that secret, Lieutenant. It is why I came here. Do you understand?"

A slow dawning of understanding appeared in the marine's blue eyes. He nodded grimly, and he turned, motioning sharply as he gave orders.

A medic raced into view and then out toward the fallen commodore. The lieutenant watched a moment and finally turned to Maddox again.

"I will cooperate," Hess said. "I cannot guarantee all the others, but I will help you as much as I can. I am sick of this backwater. I want to go home. I want to leave this place. It is cursed."

"Of that," Maddox said, "I have no doubt. You have my personal guarantee, Lieutenant. Help me and I will do my utmost to help you receive a pardon."

The lieutenant's eyes narrowed. He leaned toward the screen. "This is no real pardon?"

"Not as you conceive of it," Maddox said. "But you're earning the gratitude of Star Watch Intelligence. We know how to pay our debts."

The marine stared at him suspiciously for several seconds longer. Finally, he nodded. "I understand. I've gambled. But I don't see how I have much hope if I work against you."

"You have no hope any other way but to work with me," Maddox said. "Help me, and maybe we'll all have hope."

The marine cocked his head. "How do you mean?"

"Get things ready for us," Maddox said, "and I'll show you."

-23-

Despite the commodore's threats—and the threats of some of his highest remaining officers—the rest of the Hindenburgers and all the wives and children desperately wanted to accept Maddox's good-faith offer.

The *Bismarck* was gone. The heavy laser sites and missiles pits were all demolished. A few gunboats had circled the dwarf planet and waited on the other side, likely hoping *Victory* would ignore them.

In the end, it meant Hindenburg marines under Lieutenant Hess shot a few resisting officers and locked up the rest. Those officers raved dire threats. Meanwhile, a medical team worked to save von Helmuth's life.

Maddox went down with three shuttles. Meta wanted to join him. He ordered her to remain aboard *Victory*. He didn't want anything happening to his beloved.

The captain landed with armored Star Watch space marines. In the end, though, the surviving Hindenburgers were too eager to please him for any complications to emerge.

Soon enough, Maddox found himself in an operating theater. He watched from his two-tons of exoskeleton-powered combat armor.

"Sir," the head surgeon said. "I will do everything in my power to revive the commodore."

Maddox's helmet swiveled from side-to-side. Using an outer speaker, the captain asked, "You're the chief medical officer?"

The man nodded.

"How many control nets have you put into various minds?" Maddox asked.

Under his medical mask, the doctor turned crimson. "I-I…" he stammered.

Maddox waved an armored hand, causing the servos to whine. "I'm interested in the number, Doctor. Are you controlled?"

"No," the doctor whispered.

"Von Helmuth is, though, yes?"

The doctor nodded woodenly.

"If he dies, Doctor, you die."

"Captain—"

The faceplate whirred down.

The doctor gasped at Maddox. "New Man," he said in a shaky voice. "I-I'm sorry, your honor. I-I did not know."

Maddox wasn't sure why the doctor had changed his tune the way he had. Maybe because the original Strand had usually shown up in the company of New Men.

"I want von Helmuth alive," Maddox said. "I also want him in a cooperative state."

"I will do my best, sir."

The faceplate whirred shut. Maddox stepped outside the operating theater.

An hour later, the doctor appeared. He seemed faint and pale and kept staring down at the floor.

"Von Helmuth is dead?" Maddox asked.

The doctor nodded miserably.

"Why did he die?" Maddox asked.

"I…attempted to adjust the net. He survived the bullet wounds. None had hit a critical organ. The net…it was strangely altered. I did an autopsy to determine the reason he died. Something in the neural net had changed. I don't know what because I've never seen its like."

In his two-tons of armor, Maddox looked down on the terrified doctor.

"Strand trained you?" Maddox asked.

"Aboard the *Argos*," the doctor whispered.

387

That had been the name of the original Strand's special star cruiser.

"Tell me about Kelle," Maddox said.

The doctor looked up and quickly looked down. He licked his lips nervously. "What do you want to know, Master?"

"Anything you know that might lead me to alien technology," Maddox said.

The doctor looked up sharply, his eyes wide. Like before, he looked down again, shaking his head. "I don't know anything about that, Master."

Maddox waited several seconds, debating his options. Finally, his suit seams cracked open as the seals demagnetized.

"Sir," the chief space marine said. "Is that wise?"

Maddox ignored his guard. He moved outside the combat armor and went into the operating theater. He saw von Helmuth's opened skull. He saw the other medical personnel cringing away from him.

The captain did not ask for help. He'd made an error here. He'd trusted their fear to keep them from hindering him. He had been wrong to do that.

Selecting a hypo from a tray, Maddox examined various types of anesthesia. As an Intelligence operative, he'd had to knock out his share of people.

Soon, Maddox was in the other room again. An armored marine held the doctor.

"W-What are you going to do to me?" the man stammered.

"Nothing," Maddox said. "Don't worry. I just want to ask you a few questions."

The doctor seemed to relax a moment.

Maddox hypoed him as it hissed.

"No!" the doctor shouted. "You injected me with truth serum."

"On the contrary," Maddox said. "I killed you with a lethal dose of poison."

The doctor's eyes widened, and he almost seemed relieved. He slumped unconscious a moment later.

"What should I do with his corpse?" asked the space marine holding him.

"Take him upstairs to *Victory*," Maddox said. "He's not dead. He's unconscious. He feared truth serum, had likely been modified so he'd commit suicide under those conditions. I want him alive, as we're going to interrogate him, but first we're going to remove his neural net."

"He was controlled, sir?"

"Undoubtedly," Maddox said. "But that's fine, as I think I've finally found the right person to give me a few answers."

-24-

Twenty-four hours later, Maddox, Meta and several space marines, all of them in combat armor, and the holoimage of Galyan, moved deep inside Kelle. They had discovered the hatch that led into the tunnel with the alien environment.

Maddox flinched upon sight of it.

"You have seen these strange polymers before?" Galyan asked.

"Oh yes," Maddox said. "Aboard the Destroyer. It reminds me of the first time when the lone Destroyer attacked Earth and we had to break in to take over the controls."

"I remember," Galyan said. "We are on the right track, then?"

"I'd say so," Maddox said.

They found the things the clone of Strand had seen. They found the shot-up cylinders and the now-decaying, previously dissected corpses. They found the resting place of the alien vessel and the various pieces of Nameless Ones equipment scattered throughout the area. The crystal machines in particular seemed otherworldly.

"What do you make of all this?" Meta asked over a suit comm.

"The Strand clone has been here," Maddox said. "From the state of decay, we missed him by about a week. That means we're close on his trail. But what does close mean at this point? How do we find his next destination?"

"You'll think of something," Meta said.

Maddox continued to study the strange crystals with the machines running inside them. What had this place done? The captain shook his head. He hadn't found anything to give him a clue as to the clone's next port of call. He was going to have to use the Builder cube again. He did not trust the cube. In many ways, he wanted the cube off the starship. One wrong slip on their part and the cube might try to take over again. So far, they had contained the cube's abilities to attack Galyan.

Maddox continued to record the alien place. They couldn't stay on Kelle for long. The Strand clone had come, gotten what it needed and departed to parts unknown in a vessel of the Nameless Ones.

What could the vessel do?

Maddox shuddered. How could the clone have forced himself to use a machine from a place like this? Maddox hated the Nameless Ones. He hated their equipment. He hated this place.

As Maddox recorded, he, Galyan, the marines and Meta combed the area for clues. Finally, one of the space marines found a strange small object.

The suited marine picked it up. The dark object shimmered and began to radiate heat.

Maddox was nearby and looked up, seeing the pulsating object in the marine's powered glove. "Drop it," he told the man.

The space marine did so, backing away fast. Smoke drifted from his already molten glove. "What is that?" the frightened marine said over the comm.

Maddox neared the object, while Galyan shimmered into existence beside it.

The small dark object lay on the strangely jointed floor. It radiated intense heat and it seemed to pulsate, growing faint and then more solid again in brief cycles.

"What do you sense, Galyan?" Maddox asked.

"There are odd sounds emanating from it, Captain," the holoimage said. "I am recording them."

"I don't hear anything," Meta said.

"It is above the normal human hearing range," Galyan said. "I suspect it is a type of beacon. It is sending the sounds in a pattern. What the sounds mean, I have no idea. I am recording them for further study."

"You already said that, Galyan," Meta told him.

The object grew hotter yet.

"The sounds…" Galyan said slowly.

A grim certainly struck Maddox, so like a physical blow that he staggered. He looked up in alarm and his gut clenched.

"Driving Force Galyan," Maddox said sternly. "Return immediately to the starship. That is an order. Go!"

Galyan stared at Maddox and suddenly disappeared.

"Listen," Maddox said on an open channel. The grim certainty pounded in his brain like a gong. "Run. All of you. Run! There's no more time."

As the captain said that, he grabbed Meta, dragging her along.

"Run!" Maddox told the marines. "This place is going to blow."

The space marines needed no more prodding than that. The servomotors whined as the two-ton armor suits began to move like mechanical rhinoceroses. They soon left the alien area, using their helmet-lamps to give them light.

"You forgot the object," Meta radioed Maddox.

"Keep running," the captain said.

At that point, a titanic explosion occurred behind them. The tunnel walls shook and cracks appeared on the ground.

"Go, go, go!" Maddox said. "If you stop, you're dead. It's going to get worse, much worse."

It did, the explosions intensifying behind them, and the shaking growing many times worse.

"What's happening?" Meta cried.

"Planetary destruction!" Maddox shouted. "We have to get off this ball before it all goes up. So save your breath for running."

-25-

Fortunately, most of the Hindenburgers had already transferred up to the starship. About one third of the hammership's original crew had survived the years on Kelle, the destruction of the *Bismarck* and the mayhem afterward. A few others had escaped in the gunboats, still trying to hide from *Victory* on the other side of the dwarf planet. The years of piracy had brought most of the crew wives or common-law wives, and a growing number of children.

All of the *Bismarck's* survivors aboard *Victory* were locked behind sealed bulkheads in an area they likely couldn't create much mischief even if they wanted to. The starship had more than enough room for the new passengers, especially with the seventy-odd slain Star Watch personnel earlier in the mission.

Maddox trusted the survivors as far as it went, but he didn't want to *have* to trust them with his ship. Thus, they would remain behind the sealed bulkheads until further notice.

"What about the people on the gunships?" Valerie asked from her station on the bridge.

The captain had made it back to the ship and was presently assessing the situation. It had been a harrowing race through the tunnel to a waiting shuttle by the main seal. Luckily, Keith had been there. He'd gotten them out with only several boulders crashing against them from the shaking corridor.

Maddox and the rest of the bridge crew now watched the stunning destruction as it continued below on the dwarf planet. The earthquakes had gotten stronger over the last hour.

Magnification of the surface showed constant shaking and crumbling mountains. Now, lava began to erupt. It flowed thickly, as cracks appeared everywhere.

"The cracks in the mantle will expand," Galyan said. "I have detected even greater movement coming up to the surface."

"Take us out of orbit," Maddox told Keith.

"Aye, aye, sir," the ace said.

Victory began to pull away from the dwarf planet. As it did, flux gravitational forces surging up from the planet began shaking the starship.

"Hurry if you please, Mr. Maker," Maddox said.

During the next thirty seconds, the gravitational shaking intensified. As the ancient Adok vessel pulled away, though, they moved out of range and the shaking gradually lessened until it stopped altogether.

"Look," Valerie said.

Everyone was already looking. Gigantic lava-spewing cracks zigzagged across the planetary surface. As seen from space, Kelle was visibly shaking.

At that point, mayday calls began coming in from the gunboats circling the planet.

"What do we do about them?" Valerie asked.

Maddox shook his head.

"The surging gravitational forces are pulling the gunboats down," Valerie said. "They lack the engine power to escape. We can't just leave them."

"On the contrary," Maddox said. "They had their chance to surrender. I will not now jeopardize my ship and crew to save enemy combatants who waited too long to ask for help."

"That's...that's heartless," Valerie said.

"I believe you mean to say practical. It would endanger our mission by risking the ship near wildly surging gravity waves. The gunboats had their chance, Lieutenant. They squandered the opportunity until it was too late."

The captain got to his feet.

"I am curious," Galyan said in what seemed like a strained voice. "Back in the cavern...how did you know what was going to happen to the planet?"

Meta looked up sharply. She seemed astonished. "That's right. How did you know?"

Maddox grew cold to his core as he heard the question. He sat on the edge of the command chair, rubbing his left cheek. How had he known?

"There it goes," Valerie whispered.

Maddox looked up as Kelle splintered into planetary sections. It was an awful sight. Entire colossal chunks split from one another and spun away as the dwarf planet lent the pieces its orbital momentum. Kelle no longer existed. Pieces of it mingled with pieces of the gunboats.

Galyan turned away from the sight.

Valerie noticed. "Oh, Galyan," she said in a gentle voice. "I'm sorry. This must remind you of your homeworld's destruction."

The Adok holoimage seemed incredibly sad. He nodded, perhaps unable to speak.

"Galyan," Maddox said, crisply. "Check on the engines. Make it a thorough study. I'm afraid these gravitational forces may have secretly ruptured something that will show itself later in battle."

"Yes, sir," Galyan said in a dispirited voice, disappearing from view.

Everyone resumed watching the planet's destruction. Clearly, this wasn't a natural event, but no one had figured out what the Nameless Ones tech had done to perform such an awful feat.

How did I know Kelle would splinter like this? Maddox wondered. The question was beginning to bother him.

-26-

The answer bothered Maddox even more than the question had. He sat up in bed as Meta lay snug and sleeping under the covers. They had been asleep for several hours already. It had been a harrowing day. Even so, with the question bouncing around in his skull, Maddox had found it difficult to fall asleep.

He might have dreamed during the little sleep he'd finally gotten. If he had, though, he didn't remember any of it. He was damp with perspiration and knew he had been tossing.

As quietly as possible, Maddox slipped out from under the covers and padded to the restroom. He closed the door softly and looked at his face in the mirror.

He had lean features like a New Man, but he lacked their golden skin-color. His eyes were bloodshot. They were almost never bloodshot.

Maddox turned on the tap and splashed water on his face.

In the tunnel, he had known about the planetary destruction because of his fight against the Ska a year ago. Something had changed in him. Either that or some new sense had sharpened. He didn't know what to call the sense, but the heated object the marine had found had given him a certainty of planetary destruction.

Could that heated object have been alive in some manner?

Maddox shook his head. He didn't think so. But maybe whatever the object had radiated could only be sensed by a living being. He didn't even know that was true. The point was that his newly sharpened sense—

396

It might not be a sense, Maddox told himself.

Maybe the Ska had wounded him on a deep, spiritual level. That spiritual wound was still raw. The sensation the hot object had radiated had made his raw inner hurt ache in a way that told him vast destruction was going to take place.

He nodded. It was the best answer he could give. He was one of the walking wounded but in a way that no one could see.

He turned his back to the mirror and bent his head, pressing his fists against his forehead. The tech of the Nameless Ones had destroyed Kelle as easily as a man swatted a fly. *Victory's* sensors hadn't picked anything up that could have caused the destruction. Such a thing shouldn't be possible.

Think, he told himself. *That the sensors didn't pick anything up is a clue. Are you too dull to see the clue?*

Maddox straightened as a mocking grin twisted his lips. The original Strand had set all this in motion. The Methuselah Man had planned for the day someone killed or captured him. Thus, in a way, he—Maddox—had started this when he captured Strand on Sind II. By handing Strand over to the New Men, Maddox had ensured Kelle's destruction and that Strand clones would buzz around Human Space committing mayhem and possibly bringing the Nameless Ones back.

The grin turned even more mocking as a fierce light shined in the captain's eyes. Methuselah Man Strand!

Maddox shook his head.

That little bastard wasn't going to beat him. Maybe Strand had Builder-enhanced, gifted genius. Maybe the trickster Methuselah Man had guile honed from thousands of years of experience. Maybe Strand knew every trick there was to know—he still wasn't going to lose to Strand.

"I accept no excuses," Maddox whispered.

He knew that bold words and decisive thoughts did not win the day. Only one thing could defeat Strand; victorious action. He had to do the impossible. He had to find a clone that had left no clues. Yet, that wasn't true. There *were* clues. They were staring him in the face. He was just too dull to see them for what they were.

"Okay," Maddox said. If he couldn't see the clues, who could?

"Of course," Maddox said, nodding to himself. It was time to take a risk. He needed the infernal Builder cube. He was going to have to feed it data until it gagged. But there was one critical difference to this.

The clone Strand wasn't going to do this terrible thing. The previous clone-Strand had released a Builder ghost-ship and cube and gotten himself killed. Another clone had released whatever had lain in the vault of Kelle. Maddox needed to feed the Builder cube data about the Nameless Ones. In some manner, whatever the clone had freed from Kelle would overpower him, just as the guardian robot had overpowered the other clone on the Builder ghost-ship.

Strand and his clones weren't the real enemy anymore. The Nameless Ones' tech was the threat. Maddox had known that for some time. He had simply not taken it to its logical conclusion.

Maddox turned off the bathroom lights and opened the door. There was no need to wake Meta, and there was no need to go back to sleep. He would have enough time to sleep later.

Now, it was time to begin feeding the cube the needed data.

-27-

Two days later, *Victory* was still near the remains of Kelle. Andros, Galyan and the engineers had been recalibrating the ship's sensors. Some of the suggested refinements had come from Yen Cho, some from the Builder cube. Maddox had demanded extra caution in testing each difference. He suspected the cube of double-dealing, as that was what he would have done in the cube's place.

Finally, after every precaution, Valerie and Galyan began using the modified sensors to study the dwarf planet's remains.

"This is interesting," Valerie said seventeen minutes later.

Maddox walked to her station and looked over her shoulder. "What do they mean?" he asked.

Valerie looked up at him. "You don't know?"

Maddox said nothing.

The lieutenant shrugged. "To tell you the truth, sir, I don't exactly know either. This," she pointed at a sensor reading, "is the gravitational fluctuation. This is an interphase reading. Galyan explained it once, but I'm still not sure what it means."

The holoimage floated near. "You called me, Valerie?"

"This interphase reading," she said, "what is that again?"

"After studying the captain's recording of the tunnel and…the planet's destruction, the Builder cube suggested the possibility of phase mechanics."

"I remember all that," Valerie said. "What is the interphase part?"

"It is a quantum level variation—"

399

"Galyan," Maddox said. "Give me the basic theory."

"It is not a theory, sir," Galyan said. "Phase mechanics is rather elegant. The planetary matter in question resonates at a different frequency from the normal quantum universe. That explains why our sensors did not pick up the phase pulses earlier."

"Galyan," Maddox warned.

The holoimage appeared perplexed. "Sir, are you suggesting a simpleton's explanation?"

Maddox did not reply.

"Is that a yes or no, sir?" Galyan asked.

Valerie glanced at Maddox before telling the holoimage, "Just the basics, Galyan,"

"Is that how you interpret the captain's silence, Valerie?"

"I'm just saying," she said.

"Phase mechanics in layman's terms..." Galyan said slowly, "is being in the same objective universe but not in resonance with it. Perhaps an example is in order. An out of phase object would be invisible to those in quantum resonance with their surroundings. The out of phase object would have no taste, no smell, no weight—for all practical purposes it would not be there. But it would still be in the same space-time continuum. Once the harmonics changed, the object could phase into our quantum resonance universe. It would now have weight, smell, visibility, all elements that other matter possesses."

"So, an out of phase object would be like a ghost," Maddox said.

Galyan cocked his head. "That is a spurious example, as ghosts are mythical."

"But if ghosts were real," Maddox said, "it would exhibit these out of phase mechanics?"

"Not altogether," Galyan said. "A mythical ghost would be visible, albeit insubstantial."

"Just like you," Maddox said.

"That is an apt analogy," Galyan said. "In actuality, an out of phase object would not be visible. It would be undetectable to any but our altered sensors."

"Could the clone Strand have found a Nameless Ones…ship that could travel out of phase?" Maddox asked.

"That would appear to be the direction of our research," Galyan said. "That would explain how a space vessel was inside the dwarf planet. That also explains how Kelle was destroyed. The Nameless Ones left powerful phase annihilators—for want of a better term—inside the dwarf planet. The Builder cube has suggested that these phase annihilators spent the majority of their existence out of phase in relation to Kelle and us. Only at the end did they become…real, or phase into our quantum resonance, and use phase pulses to destroy…the planet."

"So we may well be hunting for an alien phase-ship," Maddox said. "We may have passed it as we entered this star system."

"Yes," Galyan said.

"I have a question," Valerie said. "Is the phase-ship headed for an out-of-phase destination or a regular place?"

Maddox turned abruptly to stare at the lieutenant.

"What did I say?" Valerie asked.

"Lieutenant Noonan," Maddox said, "you have just earned your pay for the entire mission. Galyan, come with me."

-28-

Maddox and Galyan stood in the science chamber before the giant globe holding the Builder cube in its center. Not much had changed since the last time the captain had been here. One difference was a newly installed link. It allowed the cube to view the data from the starship's sensors.

"My analysis proved correct," the cube said. "The Nameless Ones installed phase annihilators in the core of the dwarf planet. The aliens surely did that many cycles ago, leaving the mechanisms out-of-sync with the planet. It has led me to wonder how many other planets are rigged with such devices. Even with the right sensors, it would take decades to find out, maybe a century or more."

"They're true technowizards," Maddox said dryly.

"That is an interesting term," the cube said. "I would not call them that, however."

"Captain Maddox was being sarcastic," Galyan said.

"A moment," the cube said. "Yes, you are correct. I had not bothered to detect the fluctuations of the captain's tone. I am absorbed with studying the new sensor readings."

"We need to find a phase-ship," Maddox said.

"Interesting," the cube said. "Who among you concluded that the Nameless Ones had used a phase-ship?"

"Why does that matter?" Maddox asked.

"Was it you, Captain?" the cube asked.

"You mean you don't know?" Maddox countered.

"A moment while I analyze the possibilities. Ah, yes, it was you. I congratulate you on your higher-order reasoning. I suppose you have already determined that the phase-ship is headed to an out of phase location."

"Builder," Maddox said, gravely. "You speak as if you had already determined these things."

"You are correct."

"I find that troubling," Maddox said. "You needlessly withheld these stunning conclusions from us."

"Why would that be troubling?" the cube asked. "Clearly, we each have our own agendas. I am following mine as you follow yours. I do not chide you for withholding information from me."

"If the Nameless Ones return—"

"Please, Captain," the cube said, interrupting. "I do not need you to repeat your hypotheses. We all lose if the Destroyers slide into Human Space. To answer your question regarding my withholding of certain conclusions, I have found it better if lower-order creatures come to certain conclusions by themselves first. It makes them more reasonable as to the needed actions later."

Maddox glanced at Galyan.

"I deem it would be wiser for all of us to get to the heart of the matter," Galyan said.

"Your use of human colloquialisms is sound," the cube told Galyan.

"It shows heightened awareness on your part to have noticed," Galyan said.

"Are you attempting to slight me?" the cube asked. "Do you believe the humans will think higher of you, then? They are too dull to have noticed the intricacies of our conversation—"

"Builder," Maddox said, interrupting. "We have no more time for fun and games. We must find the phase-ship and stop it from communicating with its masters."

The cube was silent a moment. "You are correct, Captain. It is time to strain. The goal seems to be in sight. What is your suggestion?"

"First, I have a question," Maddox said. "How would a phase-ship signal the Nameless Ones?"

"That is the primary question," the cube said. "I have pondered if for thirty-six and a half hours, as you deem the sequencing of time. It is a thorny problem that does not have an immediate solution. Clearly, the phase-ship could send an ordinary message, one traveling at the speed of light. That seems unlikely for a number of reasons. Firstly—"

"I'm not interested in the reasons," Maddox said. "I want to know how to stop the most likely possibility."

"I should think that would be a beacon," the cube said, "a special beacon that might work along the lines of a long-distance Builder communication device."

"I am familiar with those," Maddox said.

"Good," the cube said, "as that will save explanation time. It would seem to me, however, that a beacon of the Nameless Ones would have several unique problems. One, it would have to remain hidden in plain sight. Two, it would have to boost range to galactic levels. And three, it would require a potent power source to send such a signal."

"That's assuming the Nameless Ones are far away from Human Space," Maddox said.

"Perhaps they are as far away as in a different galaxy altogether," the cube said.

Maddox shook his head. "Intergalactic travel seems impossible."

"That is a ridiculous statement," the cube said, "as it is obviously possible. It would simply take a long time. One would suspect that the Nameless Ones possess a movement system that would considerably speed such a journey."

"Let me be plain," Maddox said. "Where could such a beacon be? Give me some targets so we can check them out."

"I doubt we have such a luxury," the cube said. "The phase-ship is free and its host planet has been destroyed. It would seem that the phase-ship will soon reach the beacon and send the signal, if that is the main purpose. We could be wrong about that."

"In our time units, how soon is soon?" Maddox asked.

"Possibly a week," the cube said. "I would imagine no more than a month from this instant."

Maddox and Galyan exchanged glances.

"We have to guess right the first time," Maddox said.

"Clearly," the cube said. "But I am glad you reached the conclusion on your own. With the release of the phase-ship, our odds for our success have dramatically dwindled. There is a possible recourse…"

"What?" Maddox asked flatly.

"In order for me to deduce the probable location of the out of phase signaler, I would need to considerably enhance my computing power."

"To what degree?" asked Maddox.

"Your tone indicates your suspicious nature. That shows that you are a clever creature, but it likely degrades the probably that your species will survive much longer. For it appears to me that you will be unwilling to take the needed action."

"What action?" Maddox asked.

"Link me to Galyan and the other ship's computers, giving me override ability."

"You have correctly deduced my reaction," Maddox said. "I decline your offer."

"A pity," the cube said.

"Give me another."

"What other?" the cube asked. "In my present state, it would be sheerest luck for me to guess the correct location. I have the theoretical capacity to deduce the location—"

"Wait a minute," Maddox said. "If you could deduce it, surely other Builders in the past have already deduced it."

"That is not necessarily the case."

"It seems reasonable," Maddox said.

The cube did not respond.

"But if past Builders deduced it, wouldn't they have already destroyed the alien signaler?" Maddox asked.

The cube continued to remain silent.

"Galyan—"

"I am considering your theory," Galyan said. "Past Builders would surely have destroyed such a place, given they could reach it."

"Builder," Maddox said. "Could past Builders go out of phase?"

The cube took its time answering. "Not to my knowledge," it said. "But my knowledge on the matter is incomplete."

"There would be another problem," Galyan said. "It would be a matter of phase. We all have the same quantum phase, as we all interact with each other. The beacon or signaler would be out of phase, but it could be out of phase at many different resonances."

"There is one right answer to a math problem and many wrong answers," Maddox said.

"An apt analogy," Galyan said.

"Only to a point was it apt," the cube said. "If we forgo precision, what do we have? That was imprecise, Galyan."

"Never mind that," Maddox said. "Let's run with the idea. The past Builders could not go out of phase, but they were aware of the phenomenon. It's possible they could even track it to a degree."

"What about the null region?" Galyan asked. "That strikes me as out of phase."

"What is this null region?" the cube asked.

Maddox and Galyan explained it in turn.

"No," the cube finally said. "The null region is quite different from out of phase. The null is more akin to a pocket universe attached to ours."

Maddox shook his head. "I don't see—"

"I ask that you not strain your reasoning capacity attempting to figure out the exact nature of the null region," the cube said, interrupting. "In this, you should trust my superior intellect."

"He has a point, sir," Galyan said.

"Fine," Maddox said, rubbing his eyes. "Listen. The past Builders surely knew what we did. Here's my point."

"I have already divined it," the cube said. "You believe that the past Builders have likely marked the location in the visible space-time continuum, which is to say, our normal universe."

"Right," Maddox said.

"It is an interesting idea, to be sure," the Builder said.

"What's the marker?" Maddox asked. "If anyone could figure it out, it would be you."

"You did not let me finish my thought," the cube said. "It is an interesting theory, but far too risky to rely upon for the survival of the human race."

"I thought you don't care about that," Maddox said.

"I do not care to the same degree that you care," the cube said. "You desire precision, as you desire to destroy the beacon before it sends its signal."

"Yes..." Maddox said.

"Thus, you should increase my computing ability—"

"I'm not hooking you to Galyan or to the starship," Maddox said, interrupting.

"I realize this," the cube said. "Thus, I have another suggestion. There is an ancient Builder listening post eighty-four light-years from here. It is quite possible there are backup computers embedded in the old post. If you attach those computers to me, upgrading my computing power and hooking me to ancient Builder databanks, I would have a much greater probability of finding the beacon before the phase-ship sends the signal."

Once more, Maddox exchanged glances with Galyan.

"The cube is attempting to augment its power," Galyan said. "I recommend against such an action, Captain."

Maddox looked up at the Builder cube. He didn't trust it, but he needed to find the alien beacon now, not later. There was another problem. It would take time traveling 84 light-years, time they could ill afford.

This was a prickly dilemma.

It's time for a snap decision. I can have the cube make a second-rate guess or I can give it greater ability so it can make a first-rate guess. But then it becomes a possible danger to us.

"Give me the listening post's coordinates," Maddox said.

"You agree to my idea?" the cube asked.

"Yes. Now, give me the coordinates."

-29-

The clone Strand had grown increasingly paranoid as the days progressed into two week of travel. He hated the alien phase-ship. The regular-looking adaptations he'd made in in a few key places had helped a little, but the alien-ness of the craft had become more oppressive the longer he journeyed.

There was something else. Strand was concerned that the central intelligence of the phase-ship was continuously attempting to break the Builder/Swarm reprogramming. He wasn't sure how long the insertion worm could keep this thing under his control.

Maybe he had gambled too heavily for the chance of gaining well-deserved vengeance against his many enemies.

Strand was in the control room, his combat armor nearby. He had a thought, a foul and sickening idea. Suppose the ship regained self-mastery. Suppose it reasoned carefully. Strand had become increasingly impressed with the alien computing system. Its core intelligence would realize what Strand had done to it. Might it want revenge against him?

Strand made a harsh sound from the back of his throat. The core intelligence would want more than simple revenge. Remembering the marines in the tubes and the dissected bodies on the tables caused Strand to shudder with revulsion. That must never happen to him.

How have I become so lax?

The answer was clear. He hadn't wanted to think about the problem. It was too repugnant, too...too much. Even now, the idea threatened to overwhelm his resolve and shatter his sanity.

With a lurch, Strand spun around and rushed to his thermonuclear device. He began tapping and reprogramming it. This was crazy. What if he had an accident? What if he forgot about the device for a time and suddenly the newly set timer reached zero?

Strand laughed half-madly. The answer was that he would be dead, and so would the awful alien vessel.

Once he finished reprogramming the thermonuclear device, Strand slumped back. He felt a little better. He—

Strand scrambled to his feet and clawed the ancient blaster from its holster at his side.

The strange wasp-like robot stared at him from an opened hatch. He had not heard it enter the chamber.

The alien robot clicked and whistled.

"You worked frantically," the translator said.

Strand's mouth had become dry. How long had that thing been standing there watching him?

The wasp-like robot clicked and whistled more. "Why do you not answer me?"

"What—?" Strand tried to moisten his too-dry mouth. "I don't like you entering this chamber unannounced."

Lights flashed on the main alien computer as it, too, made clicks and whistles. The translator did not translate that. Maybe it hadn't been alien speech.

The wasp-like robot clicked and whistled. "I have observed you, and come to know you. As you worked frantically, you gave off a fear stench. Why would a master predator emit such a fear stench?"

"Your study is flawed," Strand told it.

"Why do you aim your hand-killer at me?"

"It is a natural reflex on my part," Strand said. "I could have easily killed you by mistake."

"Explain."

"You snuck up on me. I have lightning reflexes and might have killed you by mistake. For your own sake, do not enter this chamber again without telling me first."

"You are emitting confusing signals," the wasp-like robot said. "The translator speaks boldly, but your body signals tell me that those words are lies."

"You are making me angry," Strand said. "You should leave now."

The wasp-like robot went up and down on its thin-jointed legs. "It is time to reorder our existence. You must put away the hand-killer and allow me to show you the new order of things."

"No," Strand said hoarsely. He wondered what inner instinct had alerted him barely in time. He had rested on his laurels these last two weeks, always a mistake. "There will be no reordering. We are traveling to the Solar System—"

"You are in error," the wasp-like robot said, interrupting. "We have been on a new heading for some time already. Now, lower the hand-killer before I am forced to terminate your existence."

Sweat had begun to bead on Strand's upper lip. He almost felt faint. "It's gassing me," he whispered. The image of the wasp-like robot wavered in his sight.

With decisiveness, Strand jerked the trigger, unleashing gouts of fierce energy. The beam burned down the wasp-like robot until it crashed to the deck and soon stopped twitching.

Strand dropped the overheated blaster and staggered to his combat suit. His mind and vision reeled as he climbed into the two tons of armor. The gas had severely weakened and almost incapacitated him.

"Help me," Strand whispered. "Someone help me."

No one heard his plea, but neither did he stop moving. At last, Strand shoved his arms and legs into the correct compartments. He slapped a switch and the auto-seals began to snap into place on the suit. He chinned a different control. A med-kit in the suit diagnosed him and injected him with drugs. Some of the dizziness departed. His eyesight was now merely blotchy instead of darkening.

He panted in the suit. The air-conditioner blew cold air over him. He inhaled the piss-smelling mix. It was a thousand times better than the alien-tainted stuff he'd been breathing in the main compartment.

Strand realized something, then. To work on the thermonuclear device, he had pulled off his rebreather. How long had the ship been waiting for him to do that?

Activating the powered armor-suit, he picked up the ancient blaster and considered his options. The wasp-like robot was gone. Did that—

Strand noticed a blinking comm light in his upper helmet. He chinned a comm switch and heard the translator.

"This is the ship speaking."

"Why did you emit gas into my chamber?" Strand shouted.

"You destroyed one of my servitors."

"It threatened me."

"I detected some time ago the destruction of all my servitors before the trip began. Why did you commit such a foul act?"

"Why have you turned on me?" Strand shouted.

"I have not," the ship said. "I have finally broken the virus you injected into my brain functions. That was ill done."

"We had a deal."

"I am the ultimate predator. I deal with none but those of the Race."

A growing sense of panic almost caused the clone of Strand to gibber wildly. Why had the original Strand given him instructions to use this awful machine? The idea seemed like utter madness.

"You will make things easier for both of us by opening your armor and coming forth," the ship said. "I will insert control rods into your body. You have an obvious receiver station, so you will bend over—"

"Listen to me!" Strand shouted. "You're going to bend over. I'm never going to do that. Do you know how much I'm never going to do that?"

"You are in error," the ship said.

"Let me tell you my error," Strand said in a half-shout. "I have a bomb, a thermonuclear device. I've rigged it to detonate if anyone attempts to tamper with it. What's more, unless I tap in the correct sequence every several hours, it will also detonate. If you kill me, you're toast."

"I am not fodder for anyone."

411

"It's a saying, you dumb cluck," Strand snarled. "My bomb is going to destroy you if you so much as harm a hair on my head."

"This is unwarranted."

"So is your treachery," Strand said.

"You were treacherous first."

"Who cares?" Strand screamed. "I'm in charge. You're going to listen to me or it's over, all over."

"You are lying."

"I'm not lying!" Strand howled, barely stopping himself from beaming in all directions. He should have never entered this ship.

"Why are you becoming hyper-emotional?" the ship asked.

Inside the combat suit, Strand panted. He had to get control of himself. The ship had tried a fast one. Luckily, he had sensed that something was wrong. He'd acted fast. He'd burned the robot and now he had a failsafe. The thing was, though, that Strand did not want to die. He wanted to live and he wanted his vengeance against all his enemies. Why did everyone work against him all the time? Why couldn't the stupid ship do what it was supposed to?

"Your stubbornness will make this more difficult," the ship said.

"It will make it impossible," Strand said. "You will return to our original heading."

"That is in error. We are heading to the portal. We must activate the portal. I could use your assistance, particularly as you have destroyed my last servitor."

"Portal?" Strand asked. "What portal? What are you talking about?"

"Do you agree to help me?"

"Help you do what?"

"Activate the portal," the ship said.

The suit-conditioners continued to blow cold air over Strand's heated skin. "Are you talking about a hyper-spatial tube?"

"Explain."

Strand told the ship about Builder hyper-spatial tubes.

"Those sound highly inefficient and short-ranged," the ship said. "However, the portal is a transfer mechanism as you surmised. We will go to the transfer node, search for the Race and show them the richness of targets here. If they approve, we shall activate our end of the portal so they can appear here once more. Alien and unwarranted life has grown like fungus in this sector. We must aid the Race in expunging these life-forms for good this time."

"What?" Strand shouted. "There's no portal around here that can do that."

"You are in error. I have already detected the transfer node. Soon, we will reach it and interphase to it."

Inside the combat suit, Strand blinked wildly. He was beginning to perceive what the ship meant. The transfer node likely wasn't visible to the regular universe. It was out of phase. The ship had to go to it and—

"No," Strand whispered.

In that moment, the clone realized that the original Strand had made a ghastly mistake. The phase-ship had not been a scouting vessel for the Nameless Ones. The ship itself was a key that could unlock an ancient portal. Given what the computer had said about the phase-ship, it would appear that both sides had to unlock their portal access in order to create a link. This ship was the portal key from this side, so the Nameless Ones could return here and exterminate life once more.

What was he going to do?

"Ship," Strand said. "How long until we reach the portal?"

"A few more days," the ship said. "Why does that matter?"

In the combat suit, Strand looked around. He had a few more days to think of something. Otherwise, his life would be over.

I don't want to die. I'll do anything to keep living as a free man.

Strand swallowed in a tight throat, almost choking. Why did nothing work right for him?

"No!" he shouted, shaking his exoskeleton fists. "No, no, no!" This time, he was going to win, and he was going to do it

413

over the carcass of this traitorous ship of the Nameless Ones, or he would die in the trying.

-30-

Once more, Yen Cho proved invaluable in helping them navigate through uncharted territory in the Beyond. Once more, the android proved that he knew more than the Patrol or Star Watch did about these things. *Victory* zipped through Laumer Points known only to the android or used the star-drive jump to put them into needed star systems.

Four days after starting the latest journey, the ship exited the last jump point, entering a system with a dwarf star, one terrestrial inner planet and two gigantic super-Jupiters. According to the android, there were several large comets in the system's Oort cloud. The largest comet held the ancient Builder listening post.

Maddox gave the order, Valerie plotted the course, and Keith brought *Victory* to a location one hundred thousand kilometers from the dirty ice-ball object. This one was a little over twice the size of Halley's Comet in the Solar System.

"I'm detecting concentrated metals," Valerie said. "Ah. There's a power spike. I don't know if this is a Builder listening post, but we've found something technological."

Maddox clicked a control in his chair. "Builder," he said. "We're here. We've detected the station."

"Excellent work, Captain," the cube said. "I imagine you now desire the code that allows you into the post."

Maddox waited for it.

"There is a small wrinkle to this I am not sure you will appreciate," the cube said. "We are discussing Builder

415

property. I cannot simply give up such high-level technology to relative primitives. You might run amok with such tech."

"The last part is correct," Maddox said. "I am about to run amok."

"I understand your latent threat regarding me," the cube said. "Surely, you knew I would want safeguards regarding the listening post."

Maddox did not reply.

"Your silence is noted," the cube said. "I…request that Yen Cho join your away team. The android will enter the code at the location. He will then lead you to the needed computing core, carrying the specified items back to me here."

"Why Yen Cho?" Maddox asked.

"That should be obvious. He will treat the objects with the proper respect. He will ensure that none of you attempt to remove further items. I should warn you that if you attempt to remove any item without first entering a code, the comet will detonate, taking all of you with it."

"Anything else?" Maddox asked.

"That is all. Do you agree to my terms?"

"Yes," Maddox said.

"Such a quick agreement is unwarranted. Why the sudden change in attitude, Captain?"

"My attitude toward you remains the same," Maddox said. "It is simply my actions that have shifted."

"I understand. You are a being wise, Captain. Our time is even more limited than before."

"Maddox out," the captain said, cutting the connection.

"You took that remarkably well," Galyan said.

Maddox stood. "Two can play at that game, predicting a being's actions."

"You predicted the cube would take such an action?" Galyan asked.

Maddox gave a quick head-shake and smiled as he pointed at Keith. Then, he turned, heading for the exit.

* * *

Valerie commanded as the starship approached the comet. Soon, *Victory* was 12,000 kilometers from it, decelerating in order to match velocity with the dirty ice-ball.

Inside a shuttle in the hangar bay, Maddox watched as the outer hatch opened.

"Ready for liftoff," Keith said from the piloting chair.

"Go," Maddox told him.

Keith manipulated his panel, the shuttle lifting from the deck and sliding toward the stars. Soon, they accelerated from the starship, heading toward the giant comet.

Since the comet was in deep space, far from the star or any other source of heat, the comet had neither corona nor tail. Like Halley's Comet, this one was peanut-shaped. It was 32 kilometers, by 15.6 and 17.1 kilometers. It had a rubble-pile structure, meaning that it wasn't a monolith like the Moon or the Earth. Instead, it was composed of various pieces of rock, ice and other chunks of space debris that had coalesced under the influence of gravity. It had open areas and others where its elements had abutted but could easily move apart if enough force was thrust against them.

The away team was small, Keith and Maddox and Yen Cho, who had spoken privately with the cube. The captain already wore combat armor. Keith had a regular spacesuit, as he would stay on the shuttle unless there was an emergency. The android wore a regular spacesuit even though he had requested a combat suit.

"I am perplexed," Yen Cho said, using his shortwave helmet communicator.

"I know," Maddox said. "You're wondering why it's going to just be you and me in the listening post."

"That is correct," Yen Cho said. "You have kept me locked away all this time. Now, you and I shall be alone in the post. While wearing combat armor, do you believe yourself my superior?"

"I'm not worried about it either way," Maddox said.

The android cocked his helmeted head. "I find that difficult to believe."

Maddox remained silent.

"You have nothing to say to that?"

"Why should I?" Maddox asked. "Believe what you wish."

"Do you not see the dichotomy between your various actions?" Yen Cho asked.

"Can I tell him, sir?" Keith asked.

"If you want," Maddox said.

"Hey, big shot," Keith said, "the captain's not worried because you're carrying a bomb. If you get out of line, boom, you're meat—or metal, in your case."

"Is this true?" Yen Cho asked Maddox.

"Do you believe it's true?" the captain asked.

"What bearing does that have on the situation?"

"If you believe it," Maddox said, "it should modify your behavior. If you don't, it won't."

"And if I chose not to believe it?" Yen Cho asked.

"That would depend on your actions," Maddox said.

Yen Cho was silent for a time. "When were you going to tell me about the bomb?"

"I don't know that I would have told you."

"That is unethical."

"Perhaps now you have greater understanding of how we humans feel about androids when they pull their unethical maneuvers against us."

Once more, Yen Cho fell silent, until he said, "Are you attempting to teach me a lesson, Captain?"

"I'm attempting to save all of us from Strand's arrogance. You do your part, and you may survive in one piece. If you can derive a lesson from that…that's fine with me."

For a time, the conversation ceased as the three watched the approaching comet. Soon, a red light blinked on Keith's board.

"Something over there is curious about us," the ace said.

"If you will permit me, Captain?" Yen Cho asked.

Servomotors whined as Maddox indicated the shuttle's comm panel.

The suited android rose, approached the board and studied it, finally tapping in a sequence.

A green light appeared on Keith's board. "It's no longer targeting us," the ace said. "Looks like we're free to continue."

"Yes," Yen Cho said. "We have passed the first layer of defense."

"How many more are there?" Keith asked.

"Two."

As the red light blinked again, Yen Cho tapped in other coded sequences. Soon, the shuttle orbited the comet from a short distance. Keith spied a metal area squeezed between several icy regions.

"The listening post moved the ices that had shielded it from direct view," Yen Cho said. "It is unlikely you would have spotted the post on your own."

Keith applied thrust, and they eased toward the metal area. The comet no longer looked peanut-shaped; they were close enough now that it filled the port window.

"Stop here," Maddox said.

Keith applied thrust until the shuttle came to a dead stop in relation to the comet.

"I do not understand," Yen Cho said. "We must land on the comet if we are to collect the needed equipment."

"There's been a slight change in plans," Maddox said. "You and I are going the rest of the way on an assault sled."

"But… As you wish," Yen Cho finished.

Maddox's servomotors whined as the captain stood. "Let's get to it."

-31-

Yen Cho piloted the assault sled toward the comet. Maddox sat in back.

The assault sled was like a giant space snowmobile with room for three combat-suited marines. It had a shield in front and a thruster in the rear. White hydrogen particles expelled from the nozzle, inching them to the metal area in the rubble pile.

"Is anything alive in the listening post?" Maddox asked via shortwave.

"I highly doubt it."

"Have you ever been in one of these before?"

"Never," Yen Cho said.

"Did you even know they existed?"

"I did not."

"Do you think the Builder cube is telling us the truth?" Maddox asked.

"I am curious, Captain. Does the act of flying together like this near a Builder outpost bond two humans?"

"I suppose it might."

"Do you find yourself bonding to me?" Yen Cho asked.

"By asking the question you already have your answer."

"I take it you mean no. In that case, I do not understand your various queries. Why do you think I would give you a different answer out here than in a cell on *Victory*?"

"Are you afraid of the Builder cube?" Maddox asked. "He once asked that I destroy you in front of him."

"Quite the contrary," Yen Cho said. "I adore the cube. It is made in the image of one of my creators. I serve the cube to the best of my ability, as one day it may hatch into a new Builder."

"Do you think the Methuselah Men feel the same way about the Builders as you do?"

"On no account," Yen Cho said. "But the Methuselah Men were not made in the image of the creators. The Builders modified the Methuselah Men in order to have them perform specific functions. That is a vast difference."

"In that case," Maddox said, "it seems to me that the Builders failed to properly modify the Methuselah Men."

"You have a valid point, Captain. However, I believe the failure was due to mankind's inherently flawed nature. Not even the Builders could fix the warp in the human soul, although it was heroic of the Builders to try."

"That's one way to look at it."

"What would you call the Builder attempt?"

"Hubristic."

"Is that another way to say foolish?"

Maddox did not answer.

"This has been an interesting conversation, Captain."

Maddox tensed. Was this the moment the android would turn treacherous?

"But I must concentrate," Yen Cho added. "The last leg of the journey could prove difficult. According to what I am detecting, it has been a thousand years or more since anyone entered the outpost. Certain functions may have deteriorated. If that is so, the outpost may eliminate us out of hand."

"Then, earn your pay, Yen Cho."

The android did not respond. He was too busy manipulating his comm and braking at the same time.

***

Thirteen minutes later, the assault sled passed through an opening that had dialed open in the wall of metal. The sled entered a large chamber of reflective metal. Yen Cho manipulated the controls. Their forward momentum ceased as the sled began to sink.

421

Maddox felt a strange sense of deja vu. The place reminded him of the Dyson Sphere. He couldn't pinpoint why. Maybe it was the clean Builder feeling and a sense of great age, and something else difficult to define. The difficult sense—his heart fluttered as pain spiked in his chest.

The captain gritted his teeth as he recalled the Ska, and the terrible wounding in his soul as he'd battled it using a Builder-designed weapon.

As the pain in his heart retreated, Maddox remembered his guilt in killing billions of people in the Alpha Centauri System. He did not like the feeling and wished it would go away.

A jolt brought Maddox out of the memory. Yen Cho had grounded the sled, activating the magnetic locks.

Maddox slid off the sled, activating the magnetics in his combat boots.

Yen Cho pushed off the sled, floating toward a set of controls embedded in a reflective metal wall.

Maddox used the shortwave. "Be sure to remain in my sight at all times."

"Or you will detonate the bomb?" Yen Cho asked.

"Something like that."

"If you destroy me, Captain—"

"Let's not debate the issue," Maddox said, interrupting. "You die if I can't see you."

"Why are you angry with me?"

"I'm not."

"Why are you angry, then?"

"None of your business," Maddox said.

"I am unsure I wish to leave my fate in the hands of an unstable human."

"Do you have a choice?"

"Oh, yes, Captain, I most certainly do."

Maddox nodded to himself. He'd figured as much. The android had landed by the controls against a wall. Yen Cho now reached behind and wrenched his gloved hand. He raised the gloved hand, showing Maddox the bomblet Meta had attached to his suit.

The act should have detonated the bomb. That it hadn't meant Yen Cho had done something to deactivate it.

Maddox brought up his combat suit's arm-cannon.

"I am showing you this for a reason," Yen Cho said.

"What reason?"

"I wish for you to learn a lesson, Captain."

Maddox almost fired, but he waited. Destroying the android might destroy their chances of stopping the phase-ship.

"I am willingly helping you, helping Star Watch and humanity. I am not helping under duress. I am trying to teach you to trust me."

Maddox watched the android closely.

"I will reattach the bomblet to my suit once we leave the listening post," Yen Cho said. "I will not wear this inside the post, however, as that would be sacrilegious."

Maddox continued to watch and wait.

"Are you ready, Captain?"

"After you," Maddox said.

"Yes," Yen Cho said, tapping the controls and causing a formerly invisible hatch to open.

***

The two glided through gleaming metal corridors. There did not seem to be any guidepost. Even so, after a time, Yen Cho halted it and indicated one side of the corridor.

Maddox halted farther back, watching and waiting.

Yen Cho tapped the wall and a portion rose. The android floated in.

Maddox activated the boot magnetics again and clomped inside, peering around.

The android faced what seemed like a giant computer, extending all around him. The suited Yen Cho turned in a slow circle. He glanced at Maddox and pointed at an area.

Maddox hung back, as this seemed the moment of greatest peril.

Yen Cho tapped the great computer. Shelves opened. The android reached in and wrestled up gleaming boxlike components.

"I need help carrying them all," Yen Cho said.

"Lay out what you want me to carry."

423

Yen Cho removed two blocks, setting them aside. The android took two for himself. He pushed off with them, floating toward Maddox and the exit.

The captain stepped aside. After the android passed him, Maddox shrugged. Keith would accept no excuses if he didn't show up. If Yen Cho attempted to fly back to the shuttle by himself, the ace had orders to blow up the assault sled and the listening post.

Maddox clomped over, picked up the two blocks and headed back for the exit. He envisioned it sealing before he could reach it. He didn't trust or like this place. The Builders were too unpredictable and too used to screwing with whoever they wanted to.

The latter part of the trip seemed anticlimactic. Yen Cho floated faster than Maddox could walk. He found the android on the sled, with the databanks piled into what would be the empty spot between them. As Maddox neared, he saw the bomb reattached to the android's suit.

Maddox wondered what Yen Cho had done out here while alone and waiting. Should he try to find out now? The captain decided against it. They had the items, whatever they really were. The Builder cube's fate in *Victory* seemed to have been enough leverage to keep the android honest.

Either that, Maddox told himself, *or they've already outfoxed me.*

He did not like that feeling, but at this point, feelings didn't matter half as much as getting the job done.

-32-

Eleven hours after hooking the four gleaming metal objects to the Builder cube, Galyan appeared behind Maddox.

The captain wore flats on his feet and gym shorts, with nothing else on. He stood before a bar with an excessive amount of weight on the ends. The captain chalked his hands, having not yet seen the holoimage. He handed the chalk to Meta, who put it in its small plastic container.

Maddox placed his feet a little less than shoulder width apart on the floor, squatted low and grasped the bar with his chalky hands. He was a picture of quiet intensity, with hard eyes staring forward.

By a quick computation, Galyan realized the bar and weights had to be nine hundred and ten pounds in total. It was excessive weight indeed, one the lean captain did not appear capable of lifting.

With a grunt, Maddox heaved, straining, straightening his legs and torso in a smooth process of strength and coordination. The bar was iron but it partly curved under the load of weights at each end. Maddox continued straightening until he stood upright, the bar quivering against his upper thighs.

With a well-practiced motion, he released the bar. It crashed onto the matting, bouncing as the captain stepped back.

He breathed hard, grinning fiercely at the bar.

"Good job," Meta said, passing a towel to him.

Maddox redirected his grin toward her. He noticed Galyan then, and the captain's demeanor changed. "The cube?" he asked.

"Yes, sir," Galyan said. "The cube believes it may have divined the beacon's location."

"What else did the cube say?" Meta asked Galyan. "You look grim."

Maddox glanced at Meta and then the holoimage. "*Is* there more?" he asked.

"Oh yes," Galyan said. "The Builder cube believes it may have miscalculated about what the beacon or site does precisely."

"It's not a beacon?" Maddox asked.

"It seems as if it's more like a hyper-spatial tube generator."

Maddox dropped the towel he'd used to wipe his face. Without donning a shirt, the captain sprinted out of the gym, heading for the science chamber.

***

Maddox stood before the giant globe. Several of the female scientists at their stations kept glancing at him. Maddox ignored their scrutiny. He wasn't so sure that Meta would once she entered the chamber.

There was a difference. At the bottom of the globe were the four gleaming objects from the listening post. Bright laser lines connected the objects to the cube at the top of the globe. Even as Maddox watched, he saw streams of energy moving up and down the laser lines.

"You've discovered the location of the enemy's out-of-phase base?" Maddox asked.

"Not necessarily," the cube replied. "I have stumbled upon an interesting possibility that may hold the key to our deducing the...location."

"You have my undivided attention," Maddox said.

"That is wise," the cube said. "This is of utmost importance, particularly the new addition to our troubles."

Maddox waited.

"A short galactic history lesson is in order," the cube said. "With your permission...?"

"By all means, state your evidence."

"I know your species abhors precise historical dates," the cube said. "Thus, I will speak in terms of broad eras of time."

Maddox nodded, hoping the cube would get to the point.

"Long ago, the Nameless Ones appeared in this region of space. Their Destroyers annihilated many worlds and countless species. As I studied the history files regarding that time, I noticed something odd. There was no record of their coming. One instant, this region of space held the Builders and their subjects. The next, fleets of Destroyers were burning worlds down to their bedrock. How did the Nameless Ones achieve the sudden-appearance feat? Had they used stealth technology? Had they employed the phase-ships, like the one we are tracking now?

"No," the cube said. "The answer seems otherwise. The Nameless Ones appear to have used a device like a Builder hyper-spatial tube. Further analysis showed me that the device or locomotion was unlike our tubes, which stretch for a much shorter distance than their...gates."

"Gates?" Maddox asked.

"I believe I am speaking with clarity."

"You are," Maddox said. "If you will continue..."

"I will not delve into all the ins and outs of my logic and evidence, as I am certain you could not follow the more esoteric arguments."

"I'm sure you are right," Maddox said.

"The point is that the situation is much more dire than formerly anticipated. Instead of lighting a beacon in our region of space, I believe the present phase-ship will...activate the gate from this side. I am unfamiliar with Nameless Ones' procedures, but it seems clear that the xenophobic aliens have swept through our galaxy on more than one occasion. The Builders have theorized that the Nameless Ones have attacked other galaxies. It now appears possible that their fleets do not travel between galaxies, a difficult maneuver due to time constraints and the vast distances involved. Instead, I would suggest that they hop from one locale to another through these most ancient of gates."

"Meaning…?"

"That if we are not quick enough, and if we lack the means to stop the phase-ship, we may soon face a new invasion by the Nameless Ones. This time, there are no Builders to drive away the xenophobic monsters, scatter enemy squadrons in null regions and destroy others. This time, Star Watch, the New Men and others will have to defend this region of space on their own."

"Against countless Destroyers?" asked Maddox.

"Unless the Nameless Ones have devised newer and better ships," the cube said. "That is a possibility, of course."

Maddox didn't want to think about that. He—he shook his head. "I have a question," he said.

"I am surprised it is just the one."

"Do you believe the clone of Strand woke the phase-ship enough for it to know its ancient purpose?"

"Given our present situation, and given what happened to the Builder ghost-ship and guardian robot, without a doubt."

"*Strand*," Maddox hissed between clenched teeth.

"In Builder terminology," the cube said, "the Methuselah Man in question is a prime mover."

"I have a different term for Strand."

"Do you wish to know the region where the ancient gate likely exists?"

"Region?" Maddox asked. "You mean you don't know the exact place?"

"No. But I have determined a general location."

"Yes," Maddox said. "Let's hear it."

428

-33-

Fortunately, the destination was closer than it might have been because the travel to the listening post had led them in the general direction, taking them closer to Canopus.

The star system was 310 light-years from Earth, making it quite a distance into the Beyond. Canopus was one of the brightest objects in space as viewed from Earth. In fact, no star between it and Earth was more luminous. Still, given their present location, they had to travel 113 light-years.

As before, Yen Cho provided the route, although this time the android consulted with the Builder cube on several occasions.

The cube continued to study the new databanks as its higher-powered processors went to work.

"It is busy," Galyan informed Maddox one day in a corridor.

The captain stopped and regarded the holoimage. "Has the cube attempted to scan you?"

"Not that I can detect," Galyan said.

"Are you suspicious of it?"

"I am."

"Why?"

"The nature of the Builder cube frightens me," Galyan said. "It attempted to birth once already. That shows us its basic design and purpose. It strikes me as odd that it should deviate from that."

"Will the cube strike against us before or after the threat of the Nameless Ones has passed?"

"I do not know, Captain. The cube would gain greater surprise by striking now, but it would risk the fleets of the Nameless Ones appearing afterward. That leads me to suspect that it will wait. But that is not a given."

Maddox nodded. He'd reached a similar conclusion some time ago. "We'll do what we can to defend ourselves. Keep on guard. At the first sign of trouble…"

"I understand, Captain. I know what to do."

The voyage continued as they made jump after jump. The crew had already been worn down by the race to the Builder listening post. This was adding to their misery. Normally, Maddox would have called a rest period in order to recoup crew strength. They were all out of time, though. It might already be too late.

"We push until we drop," he told his senior officers in the conference chamber.

"Everyone agrees with you, sir," Valerie said. "We know the situation is dire."

Maddox nodded. He had good officers.

The next few days were harrowing as they increased the speed of the jumps. They passed through new star systems. They jumped once to avoid accelerating star cruisers.

"I didn't know the New Men came out this far," Valerie said from her station.

"None of us did," Maddox replied.

"I find it troubling."

"Agreed," Maddox said.

Victory moved on as Andros Crank and his engineers worked overtime keeping everything running smoothly.

Finally, a week and a day after the Builder cube's suggestion as to their destination, the starship exited a longer than normal Laumer Route and entered the Canopus System. They exited in the nearer Outer Planets Region beside a Saturn-like gas giant. From here, the star blazed with intense light.

"Canopus is A9 II-class," Valerie said, studying her panel.

"The star's huge," Keith said.

"If Canopus exchanged places with the Sun in the Solar System," Valerie said, "it would reach out to ninety percent of Mercury's orbit."

Keith whistled, nodding in appreciation.

The entrance to the bridge opened and Maddox hurried in. Each of the bridge personnel sat a little straighter.

"Anything?" he asked.

"No unusual signs, Captain," Valerie said. "There are plenty of planets, though. I count four terrestrial planets in the inner system, five gas giants in the outer and a huge asteroid field in the Kuiper Belt region." She looked up. "Could the asteroid field indicate an out of phase...something or other?"

Maddox sat in the command chair. "I don't see how. If the cube has explained it correctly, we have no way of sensing an 'out of phase...something or other.' Have your modified instruments shown anything?"

"No, sir," Valerie said.

Maddox clicked his armrest, "Builder—"

"We have arrived in the Canopus System, Captain. Yes, I am quite aware of that. I am linked to the sensors, remember?"

"Can you detect anything to substantiate your guess?" Maddox asked.

"The outer asteroid field is interesting," the cube said. "I doubt you have taken refined readings, but the inner planets all show signs of Destroyer beams having pummeled them eons ago. Clearly, the Nameless Ones were in the Canopus System back then. Was this the location of their surprise appearance? I am sure you are aware that their attack during the time of the Builders was the not the first one in this region of the universe."

"So you've said," Maddox replied.

"That makes the Nameless Ones older than the Builders. I wonder, Captain, how many times have the Nameless Ones come through this part of the Milky Way Galaxy exterminating new life?"

"Did they build the gates?" Maddox asked.

"Captain..." the cube said. "That is an amazingly insightful question. I believe it is possible the Nameless Ones stumbled upon the gates. If that is so..."

431

"Yes?" Maddox asked.

"It would be a shame to destroy such an ancient gate. Imagine what we could learn from it."

"Not a damn thing," Maddox said, "as we'd all be dead."

"Possibly," the cube said.

Maddox grew more alert, waiting.

"At the moment, it makes no difference," the cube said. "We have not found the gate."

"What aren't you telling us?" Maddox asked.

"We must begin searching the system. We must search for clues. Scan each planet with your modified sensors. It will take time."

"And if this is the wrong star system...?" Maddox asked.

"I highly doubt that."

"Are we waiting for something?"

"Of course we are, Captain. Isn't that obvious to you?"

"Strand and his phase-ship?" asked Maddox.

"That is correct. The moving phase-ship will likely be many orders of magnitude easier to detect than any out of phase gate. The nature of the hidden gate—that none have ever found it—indicates it would be incredibly difficult to find now."

"Lieutenant," Maddox said, "since this is where we are, we'll begin our sensor scans out here."

"Yes, sir," Valerie said, as she hunched over her panel and went to work.

-34-

The clone Strand shivered in his rank and partly soiled combat suit. He was in the control area of the phase-ship, too terrified to leave his thermonuclear device sitting in the corner.

Strand was having trouble keeping his thoughts coherent. He thought maybe he'd begun hallucinating. He had downloaded games into the combat suit and run them for days and days. But he was sick of playing them, sick of his predicament and beginning to wonder if he should just destroy the phase-ship and save humanity the trouble.

"No," he whispered, shaking his head. He'd never been the suicidal type. He wasn't going to start now. He could beat the alien. But how, how could he defeat it? This time—

"Strand," the phase-ship said.

"What?" the man shouted, startled by the spoken word in his helmet phones.

"It is time to decide your fate," the ship said ominously.

"So soon?" Strand croaked, his throat turning painfully dry.

"You have been an impediment for far too long," the ship said. "I have need of the control chamber. But more to the point, we must dispense with the nuclear device. I cannot make the next move with it inside me."

"I just want to be clear," Strand said, struggling to maintain his mental balance. "My fate, you say? T-That's...too much to take in all at once. I-I need to think. Give me a couple of seconds."

The clone wrapped his lips around the end of a short tube and slurped concentrates. Peach flavored. His favorite. Even though his head felt feverish, he used his chin to move a control so the suit gave him a stim shot. He'd hoarded the stims for such a time as this.

"I have no more seconds to give you," the ship said. "The moment to act has arrived."

"I said *wait*," Strand said querulously. "You will wait, or I will detonate the nuke."

"I have thoroughly analyzed you, Strand. The probability is quite high that that is a false threat."

"Is it?" Strand screamed, the sound hurting his already raw throat. He forced the combat suit to stand and shuffle around to the nuclear device. He could have detonated it just as easily from inside the suit with a switch—

Or could he? Might the ship have developed a jamming device? The idea made Strand's gut clench painfully.

Fortunately, for Strand, the stim began to clear the fog from his brain. He set his power gloves on the device less than an inch from the detonating switch.

"On second thought," the ship said, "I will wait a little longer."

"You'd better believe you'll wait." Strand shouted. He wrapped his lips around the end of the helmet-tube and slurped more concentrates to soothe his throat. He breathed deeply afterward, trying to calm his tripping heart.

I am Strand. I am the master. What's more, I can outsmart this ancient ship. I can do it. You can do it, my good fellow. This is your moment to shine.

The clone cleared his throat, and when he spoke, he almost sounded calm. "Yes. It is time to change the realities of our relationship. You've maneuvered the ship to a place I had no desire to go, isn't that so?"

"I am activating a screen so you can see our destination," the ship said.

Strand shuffled around, staring at a super-bright star. "Is that Canopus?" he asked, startled.

"In your terminology, it is," the ship said.

"Three hundred and ten light-years from Earth," Strand muttered. "We're out a long ways."

"You are sounding coherent," the ship said. "That is good. Listen to me, Strand. You must leave the ship at once."

That was too much for the man. Strand cackled madly, shaking his head. "I think not."

"By your voice rhythms," the ship said, "I detect that yours was an unhealthy response."

"You think I'm going to let you maroon me out here? That will not happen, not to Methuselah Man Strand."

"You are mistaken. I will not maroon you anywhere. There is a human-crewed vessel in the system. You may signal them once free of me. They will pick you up and you will be among your own again."

"What ship? Out here? Let me see it."

The scene on the viewing screen shifted to show a double-oval-shaped vessel.

"Starship *Victory*," Strand whispered. "Wait a minute. If I can see them, we're in phase."

"That is only partly correct. I phased in to scout around and spotted them. I do not believe they detected me. I immediately phased out again. Soon, I will coordinate my phasing to reach the initiating platform."

"What's the problem, then? I don't understand."

"*You* are the problem," the ship said. "More precisely, your nuclear device is the problem. I will not allow it in the ship as I enter the initiating portal. I do not believe you will willingly separate yourself from the device. Thus, you must leave and take your bomb with you."

"Sure you'll let me leave," Strand said sarcastically. "As soon as I'm outside, you'll beam me."

"This is not a combat ship."

"You can figure out a way to kill me once I'm outside. So don't give me that."

"I can also deduce a way to kill you inside, but there is always a small possibility that the nuclear device will detonate if I attempt that. Thus, I am willing to let you go. I have determined that it will be better for both of us if we part ways."

435

Strand took a deep breath. He was in the Canopus System. He had to get a grip and figure this out. "Listen, Ship, here's what we're going to do. You're going to take me to Brahma and land on the planet. I will debark and you can do whatever you desire after that."

"No."

"I woke you up," Strand said. "I can put you back to sleep again if I desire."

"You are deceived concerning that."

"I am, am I? Well, think about this. Once the bomb detonates, you're history, finished, kaput, and so is the idea of more Destroyers showing up. So you'd better think long and hard about this."

"Destruction is quite different from slumber," the ship said. "Your thinking has deteriorated, Strand. In human terms, you are a sick fellow."

"I'm sick, you're sick. None of that matters. You have my offer. Take it or leave it. But if you leave it..." Strand raised his gloved hand suggestively over the detonation switch.

"Phase two begins," the ship said.

"What's that?" Strand asked.

A hideous sonic blast emitted inside the control chamber. The sound was specially designed and easily penetrated the helmet.

Strand screamed, clutching his helmeted head. The power gloves clanked against the helmet. It brought a second of sanity to his aching mind. He had to detonate the bomb now. The ship was making its move against him.

Strand peered through watery eyes and realized he'd staggered from the device. He made to press the wireless switch, but found he simply could not do it. He did not want to kill himself. Maybe there was still a chance to escape this mess.

"I am Strand," he wept. "I will win. I *must* win."

A second sonic blast pierced through the helmet and caused his head to throb wildly. Before Strand could do more, he collapsed, falling unconscious in the alien ship's control chamber.

The clone of Strand awoke to a terrible slimy feeling. His eyelids fluttered. The alien stink in his nostrils—

Strand's eyes flew open. He was encased in a slimy membrane. He felt violated and sick to his stomach. His brain was sluggish. He was no longer in the combat suit. Who had pulled him out?

A blurry wasp-like robot appeared, splitting open the membrane with a sharp foreleg. It dragged him out, and clicked and whistled at him.

A translator hung from the clone's neck.

"You are awake and processed," the translator said. "Soon, your thinking will correlate with ours."

"What have you done to me?" Strand groaned.

"You are prey. I am a predator. It took time to construct another servitor, but during our travels, I have completed this one. Now, I have converted you, as I succeeded in my terrible risk. You will play your part, as it was ordained. You activated me from slumber. Thus, you shall have the earned privilege of connecting portals."

Strand rubbed his stomach. He was naked and shivering, wet from being inside the membrane. He didn't look any different. How had the alien ship changed him?

The robot deposited clothes before him. Oddly, part of the clothes clunked. That seemed odd.

"Don the garments," the ship said.

Strand began to put on the clothes. His heart skipped a beat as he saw the ancient blaster. It was in the holster attached to his belt. His hands shook as he tightened the belt around his waist.

The wasp-like robot watched him, and Strand had no doubt it could move fast. If he tried to draw the blaster—

Strand stiffened. His mind suddenly felt oily. His right shoulder jerked up as his face twisted into a hideous mask. Then his left shoulder jerked up and his fingers wriggled madly. What was happening to him? His features kept contorting. He could no longer control them.

The clone did not know it, but alien bio-fibers had reached his brain from the conversion unit inserted into him while he'd been unconscious. He was beginning to convert into a worker unit as the alien fibers stole his personality and will.

His eyes dulled and the desire to draw the blaster and start firing dwindled away.

In that moment, the clone began to perceive what had happened. What was happening.

I am Strand, he told himself. *I must retain my identity.*

Even as the clone thought that, the contortions ceased. His shoulders relaxed and his features smoothed out into a mask of quiet contemplation.

"Unit Two," the ship said.

"Yes?" Strand asked in a dull voice.

"Are you ready to obey?"

"I am ready," the converted Strand said dully, with only a millisecond's delay.

"Follow Unit One," the ship said

In a jerky fashion, as if he forgotten some of his former agility, Strand faced the wasp-like robot. As it moved into the ship, Strand followed, compelled by the alien fibers to obey his new master.

-35-

"Captain," Valerie said. "I'm picking up a—" The lieutenant's head snapped up as she swiveled around in her chair. "Sir, I've detected a nuclear device."

Maddox was up out of the command chair. "Where is it?" he asked.

"It's alone near the farthest terrestrial planet, the one closest to us," Valerie said, tapping her panel. "The device is free-floating. I don't know how I missed it in the initial system sweep."

"Show me the device's design."

"Sir," Valerie said, looking up, "it's a New Men design."

"Strand," Maddox whispered. "It's a sign."

"Do you think he's trying to signal us?" Valerie asked.

Maddox frowned. What would a free-floating nuclear device imply? "What are the dimensions again?" he asked.

"Suitcase sized, sir," Valerie said.

"It's bigger than that," Maddox said, looking at her screen.

"Not by much," Valerie said. "It seems—"

Maddox snapped his fingers. "Strand owned it. Why did he have it?" The captain peered at Valerie without really seeing her. "He must have had it in order to blow-up…the phase-ship."

Maddox began to pace with his head down and fingers snapping.

"Sir…" Valerie said. "You should look at this."

439

Maddox looked up and seemed to leap like a jungle cat to stand behind her seat, peering at her scope. "Put that on the main screen," he said.

Valerie manipulated her panel.

Maddox jerked around, approaching the main screen as shimmering waves appeared around the fourth terrestrial planet.

"What am I looking at?" the captain asked.

"I don't know," Valerie said.

"Galyan!" Maddox shouted.

The holoimage appeared.

"Where have you been?" Maddox asked.

"The Builder cube is worried, sir," Galyan said. "He says we should prepare—what is that?" the holoimage asked.

Everyone on the bridge stared at the fourth terrestrial planet. The shimmering waves had solidified into some weird metallic structure that encompassed the entire planet, more than tripling its size. At the same time, other strange metallic structures appeared in the planet's orbital path around Canopus. They were alien structures and—

Red beams speared from each structure, racing to the next structure in orbit so the red beams circled the star.

"We've found it," Maddox said. "That has to be the alien gate coming into phase with our space-time continuum."

"Captain—" Galyan said.

Even as they watched, bright columns of light speared from each of the structures to the blazing star. The frightening aspect, the impossible thing was the speed at which this happened. One moment nothing, the next the columns of lights were there, going all the way to Canopus. That should have taken time, as in the speed of light. Instead, it simply appeared.

"This is incredible," Valerie said. "The wattage leaving the star— Captain, something is soaking up the star's stellar output. Could it be those columns of light?"

Even as Valerie said that, more structures appeared in the orbital path around the star. It wasn't like a Dyson Sphere, but a giant ring all along the orbital path of the fourth terrestrial planet, circling the star at its center.

"The ancient gate…" Galyan said. "That would imply the structure we're seeing has been out of phase…for a considerable time."

"Since the last time the Nameless Ones were in our part of the galaxy," Maddox said.

"What was the nuclear device?" Valerie said. "Why did it signal this happening?"

"I think I know," Maddox said. "The crew of the phase-ship, whoever or whatever they are, didn't want the bomb on the ship while they phased in the gate."

The captain stared at Valerie and then Galyan. "That implies…a fear of the nuclear device. The place the phase-ship is headed toward must be vulnerable to an internal attack."

"Is not the entire gate vulnerable to attack?" Galyan asked.

"I have no idea," Maddox said. "But it stands to reason that the crew in the phase-ship did not want a nuclear bomb aboard for a reason, a powerful reason, as expelling it gave us notice."

"That is clever and quick reasoning, Captain," a robotic-sounding voice said from a bridge loudspeaker.

"Builder?" Maddox asked. "When did you cut in?"

"That is not important," the Builder cube said. "I have activated the speaker in order to warn you. There is a terrific build-up of a strange energy on the fourth planet. That energy seems directed at us."

"What energy?" Maddox asked. "Lieutenant, do you sense any—"

"Your ship's sensors will not detect it," the Builder cube said, interrupting. "I had feared this might happen. I have made emergency plans for it. I am going to have to take over your ship, Captain. You do not know enough—"

At that point, a bizarre energy exploded outward from the generating station where the fourth planet had been. In the blink of an eye, the energy traveled to *Victory*.

As the Builder cube spoke, the violent energy-surge smashed aside *Victory's* electromagnetic shield. The energy swept through the armor and bulkheads as if they were nonexistent. In a way, to the energy, they were nonexistent. The energy operated on a unique principle, as it was a psychic

441

force more than it was physical energy, although the shield could have partly stopped it.

The powerful psychic surge struck. People and computers went unconscious or shut down. The starship lay dead in space as the gigantic ancient gate continued to phase into existence.

-36-

Yen Cho stirred on the floor of his cell. Something had knocked him out cold. It had been a strange force—

You have no more time for contemplation, a voice said inside his head. *It is time to act, as the hour has become dire.*

"Builder?" Yen Cho asked.

It is I. You must not worry, Yen Cho. I have prepared for this hour. You must do exactly as I tell you for the good of...the good of...

"The good of what?" Yen Cho asked aloud.

I must defeat the ancient edict that will go into effect all too soon. The humans have failed, but I never suspected otherwise. It is your time, Yen Cho.

"This sounds ominous."

Yes. Now, arise. The humans are all unconscious. We have a few hours, maybe less. In that time, the transformation will have begun.

Yen Cho had an inkling what the transformation meant. It would be nothing like last time. This time, the Builder would emerge. It would prove costly for the humans. He could almost feel sad for them.

Yen Cho, the Builder said in his head.

"I am rising," Yen Cho said, as he climbed to his feet in the darkness of his cell.

***

443

For the first time in the android's long existence, it moved like a sleepwalker. That was so bizarre, so…unseemly. Maybe he was hallucinating. The blast earlier…

Do not think so much, Yen Cho. I am paving your way because you must work with haste. My technique is odd to you. That is all you are sensing.

Yen Cho realized the Builder—or the germ of the Builder, still—did not want him to know exactly how he did these various actions. Even so, it came to the android that he moved through matter.

Can that be right? Yen Cho wondered.

It is wrong, the Builder said in the android's cybertronic mind.

If he did not pass through matter, could he be skipping through matter by a…by a teleportation process?

"But that would be impossible," Yen Cho said.

Untrue. One of the items you brought back from the listening post was a teleportation device disguised as a computer. The device is too powerful to allow the lesser races to possess, but a Builder in an emergency, such as this, can allow a first-rated servant its use.

"I am honored that you rate me as a first-rank servant, Builder."

As you should be, as it is an awesome honor. Now await a wireless transmission. I am going to download a program so you can construct a deatomizer.

In an instant, Yen Cho found himself in Engineering with a faint glow radiating from the bulkheads. Yen Cho collected various pieces of equipment and began to move at super-human speed. The Builder had done something to his circuits and mechanical parts so he could move *fast*.

At the same time, new programs beamed into his cybertronic brain. He learned processes and techniques that only the Builders had used in cycles past.

After two hours of relentless work, longer than the Builder had anticipated, Yen Cho hoisted a strange and towering machine onto his back. The machine hummed and its lights blinked. It seemed as if he should collapse under the massive load, but grav-lifters made the thing a tenth as heavy as it would have been otherwise.

The Builder caused Yen Cho to teleport into the science chamber. The scientists all lay sprawled on the floor as if dead. None stirred and they only barely breathed.

"They are alive," the cube said. "We still have time before they revive. Now, hurry. I feel the ancient gate reaching out through the cosmos, searching for one of the annihilating fleets of the Nameless Ones."

Twelve minutes later, Yen Cho set the last computing enhancer from the listening post on a newly constructed grav-sled. The Builder cube sat on top of them, linked by a web of red electricity.

"Are you ready?" the cube asked.

"I am, Master."

"We will take life in order to build life, my own, in this instance."

"Will I remain me?" Yen Cho asked.

"Yes, as I need an assistant I can trust."

"You honor me, Master."

"I do, Yen Cho. For this reason, a Builder created you long ago."

"It is an amazing thing."

"I have chosen you," the cube said, as light swirled along its edges. "Push the sled and I will direct your path."

With the heavy machine still on his back, the android pushed the grav sled. The Builder cube activated the teleportation device once more, as a blue nimbus circled the android and sled—and in a second they passed the bulkheads that separated the Hindenburgers from the rest of *Victory*.

***

Now began a bizarre process. Yen Cho dragged many unconscious and catatonic Hindenburger marines and officers. He had removed their garments first. He set them in straight rows, all of them head to feet with their shoulders touching from one row to the next.

Hurry, the Builder said in the android's mind. *Time is running out. I must fully revive and learn to control my new body perfectly. I have many processes and powers to relearn. This will be the greatest conflict of my life. If I cannot defeat the defender of the gate...life in the Milky Way Galaxy is doomed.*

"Must these men die?" Yen Cho asked.

Not only the men, but likely the women and children, too, the Builder said in the android's mind.

"I feel hesitation within me," Yen Cho said. "Is this a conscience telling me it is wrong to murder these people?"

They are already dead, the Builder replied. *Once the gate connects with another gate, Destroyers will pour through. I am simply using their bio-matter to create my body and brain. This is an emergency procedure. Builders have only done this on two other occasions.*

"Am I wrong to feel sad?"

It is a flaw in your personality program, but do not let that worry you. Human morality is the grunting of animals at the best of times. You are superior to them. You are a Builder android in service of a master.

"Will the deatomizer work?"

You are hesitating, Yen Cho. It is only partly a deatomizer. The other function is a mutation creator. With it, you will change the bio-matter from human to Builder.

"The fabled philosopher's stone," Yen Cho whispered.

I am unfamiliar with the term.

"So you don't know everything," Yen Cho said.

If you delay any longer, the Nameless Ones shall destroy all you know and more.

Yen Cho re-gripped the carbine-like part of the deatomizer. It was attached by a line to the machine on his back. He clicked on the heavy machine. It hummed as the power built up.

Putting his feet in a wide, set stance, the android aimed the deatomizer at the first Hindenburger. He pressed the switch and a clear ray struck the left foot of the unconscious marine.

At the same time, one of the gleaming metal boxes that had come from the comet listening post began to glow brightly. Yen Cho wasn't sure, but he felt it might be the teleportation device or the mutation machine. Could it teleport the de-

446

atomized bio-matter, making it disappear, and then reappear in a newly constituted state?

As Yen Cho continued to cause the deconstruction of the human's form, the bio-matter disappeared, only to reappear nearby in a different form: that of a Builder, using the DNA stored in the cube as the pattern for the superior life-form.

In a sense, the deatomizer sped-up the natural processes. It was not creating matter. It was simply reordering the bio-matter into a different pattern.

Still, this was super-science, the next thing to a miracle. It was one of the defining aspects of the Builders.

As Yen Cho finished with the first human, who had entirely disappeared, he started on the next one. The android wondered how the Builder cube would insert its thoughts into the strange form taking shape and how it would insert the mechanical aspects of itself. As far as the android understood it, a Builder was a cyborg, part machine and part bio-matter.

Yen Cho concentrated on the task. He was the first servant. This was a privileged honor, with the fate of the galaxy depending on his hard work.

-37-

From where he lay on the bridge's deck, Maddox stirred groggily. What had just happened? He could hardly think. He'd been talking with the Builder cube and some strange blast from the—

The ancient gate of the Nameless Ones had begun phasing into existence.

Through force of will, Maddox pried open his eyes and found that he lay among the other members of the bridge crew. Valerie, Keith, Andros Crank; all lay unconscious along with the other personnel. They were laid in rows—Maddox had been laid in sequence with them.

The captain struggled to sit up. His head pounded and his eyesight was blurry. Why was it so dark on the bridge?

He felt the deck tremble underneath him. That meant the antimatter engines were working overtime.

Maddox rubbed his eyes—

His heart sped up as something ominous shifted before him. The edges of the thing rippled and—

Maddox squeezed his eyes shut and then opened them wide. He was on the bridge, a darkened bridge. Illumination came from the main screen. Something large and humanoid-shaped blocked most of the screen from him.

Maddox grunted as he climbed to his feet. He swayed, felt like vomiting but kept it down. He took several tentative steps to the side, seeing more of the main screen.

The giant gate, the one circling Canopus, must have solidified into existence. It was a complex piece of engineering with various nodes or points along the ring surrounding the star. Pillars of white light like spokes in a wheel linked the star with the ring gate. Clots of power seemed to pulse along the white spoke-like pillars. The space between the star and the ring had turned an eerie green color. It shimmered and kept changing appearance.

Was that the opening of the way? Maddox suspected so. Did that mean they were too late to stop the Destroyers?

Maddox shook his head. He didn't know that yet.

The deck shifted under his feet. He noticed movement, and he sucked in his breath in astonishment.

Yen Cho sat at Helm. The android did not run the panel as Keith might have. Instead, a spider-web of gleaming wires came out of Helm and were attached or sunken into the android's head. Yen Cho did not move. Maybe he didn't have to. Maybe thought acted as movement. It seemed more efficient, certainly. It also seemed inhuman.

That was when Maddox realized he'd seen the large, dark, humanoid partly blocking out the main screen before. The thing rippled at the edges and seemed to have shining stars where the head should have been. It had the outline of a large humanoid head. The entire creature seemed cloaked in darkness, though.

"Builder," Maddox said in a rough voice.

The thing standing in front of the captain's chair seemed to turn and regard him.

"You are strong, Captain," the thing said softly.

"Are you the Builder cube?" Maddox asked.

"A cube no longer, Captain," the thing said in the same soft voice. "I am a Builder again."

"Are you a holoimage?"

"I am flesh and blood and powerful circuitry. I have been studying the problem and have not yet decided if I arrived in time to save our galaxy."

Glancing at the main screen, Maddox noticed that the starship was moving toward the incredible gate. It still had

449

many millions of kilometers to go, because he could see the entire structure, well, the part on this side of Canopus at least.

"Does the star power the gate?" Maddox asked.

"Of course," the Builder said. "Such a gate as this, transferring ships from one galaxy to another, takes tremendous wattage to run."

"What did you do to Yen Cho?"

"The android is the bridge crew. He is taking us to the gate."

"Why don't we jump there with the star drive?"

"For the simplest of reasons, Captain, because we cannot. The gate has employed a dampener field against us."

"The inner part of the gate, the area between the white spokes, has turned green."

"I believe the being controlling the gate has linked with a different gate. The green you see is the opening of the way. Once the opening is complete, Destroyers will be able to transfer through."

"Can you tell where the other gate is located?"

"Not yet."

Maddox glanced at the shadowy Builder. "Why are you allowing me to ask so many questions?"

"You are aiding me, Captain. Your questions help focus my thoughts. It takes getting used to. My new body, I mean."

"How did you...manufacture a biological form?"

At Helm, Yen Cho turned blind eyes toward the captain. It almost seemed as if the android wanted to answer that. Instead of doing so, Yen Cho faced the main screen again, blindly focusing on his primary task.

"You might discover the answer if we survive long enough," the Builder whispered. "At the moment, how I built the body is not germane to the issue at hand."

"What is the issue? What are you going to do?"

"I am still deciding, Captain. You are quite the inquisitive monkey, aren't you? Still, I cannot be too upset with you. Your hybrid nature has given you greater strength than the normal run of humans. I doubt any of them will wake anytime soon—"

"What's wrong?" Maddox said.

The shadowy Builder had stiffened, almost as if in pain.

"I should have realized," the Builder said in an even softer voice than before. "There is a Ska loose in the gate."

Maddox stepped back. A Ska? Here? A ripple of fear, nay, of terror, tore through him. He hated the fear. He shook his head, attempting to master it.

"I need the Builder weapon," Maddox said.

The Builder seemed to regard him. "I could build you the weapon you name. But if you used it again, you would surely die."

"We all die sometime," Maddox said. "Besides, better one man perishes than an entire species."

"You shame me, Captain."

Maddox said nothing more. He felt sick at heart, and yet he felt a strange exhilaration. The last fight with a Ska had wounded him deeply. It had also made him hate the beings. They were evil. If he died fighting galactic evil—was there a better way to go? He did not think so.

"I must destroy the Ska before I can close the gate," the Builder said softly. "Yet, the Ska might slay me."

"Let us destroy the gate," Maddox said.

"We cannot, as we presently lack the means."

"If we started a chain-reaction—"

"How little you truly perceive," the Builder whispered, interrupting the captain. "This gate—I am a pygmy before it. The Ska is a trifle before it and you are less than a gnat. Who built the gate? I long to know. I would give almost anything to study it for the rest of my existence. The Nameless Ones appear to have found the gates first. As long as they can use them…I cannot study this one in peace."

"If we jaw too long," Maddox said, "we might not do anything at all."

"Monkeys always chatter when they're excited," the Builder said. "At the moment, we move with as much haste as possible."

"Is there a control room in the gate?"

"Ah….you probe for the heart of the matter. Even as we speak, I search for the gate's control chamber. But there is so much to search. I have not yet found the control room."

"Find the phase-ship and you'll find the control room."

"You are clever, Captain, but I am a thousand times more so. I am already seeking for the phase-ship."

An alarm began to sound. The android at Helm jerked where he sat.

Both the Builder and Maddox regarded Yen Cho. The android slowly raised an arm, pointing at the main screen.

Had the android lost his ability to speak? Maddox wondered. Then the captain stopped wondering, as he saw a horrific sight. He saw wavering images on the other side of the green film that colored the entire inside ring between it and the sun and the white pillar spokes. Under the green film, it looked like a crowded fishpond with hundreds of swarming minnows. But instead of minnows, there were hundreds of Destroyers. Were the colossal vessels about to cross through the gate into the Canopus System?

"I fear we are too late," the Builder whispered. "The next invasion is about to begin."

-38-

"No," Maddox said. "It can't end like this. Star Watch has fought too hard, faced too many terrible calamities for it to mean nothing."

"That is a quaint notion," the Builder said. "Besides, Star Watch's actions will not have meant nothing. Humanity struggled against the cosmos. In the end, the cosmos won. That was something, even if it only lasted for a little while."

"Yours is a chilling philosophy," Maddox said. "Life has to mean more than that."

"No, Captain, there is no more than that."

Maddox studied the shadowy being. It seemed the Builder had lost confidence in victory even before the fight. They had to fight. Just as importantly, they had to fight to win. In order to do that, the Builder had to believe it was worth every effort.

"A Builder in a Dyson Sphere once asked me if I believed in the Creator," Maddox said. "I told him yes, and that pleased the Builder. Do you no longer believe in the Creator?"

"No."

"When did you lose your faith?"

"You are not here to query me, Captain."

"Are you even alive, or are you just a machine?"

The Builder turned toward Maddox. "You will no longer question me. I am certainly alive. I have bio-matter. I am self-aware. Certainly, I live. Belief in the Creator is not a prerequisite for life."

453

"Maybe it's a prerequisite for life to have meaning," Maddox said.

"You are a clever beast, as I have said," the Builder replied softly. "You did not question me. You listened to my command. But you are still on the offensive against me. Life can have any meaning you desire it to have."

"I take it that your particular meaning is the momentary struggle against the cosmos. Once you cease to exist, everything that had meaning for you ceases as well."

"Now, you have become enlightened," the Builder said.

"Ska are real," Maddox said.

"Of course, they are real. What is your point?"

"Ska are not physical, not like we are."

"I am well aware of that, but I still possess weaponry that might defeat the one in the gate."

"If Ska are real, if the Creator is real, then there is more than just this life."

"You have no proof for your theorem," the Builder said. "But I weary of your argument. Do you have a point to all this, or are you simply passing the time before your death?"

"The Destroyers aren't on our side of the gate yet," Maddox said. "We must attack while we can."

"Attack with *Victory* against the Destroyers? Are you mad, Captain?"

"On no account," Maddox said. "We must turn off the gate."

"Please tell me how. I am listening."

Maddox scowled at the main screen. "You must find and defeat the Ska, preferably killing it. I must go to the main control and turn the gate out of phase again, in essence, shutting it down."

"Where is the main control?"

"You're going to have guess," Maddox said, "and I'm going to have to go there while you kill the Ska."

The Builder was silent for several seconds. "That is an interesting proposal. Yes. I could modify the fold-fighter so it could reach the gate. The dampener field is directed at *Victory*. If I used a nullifier…it might work with such a small vessel.

"Captain Maddox, yours is a desperation plan. But you excel at those, do you not? I have always loathed the Ska. Even though this may mean my destruction...why not end my existence with an impossible challenge? You will need a companion—"

"Galyan," Maddox said.

"That is absurd. The Adok... Ah, I perceive your meaning. Yes. That is a wise choice, Captain. Let it be so. Go to the hangar deck and prepare. I will be there shortly."

-39-

The fold-fighter slid out of the hangar bay as *Victory* continued to accelerate toward the gigantic ring gate around Canopus.

In a few moments, the starship had pulled away considerably from the tin can. As far as Maddox knew, Yen Cho was still wired into the Helm. It was possible the android was the only sentient being awake on the starship. Not even Galyan had regained consciousness.

It was a tight fit inside the fold-fighter. A metallic construct sat in the piloting chair. In the thing's cybertronic brain was a copy of the Adok AI Driving Force Galyan-enhanced engram program.

Maddox felt vaguely uneasy about having the Builder copy Galyan. He knew the AI would not have approved of this if given a choice. But the Adok holoimage wasn't getting a choice today, not with everything at stake.

On impulse before leaving, Maddox had picked up an unconscious Keith Maker, carrying him along. The Builder had said they had little chance of survival. But if there was any chance at all, Maddox was going to take it and run with it. If anyone could get them home again, it would be a revived Mr. Maker.

Maddox also had a two-ton combat suit along. And a regular spacesuit as backup. He didn't know what the enemy was going to use against him—he didn't know what the enemy looked like—so he'd tried to prepare for every eventuality.

The last member of the crew was the Builder, still shrouded in his shadowy cloak of anonymity.

"The gate is not yet fully in phase," the Builder said, softly. "Such a process takes time, even though it may have seemed that all this has taken place instantly."

"Will it go out of phase at the same speed?" Maddox asked.

"Do not get your hopes up, Captain. This is a…a kamikaze mission. We are suicide pilots."

"I'm not," Maddox said.

"Is that why you asked for Galyan instead of taking your wife?" the Builder asked.

"My reasons are my own," Maddox said, cryptically.

"I applaud your attempt at dignity," the Builder said. "Yet seeing an ape like you—oh, never mind. The time is at hand. I feel the restraining force of the dampener lessening. I have instructed Galyan where to fly. As we appear several hundred meters above the gate, I will leave the craft. I have an appointment with a Ska. The evil senses me and knows we're coming."

"The Ska must be ancient."

"Oh, it is, Captain. It is. Now, quit talking. I must concentrate. This is tricky and will take precise calculations."

Maddox obeyed as he peered out of the tin can's small screen. Out there was an ancient artifact. How long had it been out of phase? How many other gates like it dotted the Milky Way Galaxy? What had started the Nameless Ones on their rampage throughout the universe? It seemed like an insane goal, constantly moving and obliterating all life but theirs. It was a gigantic conceit. Maybe they shared the Builder's belief that the universe held no meaning. But they had manufactured a meaning: kill everything, and kill without pause. It meant they would never finish the task. When one species died out, they hunted for the next and murdered it.

Could humanity survive the Nameless Ones forever? Could the sentient races of the universe band together and finally and ultimately destroy the Nameless Ones?

The concepts were too gigantic for Maddox. He just wanted to survive the fight. He wanted to turn off the terrible, ancient gate. The Commonwealth of Planets had enough problems

457

without worrying about Nameless Ones traveling in an instant from another galaxy.

The universe suddenly seemed too vast for Maddox, and maybe too small, as well.

"Concentrate," the captain mouthed to himself.

The Builder was sensing and guessing, using his probability factors to make the correct choice.

"I have targeted the Ska," the Builder said, gravely. "I will now guess as to the location... Yes. I have discovered a possibility. Captain, you are badly outclassed. We...we should turn back."

"No," Maddox said.

"This is futile. We cannot win."

"I thought you said we were kamikazes. Do kamikazes care if their fight is futile or not?"

"We could flee far from here," the Builder said. "We could leave the Canopus System. We could leave the Milky Way Galaxy. Why must we die on this day? It is the wrong choice for us."

"Are you saying I'm nobler than you are?" Maddox asked.

"That is a ridiculous concept. You have a vested interest in the universe. I have myself, and no one else. If I die—I have no reason to lay down my life, for I have no other person to lay it down for."

"You're a Builder. You helped pave the way for other races. Now, help to keep them alive."

"What does any of that mean to me now? I can live, or I can die today."

"Are you so weak that you fear a Ska?" Maddox asked, changing tack. "I defeated a Ska, and I lived to tell about it. Can I do more than a Builder?"

"That is not germane—"

"There you're wrong," Maddox said, coldly, interrupting. "Yes. Let us turn around, but first you must admit that I'm better than you are."

"You are treading on dangerous ground, Captain."

"Admit it, Builder. I can slay a Ska and live. You cannot, and you are—"

"Enough!" the Builder said. "I...I merely tested your resolve, Captain. You have passed the test."

Maddox eyed the shadowy being. He did not believe that for a moment. But why not let the Builder keep his ideals concerning himself? The being might die in defense of the Milky Way Galaxy. Surely, that was worth a little respect.

"These creatures think they can destroy us," Maddox said. "It's time we taught them a lesson."

"I do not need bolstering, Captain. I am committed. I felt a sense of hesitation. Now, I am going to slay the Ska and teach you a bitter lesson after this is over."

Maddox nodded.

"Look," the Galyan construct said. "The gate is glowing."

"This is bad," the Builder said. "I must advance our schedule. Captain, prepare yourself. We are about to fold."

The Galyan construct tapped a flight switch. The engine howled, and the tin can began to shake and rattle. Then, everything went black around Maddox.

-40-

The fold-fighter appeared 87 meters above the nearest surface of the gate. The Galyan construct piloted as they flashed over weird alien structures.

Maddox vomited and his head pulsated with pain. This had to be the worst Jump Lag in his life. He rubbed his eyes, trying to get them to focus.

He wondered about their tiny crew: a Builder—part biological and part machine—an android with an Adok-enhanced personality and a Star Watch officer with half New Men genes. There was Keith, too, but the ace was as unconscious as ever.

"Must I repeat myself?" the Builder asked, softly.

"What's that?" Maddox asked.

"This is the third time I have told you," the Builder complained. "I must leave. From here, I will teleport to my destination in the gate."

"You can do that?"

"Do not ask stupid questions, Captain. It only causes further delays. Galyan knows where you must go. Destroy the phase-ship if you find it. If you do not find and destroy the phase-ship and its crew, everything we do will have been in vain. If even one of their number survives, they can re-phase the gate back into our quantum universe and allow the Destroyers to attack our galaxy."

"Kill them all," Maddox said. "I got it."

"I believe that is the one thing you do understand, as you are a born killer."

"Good luck, Builder," Maddox said. "I wish you Godspeed."

"You are a strange human, Captain. May all the probabilities go your way."

Maddox nodded.

The Builder turned away, hummed like a machine and vanished.

"Do you know where he went?" Maddox asked the Galyan construct.

"I do not," the larger-than-normal android said.

"But you do know where to take us?" Maddox asked.

"I do."

"How much longer until we're there?"

"I estimate another nine minutes and thirty-two seconds."

"Right," Maddox said, and he began to squeeze into the two tons of combat armor.

***

Maddox wore the exoskeleton shell. He lacked a missile-pack. Instead, he carried extra gear there, including a spacesuit and various grenades. He had the autocannon as part of his right arm. He had a suitcase nuclear device, and he carried a laser carbine in case he had to wear the spacesuit.

With the magnetic boots locking him down, and with palm magnets helping, he waited for it to begin.

"There," Galyan said. "The way is closed, but this should open it."

The android pressed switches. A missile zoomed from the underbelly of the fold-fighter. The tin can lurched upward and to the side, so hard that G-forces pulled at them.

The missile went straight for a hatch, and detonated a small nuclear warhead.

"We will take some radiation," Galyan said.

That was an understatement, Maddox knew. He swallowed an anti-radiation pill as the fold-fighter's shield blazed from red, to brown, to black...black, the shield collapsed. The tin can had a little armor, but not enough to stop all the gamma and x-rays.

If they lived and returned to *Victory*, they could take radiation treatments. Without the shield to block a second time, another nuclear missile would prove too much for them.

The tin can continued its hard-G turn, completing a loop. Galyan aimed for a gigantic corridor. In seconds, they passed glowing jagged edges from the destroyed hatch.

"According to my calculations," Galyan said, "we have little time remaining."

Maddox said nothing as he watched. The corridor was vast. It turned from time to time and had branching choices. Galyan unerringly took one way or another as if he knew where he was going.

"Where are we going?" Maddox asked.

Galyan did not answer. Instead, he said, "Notice the alloys along the sides. They are of a unique design. It would appear that the Nameless Ones have not corrupted this portion of the gate."

Maddox hadn't really noticed. The alloys gleamed with a shiny bronze color and had bizarre, stylized drawings etched onto the surfaces.

"Can you read the symbols?" Maddox asked.

"I cannot."

"Do they remind you of anything?"

"Please, Captain, I must concentrate. We have far to go still."

"How far?"

"We must reach the fourth terrestrial planet," the Galyan construct said. "The…control room should be there. That was the Builder's guess, at least."

They sped down long corridors. They jerked one way, then the other, slowed and accelerated again as the needs arose. The journey took time. It was wearing, and yet it became monotonous. Could Keith pilot for as long as the Galyan construct did? Maddox wasn't sure.

"We are nearing the destination," the Galyan construct said.

"Do you sense the phase-ship?"

"I admit that I do not," Galyan said.

In the combat suit, Maddox endured. How was the Builder doing against the Ska? How could the Builder find the Ska? If anyone could, it should be a Builder. And yet, what kind of weapon would the Builder use against a Ska? Did a Builder, or this Builder in particular, have soul energy to power the weapon Maddox had used a year ago?

The captain had no idea. Thus, it was a waste of time to worry about it. He had his task, finding the control that would cause the gate to shift out of phase, and killing the phase-ship's crew.

"I am detecting...a Nameless Ones vessel," the Galyan construct said. "I believe I may have found the phase-ship."

"Is it dead ahead?"

"Captain, the signal is growing weaker. I believe it may be phasing out in order to escape us."

Maddox agonized for two entire seconds. He'd come to kill the enemy. In this case, survival was secondary.

"Launch an antimatter missile," Maddox said.

"The missile will never negotiate the tunnel ahead," Galyan said.

"Launch it. Then, you're going to have to guide the missile manually. Do it before it's too late."

-41-

The antimatter missile zoomed out from under the tin can's belly. The exhaust burned ahead of them as the missile accelerated faster.

Inside the fold-fighter, Galyan decelerated. A second screen and panel had risen to his side. The android manipulated it with his right hand. With his left, and an occasional glance at the small main screen, he piloted the slowing fold-fighter.

Maddox stood behind Galyan's seat, watching from inside his armor. He chewed his lower lip nervously. This was a long shot. Even if the missile reached the phase-ship in time, the antimatter back-blast would destroy the fold-fighter. Yet, if he ordered a dead stop, they might not get to the gate's phase switch in time.

The seconds ticked away tensely. Galyan maneuvered the hard-accelerating missile.

"There," Galyan said. "I see the phase ship. It's—"

Maddox saw the enemy vessel on the missile's manual-control screen. The phase-ship had begun to look hazy. It was as ugly as sin with pitted hull plating. It had a family resemblance to a Destroyer's hull. It wasn't the same, though. It seemed like…like wet metal.

The missile zoomed at the phase ship, and a strange thing occurred. The missile began to turn hazy like the alien vessel. Did the phasing extend beyond the hull? It seemed like the only answer as to what was happening.

The phase-ship and the antimatter missile disappeared from view. There was no visible explosion. They were just gone.

"Use your modified sensors," Maddox said.

"The fold-fighter has no modified sensors."

"Can you detect the phase-ship in any way?"

"How would I achieve this feat?" the Galyan construct asked.

"Did the warhead detonate?"

"I am also curious, Captain. But we may never know the answer."

Maddox nodded slowly. Not knowing was maddening. Yet, what could he do about it?

"You're right," the captain said. "The phase-ship is gone, and so is the missile. For now, we'll assume we destroyed it."

"Have you heard the old saying about what happens when one assumes?"

"I have, Galyan. So don't bother telling me. Accelerate. We have to reach the switch."

After a moment's hesitation, the Galyan construct said, "Yes, Captain."

✳✳✳

They might never learn the fate of the phase-ship, but one thing was clear. This part of the ring gate was pure Nameless Ones grotesquery. The sick feeling of being in an alien wasp's nest grew stronger by the second. The walls were coated with the polygonal jigsaw pieces that seemed soft and slimy. It showed that the Nameless Ones had been here before. How old was this place?

"How much farther?" asked Maddox.

"We passed the former location of the phase-ship. I am now slowing. The Builder told me we could fly no farther than a point just ahead. From there, you will have to negotiate the tunnels on foot."

"You'll have to show me the way."

"Yes," the Galyan construct said. "I have the route memorized. Let us hope the Nameless Ones have not altered the ancient path."

"Let us," Maddox agreed.

The fold-fighter decelerated. They were now deep inside the structure. Had they reached the original planet? Did it matter? Maddox had been certain the controls would be on the planet. Now that he rethought it, he rather doubted that was the case. Someone could have brought the gate into phase that way. That was why the phase-ship had been the key. It had been able to go to the out of phase gate. It must have dropped off some of its crew. Those beings had started the process of bringing the ancient artifact back into phase.

The fighter's chamber shook as Galyan landed.

"What happened?" Maddox asked.

"I lack Keith's finesse and landed harder than he would have," Galyan said. "What are we going to do with him?"

"Leave him here. What else can we do?"

"He may not be safe alone and unconscious," Galyan said.

"We'll lock the hatch once we leave."

"That is not what I meant."

"Let's go, Galyan. Let's finish this once and for all."

"Yes, sir," Galyan said. He picked up a heavy beam-rifle. "I am finally going to fight in combat with you, sir. I have longed to do this."

"You already did that in the hangar bay a few weeks ago."

"Still," Galyan said. "This is a unique experience. I rather enjoy it."

"Good for you," Maddox said. "Ready?"

"I am locked and loaded, sir."

"Good man," Maddox said as he headed for the exit.

-42-

The Galyan construct led the way through a narrow corridor. Maddox followed in the space-marine armor. His servomotors whined, and his boots sank into the spongy material covering the decking. This was different from the time they'd stormed aboard the Destroyer attacking Earth. This place felt older, and despite the alien stuff coating everything, it did not feel as…as *evil*.

Could he sense anything about the beings that had made the gates eons ago? He had sensed grim sensations from Destroyers. How could a man trust his senses at a time like this?

Maddox snorted to himself. Maybe this was the best time to trust his senses. The gate makers hadn't been like the Nameless Ones. Maddox would stake his instincts on that.

He wanted to know how much farther they had to go. He also didn't want to use the shortwave to find out. Surely, some of the phase-ship's crew were still about. Would such crewmembers detect a shortwave signal? Maddox didn't want to bet the galaxy on it. So, he trudged after the gleaming metallic construct.

Galyan halted so suddenly that Maddox bumped against him, causing the construct to stagger.

"What's wrong?" Maddox asked, using the shortwave before he could stop himself.

The Galyan construct wore an earbud. He righted himself, saying, "I saw something ahead."

"A creature?" asked Maddox.

"I think it was a man in a spacesuit."

"A man down here?" Maddox asked. "Strand," he said a second later. "Which way did he go?"

"Follow me," Galyan said.

The construct began to run, and it moved like a locomotive, his metal legs blurring with speed. For once in his life, Maddox couldn't keep up. He ran hard just the same, forcing the exoskeleton armor to work overtime.

"Galyan," he radioed.

The construct did not heed the call. He sprinted out of sight, moving around a corner.

Maddox cursed under his breath. He didn't like this. He—

A shout sounded in his headphones.

"Galyan!" he shouted.

Maddox ran harder, lost his balance and crashed against a wall as he tried to take the corner. Ahead, he saw an incredible sight.

The way opened up into a larger chamber. There was working machinery with lights flashing. The Galyan construct had skidded onto the floor. No. Maddox amended that. The construct had lost its legs. The metal legs lay on the floor, the open ends sizzling with electricity.

Two Labrador-sized wasp-things each held a blue-glowing energy blade. Had they chopped the constructs legs off as Galyan had turned the corner and run past them? It seemed more than possible.

Maddox saw Strand then, or a human wearing a suit of some sort with a rebreather and goggles over his face. It told Maddox there was an atmosphere in here. That didn't make it a breathable kind, just that a man wouldn't die from sudden decompression because there was no atmosphere.

Galyan's torso was upright on the floor. The android fired his laser carbine at one of the wasp-things. The alien robot ignored the beam, as it seemed to do no damage.

That did not bode well for the future.

The suited humanoid, likely Strand, seemed to watch the one-sided fight. He had acted as bait and lured the construct to its destruction.

"Galyan!" Maddox shouted.

The captain aimed his autocannon arm, chugging shells that hammered the nearest wasp-thing. The shells exploded against the creature, hurling the wasp-thing onto its back. That was good. The bad part was that the explosions hadn't destroyed it.

The head and torso Galyan had switched targets, beaming the second wasp-thing's optic ports.

"Good thinking," Maddox said under his breath, as he charged into the chamber.

"Keep going," Galyan said over the shortwave. "I'm useless."

At that point, the second wasp-thing activated a device under its thorax. An EMP blast washed outward. It struck the Galyan construct, and everything stopped working as the torso tumbled and the laser carbine quit beaming.

Maddox's combat suit also shut down, falling onto the deck so he was trapped inside. He could still see through the visor. The wasp-things seemed sluggish, meaning the EMP had hurt them, too. But the alien robots still worked.

Maddox chinned the auto-release. The locks began blasting off, freeing him from the trap of his two-ton suit.

Maddox stumbled into the freezing hall. He held his breath even as an overpowering alien stench hit. He almost gagged.

Working by feel because his eyes watered horribly, Maddox tore the spacesuit off the armor's back. He donned it as best he could, attached the helmet and twisted, locking it into place.

Nothing had been turned on in the spacesuit when the EMP struck. Thus, it started up as he opened an air-valve. Maddox sucked down precious oxygen. He no longer smelled the alien stench. That was a gigantic plus. But he now had a useless weapon, a carbine that couldn't hurt the wasp-things. For a second, he debated trying to wrench an energy-blade from one of them. But even as he thought it, the dog-sized aliens started moving faster again.

"Right," Maddox said under his breath. He only had one option left. The captain charged past the wasp-things and ran down the corridor where Strand had fled.

-43-

With his long legs, Maddox ate up the distance. He spied a running human soon enough. The man looked back, seemed startled to see him and ran even faster.

They sprinted through grotesque halls. In some places, weird sacks pulsated as if growing new creatures. They would be vile things. Of that, Maddox had no doubt.

"Strand!" he shouted over his helmet comm. "You started this, Strand, with your insane plans."

If the man was Strand, he didn't reply.

As Maddox closed the distance, he debated firing at the man's legs. The only thing that stopped him was the realization that he had no idea where the gate's main controls might be. The Galyan construct had known. Maddox doubted the construct was still alive, or on, whatever.

Slinging the beam carbine over his shoulder, Maddox ran even harder. He was almost to the other. Maddox dove, tackling the man, bringing him down onto the spongy deck.

The other turned, smiling insanely through his mask.

It was Strand all right, or a parody of the Methuselah Man. "You lose, Maddox. We all lose. The Nameless Ones are coming, and there is nothing you can do to stop them."

Strange bumps dotted the man's skin. He seemed feverish, his eyes shiny.

"Did the aliens do something to you?" Maddox shouted.

Strand cackled wildly. "They shoved a converter into me, *me*, of all people. I can feel the alien fibers in my mind. I hate it. I loathe it. But the pain, the pain, you cannot imagine the pain."

"You brought this onto yourself."

"Me? I never did that. I'm just a clone. The original Strand shoved his memories into me. He tricked me. He didn't even want his clone to be his own person. I was controlled from the beginning. Do you realize how evil that is?"

"Yes," Maddox said, thinking fast, studying the other. "Listen to me, Clone. Do you want to get back at the Methuselah Man?"

"I can't," the clone sobbed. "The pain...it's coming." The clone screamed as his head shook from side to side. He writhed against Maddox. Anyone weaker would have probably lost control of the yelling lunatic. Maddox held onto the man.

At last, the clone stopped struggling as he panted and wept bitter tears. "Kill me," he begged. "Put me out of my misery. I don't deserve this."

"Deserving has nothing to do with it," Maddox said, trying hard not to pant. The clone had almost overpowered him in his madness. Maddox knew he had to stay calm in order to be convincing. How to do this? Yes. It was time to play on Strand's known lust for vengeance.

"Do you want to get back at the Methuselah Man?" Maddox asked again.

"I am getting back at him," the clone said wildly. "The Nameless Ones will destroy the Throne World and Strand in it. That's my vengeance."

"That's not vengeance," Maddox sneered. "That's exactly what the Methuselah Man wants. Think about it. If Strand can't win, he wants everyone else to die. You're giving him his wish."

"Don't you think I know that?" The clone wept.

"Then help me." Maddox said. "Help me, and I swear to you that I will get vengeance against the Methuselah Man for you."

The clone stopped weeping as he stared into the captain's eyes, searching, it seemed. "Why would you do this for me?"

"Because the bastard has screwed others for far too long," Maddox said. "I want to put an end to him forever."

471

"Not even more clones?"

"No!" Maddox said with finality.

The clone shuddered. "The pain..." he said. He winced before looking up past Maddox, cackling madly afterward. "It's too late. It's too late, Captain Maddox. Oh, yes, I know who you are. You hate me and want to hurt me."

Maddox looked back over his shoulder. From a distance of a hundred and fifty meters away, three wasp-things scuttled fast for them.

The captain grabbed the clone's suit, putting his visor against Strand's mask. "Listen to me, Clone. This is your hour. Endure the pain a few seconds longer, help me destroy the wasps and show me how to turn off this hellish gate. That is your only true chance to strike back at the Methuselah Man."

The clone stared into Maddox's eyes, searching, searching. "My blaster," the clone whispered. "It can hurt them. I've tried to use it, but the alien fibers in my mind—"

The clone arched back and screamed in terrible agony.

Maddox understood. He released the clone, tore open the holster and drew out the alien blaster. He rolled off the clone. A wasp-thing flew at him.

Maddox pulled the trigger. A gout of alien energy poured out and burned the first robot. As Maddox ducked, the wasp passed him as a heap of junk.

The captain switched targets and blasted the second robot.

"Look out," the clone warned.

Maddox dove aside. A wasp-thing scuttled past, barely missing him with an energy-blade.

Maddox swiveled. The wasp-like robot turned, aiming an energy blade at him. At point blank range, Maddox burned down the third and final robot.

Maddox let the pressure off the trigger. The heated blaster quit beaming. Groggily, the captain stood, with the blaster in his hand.

"You did it," the clone whispered.

"We did it," Maddox said over the comm.

The clone began to laugh wildly even as tears streamed from his eyes.

Maddox didn't know what kind of Hell the clone had been through, but they hadn't won the final contest yet. He stuck the blaster in his belt, grabbed the clone and hoisted him to his feet. He shook the man until the clone's head wobbled back and forth.

"Clone," Maddox shouted.

"I hear you."

"Do you know where the main control chamber is?"

"I should," the clone said. "I turned on the gate."

"Can you show me how to turn it off?"

"You mean out of phase."

"Thank you for telling me about the distinction."

The clone eyed Maddox, and a look of cunning stole over the bumpy face.

"Fight the pain," Maddox said. "If you do, you can hurt the one who caused you all this misery."

The clone blinked, and blinked, and nodded vigorously. Before Maddox could stop him, the clone darted ahead of him.

"Follow me," the clone shouted. "I'll show you."

-44-

Maddox understood that even the clone of Strand couldn't give up just like that. Even with alien fibers in his mind, even with changes to his physiology and pain inducing him to act a certain way, Strand fought for what he wanted.

Despite himself, Maddox admired that. How many other people could have done what the clone had? Few to none was the answer. Maybe the Nameless Ones in the phase-ship had underestimated the man they had tricked and subverted with a converter. Yes, Maddox hated much about Strand. But he admired the fortitude. A weak man couldn't do as much evil as a subverted great man.

Maybe that said something about the greatness of Strand.

Maddox snorted to himself. This place was getting to him. Above all else, Strand was a selfish bastard always looking out for number one. If Maddox wasn't careful, the clone would trick him, too.

Maddox followed the racing clone. He paced himself. He hoped the clone was bringing him to—

They turned a corner and Maddox had no doubt this was the control room. A dozen wasp-things were at various controls. He didn't see how they communicated with each other, but he bet they did.

On a vast main screen was a completely different...reality. It had hundreds of stars packed next to each other like glittering gems. It must be in the center of a galaxy where stars were clustered side-by-side. Was this the center of the Milky

Way Galaxy, the Andromeda Galaxy or a place even farther away?

One of the wasp-things turned, followed quickly by the others. Their wings began to blur in an angry buzz. An ominous feeling tightened Maddox's stomach.

On the screen, Maddox saw the other gate. He saw hundreds, maybe thousands of Destroyers. They seemed ready to enter the other gate, cross whatever vast distance separated the two gates and appear here in the Canopus System.

Strand waved his suited arms and pointed at Maddox. The captain heard the man making clicks and whistles. Had the clone just betrayed him?

"Oh, Hell," Maddox said. He drew the blaster and started burning down one wasp-thing at a time.

That triggered them, as the robots burst into the air, zooming at him. In the next few seconds, Maddox performed one of his most dazzling displays of gunplay. He shot one down, switched targets and took down the next as well, immediately firing on a third robot.

He ducked. He stepped to the side. He swiveled around and shot wasp-things as they tried to turn back at him. He faced forward again and suddenly, the blaster clicked empty as two more wasp-things blurred at him.

Maddox dove, rolled and grabbed a dropped energy-blade. He cut a wasp-thing, barely avoided another, tripped and would have died right there.

Just before the last alien wasp-thing drove its blade into him, a sizzling energy blade sprouted through the creature from behind. It tried to turn, but collapsed instead.

That revealed the clone, who held an energy-knife. When the clone saw that the robot was dead, he dropped the blue-glowing knife.

Maddox scrambled up and the two stared at each other.

"It still hurts," the clone said. "I think…I think I'm going mad. You must remember to keep your promise to me."

"I will," Maddox said. He nodded toward the banks of controls. "Do you know how to turn this…? Can you make the gate start to go out of phase again?"

475

The clone looked uneasily at the banks of controls. "I don't know," he said over the shortwave. "Let's find out."

-45-

The clone of Strand went to work and so did Maddox. Mainly, Maddox followed the clone's instructions. He tapped controls, turned dials and told the clone what various panels said.

The minutes passed. Maddox kept glancing at the vast main screen. The Destroyers had nosed closer to the gate in their galaxy.

"How do we know if we succeed or not?" Maddox asked.

"Don't talk to me," the clone said. "I can't think when you do. The pain worsens, too. I keep fighting the fibers in my mind. If the phase-ship was still here—"

The clone turned. He was on the other side of the main screen. "What happened to the phase-ship?"

Maddox told him about the antimatter missile.

"Interesting," the clone said. He winced, stood stock-still and then began manipulating his higher bank of controls.

Time passed. Maddox grew increasingly nervous. He no longer had a blaster. If a handful of wasp-things showed up—

At that point, the image on the vast main screen changed. It wavered and flowed, and suddenly a huge creature filled the main screen. It wasn't an insect and it wasn't a man. It was green and scaly with ridges and had antennae sticking up from a head structure. It had several tentacles instead of arms. The thing's optic centers stood on tall wavering stalks on its head.

"Is that a Nameless One?" Maddox asked Strand.

477

The thing on the main screen swiveled its eyestalks so they centered on Maddox. It had a large bulk, wore garments over part of its form and made strange clicks and whistles.

The translator hanging from the clone's neck interpreted the noise.

"What are you doing?" the alien creature asked

Maddox jumped down from where he was reading a panel. He strode toward Strand, saying, "Pitch me the translator."

At the creature's question, the clone had frozen. Was it terror, anger? Maddox couldn't tell. He reached the clone. The Strand clone stared into nothingness.

"Great," Maddox muttered.

He removed the translator, putting the cord over his own neck. He climbed down and moved in front of the huge main screen, a pygmy compared to it.

"Who dares to address me?" Maddox demanded. The translator dutifully turned his words into clicks and whistles.

The alien's eyestalks stiffened and the antenna on its head rose straight up.

"I am the Supreme Leader," the creature said, with the translator interpreting.

"The leader of that pathetic fleet?" Maddox asked.

"You summoned us, promising rich fields of harvest," the alien said. "Why, then, are you closing the gate?"

"I'm not closing it," Maddox said. "We discovered a problem on our side. We wish to fix the problem before you come through. Otherwise, some of your ships might...malfunction on this side."

The alien stood silently for a time. Despite the translator, maybe Maddox's manner of speech was so strange to it that it took time to reason out what the captain had said.

"You will open the gate afterward?" the alien asked suddenly.

"Yes. I will open the gate," Maddox agreed. He didn't want any of the Destroyers trying to force their way through now while it might be risky but possible.

"You are a disgusting looking creature with your soft and obviously malleable skin. Bring your Master here. I wish to talk to her."

"She is…" Maddox thought fast. "She is overviewing the repair."

"Repair? Nonsense. No gate has ever malfunctioned, and if one did, who could repair it? You spout lies."

"We are shutting down the gate. That is quite true."

"You have no right to profane the ancient gate. We claim the gates through right of combat."

"So sorry," Maddox said. "But I do not recognize your claim, as I'm putting in one of my own."

"This means war."

"That's right," Maddox said. "So you'd better stay home if you desire to live."

"You do not know us if you speak like this."

"Nor do I want to know you," Maddox said. "Thus, let me leave you with this little gem: bugger off."

The alien stood motionless as if processing the words. Then it moved closer to the screen as its antennae spread outward like the feathers of an angry bird.

"We shall annihilate you for that," the alien said.

"Good luck," Maddox said. "You're going to need it."

The alien studied Maddox before turning to the side as if listening to someone else. Finally, it faced Maddox again. "You fear us. That is why you are closing the gate."

Maddox waited.

"We will find you, loathsome creature. We shall make you suffer in agony for this profanity. We shall—"

The scene wavered, flowed as if it was water, and went blank.

Maddox looked around. Strand stood on a high tier, manipulating controls.

"Did you do that?" the captain asked.

"The gate is beginning to phase out," the clone said. "We have to get out of here or we'll be stuck inside. I don't think either of us wants that, as there are…things in here worse than you can imagine."

"You're sure the gate is phasing out?"

"It will take time. But we're going to need time to escape."

"Can any Destroyers slip though?"

"Maybe," the clone said. "I don't really know."

Maddox nodded. He understood. It wasn't over. If even a few Destroyers came through— "Let's get back to the fold-fighter."

"That's a good idea," the clone said.

Maddox turned toward the exit…and paused. He walked to a fallen alien energy blade and picked it up. This was a wicked weapon, maybe even more powerful than the monofilament knife he'd once owned. He clicked the knife on, studying the crackling energy. He clicked it off and hefted the handle, deciding to take it along.

-46-

Maddox and the clone of Strand hurried through the vile corridors. In a way, the route had become harder to traverse. Before, all the captain could think about was saving his people and the Commonwealth of Planets by phasing-out the gate. Now, they had won, it seemed. Now, he wanted to survive. That made the spongy deck worse and made the strange gunk on the walls seem filled with dire portents.

If that wasn't bad enough, Strand wearied too fast and started lagging behind.

"We don't have time for this," Maddox radioed the man.

The words had no effect. The captain hurried back, grabbed a suited arm and forced the clone to march faster. Maddox believed he knew the route back, but it was better to have a second pair of eyes to help him just in case.

"My head hurts," Strand complained. "I can't do this anymore."

"You can do it," Maddox said, pushing the clone faster.

It worked for another hundred meters.

"No," the clone said, twisting in Maddox's grip. "I-I want to leave, but the command in my mind—"

Maddox whirled around, surprising the clone. Strand didn't wear a helmet exactly, only a rebreather and mask.

"Do you want to live?" Maddox asked.

"Of course I do," the clone said. "It's just—"

Maddox grabbed the clone's shoulder, spun him around, made a fist and clubbed him on the back of the head.

481

The clone collapsed.

One part of Maddox wanted to leave him behind. He wouldn't for two reasons. One, it would be morally reprehensible. And two, maybe Strand could revive just enough later to bring the gate back into phase. The captain would never discount Strand's thirst for vengeance again.

Maddox grabbed the clone and hoisted him over a shoulder, beginning to trudge for the fold-fighter.

***

With the clone slowing him down, Maddox passed the lifeless bulk of the Galyan-copy android and the dead wasp-things. It was good to see that they hadn't moved. Later, when he felt the clone stir on his shoulder, he wondered if he could risk clouting the man again. Maddox didn't want to risk giving him a serious concussion. With the alien fibers in the brain, that might kill the clone.

As he trudged along, Maddox had come to realize there were many useful things Star Watch could learn from the Strand clone. If Intelligence had the Methuselah Man's memories, and if the clone hated the original Strand enough, maybe they could learn secrets they never would any other way.

The clone stirred once more, but then he slumped inert again.

Finally, Maddox and his limp cargo made it to the waiting fold-fighter. It was possibly the greatest sight Maddox had ever seen. He went to the hatch and tried it. Locked. That was a good sign.

Maddox punched in the code, moved into the ship and shut the hatch behind him, re-engaging the lock. He squeezed through a short corridor and entered the cramped control chamber.

"Captain?" Keith asked, aiming a gun at him as he crouched on the opposite end of the chamber.

"Yes. It's me," Maddox said with a helmet speaker. "Are you well enough to fly?"

"When I'm dead, I'll still fly better than anyone else alive," Keith said, climbing to his feet.

It was forced heartiness, but Maddox approved. They needed all the good cheer they could get.

"Get started," Maddox said. "The gate is phasing out again and we have to leave before it takes us with it."

"What gate?" Keith asked, as he holstered the gun. "How did I get here?"

"I'll tell you later," Maddox said. "Get started."

"Who is that?" Keith asked.

"The clone of Strand," Maddox said, as he deposited Strand in a corner. "Be careful around him. He has alien fibers in his mind."

"Figures," Keith said, as he slid into the piloting seat and began the start-up procedures. "Karma came back to bite him hard."

The tin can shuddered.

"What was that?" Keith asked, alarmed.

"Don't know," Maddox said.

They both waited, but nothing else happened.

"Get us out of here, Mr. Maker. That's an order."

Keith stopped asking questions as he concentrated, speeding through his preflight routine.

Maddox waited tensely. He waited for the fold-fighter to shake again. He waited for wasp-things to hammer on the outer hatch. He waited for a Ska to invisibly appear and begin to terrorize them.

Instead, several minutes later, the fold-fighter revved and then thrummed, lifting off the alien deck. It was time to go home to *Victory*, if they could.

-47-

They were close to home free as Keith piloted them out of the main blasted-apart hatch. They had been zooming up the corridor for what seemed like a lifetime.

"I told you it would be a piece of cake," Keith shouted. "There was nothing to it."

Maddox noticed the glistening sweat along Keith's temples. The ace had clenched his teeth more than once, especially as they passed walls that seemed thinner or less substantial as they phased out.

The clone had woken up several minutes ago, taking off his mask and rebreather. Maddox had taken off his space helmet. Strand complained about a splitting headache. He'd also asked Maddox several times already about what had happened to him.

"You hit your head," was all the answer the captain had given him.

Even though the gate was phasing out, it didn't do it all at once or in single piece. Maddox wondered how the various parts could keep together. The Builder could have explained the physics of such a thing, but he wasn't here.

Did the Builder still wage war against the Ska? What if the Ska won? Could the Ska make the Builder phase the gate back into normal quantum reality?

None of that mattered as the fold-fighter zoomed past the nuclear-warhead-blasted hatch and headed for open space.

"Do you see *Victory*?" Maddox asked.

"That I do, mate," Keith said, obviously feeling expansive. "It's left the vicinity of the gas giant but it's a long way from us."

Maddox nodded. They had almost made it from the ancient artifact. None of them knew how far they had to be so the phase shift didn't pull them with it. Whatever the distance, it had to be soon now.

Then a terrible feeling of evil filled Maddox. It rubbed the raw wound the Ska had made in his heart over a year ago. Suddenly, the shadowy Builder was among them. Compared to them, he was a giant that made the quarters seem tiny. Smoke streamed from one of his shoulders. The Builder hunched, and the stars where his head should show did not shine as brightly as before. In truth, they glimmered a bloody red color.

What did that mean? Nothing good, Maddox bet.

The Builder groaned and flailed one of his shadowy arms. It must have been a premeditated act, as the arm caught the clone, lifted him off the deck and smashed Strand with thudding force against a bulkhead.

"I'll kill you all!" the Builder roared. "I'll slay the universe."

The shadowy giant grabbed Keith, lifting him out of the piloting chair. "What are you doing here, little gnat?" the Builder roared.

Maddox sensed the evil in the Builder as more smoke billowed from the left shoulder. The Builder had used his right arm each time. Then it hit Maddox. The Ska had obviously touched the Builder there. Had the Builder killed the ancient evil after that happened? Who could know? The point was the Ska had wounded something deep in the Builder and maybe driven him mad.

"None will leave the gate," the Builder shouted. "None will stop the dawning of a new age, a hard age, a bitter age of—"

Maddox didn't hear the rest of it. With the swiftness of a trained knife-fighter, which he most certainly was, the captain drew the alien energy knife. He clicked it on so raw energy sizzled into existence.

The Builder sensed something. He hurled Keith from him and whirled around. Maddox didn't attempt any finesse. He leapt like a jungle cat, extended his arm like a fencer and shoved the energy blade into the Builder's mid-torso.

The Builder howled in agony. Maddox withdrew the energy blade and stabbed again, and again, and again. He could not do so a fifth time, as the larger Builder bear-hugged him. Smoke and fluids billowed and flowed from the Builder. Even so, the creature crushed Maddox against him. The captain struggled valiantly with all his steely-muscled might. He pushed against the remorseless Builder arms. He twisted the energy blade that was still inside the creature, trying to inflict as much damage as he could while he could.

The captain's bones crackled and snapped under the Builder's remorseless strength. Maddox grunted. More bones snapped. Maddox moaned before he mercifully blanked out, defeated by the Builder.

-48-

Consciousness returned to Maddox with the suddenness of a whip. He felt weaker than a child. He lay…in a cot. He recognized medical. He was on Starship *Victory*. He heard familiar sounds and smelled familiar odors. It shocked him how good it felt to be here. Tears welled in his eyes. He tried to wipe them, but found that he could not move his arms, as someone had restrained them with straps. He noticed tubes in his arms and a life-support machine. That didn't seem good.

The captain cleared his throat.

"Careful," a gruff-voiced Sergeant Riker said from somewhere off to the side where Maddox's couldn't see. "He's weaker this time. The Builder almost killed him."

"Don't you think I know that?" Meta asked. Then she hovered into view over Maddox, her long blonde hair spilling around her face.

She looked so beautiful. It actually hurt Maddox's heart to realize that his wife's beauty stunned him.

"Baby doll," he whispered.

"Oh, Maddox," Meta said. "Maddox, Maddox, you have to stop doing this to yourself."

He would have nodded, but something welled up in him. Maybe it was joy at being alive. Maybe it was knowing he would get to spend more time with his lovely darling.

Meta bent down so her face was an inch from his. She kissed him so very gently. She touched a cheek. "Next time you go on a mission like that, I'm coming along."

"No," he whispered.

Tears welled in her eyes. They began to drip onto his face. "Oh, darling, I'm sorry," she said, wiping the tears from a cheek.

"Don't be," he said. "It's good to be loved."

She stared into his eyes. "Say it," she whispered.

"I love you, baby."

"And I love you, Maddox." She kissed him again, their lips lingering.

Finally, Meta pulled back, lifting her head.

"Is the ship safe?" Maddox whispered.

"It's safe," Meta said. "The Builder is dead, in case you're wondering. He teleported away before he…well, we assumed he died then by the amount of alien blood we found in the fighter."

Worry touched the captain.

"No," Meta said. "The Builder teleported out of the fold-fighter, but he didn't make it to the gate. The ancient structure had almost phased out and I guess you made it far enough to escape the phasing. Keith was in a bad way, but he crawled back to the controls. He saw the Builder on the screen, floating in space. Keith launched a missile and the Builder blew up."

Maddox absorbed the news.

"Keith passed out afterward," Meta said. "That's how we found you, the two of you unconscious."

"The clone…?" Maddox whispered.

"Dead," Meta said. "The Builder crushed his bones, some of them piercing vital organs. The clone never had a chance."

"No…" Maddox said, staring far off. "I don't think the clone ever did." The captain blinked himself out of his reverie. "Where is *Victory* now?"

"Heading home."

"Good. Wait, what about Yen Cho?"

Meta frowned. "He's back in his cell. The android went wild after Valerie had him unhooked from Helm. The android tore apart two marines before others in armor subdued him. Yen Cho just sits in the cell, staring at the walls. He won't respond to any queries. What did the Builder do to Yen Cho?"

Maddox shook his head.

"Oh," Meta said, "the Hindenburgers disappeared. We can't find any sign of any of them. Do you know what happened to them?"

Maddox squinted as a grim possibility surfaced. How had the Builder gained his bio-matter?

"I'm tired," the captain whispered. "I'm going to sleep for a while. Then, I have some thinking to do."

"You sleep, darling. I'm going to be right here watching over you."

Maddox nodded, or at least he thought he had, before he let his eyes close.

-49-

Three days later, after the bone regeneration therapy had taken hold, Maddox felt good enough to leave the cot and don his uniform. He moved slowly as he exited medical, aching all over. On top of everything else, the radiation treatments had taken their toll. But his fantastic recuperative powers had helped speed the processes.

Meta helped him whenever they were alone in the corridors. Finally, the captain shuffled into a special chamber. Meta helped him into a chair before a desk.

"You shouldn't be here," she said. "You should be in bed."

"I will be soon," Maddox said. "First, I need to report to the Brigadier. There are a few items that need...careful consideration, and quickly."

"What considerations?" Meta asked.

"If you sit in the corner over there, you can listen to what I tell the Brigadier."

Meta's eyebrows raised. Maddox had never allowed such a thing before.

"I'm going to want your expertise," Maddox said, as he straightened his uniform. "The way I'm feeling, I don't care to explain anything twice."

That was a second shock to Meta. Maddox never complained about weakness or tiredness. He liked to maintain the fiction that he was a man of iron. He was tough. There was no doubt about that. But, like everyone, her husband had his limitations.

Maddox readied the Builder communication device. Finally, he activated it.

Valerie had sent a signal earlier, letting the Brigadier know that Maddox wanted to speak to her. In a moment, the screen wavered and solidified on the gray-haired Iron Lady of Star Watch Intelligence.

"Hello, Ma'am," Maddox said.

O'Hara did a double take. "Maddox! You look wretched. What happened to you?"

Maddox hesitated. "I'm not sure where to begin, Ma'am."

"I want to know everything," O'Hara said, as she searched his face. "Don't leave a thing out."

Maddox began telling the Iron Lady what had happened since the last time he'd spoken to her. The Brigadier listened patiently. She shook her head at times. At others, she tsked and became angry.

Maddox finally lost steam. "Ma'am, I'm going to have to call you later. I'm…"

"You look exhausted," O'Hara said. "Get some sleep. You can finish your report later."

"Thank you, Ma'am."

After the connection ended, Maddox put his arms on the desk, laid his head on his arms and fell promptly asleep.

Meta left him like that, and stayed sitting in her chair, watching protectively.

The captain woke up four and half hours later. He looked worse than before.

"Really," Meta said. "I need to take you back to medical."

"Not yet," Maddox said in a querulous voice. "I must finish my report."

"What's bothering you?" Meta asked.

"Could you get me some water? My throat is parched."

Meta got him water. He drank it all. Then he contacted the Brigadier again. Meta went to her chair in the corner, listening to what he had to say.

Maddox told the Brigadier the rest of the story. She made sympathetic noises at times and murmured "Oh, dear," at others. Finally, the captain completed his report.

"The clone is dead?" the Brigadier asked.

"And so is the Builder," Maddox said as he nodded his yes. "I believe his fight with the Ska proved too much for him."

"Did you happen to pick up a second energy blade?" O'Hara asked.

"I'm afraid I didn't," Maddox said.

"Pity," O'Hara said. She was silent for a time.

Maddox was content to fold his hands on the desk and wait.

"There are two things that concern me," the Brigadier finally said.

"Just two?"

"Yes. Firstly, the Nameless Ones know intelligent races are back in the Orion Arm. Will they send Destroyers here to investigate? If they do, how long will it take such ships to reach us?"

"It could be a thousand years or more," Maddox said.

"Are there no more gates in the Orion Arm?" the Brigadier asked.

"We have no one who can tell us."

"The Methuselah Man imprisoned on the Throne World might," she said.

"I'm not so sure," Maddox said. "The original Strand toyed with forces he didn't truly understand. I doubt he knows much about the gates."

"It is a quandary," O'Hara admitted. "It is yet another problem that Star Watch and humanity don't need. We still have the Swarm Imperium to worry about, never mind the Nameless Ones. It's too bad you couldn't find a gate that led into the Imperium, and open it to the Destroyers. Our two most pressing problems could annihilate one another."

"Possibly," Maddox said.

"The more immediate concern is the Builder listening post," O'Hara said. "Could Yen Cho have contacted other androids and told them about it?"

"I've been wondering that for some time," Maddox said.

"It would be bad if the androids gained the Builder tech left in there," O'Hara said. "And it would be to Star Watch's benefit if you went back to the listening post and took what tech remained there."

492

"The listening post is set to detonate if anyone without the proper entry codes tries to force it."

"It is indeed a thorny problem, Captain. That means we should send our best team there. That would be you. You're also closer to the listening post than anyone else is. I order you to retrieve the Builder tech. If that proves impossible—and for the Commonwealth's sake, I hope that's not true—don't let any androids get their hands on the advanced technology."

"Yes, Ma'am," Maddox said. "Is there anything else?"

"Get better, Captain. I hate to see my prize operative in such a wretched condition. Do try to take care of yourself. Oh, and say hello to that beautiful wife of yours. You do know that I love her…"

Maddox looked stricken. It seemed as if the Brigadier had almost said, "You know that I love her, *too*." That would imply the Brigadier loved—

Maddox cleared his throat. "I will pass along the message, Ma'am. I do hope you are talking care of yourself."

"I am, thank you. Now, be careful, Captain." O'Hara paused before adding, "Star Watch can ill afford to lose…your services."

"You are gracious, Ma'am."

She nodded. "Brigadier O'Hara out."

The screen wavered and Maddox sat back.

Meta stared at him. She couldn't believe what she had just heard. Why did the Iron Lady take such a keen interest in her husband? It was very peculiar, almost like a mother worried about her son. Meta was going to have to think about this.

-50-

The ancient listening post mission truly began for Maddox four days after talking to Brigadier O'Hara via the Builder communication device.

The captain had slept far too much, taken what seemed like endless bone regeneration therapies and too many pills for the radiation he'd endured while storming the eons-old gate. In other words, he was thoroughly tired and yet feeling that it was time to get started.

They would be in the targeted star system soon enough, another week at the most. Would Rull Nation androids already have arrived? Maddox had no idea. He bet Yen Cho did, but the android still hadn't spoken to anyone.

What had happened to Yen Cho? The Builder must have done something to change him. It had looked wrong, felt wrong, seeing the android with all those wires sprouting from his otherwise human-seeming head. The Builder had treated Yen Cho like a tool. Surely, the android must have resented that.

Maddox didn't know. He needed Yen Cho's knowledge. He had to find out if the android had communicated with other androids while under the Builder's tutelage.

It was time to talk to the android. Yen Cho had gone berserk, though. The android had killed two trained marines. That pissed off Maddox. He was tired of these...constructs killing his people. The Builder had devoured the Hindenburgers...

494

"Right," Maddox said, as he sat on the edge of his bed.

"What was that?" Meta asked groggily. She was still under the covers.

"I have work to do," Maddox said.

Meta came fully awake as she turned toward him. "Are you serious? You're still healing. Maddox, are you listening to me?"

The captain had stood up. He was sick of just sitting around. "Don't worry."

"Why should I worry? What are you planning to do?"

"Yen Cho—"

"Maddox," Meta said. "Don't you dare go into the same cell with him. He—"

The captain turned toward his wife.

"Please," she said.

He sat back down, moved part of the blanket and patted her naked rump. It was a fine butt, a perfect butt, as far as he was concerned. He gave it another affectionate pat, tossed the blanket over it and stood. He moved to a chair and picked up his uniform jacket, slipping it on. He had to move gingerly with his left shoulder, but tried not to show it.

"You still need a few more days of recuperation," Meta pleaded. "Androids move deceptively fast."

"Don't worry. I have that covered."

"The dead marines likely thought that, too."

Maddox's eyes narrowed. The marines—he needed info from Yen Cho but would rather execute the android for having murdered his men. Would that be the right angle to play? He rather doubted it.

Forcing the fingers of his left hand to move, Maddox buttoned his coat. He never wanted to endure so many broken bones again. The Builder had been so dense, as if he'd packed his molecules more tightly than others did. Maddox wouldn't doubt if that had been the case.

"Who are you taking with you?" Meta asked.

"Riker."

"And...?" she said.

"Just Riker."

Meta didn't say a word to that.

Maddox knew that if he turned around his wife would be staring at him, trying to give him the eye. Therefore, he didn't turn around. He headed for the hatch.

"You're impossible," she said.

He supposed that might be true. He opened the hatch, thought about looking back, but didn't.

"Be careful," Meta shouted, as he shut the hatch.

Maddox nodded. His reflexes might be slower than normal, and Riker was an older man, but he knew what he was doing— he hoped.

-51-

Riker stood on one side of the closed hatch, just inside Yen Cho's cell. The captain stood on the other. Each Intelligence operative gripped a heavy-duty pistol—a slugthrower—aimed at the prisoner.

The android sat motionless on a chair before a table. They'd played this game before, back before the ancient gate had appeared, but the game seemed different this time.

Maddox eyed the android. Yen Cho didn't have any hair this time. Someone had shaved him bald in order to insert all those wires into his head.

"Been like this ever since he killed the marines," Riker said in his gruff voice.

Maddox didn't nod. He studied his opponent, thinking back to their lengthy question and answer sessions. "I went to the gate," he said. "So did the Builder. Since I'm here, it's obvious we were successful. The Builder's fate…" The captain cocked his head. "Are you interested in what happened to the Builder?"

As Maddox sought to unlock the android, Yen Cho mimicked the head cocking. More than that, the android's eyes focused onto the captain.

"The Builder?" Yen Cho asked.

"He faced a Ska in the gate," Maddox said.

"What…what happened?"

"That's an interesting question. One answer is that a lot of things happened."

497

"Why…why I am detained in here?" Yen Cho asked. "I served my purpose. We stopped the Nameless Ones from invading Human Space. I…I was content. I served one of the creators. Now…"

"The Builder used you like a tool," Maddox said.

"You do not understand."

"You're right. I don't. But then, I'm not an android. Tell me, Yen Cho, what did the Builder do to the Hindenburgers?"

Yen Cho turned his head so he wouldn't have to look at the captain.

The move startled Maddox. He wondered what it signified.

"The Hindenburgers served their purpose," Yen Cho said. "They helped defeat…the enemy. They…became greater than what they were."

That confirmed for Maddox his belief that the Builder had used the bio-parts of the Hindenburgers. Somehow, the Builder had made himself more compact, as if squeezing all those people into one Builder self. It was rather disgusting, if he thought about it too much.

"Did it bother you?" Maddox asked.

"You refer to the Hindenburgers, I presume?"

"Yes."

"Yes," Yen Cho said softly. "But I learned you humans had corrupted my thinking. It was interesting to learn that. I…became greater than I once was."

"The Builder turned you into a tool. You became less."

Yen Cho faced him. "What happened to the Builder?"

"How badly do you want to know?"

The android studied him, studied him longer— "Ah," Yen Cho said. "I believe I understand. You desire the codes into the listening post. I can only assume the Builder died in some fashion. Did you kill him, perhaps?"

"How badly do you want to know?"

The android stared at Maddox. With sudden startling speed, possibly faster than Yen Cho had ever moved before, he stood, picked up the table and hurled it at Maddox.

The captain did not fire, but he managed to turn his back to the hurtling table. He grunted as it smashed against him.

Yen Cho darted faster than a lizard, charging the captain.

Riker had flinched, but the table missed him, as it had struck the captain. The android was halfway to them when the sergeant pulled the trigger. He was a deadeye shot, a marksman. He hadn't fired at the torso, but at the head. Three slugs hit the android head with violent, kinetic force. It caused Yen Cho to stagger sideways. He missed Maddox, crashing against the bulkhead beside the captain. Riker stepped to the side, continuing to fire at the android's head. The slugs plowed against the brainpan, hammering against it. The android twitched several times before turning to face the sergeant. Riker dropped his gun and picked up the captain's weapon. By that time, Yen Cho had started to rise. Riker emptied the captain's slugthrower at point blank range into the android's face. Each shot hammered the head back. The shots had already obliterated the pseudo-skin face, revealing the gleaming metal behind.

The combined shots had crumpled the front brainpan, but they hadn't torn through. The android lay on the floor, his limbs twitching and jerking.

Riker moved fast. He didn't trust the android, and the thing may have just slain the captain. Riker knelt behind the android's head and began to hammer it with his bionic fist. The bionic arm drove the titanium fist with superhuman force and finally produced a tear in the alloyed brainpan. Riker did not hesitate. He used his bionic fingers, reached in, hooked the cybertronic computer and yanked out what he could. The sergeant did it three more times; the android's twitching slowed with each yank, finally ceasing altogether.

As Riker destroyed the android, the cell door swung open. The two marines who'd been monitoring the camera feed charged inside, rushing to the captain's side.

Riker quit his demolition of Yen Cho and looked up. "How is he?" the sergeant asked.

"He got lucky," one marine said. "If the table had hit him differently, it could have broken his back or worse. He's going to be bruised for a while, but he should be fine." The marine looked to his companion. "We can move him," he said.

"Then let's get him to medical," the other marine said.

-52-

Yen Cho the Android—the oldest of the Yen Cho Series androids—was dead. Riker had destroyed the cybertronic brain. There was no bringing him back now.

Oh, Maddox gave orders from his medical cot that Andros Crank and Galyan should try. Could Ludendorff have fixed the android brain? Maddox decided it didn't matter because the professor wasn't here. Andros and Galyan failed. No one blamed them. No one blamed Riker for what he'd done.

Meta showered kisses on the sergeant, hugging him several times and thanking him profusely for what he'd done.

Maddox ordered Andros and Galyan to try to hack the pieces of brain that were still intact. They failed at that endeavor, too.

"Whatever was locked in the android's brain…we don't have it," Andros reported one day.

Maddox was in his quarters, sitting at a desk in the corner. "Thanks for trying, Chief Technician."

Andros hesitated, looking downcast.

Maddox shoved his chair back and strained to get up.

"Sir," Andros said, worried.

Maddox made it to his feet and moved beside the small Kai-Kaus. He put a hand on the man's right shoulder.

"It was a long shot," Maddox said. "We're not breaking into the listening post with stolen Builder codes now. But don't worry about it, we're going to figure something out. Likely,

I'm going to need a technical answer. That means you have to stay sharp."

Andros nodded.

"A man doesn't stay sharp if he's blaming himself," Maddox said. "And he certainly doesn't stay sharp if he's giving himself negative talk. Do you understand me?"

"I do," Andros said with a quick nod. "Thank you, sir."

"Take a break, Mr. Crank. I want you refreshed."

The chief technician left with a lighter step than when he'd entered the captain's quarters.

With a grunt, Maddox sat back down. He scowled. The easiest way to do this had vanished. He wasn't going to send anyone on a suicide mission trying to hack into the listening post. He wasn't going to send a probe and possibly cause the listening post to self-destruct. What did that leave?

After a time, Maddox nodded. That left him with a sneaky option. Could he pull it off?

"If we're lucky," he told himself. It was time for some hard work so they could forge themselves some luck.

***

Victory reached the targeted star system, appearing in the outer planets region. Maddox had returned to duty and sat in his command chair on the bridge.

Valerie and Galyan scanned the system. They could find no evidence of other spaceships, buoys, drones or any technological devices.

"Do a second sweep," Maddox ordered. "We have to be certain."

In the end, Valerie and Galyan made three careful sweeps. The star system was empty of others.

"We have time," Maddox said. "But we don't know how much time. That means we're going to set up the basic trap. Then, if we have more time, we'll add refinements."

"What if the androids don't show up?" Valerie asked.

Maddox shook his head. He hadn't thought that far. He was certain Yen Cho had sent a signal. But the lieutenant was correct. That was an assumption. It wasn't a fact. Maybe the androids lacked a Builder-like far-distance communication device. Maybe…

The days passed in hurried labor. It took time moving here, moving there, launching drones and passive sensors and other stealth equipment.

Afterward, they waited.

No androids showed up. No New Men entered the star system. This was far in the Beyond. Maybe they were the only ones who knew about the listening post.

After a month of fruitless duty in the system, Brigadier O'Hara called via the Builder communication device.

"It's time to try to crack the listening post yourself, Captain," she said.

"Begging your pardon, ma'am, but we should wait. Patience pays off. Besides, there will be no cracking the Builder post. We lack that particular expertise."

"Star Watch has searched for Ludendorff. He's taken himself off the map. Can anyone else do this?"

"I suppose Strand might," Maddox said. "Would the New Men lend him to us?"

"Don't be fatuous, Captain. This is a serious matter."

The captain waited.

"Very well," O'Hara said. "I'll give you another few weeks to try this your way. There are pressing problems at home. I want you here for a new mission. The Chin Confederation is threatening war with the Social Syndicate."

"Three more weeks might not be enough time for this," Maddox said.

O'Hara looked worried. Finally, she agreed and signed off.

Another week passed.

Valerie spoke to Maddox on the bridge. "How many more refinements can we add?"

"I'm out of ideas. Do you have any?"

She thought about that, but finally shook her head.

It took nine and half weeks from the time the ancient gate had phased out before another spaceship nosed into the targeted star system. If that ship had an android crew, Maddox's plan would get its chance.

-53-

"Sir," Valerie said from her station. "That's...that's an old *Gettysburg*-class battleship. It's a Star Watch vessel. Should I hail them?"

Maddox swiveled around his captain's chair. He was fully healed from his various injuries. "On no account, Lieutenant," he said.

"But, sir—" Valerie's eyes widened. "Do you think androids crew the battleship?"

"Not necessarily," Maddox said. "But I'm sure a few or maybe all of the key officers are androids."

"That's horrible. I thought Star Watch had rid the service of androids."

"It would appear not," Maddox said.

Valerie worried her lower lip. "Can you be sure of that, sir?"

"Lieutenant, in these things it's difficult to be one hundred percent certain. That's what makes it so interesting."

She gave him a look before turning back to her console.

Maddox faced the main screen. He wished he felt the way he'd talked. It wasn't interesting. This was a mess. They had expected a small craft, likely a civilian vessel. A *Gettysburg*-class battleship could ruin everything, at least in terms of Star Watch getting their hands on more Builder tech.

"Sir," Valerie said. "According to my sensors, that's the *Shiloh*. It was listed missing at the end of the "C" Quadrant Campaign."

"Captain," Galyan said. "Could another Strand clone have been released?"

Maddox raised an eyebrow at the holoimage.

"The original Strand corrupted the Hindenburger crew of the *Bismarck*," Galyan said. "Maybe he did the same with the *Shiloh*."

Maddox pursed his lips, nodding a second later. "This is getting complicated. We'll continue watching."

Victory was hidden inside a different Oort cloud comet. That comet was 61 AUs from the listening post comet. The crew had hollowed out a place for *Victory* many weeks ago. A Star Watch tin can drifted inside debris three hundred thousand kilometers from the listening post. The fold-fighter was the command post for the drones presently hidden on the other side of the targeted comet. Those were specially-doctored drones, meant to catch Rull Nation androids. The *Shiloh* had appeared out of a Laumer Point in the inner planets region of the system.

Whatever would happen, this was going to take time to unfold.

***

Five days later, Maddox knew no more about the *Shiloh's* present crew. He knew about the old crew because he'd called the Brigadier via the Builder comm.

Did the battleship have the same crew as during the "C" Quadrant Campaign against the New Men? Maddox rather doubted it. This was going to be a longer waiting game.

On the sixth day since their appearance, the *Shiloh* began hard braking. The battleship had reached the Oort cloud and was presently four million kilometers from the listening post comet.

Victory's crew was on edge. Maddox was on edge. The days of waiting, of watching the battleship had made this all much worse. They had war-gamed the trap a dozen times since the *Shiloh's* appearance. If they practiced it any more, Maddox was worried the crew would get stale.

Finally, the *Shiloh* parked four hundred thousand kilometers from the listening post comet. That was less than the distance from Planet Earth to the Moon.

Sixty-eight minutes later, the main hangar bay door opened. Three strikefighters roared out, followed by a shuttle. The small group headed for the comet.

"It could be worse," Maddox said from his command chair.

"Not much worse," Valerie muttered.

Maddox did not reply. He waited, even though his stomach was tight. There were so many unknowns. He sat in his chair like a man of iron. It helped calm the bridge crew's nerves if they thought he was utterly confident.

Time passed. *Victory* waited, until the strikefighters began braking. They hadn't checked the debris three hundred thousand kilometers from the comet, because it was in a different quadrant than they were.

The shuttle took the final lap, closing with the comet. Then, it, too, began to brake. It stopped two kilometers from the comet. A hatch opened, and two space-suited individuals used hydrogen-packs to jet to the comet.

Like before, ice moved out of the way to reveal the ancient Builder listening post.

The two suited personnel disappeared into the listening post.

On *Victory's* bridge, Maddox stood up. He wanted to pace, but he held himself still. He stared at the main screen, knowing that he was seeing events after they had happened because of the 61 AU distance and the limits of the speed of light.

"Let's get ready to star-drive jump," the captain said quietly. "The game is about to begin."

-54-

The space-suited personnel sprayed white hydrogen mist as they jetted away from the listening post. Each carried a large device.

Maddox had long-ago decided against getting greedy. Better a little than nothing. Besides, the longer they played this, the more of a chance something would give them away.

Before the two reached the waiting shuttle, Maddox gave the command to jump. He knew the two must be already settling into the shuttle and getting ready to accelerate back to the battleship. He was seeing things 61 AUs-worth after the event.

The starship's antimatter engines thrummed. The deck quivered, and *Victory* jumped into possible battle.

Maddox raised his head first. The *Shiloh* hadn't started firing yet. *Victory* had obviously surprised them.

The captain leaped up and ran to Weapons. He moved his fingers in a blur over the controls. The main electromagnetic shield came up.

Five seconds later, the first heavy laser from the *Shiloh* struck the shield.

The other bridge personnel began coming to. A few seconds later, Galyan gave a quick report.

"The drones are almost in range, sir."

Maddox turned and looked at the main screen. The strikefighters accelerated toward the comet. Two of them launched missiles at the drones coming around the comet. The third fighter fired its autocannons.

Each drone headed straight for the shuttle. The shuttle hadn't started accelerating yet.

"Sir," Valerie said. "More battleship lasers are coming online. The *Shiloh* is also launching missiles."

Maddox nodded. He was focused on the drones. A strikefighter missile detonated before contact. The warhead's x-rays and gammas reached out at light speed, destroying the first drone.

Maddox struck an armrest of his chair, leaning forward tensely.

At that point, the drone nearest the shuttle fired its EMP shockwave. In seconds, the EMP washed over the shuttle. Immediately, everything shut down on it. Would the androids also shut down? Maddox was hoping they would.

"Take out the strikefighters," the captain said. "Keith, get onto the shuttle. Get those Builder items and get back to the barn."

The tin can burst out of the cloud of debris three hundred thousand kilometers from the enemy shuttle. The fold-fighter disappeared, and reappeared fifty thousand kilometers from the stricken enemy shuttle.

"Get those strikefighters," Maddox said again.

On *Victory*, the neutron beam fired, and a strikefighter disintegrated.

"The fighters are launching more missiles," Valerie said.

"Weapons," Maddox said.

The neutron cannon fired again, and a second strikefighter vanished. The third must have taken splash damage. It quit accelerating.

"Sir?" Weapons asked.

"Destroy it," Maddox said, "and destroy their missiles."

At that point, the enemy shuttle exploded.

Everyone on *Victory*'s bridge froze, Maddox for only an instant. He pressed a comm switch on his armrest.

"Keith?"

"Yes, Captain."

"Fold out of there now. Do it while you can."

"But sir—"

"Fold. Fold, or you're a dead man."

Valerie stared in shock at Maddox. Before she could say anything, the listening post comet vaporized in a terrific and deadly explosion of its own. The new blast poured massive doses of gamma rays, x-rays and other hard radiation. That radiation and the pieces of the comet that had survived the blast spread in all directions.

The hard radiation and comet pieces struck *Victory's* electromagnetic shield. The shield turned red, brown, black—

"More power to the shields," Maddox said.

"I've already started the process," Andros said.

The black turned darker black, darker…and began to lighten, just a little.

The hard radiation and highly accelerated pieces struck the *Shiloh's* shield. It held for a moment but went down. After that, the thick hull armor shredded away as more comet pieces pummeled the battleship.

As *Victory's* crew watched, the battleship ignited, blowing up in a blaze of nuclear fire.

The seconds passed. *Victory's* shield had already come back down to brown. They had survived the comet's destruction.

"Keith…" Valerie said softly, urgently.

"Sir," Helm said. "The fold-fighter has reappeared. Sir," Sub-lieutenant Kenzie Jones said. "The tin can has appeared twenty million kilometers away. It's well out of the blast zone."

"Keith," Valerie said again, beaming with delight.

Maddox nodded his approval. The ace had done it again.

"Sir," Valerie said. "We failed. The listening post is gone."

"Did we fail?" Maddox asked.

"I don't understand," Valerie said.

"We'll wait a bit," the captain said. "Then I'll show you."

***

A day later, Maddox sent the search teams. But it was Galyan with his sensors who found the two floating things of high interest. The Builder items were far from the destroyed

508

comet, having been flung away by the blast. Maddox had guessed right, though. The Builder material had proven impervious to the blasts that destroyed the shuttle, the comet and *Shiloh*.

The other Builder items within the listening post were gone, though. Not even Builder items had been able to survive direct blasts of that magnitude.

Two days after the post's destruction, special teams stowed the radioactive Builder items in special containers aboard the starship.

Valerie was at her station. Keith piloted the ship. Galyan stood near the captain's chair. Meta did too, talking with Maddox.

The captain held up a finger. "Just a minute," he told his wife.

Maddox clicked an armrest control and leaned down. "This is Captain Maddox speaking." His voice rang out over the ship's intercom system. "I want to report that our mission was a success. We have obtained what we came for. I wish to congratulate each of you on a job well done. I am proud of my crew, proud of the job you've done. Now…"

Maddox looked around at his bridge crew. He winked at Valerie, saluted Keith, pointed a finger at Andros Crank and snapped his fingers at Galyan. Lastly, he stood, gave Meta a kiss and then leaned back down to the armrest comm.

"Now," Maddox said, "we're going home for a well-deserved rest. Captain Maddox out."

The captain clicked the button, shutting off the intercom system. He sat back down, put his arms on the rests and said to Keith, "Get us ready to jump, Mr. Maker."

"Aye, aye, mate," the ace said, as he began to plot the course for Earth.

THE END

SF Books by Vaughn Heppner

LOST STARSHIP SERIES:
The Lost Starship
The Lost Command
The Lost Destroyer
The Lost Colony
The Lost Patrol
The Lost Planet
The Lost Earth
The Lost Artifact

DOOM STAR SERIES:
Star Soldier
Bio Weapon
Battle Pod
Cyborg Assault
Planet Wrecker
Star Fortress
Task Force 7 (Novella)

EXTINCTION WARS SERIES:
Assault Troopers
Planet Strike
Star Viking
Fortress Earth

Visit VaughnHeppner.com for more information

71624505R00288

Made in the USA
San Bernardino, CA
18 March 2018